TIDE

Also by Daniela Sacerdoti

WATCH OVER ME
DREAMS
REALLY WEIRD REMOVALS.COM

TIDE

The Sarah Midnight Trilogy

Book 2

Daniela Sacerdoti

Daniela

BLACK & WHITE PUBLISHING

First published 2013
by Black & White Publishing Ltd
29 Ocean Drive, Edinburgh EH6 6JL

1 3 5 7 9 10 8 6 4 2   13 14 15 16

ISBN: 978 1 84502 539 7

ALBA | CHRUTHACHAIL

Typeset by Creative Link, North Berwick
Printed and bound by Nørhaven, Denmark

This book is for Lindsey

Acknowledgements

Thank you Ross, Sorley and Luca, for putting up with me writing, writing, writing, and then writing some more! I couldn't do it without you three cuddling me, feeding me, making me laugh and being so understanding when my head is somewhere else for days at a time.

From the bottom of my heart, thank you to my editors, Janne Moller and Kristen Susienka, and to everyone at Black & White Publishing. Thank you to my agents, Lindsey Fraser and Kathryn Ross, my velvet and steel fairy godmothers – what would I do without you?

Thank you to my families, the Sacerdotis and the Walkers, for their belief in me. Thank you to Irene, my best friend and little sister – our daily emails keep me (relatively) sane. Thank you to my amazing girlfriends and their warm, generous support (and help with the school run when I'm overwhelmed with edits!).

Thank you to the musicians who soundtracked many hours of writing: Julie Fowlis, The Treacherous Orchestra, Runrig, Manran, Corquieu, and as ever for many years, the wonderful Maire Brennan. Thank you to Kirstyn Knowles and Jenny Masterson for Sarah's song, "Do it Alone", Martyn Bennet, Margaret Bennet and BJ Stewart for the lyrics of Niall's song "Grioghal Cridhe", Pentangle for their rendition of "Cruel Sister" and Sting, with Robert Louis Stevenson, for the musical version of the poem "Christmas at Sea".

Thank you to Jim Sutherland, David Stanton and Peter Kerr for Gaelic help.

And finally, thank you to Linda Norgrove, one of the women of courage and belief who inspire me to be *braver*. www.lindanorgrovefoundation.org.

Contents

Prologue
Salt and Lilies

Islay, October 2002

It was the first time that Sarah ever felt close to Morag Midnight, and the last time she saw her alive.

The beach was vast and windswept, and the black-haired girl wrapped her scarf around her neck twice, struggling to keep up with her grandmother as they strode towards the sea.

"Come on, Sarah!"

Sarah broke into a run. She didn't understand what the rush was, and she didn't know why her grandmother was desperate to take her for a walk on the beach all of a sudden. Her parents had driven over to the other side of the island – Secret business, as usual – and they had left her with Morag, in spite of the fact that Morag's behaviour was becoming increasingly erratic. As soon as Sarah reached her grandmother on the shoreline, Morag took the girl's hand.

"The water is very cold," the old woman said.

Sarah felt a flutter of apprehension. The sea was wide and grey, and choppy under the wintry wind. She didn't like to

1

think how cold the water would be, how freezing the white-topped waves. Her skin puckered into goosebumps.

"Have you ever swum in the sea in winter?" Morag asked. Sarah noticed how the water was lapping their boots now. The bottom of her jeans was wet already.

"No. My mum and dad wouldn't let me. It's too cold."

Morag laughed, a brittle laugh that made Sarah shiver. "Of course! Imagine your mother letting you swim in there at this time of year. That would be crazy. What mother would do that?"

Morag's grip was tight around Sarah's hand, and Sarah flinched but she didn't say anything. She knew better than to provoke her grandmother. Her temper was such that she would fly off the handle at the slightest provocation.

"It's so cold that you wouldn't drown. Your heart would just stop," Morag continued. Her once blonde hair, now grey, was coming loose from its bun, and long strands framed her graceful face. Morag's eyes were big and blue, and her features as stern as a northern goddess. She was tall, and always stood very straight. Everything about her spoke of pride and strength.

Sarah swallowed hard. She fought the instinct to free herself from Morag's grip and run. She didn't want to be standing with her feet in seawater, with her grandmother holding her hand so tight it hurt; she wanted to be home with her mum and dad.

"Gran, I'm cold. Let's go home."

Morag turned to look Sarah straight in the eye. She softened her grip on the child's hand and bent down, her face now level with Sarah's. Unexpectedly, she stroked Sarah's cheek.

"The world is changing. I won't be here to see how things

map out, but you will be. Remember this, Sarah: whatever happens, the Midnight family must be protected and preserved by all possible means."

Sarah didn't know what to say. Though she was only eight years old, she was an old soul, and could see and feel things much beyond her years. Morag's intensity petrified her. She nodded.

"At your age, Sarah, I was hunting already. But maybe you're not meant for the hunt . . . like *she* wasn't. Maybe there's something else you need to do. Had I known . . . had I known what was happening, back then . . . what I was about to lose! But it's too late now. It's your parents' time. And soon it will be your time, Sarah. Come," she said, grasping her granddaughter's hand tight again.

"Where are we going?"

"Back to Midnight Hall. There's something I need to show you."

The next morning Sarah awoke to find her mum sitting on her bed.

"Wake up, darling. Wake up . . ."

"Mum?"

Sarah was startled to see her mother's face streaked with tears.

"There was an accident," Anne began.

"Gran is dead," Sarah said. "She walked into the sea."

"Sarah . . . How do you know? Did you dream? Already?" The little girl shook her head.

"Then how . . . Did you hear your father and me talking? Were you awake?"

"No. She told me."

★

Morag had kneeled down and held Sarah tight all of a sudden – the little girl had stood tense, breathing in her grandmother's scent of salt and lilies. "Sarah . . . They say that people from these islands belong to the sea. I think it's true. Tomorrow I'll go back where I belong."

A teardrop had rolled down Morag's cheek, and Sarah had wiped it away with her small finger. "Don't cry, Gran," she'd said.

"No. Of course not," Morag had whispered. "I won't cry anymore."

1

Without You

For all the lovers who had no choice
Choose now which heart to break

Sean

Every night I watch over Sarah, invisible, concealed in her garden. As December approaches it gets colder and colder, but I don't care if my hands are frozen and my lips turn blue. I must be there for her. The threat is far from over, Sarah is still in danger and Nicholas Donal is not the right person to protect her. I can't trust him. Even though he saved our lives many times.

Who is he, anyway? He says he's the heir to the Donals, a Secret family I've never even heard of. Hardly a satisfactory explanation. I watch him walking up the steps that lead to Sarah's door and follow her inside. It's clear enough that they're together.

Just thinking about it makes me ill.

Only a few weeks ago, Sarah had feelings for me, before she discovered who I really am . . . I know she did. How can those feelings have changed so quickly? There's something strange about the sudden hold Nicholas has over her. And she looks so pale, so thin. Even from the distance I keep she seems . . . *dazed*. She walks to and from school with uncertain steps, with her head lowered. Of course, she has been through so much, but even so. She is not the Sarah I know. Or knew.

Maybe I'm flattering myself that I'm better for her, when what's between the two of them really is love.

No, it can't just be jealousy; it can't just be the fact that he took Sarah for himself the night he saved her life – him and those ravens, and those cold blue flames that sprung from his fingers. It can't just be my spite at having lost her to him – not when I see Sarah as she is now.

What has he done to her? And how could I have allowed this to happen?

It was Harry Midnight, Sarah's cousin, who entrusted me with her life. Just before his death at the hands of the Secret Council, the Sabha – the very people who were supposed to lead the Secret Families – he sent me, his Gamekeeper, his best friend, his brother in all but blood, to Scotland to watch over Sarah. Harry gave me his name and his identity – Sarah was just a baby when she'd seen him last – because he knew that it was the only way that she would trust me. And she did, until she found out about our deceit. And now she hates me for it. Even though it was all done to keep her safe.

We're apart, and it's killing me.

Crouched night after night in Sarah's garden, I wonder what has happened to Harry's friends – our friends. Elodie, his wife, was sent to a safe place in Italy, to guard the last of the Japanese Secret heirs. Mike Prudhomme, a Gamekeeper like me, was sent to Louisiana with Niall Flynn, the heir to the Flynn family. For a while we were able to keep in constant touch via secure phone lines, but the lines have gone dead now. There has been no signal – the short message we used to send each other at the same time every day – for weeks. I try to believe that it's too dangerous for them to be in touch with me right now, because I can't contemplate the alternative: that they have been killed. Murdered by the Sabha, or by demons, take your pick. The whole world seems to be against us, in one way or another.

Every day I check our dead drop. Mike knows that if everything else fails, as a last resort I'll have left them a message folded inside a plastic pocket, hidden in a fissure in Sarah's garden wall – the north wall. The exact place is marked by a small symbol I've painted in such a way that it's visible, but doesn't attract too much attention.

Every day I pray that I'll find the envelope gone, that they'll come looking for me at Gorse Cottage. Losing hope is not an option.

I spend every night in Sarah's garden, invisible. I can make myself unseen, unnoticed – nobody rests their eyes on me twice, nobody remembers my face. They see me, but their gaze slips away from me like rain trickling off glass. It works best when I'm still, but I can be invisible when I'm moving too, although occasionally my shadow is perceived like a flicker in the corner of somebody's eye. From my hiding place I can see Anne Midnight's herb patch, where Sarah found the diary her mother had kept for her. The image of Sarah kneeling in front of the thyme bush, clutching her precious discovery, her hair loose round her shoulders and the full moon above us, is burnt into my memory. She came into my arms, crying for joy; it was me she shared that moment with, me and nobody else. I remember how soft her hair felt under my lips, threaded between my fingers . . .

When dawn breaks and cold and hunger have the best of me, I walk home. The sky is grey over my head, and it's so, so cold. Every step is agony on my frozen feet.

How long can I keep this up? I want to be with Sarah, I want to know what's happening to her, what Nicholas is doing in her life. But what about the bigger picture? How many Gamekeepers are left, how many heirs? My promise to Harry was to protect Sarah – but my promise to the world is to fight the bigger fight. Can I spend all my time, all my energy, guarding Sarah and only Sarah, when the survival of everyone is at stake?

Gorse Cottage is a near-derelict building at the edge of the moorland, as far as possible from any other house, hidden and unkempt. Ivy climbs up the wall and nearly hides the windows, the grass is high and littered with weeds, uncut for what seems like forever. I want to keep it this way – the fewer people who know it's inhabited, the safer it is for me. My stiff, frozen fingers struggle to turn the key in the lock. Immediately, I sense that something is wrong. I sniff the evening air; it smells of peat. There's a peat fire, somewhere close – and suddenly I realize, it's in *my house*.

I grip my *sgian-dubh* at once – James Midnight's *sgian-dubh*, with its silver handle engraved with Celtic patterns. The red painted door creaks as I make my way in. The house is warm, and the smell of peat even stronger as I step into the entrance hall . . .

There's a light coming from the living room.

There shouldn't be.

My heart is in my throat. I stand for a second, listening, waiting for a sound, a breath, a whisper to reveal who – or what – has made its way into my cottage.

I don't have to wait for long, because a girl with long golden hair steps out of the living room towards me. She's a lot thinner than she used to be, and there's a guarded, tired expression on her face that used to not be there, but it's *her*.

"Elodie," I whisper, and before I know it she's in my arms and we're holding onto each other as if we're all that's left to hold on to. Which might as well be the case.

2
From Within

To return and see
What went before me
The reasons for my heart
To beat the way it does

The last notes of the young man's accordion seeped from the audition room. Sarah sat upright, her back rigid, her hands clutched together, her eyes lowered in concentration. Beside her, her cello in its purple case, and beside the cello, Aunt Juliet, tapping her foot, *tap*, *tap*, *tap*, in rhythm with the music coming from behind the closed door.

There was no way Sarah could have stopped Juliet coming – her aunt had her heart set on it. But if she was honest, she did want Aunt Juliet with her, for moral support. Nicholas had offered to accompany her too, of course, but Sarah couldn't risk being distracted by him on the day of her audition for the Royal Conservatoire of Scotland, the day where she was playing her most precious card: her music. When she was with Nicholas, her mind floated, her thoughts unravelled, and she couldn't have that happening. Today was her day, and hers only. She didn't want to be reminded of all that had happened since her parents were killed, she didn't even want to be a Midnight – just a musician.

Sarah was determined to win a place at the Royal Conservatoire – she just had to. There was nowhere else she wanted to be, nothing else she wanted to do. Her rational mind told her over and over again how hard it would be to keep up with her music studies and be true to the Midnight mission at the same time, but she refused to acknowledge that set of thoughts. She wanted to be a musician too badly to ever be able to accept that it might not happen.

And now, the accordionist was finished. Out he walked, his young face flushed, hurrying towards his mother. The woman rose on her toes and ran a hand through the young man's hair – it was a hesitant, self-conscious sort of gesture, but she couldn't help herself: that tall young man used to be her little boy, after all. Sarah looked away, a stab of pain through her heart.

Mum, you should have been here with me.

"Sarah Midnight."

It was her turn. No time to remember the past, no time to think of anything that hurt. It was time for her music to make its mark, at last.

Sarah picked up her cello and walked into the audition room, heart steady, eyes clear. All of a sudden, her nerves were gone.

All of a sudden, she believed.

"So, how do you think it went?" Aunt Juliet stirred her cappuccino. The Glasgow city centre was bustling with early Christmas shoppers. They had been lucky to find a seat in the John Lewis café.

Sarah shrugged, staring into her hazelnut latte. She was tired after the strain of the morning, but buzzing with the excitement of it. Her dream was so close she could almost touch it. "I don't know. I can't really say. It went well, I think. I just need to wait for the letter now."

Sarah caught Juliet looking at her hands, red and rough. She curled them into fists, trying to hide them away. "My eczema is back," she whispered. She had lied about her hands so many times it had become an alternative truth. Sarah's obsessive cleaning rituals were an open secret, but one she had always refused to discuss.

Juliet nodded, stirring her cappuccino.

Sarah looked away and out of the window at the steps of the Royal Concert Hall. A small group of tourists reading a map, a few seagulls, and a bit further down, a little band of long-haired, kilted pipers and drummers. A sudden memory came back to her: Harry, or the man she used to know as Harry, rubbing cream tenderly into her chapped hands. The sadness of the reverie must have been visible on her face, because Juliet reached out to her and touched her hair gently. Aunt Juliet would never stop trying to do what Sarah's mother should have done.

She cupped Sarah's cheek briefly. "Listen, why don't I treat you to something new to wear? It was a big day, you deserve it."

"It's OK, Aunt Juliet, really."

The older woman pursed her lips. "All right. Maybe you and Bryony could come up to the house later? I'm sure your friend would love to know how your audition went. How is she?"

"I haven't spoken to her in a while."

Juliet was astonished. "You haven't spoken to Bryony in a while?" Sarah and Bryony had been inseparable since they were in nursery. Still, since her best friend Leigh's death . . . nothing had been the same.

A pause, with Sarah taking a sip of her latte, glad of the chance to hide her face behind her long black hair.

"Sarah . . ." Juliet continued. Sarah knew at once what was coming. "Any news of Harry?"

Harry is dead.

Sarah looked out of the window, her gaze resting on the Christmas lights hung across Buchanan Street. "He should come back soon," she replied without missing a beat. "I spoke to him last night." A lie, of course. Lying was something the Midnight family was exceptionally good at. "And he says he has more or less done all he needs to do in London."

"That's great news. So when is he coming back?" Juliet insisted.

"Like I said, soon."

Juliet raised her eyebrows. "Before or after Christmas?"

"After, probably."

Juliet sat back and sighed. "Sarah, that's over two weeks away. You know you can't stay in that house alone, it's stated in your parents' will."

"Well, who'll tell the solicitor? Nobody. Unless you do."

"You know I agree with James's and . . . Anne's decision." Juliet closed her eyes briefly. She still found it difficult to mention her dead sister's name. "You can't live alone. It's not safe."

"Two months is not long. And anyway, I'm going to Islay for Christmas." Now was as good a time as any to tell her aunt that piece of news.

Juliet frowned. "What? On your own?"

"No, of course not. With Nicholas." She made it sound as if she were surprised her aunt hadn't worked that out for herself. She hadn't asked Nicholas yet, but she was in no doubt that he would agree.

"Oh, Sarah. You're not spending the first Christmas after ..." Juliet took a deep breath. "We want you to spend Christmas with us. We're your family ..."

"I know, I know . . ." Sarah felt a pang of guilt. But the first Christmas without her parents, in the company of Juliet and Trevor and her giggly cousins was too much to bear. She wrung her fingers.

"Sarah, please. Do it for me, at least." Hurt and disappointment were painted all over Juliet's face, and Sarah's determination wavered for a second. But no. She had to do this. She had to go back to Islay and try and unravel the mysteries that surrounded the Midnight family. She needed to know the truth about Mairead Midnight, the aunt Sarah didn't know she had until Sean told her. Before that, nobody had mentioned Mairead. Sean didn't know anything about the circumstances of Mairead's death, aged only thirteen, because Harry himself didn't know. Why had it all been kept secret? Why had any memory of her aunt been erased, as if she'd never existed?

Sarah hoped that on Islay, in their ancestral home, she could unravel Mairead's story, and her own story too. Maybe she would begin to understand herself better. She had been a sheltered little girl, and all of a sudden she was a young woman, alone to face a world full of secrets. She was a huntress, bearer of powers she had to learn to control and use to save her own life, and the lives of others. The changes in Sarah's life, in her perception of herself, had been too fast to allow her to grasp and fully own her new identity. She needed to stop and look back, to get her bearings before taking the next steps. Islay was the place to do it.

How could she convey all that to Aunt Juliet, who knew and understood nothing about the world of the Midnights?

She couldn't.

Sarah gathered their empty cups and put them on a tray. She had to stop the compulsion to wipe the table, clearing the crumbs away. "Aunt Juliet, I need to go back to Islay. I need to be . . . near them. I hope you understand."

Juliet sighed. "I *don't*. We might not be Midnights, but we still love you. We want you to be with us. And we do our best, you know."

A touch of resentment had seeped into Juliet's tone. When James Midnight had appeared on the scene all those years ago, her sister's life had immediately shifted to focus on him and his charismatic family. Juliet and her parents, who had died one after the other not long after Anne's wedding, had felt side-lined, forgotten. As if they couldn't quite match up to the golden clan, the charmed Midnights. James never paid much attention to Anne's family. To him, they simply didn't exist. They were a blur at the edge of his perception.

Sarah turned her head away. A woman with a fiddle case strapped across her back was walking up the steps of the Royal Concert Hall. One day, that would be her.

"Is your heart set on this?" asked Juliet.

Sarah nodded.

"Right." A moment of silence while Juliet absorbed her defeat. "I just wish we could come with you. To Islay. But Trevor and the girls, spending Christmas up there . . ."

"No, no. That just wouldn't work," Sarah hurried to reply. No way. She wouldn't be able to do what she had set out to do with the McKettricks there too.

After a moment, Juliet tried again. "But going alone with Nicholas . . . are you sure it's a good idea? He seems like a nice lad, but . . . You've been with him what – only a matter of weeks? Do you know anything about him?"

He saved my life.

"He comes from a good family, Aunt Juliet, I told you. His parents are both lawyers. They're based in Aberdeen, but they're abroad all the time. He's alone for Christmas."

"Oh. Oh well. I suppose it's a bit early for us to meet his family . . .?"

"I haven't met them either," Sarah said quickly, adding, "but I will, soon." Another lie.

She was surprised herself at how quickly her relationship with Nicholas was moving. Sometimes it felt as if someone else was making all her decisions. It was almost puzzling.

"That house is in the middle of nowhere. How will you manage?"

"We'll be fine, Aunt Juliet!" Sarah pulled her jacket from the back of the chair and swivelled her cello case so that she could shrug the straps over her shoulders. "Better go. Nicholas will be waiting for me. He'll want to know how the audition went. There's no need for you to take me home, I'll just take the train."

"Sarah . . ." Juliet put a hand on Sarah's sleeve as they got up. Her eyes were warm, but her voice was steely. "Harry must be back by Christmas or just after, or you're moving in with us. It'd only be until you're eighteen. But that's the way it must be."

The thought of being removed from her home made Sarah's stomach churn. "You'll report me to the solicitor?" Her voice trembled with hurt.

"I'll protect you, Sarah. It's for your own good."

Sarah threw up her hands. "You'll protect me? Like my parents did?" she spat. "This conversation is over." She strode off, leaving Juliet to hurry after her through the shop.

★

Neither of them noticed the hunched, thin figure who'd sat at a table behind them, at such an angle that he wouldn't be seen, but he could see them. Neither of them, therefore, was aware of the fact that the figure's eyes had never left them throughout the conversation, that he'd heard every word Sarah and Juliet said, and that he'd followed them on their way out.

3
Stolen

I saw you falling slowly
For many years
Death told me
She'd come for you first

Of course, Juliet insisted on driving Sarah home. There was no chance Sarah could convince her aunt to let her go back by train.

Sarah didn't say a word as they travelled along the motorway, her cello resting on the backseat and her thoughts all tangled up. *My parents' will. Selfish, selfish and stupid.*

But it wasn't, really, it wasn't stupid or selfish. A girl alone in a huge house – it was a risk in any circumstance, even more so if the girl in question was a precious Secret heir, and a Dreamer. The selfish thing had been not to teach her to fight – to leave her helpless and force her to learn fast, and alone.

So much for protecting me, she said to herself. All she knew when they'd died was that she was a Dreamer, and that her parents used her dreams to know if there were demons around, and where. That was her knowledge of the Midnight mission, in a nutshell. A drop in the sea of what she should have learnt.

Each Secret Family has one Dreamer whose gift awakens at the age of thirteen – and they all pay a terrible price for it. Their nightmares are a torture they can't escape, and one over which they have no control. They dream of the demons – or Surari, as they're known in the ancient language – that seep into the world. Sometimes the Dreamers themselves become victims, hurt or even murdered in the course of their visions, and although they suffer no physical damage, they have to endure the pain and the panic as if it were happening for real. In her dreams, Sarah had been burnt, drowned, buried; most nights waking up screaming in a house that was often empty, with her parents out hunting. The constant terror had heightened Sarah's obsessive nature. She'd wake up from some terrifying ordeal to clean and tidy and straighten anything she could put her hands on. Her rituals were her protection against the chaos in her life.

Every night, alone in her huge, silent house, waiting for her parents to come back from the hunt, she performed her routines of wiping and sorting and aligning. If she did everything perfectly, in the right order, the correct number of times, her parents would return. If anything was out of place, if she neglected the smallest detail, her parents would be killed, and it'd be all her fault. It was on that basis that she had lived her life.

Her pact with God hadn't worked. In the end, her parents were dead. But if she stopped, more tragedy might befall her.

The Dreamer's duty was to write everything they saw in their dream diary, so that the hunters of the family would know what and where to hunt. Sarah's diary was a black, leather-bound volume that had caused her endless anguish and symbolized all the fear she'd had to endure throughout her childhood. That volume was now a mound of cold ash in the fireplace, and its leather cover had floated down the nearby river towards the sea. Sarah had torn it page by page in a fit of anger towards her parents, towards her destiny. Burning her diary and throwing the remains into the river hadn't changed her predicament, but it had freed her from so many terrible memories. There didn't seem to be any need for another dream diary. Since the Scottish Valaya had been defeated and its leader Cathy Duggan killed, Sarah's dreams had all but disappeared. At first it had been a relief, after the fraught few weeks when she'd been under nearly constant attack and dreaming like never before – but the truth was that the eerie silence that filled her nights was making her increasingly uncomfortable. Was it the quiet before the storm?

Sean would know. In those few short months he, as Harry, had become her family, her world. Because her "cousin" was living with her, Juliet allowed Sarah to stay in her home, abiding by her parents' will. She would never forget his arrival during these worst of times, to give her a ray of hope in such darkness.

But he had lied. Harry Midnight was dead. Sean Hannay was his real name. Sean Hannay was the man who had pretended to be her cousin, had stolen his identity, the man who might have killed him, too. She couldn't be sure.

Sarah's anger at Sean's betrayal had been so great she had nearly used the Blackwater on him, the deadly Midnight power that could dissolve any living creature, but she had stopped herself in time. She shuddered at the memory of how close she had come. She refused to listen to his reasons, she refused to speak to him at all, and had sent him out of her house, out of her life. The night Cathy Duggan was finally killed was the last time Sarah had seen Sean.

She missed him terribly.

Despite everything, she missed him every day, every hour. Not even Nicholas could fill his absence, even as persistent and as heady as his presence could be. But Sean was a liar. He had made his way into her home, into her heart, on false pretences. He wasn't her cousin, he wasn't a Midnight – he was someone else, of whom Sarah knew a name and nothing more.

Sarah felt that her upset must be written all over her face, and turned towards the car window, letting her hair fall between her and Juliet and cover her like a curtain.

She didn't want to have anything to do with Sean ever again.

She wanted to hear his voice.

She wanted him to come back.

She wanted him to go away, and disappear forever.

She didn't know what she wanted.

And in the middle of this swirling galaxy of Sean thoughts stood Nicholas.

It was Nicholas who'd explained all that Sarah's parents and Sean hadn't told her, in their vain attempt to protect her. He had told her about the existence of other Secret Families, about the Sabha, the Secret Council that bound them together, and how the Scottish Valaya, the coven they had destroyed, was just one of many throughout the world.

She was still in danger; Nicholas had made that clear. But she had him on her side. Of all the humans and Surari she had encountered over the past months, nothing and nobody could compare to him. The way he mastered the Elementals, the spirits of the elements, bending them to his will; the way he could call those blue flames to burn from his fingertips; the way he seemed to make her forget everything just by looking into her eyes . . . He had saved her life by killing Cathy, and now he was saving her from being completely alone. He had proved himself to her, over and over again.

And still there were times, even now, when Sarah felt utterly bereft, as if there was an abyss opening right in front of her feet.

Is this what love is?

Sarah had no answer. Nicholas was, after all, her first boyfriend. *Was this love, this heady feeling, this sense of burning up and not caring about anything, anyone but him?* Not caring for herself, either. Still, in spite of her doubts, she couldn't stay away from Nicholas. He had been there for her when nobody else was. And she was happy, wasn't she? As happy as she could be in the mess her life now was.

"Hey, sweetheart."

And there he was, Nicholas, waiting on the stone steps of her house. Sarah could feel Juliet's gaze burning into her back as he put his arms around her and kissed her.

"Well done." Nicholas waved to Juliet over Sarah's shoulder. Sarah turned to see Aunt Juliet waving back, a smile on her face. Her stomach knotted all of a sudden, and a feeling of sorrow, of loss, overcame her for a moment. She watched Juliet drive away as if you'd watch a drowning person sink underwater. She closed her eyes for a second, astonished at the intensity of the grief, wondering where it'd come from.

"Sarah?"

"Yes?"

"You're a million miles away. I said 'well done'."

"Thanks. Thanks." Sarah stretched her mouth into a smile,

but the dreadful feeling of loss was still gripping her. "But I don't know how it went yet. I won't know until March."

Nicholas took her cello from her as she unlocked the door. "*I* know," he told her. "I've got a feeling your performance today knocked them all out."

"I hope so. Come on in." She opened the door and removed her shoes before walking in to the hallway. Nicholas knew by now of her rituals. He stood back as she hung up their coats, trying in vain to make them sit straight. Sarah's obsessions amused him, like a charming eccentricity

"Would you like something to eat?" she asked.

"I'm not hungry, thanks." He slipped his arms around her waist. Sarah tensed for a moment – she had never enjoyed being touched. *But shouldn't it be different, with your boyfriend?* Nicholas kissed the top of her head and she breathed in his signature scent of soil and woodsmoke.

"Actually, I need to talk to you," she began.

"Talking is not what I had in mind!" he laughed. "But sure, let's go."

Sarah ignored the pang of hunger in her stomach. She was ravenous after her long day, and she would have loved to cook something. But it was somehow easier to take Nicholas's lead. That was the way things seemed to work between them.

Nicholas had appeared in her dreams over and over again, before they ever met in real life. She used to call him "Leaf", because he'd leave autumn leaves on her pillow, on her doorstep, among her books, for her to find. She treasured them, pressing them into the silver photo album Juliet had given her for Christmas. Nine transparent pockets, nine leaves – red, gold and yellow. She'd kept them hidden under her bed so that Sean wouldn't find them. Sean was always wary of him.

Nicholas hunkered down in front of the fireplace, fuel briquettes and little twigs piled up, ready to light. He touched them with his long, pale fingers, and blue flames started burning at once, silently. Sarah wasn't sure if she loved those blue flames or if they spooked her, dancing blue in place of a hot, red fire.

"Nicholas."

"Yes? What's on your mind?"

"It's not over, is it?"

"Between us? It's just started, are you ditching me already?" he said in mock alarm.

"Please, be serious. You know what I mean. You said you'd tell me everything, but there's still so much I don't understand."

"OK, OK. Sorry. No, of course it's not over. But I'm here to protect you, so what's the problem?"

"Cathy's Valaya . . . you said it's not the only one."

"No. There are many of them."

"Why now? What has happened to . . . to organize the Surari in this way?"

Nicholas hesitated for a second. "I see no point worrying about that. All we need to do is stay alive, and with me here, nothing can hurt you, Sarah."

She tried to read his expression. His black eyes were very lucid, very bright – but impenetrable, like the surface of a still, dark loch – it was impossible to gauge what lay underneath. He took her in his arms and she rested her head on his chest, thinking she'd only stay there a minute, time for the world to stop swirling.

An hour later, she was still curled into him, as Nicholas stroked her hair slowly, hypnotically.

"Nicholas . . ."

"Yes?"

"There was something else." Sarah tried to feel her way out of the fog that enveloped her thoughts.

"Tell me."

"I need . . . I need something to eat first."

"Is that what you wanted to say?" he laughed.

"No, no. Just, I haven't eaten since last night. Come on." Nicholas followed her into the kitchen, where she stood in front of her cupboards, and sighed. When Nicholas was around, cooking seemed a huge effort somehow. And to get her kitchen dirty filled her with dread. She'd have to wipe each surface a million times over.

"Nicholas," she began.

While she was trying to decide how to ask him to go to Islay with her – so difficult, when her brain felt as if it was full of cotton wool – a little black ghost with a white paw crossed the room, as quick as lightning, and jumped onto her lap.

"Shadow, my sweetie." The cat purred and burrowed into Sarah's neck. Since the whole Cathy business, she had become very clingy, especially when Nicholas was around. She liked Nicholas even less than she liked Sean, who had sent her to sleep when he'd first arrived at the house. He had touched her between her eyes and put her out cold. Shadow had never forgotten that, let alone forgiven it.

Sarah cuddled the cat for a bit, placing little kisses all over her fur under Nicholas's impatient gaze. He didn't like Sarah giving attention to anything else but him. Finally she let Shadow go, and put the kettle on. A cup of tea with lots of sugar was the safest option.

"What did you want to talk to me about?" asked Nicholas as Sarah wiped away stains only she could see.

She took a deep breath. "My parents' will." She moved on to polishing her already spotless kitchen table. "You see, I am not allowed to live in this house on my own. Not until I'm eighteen." Her hands were shaking with nerves and hunger.

"I don't understand. What happens if you live here on your own?"

"I'd have to renounce everything, including this house. The condition for me to inherit is that I don't live alone. And I can't lose this place. I just can't."

"Are you asking me to move in, Sarah?" Nicholas touched her arm.

"No, no way!" she said vehemently, and then blushed when she saw his stricken face. "We've been together a month!"

"Yes. But one day . . ."

Sarah blushed even more, her cheeks and neck blotched red in a way he found impossibly cute. Suddenly he remembered someone else – someone else he had loved who blushed just like that, red roses on her amber cheeks.

He swallowed. "Sorry, I don't mean to put you under pressure," he said. "It's just that with my parents being abroad so much, and your parents . . . gone, and the dangers that surround us, we might as well stick together."

I need sugar now. The room was spinning again. Sarah assembled her cup of tea quickly – teabag, sugar, milk – before Nicholas could interrupt her, before her thoughts could go adrift again. She took a sip of it at once, scalding her lips.

"I told Aunt Juliet that *Harry* is in London for business."

"Right." Nicholas nodded slowly, never taking his eyes off her.

"That he'll be back after Christmas."

"And it's a lie."

Sarah nodded, looking away.

"The guy is crazy, Sarah. Who in their right mind would pretend to be your cousin?"

"Cathy said . . . She said Sean killed Harry to steal his identity."

Nicholas shrugged. "Does it matter at this stage? The point is that he lied to you. You can't trust him."

"No. No, I can't. I know that."

"You're with me now. Don't forget that."

"No, of course."

"So what are you going to do? About the house, I mean?"

"I have no idea. I'll be eighteen next October. If I manage to throw Juliet off the scent until then . . ."

"Why don't we . . . pretend? Why don't we tell her I moved in? I'll still be sleeping in my house – mostly . . ." Sarah looked away. The mention of "sleeping" made her heart beat faster. "But we tell her I'm staying here. That we're serious."

"That would freak her out!"

"Yes, but better than you moving in with them and bringing who knows what to their doorstep! And anyway, we are serious, aren't we?"

"Yes. We are." Sarah drew a breath. He was right. That was the worst-case scenario, but a possible one. Not only having to leave her home and all that it contained, but also putting Aunt Juliet and her family in danger. That couldn't happen.

"Okay," she whispered.

"Settled, then. Don't worry, I'm a good liar." He laughed.

"So am I," she replied seriously.

Nicholas took her face in his hands, and kissed her – so gently, so slowly, that she forgot all about her sugary tea. When he let her go, she was too dazed to swallow anything. Her hunger was gone. Again. She felt she might faint. *I know that love is supposed to make you lose your appetite, but this is a bit much.*

"I've got to go."

"Don't go," she heard herself pleading. A knot of unease

settled in her stomach. This wasn't like her. She was turning into someone else, someone she didn't know.

"I'll be back tomorrow!" he reassured her, smiling.

Sarah followed him down the hall and watched as he pulled his jacket from the hook. She couldn't put off asking him any longer.

"One last thing, Nicholas."

"Yes?"

"When school finishes for Christmas, I'm going to go to Islay. For the whole holiday. My family has a house there. I was wondering . . ."

He kissed the tip of her nose. "Of course. I'd love to go with you. Is that what you meant to ask me?"

"Yes, yes it was."

"Deal."

"Are you sure?"

"Well, you know my parents won't be around, and I can't let you out of my sight, can I? It'd be too dangerous." He slipped his arms around her waist again.

"Settled, then. Christmas on Islay," she said, her face against his chest once more.

"I can't wait."

He walked down the stone steps, Sarah following him with her eyes, leaning on the doorframe. She watched him go, then closed the door. There was still the cleaning to do – weird how much mess making a cup of tea could generate – and then she could drag herself to bed, to a dreamless sleep.

4

Shadows in Edinburgh

Is this love
If every time you go
I fall?

The night was busy and full of sounds, as always around the Royal Mile approaching Christmas time. Bright shop windows, people coming in and out of restaurants and pubs, voices in many languages and the inevitable piper entertaining the tourists. And still, there was something in the mist curling around the stones of the ancient buildings, something in the white moon above and in the dark winding streets, that made Edinburgh look mysterious and slightly sinister even on the busiest, liveliest of nights.

Nicholas felt at home there. Nowhere else in the world, no other places he had passed through or lived in during his years of wandering resonated with him as this Scottish city did. There was something black and rotting in the heart of Edinburgh, a taste for death that called to him. He often walked the streets and closes and wynds until late, and sometimes until dawn – he hardly needed any sleep to sustain his human body – letting the cold and dark seep into his bones.

As he strode down the Royal Mile, Nicholas attracted quite a lot of attention – with his black clothes and his height, he towered over the passers-by. He always got a few second glances, especially from girls and women mesmerized by his perfect, flawless face and his muscular frame. Nicholas never seemed to have to yield to anyone in his path. People moved left and right to avoid bumping into each other, with unspoken agreements of looks and body language, but Nicholas walked straight on. He wasn't aggressive with it – he didn't elbow people, he didn't glare at them, he didn't even look at them. They seemed to move of their own accord to let him pass, the stream of people opening up in two wings, with the black-clad young man in the middle.

That night he felt unusually peaceful. Things with Sarah were going according to plan. He hadn't lied to her about her safety; she would be spared. She was no longer in danger of losing her life by the hand of that deranged woman, Cathy Duggan and her Valaya. She wasn't in danger of being attacked by the Surari at all. They'd keep coming at her, but it'd just be a well-rehearsed dance, under Nicholas's supervision.

They won't touch a hair on your head, my Sarah. You'll follow me to the Shadow World, and be my wife for the rest of days. You and I will guard the opening between worlds, and my chains will be so much more bearable, and the darkness less daunting because of you. Your skin will turn as pale as mine, and you'll dream more than ever – you'll hardly ever be awake.

But Nicholas knew that there was some way to go before he could call Sarah his own. He needed to convince her that going with him was her only choice. No woman could be forced to be the King of Shadows' bride. She wouldn't be able to be tied to the Shadow World then. No, she had to come willingly, as his mother had.

Once again, his mother's face came to haunt him, shimmering in the shop windows, in the moonlit puddles, in every woman he saw. It was the face that appeared in his sweetest dreams, a distant memory of happiness never to come back.

Ekaterina Krol *chose* to marry the King of Shadows. He'd used her newborn baby, little, vulnerable Nicholas, and the desperate need of mother and son for each other as a bargaining tool to convince her. Her whole family had warned her of the dark stranger, a man who often disappeared for days without a word – even the King of Shadows, with all his powers, couldn't be away from the Shadow World for long periods at a time. She didn't listen, of course. Nicholas's father had used on her the same mind-moulding that Nicholas was using on Sarah, and it didn't take long for him to own her mind. By then, he knew Ekaterina's thoughts inside out; he came to believe that the best way to break her would be to make her a mother, and use the baby as a way to lure her into the Shadow World.

And he was right. Ekaterina's and the King of Shadows' son, the heir of Shadows, came into the world not long after. Ekaterina was smitten with her son; she called him Nicholas, after her own father, and for a short moment she was happy.

But one night, when the baby was only a few days old, she woke up to find him gone. She and her family searched everywhere, day after day and night after night. Ekaterina wandered the woods in despair, calling her son's name. It was on one of these lonely expeditions that the King of Shadows appeared to her and told her the whole truth: who he was, where he'd taken Nicholas, and how the only way for her to ever be with her son again was to shed her body and follow them both, son and father, into the Shadow World.

Many long years of life in the darkness as a spirit, with the man – or *what* was he? – who had betrayed her was a horrifying prospect, but a life without her son, or even one more day, one more hour without him – was worse.

And so Ekaterina shed her body and was bound to the Shadows.

Sarah Midnight, Nicholas thought dreamily. *I'll be the one who saves you over and over again, from the Surari, from your family's interference, from feeling alone, with nobody knowing what your life is really like. I'll be the only one who knows your secrets, I'll be your lighthouse in the storm, the one you can rely on in a chaotic world. I'll make you weak so that I can be strong for you. I'll make you unable to stand on your own two feet so that I can be the one who props you up. I'll make your body ill and worn so that you'll long to be free of it. I'll make sure you're alone, and then I'll be the one who rescues you from the ice in your heart.*

The thought of Sarah broken and dependent on him filled Nicholas with anticipation. He walked on, revelling in his human body and his god-like powers. The night enveloped him and filled him with blessed, welcome darkness. For a moment, the constant whirlpools of his mind had stopped, giving him some relief – and life, and his predicament, and his future, seemed nearly bearable.

And then, the flames in his mind exploded again. No warning, no hint that it was all about to start. It was a sudden explosion of voices, screaming at him from inside his brain. His head spun for a moment, the night sky and the pavement swapping places, and the familiar smell of burning and of rotting, hidden things hit his nostrils. The smell of death. The smell of home.

The voices from the Shadow World were screaming, calling, clamouring for attention. And among those voices, the one that had no need to scream, the one that would always be listened to, the one that claimed his life, his will, his very own soul: that of his father, the King of Shadows.

Nicholas regained his balance and walked on, wincing, trying with all his might to keep his thoughts on the Edinburgh night, on his steps, on the people around him. On reality. He just didn't want to be cut up inside again, he didn't want to open his mind to his father. Not that what he wanted mattered at all. Peace, for Nicholas, never lasted long.

There was only one solution, one way to block out the voices at least for a little bit: human company. Human voices and human bodies to keep him tethered to this world, away from the shadows.

Nicholas made his way into a club and came out not much later with a small, blue-haired, bird-like girl on his arm. It was as simple as that for him. Like picking a flower from a field. It wasn't entirely natural, of course. Some of Nicholas's charisma was very much about mind-moulding – and often the girls would have flashbacks for weeks and months afterwards, wondering what made them follow the tall, dark-haired man who whisked them away so easily and then didn't speak a word the next morning.

Her name was Laura. Nicholas held her hand tenderly on their way to his townhouse. For all the hatred in his heart, for all the anger he felt and that terrible, irresistible desire to destroy that ran in his veins, he would not harm her. He kept the anger for himself and burnt silently. For one night he would caress her, and touch her hair as gently as a mother, and kiss her as if he was in love.

Love was part of the fantasy. Tenderness was something he looked for in them, the girls he couldn't tell one from another. They had to be beautiful, and none of them could have long black hair; he couldn't bear that, he couldn't bear to be reminded of the girl from long ago. Only Sarah would do that for him and still be there the next morning, still be his.

Laura. She would talk about her job and her family, she would laugh nervously and accept another vodka. She would be wholly and entirely human, with her worries about make-up and a compact mirror falling out of her bag and a run in her tights, and the photo of her nieces in her wallet. He would hold her and speak to her long into the night, and prevent her from falling asleep so that he would not be left alone to the calls of the Shadow World. Until her eyes would close, and eventually he'd have to give up and answer his father's call, as the noise in his head grew louder, unbearable.

Nicholas couldn't stop thinking of Sarah as he kissed the blue-haired girl. It would have to be just Sarah and him in the world soon. Nobody else for her, nobody else for him, ever again. So this is what he'd have to do: the people closest to her would have to die. They'd just distract her otherwise. She'd have to be properly alone but for him, and she couldn't be if she had aunts and best friends and all that bloody farce of a family, could she?

I'll take my time, and when you're ready, the journey will begin. From Scotland to the gate of the Shadow World, every step forward will be another drop of your faith in life trickling away. Shame I couldn't just move in with you now. It would be so good to spend all my time with you, day and night. But it'd be too soon. My control of your mind is not strong enough yet, though it seems to be working extremely well – and you might get suspicious. I hardly sleep, I hardly eat, my father contacts me when I least expect it. And I'm often surrounded by my Elementals. How much I would have loved it to be me and you, as good as married already . . . but I have to be careful.

The last time they had worked on breaking a chosen wife . . . It didn't end well, and all their plans were shot to pieces. They couldn't make that mistake with Sarah.

The girl from long ago.

For a second, the blue-haired young woman resting on his pillow looked at him with black eyes, and not her own blue ones – and the arms entwined around his back were amber-skinned and not white. For a second the girl from long ago, the one chosen before Sarah, the one he'd loved . . . she lay on his bed and called his name.

Laura lay asleep beside him, her dress draped over the end of the bed, her shoes and her coat abandoned on the wooden floor.

Another girl he wouldn't remember the name of, who held no meaning, who left him with no memories. Just a short-lived relief from the voices that screamed constantly in his mind, from the terror that grasped him more and more often as the time to be bound in the Shadow World grew closer. A desperate way to grab some crumbs of human life for himself before he'd have to shed his human form and his spirit life would begin. A warm body, lips that smiled, the need to eat and drink and sleep – a girl who smelled and felt like life.

Until she fell asleep, and the dark closed on him again. He considered waking her up and throwing her out, but he had no energy left for that – the voices were crippling him already.

There was no escape.

You might think that being a Dreamer is a curse, Sarah, and it is – but you have no idea what it's like to be born of a mortal woman and of the most powerful Surari of all time. Try that, then you'll realize that in comparison, being a Dreamer is as easy as breathing.

Nicholas sat up on his bed and took his head in his hands, moaning softly. The voices from the Shadow World were ripping his mind, refusing to be silenced any longer.

The night was spent in agony.

A few painful, burning hours later, the blue-haired girl woke with a smile, make-up strewn on her face. With her eyes still closed, she stretched out her arm and felt the sheet beside her, looking for Nicholas. But the bed was empty.

He was sitting on the floor in a corner, his arms around his knees, sunken, red-rimmed eyes. When he saw she was awake, he got up without looking at her, crossed the room in his bare feet and stood framed in the doorway.

"I'm going out. By the time I come back I want you gone."

5
Evening Star

A hidden place
Heather and myrtle
Gorse and mist
The in-between
Take me there with you.

Sean

I hold Elodie against me again. My mouth feels strange, stretched into a smile like that. How long has it been since I last smiled? Or laughed? Even the sound of my voice right now, so happy, seems to belong to someone else.

And then a terrible dread hits me: that the heir Elodie was protecting, Aiko Ayanami, is dead, and that's why she's here.

I take her by the shoulders and look into her eyes. "Aiko?"

"Aiko is alive." And then she corrects herself. "She was alive when I left. One of the Gamekeepers I lived with is looking after her. But . . ."

"What happened?" I urge her gently.

"A Gamekeeper – a *friend* – was killed." Elodie clasps her

hands over her mouth, her voice laden with unshed tears. "She was so young. Marina Frison was her name. I had to go, Sean. I couldn't hide away any longer. We must do something more than just protect the heirs. We must do something more."

She's getting distressed, her eyes feverish all of a sudden. I hold her hands against my chest. "Yes, yes. We must. But first, come on, come and sit near the fire. You need something to eat, and some sleep. You look terrible."

"Thanks!" She smiles in the midst of her tears.

"No, no, that's not what I meant . . ." I lead her to one of the worn, threadbare sofas.

"I know. I do look terrible, though." She leans against me as we sit. "I've been feeling strange lately. I'm sure it's just the strain of hiding, watching, waiting . . ." She shakes her head. "Never mind. Sean, there's something I need to tell you." Her brown eyes burn into mine. "I have seen Sarah's death in a vision, on my way here."

I stop in my tracks, my heart in my throat.

"She was being murdered. I couldn't see his face, the killer's, I mean. I don't know what he was doing, but Sarah was dying right there, slowly in front of him."

I feel a terrible cold invade me, sharper and crueller than the winter cold outside, in spite of the sweet-smelling peat burning on the hearth. I stand and stoop in front of the fire to turn the peat with the metal tongs. "When?" My voice is deadly calm, deadly quiet, though my heart is beating so hard I think the whole world can hear it.

"I don't know. I couldn't spot any clues, when, or where."

"And the man? Who was he? A demon?"

"I don't know. I couldn't make out his features."

How far in the future is Elodie's vision? And who is the man, or demon, who's destined to do it? I walk to the window, watching the purple sky turning orange over the hills as dawn breaks slowly. "I must go and see Sarah. I must tell her. She's not . . ." I take a deep breath. "She won't speak to me."

Elodie is aghast. "Why? What happened?"

"Harry had asked me to take his place. His identity. Did you know?"

"Yes. He often mentioned how distrusting the Midnights are. I think he felt it was the only way."

"It was. But when Sarah found out . . . You see, the woman who told her, Cathy Duggan" – her name is so odious to me – "was the head of the Scottish Valaya. She's dead now. She told Sarah that I killed Harry to take his place."

"Oh no . . ."

"I don't know if Sarah really believes that. But she knows I've been lying. She threw me out of her house, she doesn't want anything to do with me. I'm still guarding her, of course."

"Is that where you've been all night?" Elodie crosses the room to stand beside me. She takes my still icy hands in hers. "That's why you're freezing."

"Yes. I was keeping watch."

"We need to tell Sarah everything. No more lies."

"I know. I know. You see, someone is . . . with her."

"Someone? Another heir?"

"He *says* he is. I don't know if it's true. His name is Nicholas Donal."

Elodie frowns. "I've heard of the Donal family, yes, but I never knew any of them, and I don't think Harry did either."

"The thing is . . . There's something strange going on. Nicholas and Sarah are together now. It happened so quickly."

Elodie looks at me as if to say *what's so strange about that?*

"You don't know Sarah. She is . . . she was . . . It's just that I think this Nicholas has some kind of a weird hold on her. I don't know. I . . ." I stop myself from saying any more. I just can't tell Elodie about my feelings for Sarah.

"I'll come with you. I'll speak to her."

"No. I've got to do it. You can come with me, but I need to speak to her alone. I need to convince her to let me back into her life. "

"Fine." She shrugs in a very French way. "I need to show you something. Wait." Elodie takes hold of the brown canvas rucksack she had left beside the fireplace, and takes out something wrapped in a linen cloth. "I took this from Harry's desk." She unwraps the book, carefully holding the linen cloth. I notice it's embroidered in red thread with the letters MF, intertwined in a delicate pattern. I take it gently from her hands and examine it. On the cover there's a grim illustration: a girl in a long dress, wandering in a wood at night. The girl holds a stick with a skull perched on top of it, and blue rays of light are streaming out of the skull's eyes.

"I went through Harry's things, looking for a hint, a clue about what's happening. I found this. And now I think he *wanted* me to find it. It was in a box on his desk, under lock and key. I took it, together with some letters he sent me. I wanted to keep a part of him with me."

I nod.

"I read it over and over again, but I just couldn't understand why this book was precious enough to be kept in a locked box. And then, on the way here, I saw something. Look—" She takes the book from my hand and opens it a few pages in. "Look at this word. There's a little dot under the S. It's so tiny, I didn't see it for ages. And look, there too."

"Oh, yes."

"And there are others throughout the book. When I made a list of all the letters that had been marked, I didn't recognize them as anything English or French. I can't even pronounce them. So I began to think it could be Gaelic. You see, Harry's family spoke Gaelic, and Harry had a few Gaelic books around. I'd seen the language before. Harry has used asterisks here and there, and I think they mark the different words." Elodie takes the book from me and opens to the last page. She's scribbled a few words on the back cover.

Sann*an*Ile*a*tha*n*fhreagairt*cum*faire*air
Morag*airson*gur*ise*an*iuchair.

I recognize it as Gaelic, but I can't pronounce it either, and I have no idea what it means.

"The only word I understand is . . ." I begin.

But Elodie is quick. ". . . *Morag*," she says. "Could it be Morag Midnight, Harry's grandmother?"

"Yes. I'm certain that it is. Sarah told me that Morag used to speak Gaelic with her dad, and she can speak it a bit herself. She'll know what it means. But why did Harry leave you a message in Gaelic, knowing you wouldn't understand?"

"Maybe it was a way to tell me that I needed to go to Scotland and find Sarah. And you. I mean, I couldn't risk asking anyone, or Google it or something. The Sabha's people are everywhere, and he was aware of that."

"I'll show it to Sarah when I go and see her."

"I won't be parted from this book, Sean. *We'll* show it to Sarah together if she agrees to listen to you."

"Yes." I know Elodie is right. What if something were to happen to me tonight and the book fell into Nicholas's hands? Or got lost?

"What about Mike?" Elodie asks. "Have you heard from him? Is he still in Louisiana with Niall Flynn?"

"I don't know. We were in constant contact until a few weeks ago. Then, nothing."

Elodie wraps her arms around herself. "Maybe they're hiding somewhere else. I can't think that ... I can't believe ... Harry had complete faith in Mike. I'm sure they're alive," she says. She doesn't sound sure at all.

"Yes. Of course. Harry always told me that Niall wa— *is* – amazing." *Is.* He *is* amazing. There's no way I'm using the past tense until I know for sure what's happened. I shake my head. "I can't believe you're here, Elodie."

She smiles, her shy, bashful Elodie smile. "It's so good to see you, Sean. I didn't think I'd ever see you again." She looks so young. And so weary.

"You need some rest now."

"So do you."

I shrug. "You know me, I never sleep."

"You must. Hey, you must." She looks at me, concerned. "I'll have a quick shower and make us something to eat, then I want you to go straight to bed, *d'accord*?"

I look into her face, and her features are so familiar, so ... Elodie. My kind, old friend who's been with me since the beginning of it all.

"Deal. But I'll cook," I warn her.

"Oh, not that again!" she laughs, and the sound of her laughter is so inconsistent with the situation – a ray of sunshine in the middle of a storm. "I'm not that bad!"

"You're a terrible cook, Elodie Midnight. Terrible. Admit it."

"I'll never admit it!"

"Even Harry used to say—"

I don't finish the sentence. Elodie's face is frozen, her mouth open in a little "o". I've hurt her. I shouldn't have mentioned him like that, laughing.

"At last," she whispers.

"What . . . what do you mean?"

"It's the first time I hear his name spoken like this. You know, in a normal conversation. Not about the Sabha, or his death or whatever. Like we actually used to have a life, me and him. Not a normal life, but – well, it was our life. And there was more to it than all this . . . destruction."

I wonder if any of us will ever lead normal lives again. Or a life at all.

6

When You Return

If only you and me
Meant something more
Than bittersweet memories

Sean

It's nearly midday. Elodie is sleeping, snug among the sofa cushions, like a child. I have wrapped the duvet around her and brushed her hair away from her face. I should sleep too – I've been awake for nearly twenty-four hours now – but of course I can't. My days and nights are a daze, mixed up in what seems like a constant, freezing twilight. Making myself invisible for such long periods has a strange effect on my body. My breathing gets slower, my blood goes cold, my metabolism slows down: like a sort of frozen state, a kind of sleep that gives no rest to the body, but instead wears it out. I'm not sure how long I can keep my vigil up.

I watch Elodie as she sleeps. She couldn't stand being hidden in Italy, waiting and hoping to come out of this alive. She couldn't stand it, and neither can I. The Secret Families are being decimated, the Surari are stronger than ever – soon there will be nobody left to protect humanity from them. We need to rise up and confront the Enemy, not just try and survive, hiding away like mice in their holes.

My fingers close around the protection charm Sarah made for me. I always carry it around my neck – to keep a piece of Sarah with me.

Finally, I shake myself and take a hot shower. Changing into clean, warm clothes is such a relief. After that, I'm at a loss, as I wait for night to fall again so I can look for Sarah. It's her audition for the Royal Conservatoire, today – the eighth of December. I remember when she got the letter confirming the date – in the middle of Cathy's attack, not knowing if an hour later we'd still be alive. That letter meant so much to her. Music means so much to her.

Sometimes, as I sit still and hidden in her garden, I build a little world in my head. A world with no Surari, no Secret Families, no Gamekeepers. A world where Sarah and I meet like two normal people – a doctor and a cellist – somewhere in the world, here in Edinburgh, or Christchurch, or Tokyo, who cares? Anywhere in the world where we can be ourselves.

Just Sarah and Sean, no lies, no secrets.

I might as well try and get some rest. I force myself to lie on my bed, trying without success to invoke sleep. Out of the window I can see the top of the pines, swaying in the breeze against the milky sky, and wonder if it's going to snow soon.

"Hello." Elodie's face, framed by her blonde hair, appears in the doorway.

I sit up, propping myself against the pillows. "You're awake. Enjoyed your nap?"

She crosses the room to sit beside me, her footsteps silent on the dusty floor. She smells fresh, of shampoo and mint shower gel. She's wearing clean clothes too, a white top and jeans – she loves wearing light colours, she always has. Her hair is hanging in long damp strands. She looks better than when she first arrived. Her face is not as tired, not as lined, but there's still a pallor, a frailty about her that used to not be there.

"I had a dream."

"An attack?" I ask, alarmed.

"Not exactly. It's strange. I dreamt of a woman, a girl with silver hair. She was swimming in the sea. I was in the sea too, the water came up to my neck." She touches her white throat with her fingers. "And then a wave came, a weird wave that seemed to have . . . arms. Out to get me." She trembles for a second. "The wave took me under, but the woman with the silver hair saved me. She held my head out of the water and took me to shore."

"Do you have an idea of who she was?"

"I'll find out sooner or later, I suppose. You can't sleep?" Elodie asks, but she knows the answer.

"You know me." I rub my forehead.

"Yes. I remember the way you were in Japan. I don't know how you keep going on no sleep."

"I don't know either."

"Harry always said he only slept when he was happy."

"No chance for me, then!" I try to smile, but it's more like a grimace.

"Why don't I sit here with you, and you can give it another try?"

Elodie walks over and perches herself on the windowsill, hugging her knees. An invisible hand squeezes my heart – Sarah loves doing that, sitting on her windowsill looking out to her garden, wrapped in that white jumper she has.

I'm about to tell Elodie that there's no point, I'm awake, it's not going to happen, but I'm tired, so tired, and my eyelids start feeling heavy. Elodie's profile looks exquisite, nearly angelic against the white sky and the black, swaying trees. She's humming a tune under her breath, a slow, soft song I've never heard before, sweet as a lullaby. I feel myself relax ... and then my heart flutters, my limbs tense up in sudden alarm – they don't want to let go, they don't want to give into sleep.

But I haven't rested for so long, and Elodie's voice is cradling me. Before I know it, I drift away with it. At last.

I wake as gently as I fell asleep, without the usual jolt of panic. My mind goes straight to the first thought I always have when I awake – where's my *sgian-dubh*? I check – it's on my bedside table.

Next, as ever, is a thought of Sarah. I need to see Sarah.

"*Ça va?*"

I rub my face with my hands. Elodie is sitting on my bed. I notice her fingers curled around her silver star necklace – the one Harry gave to her. I was with him when he bought it. Only yesterday, it seems.

"What's the time?"

"It's just past midnight. British time."

"I haven't slept so long in months."

"Maybe you just needed some company." She smiles.

"I'm going to see Sarah." I jump out of bed and slip the *sgian-dubh* in the leather strap tied around my ankle.

Elodie's smile wanes, replaced by an anxious expression. "Now? In the middle of the night?"

"Sarah is very powerful. She has the Blackwater and the Midnight gaze. If she uses her powers on me, I'm gone in a minute. I need to come back in one piece. My best bet is to catch her asleep." I laugh, a hollow laugh, slipping my trainers on and making my way down the stairs.

Elodie follows me, grabbing her jacket hanging on the banister. "Would she hurt you?"

I hesitate. "I don't know. I'd like to think not, but I can't take any chances. There's something strange going on with her. Remember what Harry used to say about Morag Midnight? Well, they seem uncannily similar."

"Oh. I see."

We make our way through the silent, still night. The sky and the air all around us are now dark purple, with the orange tinge of the lights over the city of Edinburgh. I feel full of energy after my sleep, as if I'd shaken off a lead suit I'd been wearing for days.

"Come," I call, striding down the overgrown path. "We're walking. I don't want anyone to spot my car."

Elodie looks around nervously. "I wonder when they'll come next," she whispers. "It's just a matter of time, isn't it?"

There's no need to ask who "they" are.

"True. And they will get Sarah if I'm not there."

"You said she's very powerful."

"She is. But she's also new to the fight. Sometimes she sort of . . . forgets she's a huntress. I always have to convince Sarah to fight. She's been so sheltered by her parents."

"Not a wise idea, to shelter a Secret heir. With all we need to face . . ."

"Well, she's a Dreamer, so she knew what she was going to have to face one day. I suppose her parents were trying to protect her. Maybe because of what happened to Harry's aunt . . . They never even told Sarah about that."

"They never told Sarah her aunt died?"

"They never even told her she existed."

"Seriously?"

"Weird, I know. And Sarah even reminded me of Mairead . . . the way Harry used to describe her. His father, Stewart, was very close to Mairead and he often told Harry about her. She was shy, sensitive. Very quiet. Just like Sarah. But something happened, just a few weeks ago. That's when she changed." I take a breath, remembering the terrible day Leigh was killed. "One of Sarah's best friends was murdered by a Surari. The bastard said that if Sarah sacrificed herself, he'd spare Leigh. Sarah agreed, of course. But I was there. I couldn't allow it to happen. So it was Leigh who died."

Our feet make a crunching noise on the frosty grass. There's silence all around and darkness as we walk across the moorland towards the outskirts of the city.

"After that Sarah changed. The Surari's slave had possessed a woman – she was the one who killed Leigh. The woman turned up at our door, and well . . . Sarah slaughtered her. I mean, she *slaughtered* her. The look in Sarah's eyes when she finished . . . It was as if she really was Morag Midnight."

I haven't quite managed to finish explaining when the ground rises up to meet me. I hit my face, hard, on a tree root. I taste my own blood as a voice rasps in my ear.

"Back . . . soil."

7
The Night Has Eyes

I hope you never know what crawls
In places of the soul
I keep under a shroud

Sean

"Elodie!" I try and warn her, but it's too late. She lands with a thud beside me. I struggle as hard as I can – the creature's fingers are wrapped around my ankles, and they're pulling me under. My eyes meet Elodie's; she is mute and staring as she too struggles to free herself. I see her reaching for the dagger she carries strapped to her chest. She manages to slip the knife out, but right at that moment the Surari pulls her down another inch, and the blade falls out of reach. I try to take a hold of the dagger strapped around my ankle, but I can't quite stretch far enough. Maybe Elodie . . .

"My *sgian-dubh!*" I mutter, my hands grabbing at the frosty leaves, at the soil, trying to hold on to something, anything. I spit blood.

Elodie understands at once and lifts herself up on her

arms, kicking back as hard as she can. She twists herself at an impossible angle and reaches towards my legs. She must have freed one of her ankles, because I see her leg is bent behind her. Her heavy breathing is in my ear as she grabs at my knee, my calf and finally my ankle – I feel her fingers working around the strap, but the demon pulls down again and both my feet are buried deeper. I'm slowly being buried alive.

"I lost it!" cries Elodie. Her head jerks backwards, and I realize the demon must have both her ankles again and is pulling her down too.

"Back. Soil," says the rasping voice again. It's coming from underground, somewhere between Elodie and me. I can sense the thing's head just there, under a shallow layer of earth.

I dig with one hand, under the leaves, under soil, until a mop of black hair appears. I pull at its hair as hard as I can, and the creature growls in anger. I look over at Elodie, and our eyes meet – she knows at once what I'm trying to do.

I feel the ground frantically with my hands – Elodie is being wrenched further and further underground. "Sean!" she calls. It's dark, but her face is so white it's glowing.

Please don't let Elodie die like this.

Rage burns through me, and with a sudden burst of strength I grab at the black hair again, yanking and ripping until the creature does what I want it to do – it comes to the surface with a jump, in a shower of leaves and earth. Elodie is free – she scrambles to her feet as quickly as she can, panting.

I have a split second to take in the Surari's face, its sickly white skin that has never seen the light of day, the unseeing eyes, the mouth crowded with black and broken teeth – and then Elodie is on it, with a roar you wouldn't believe could come from a woman so slight. She lands on the Surari's stomach, sinking her knees into its chest.

Right at that moment, a second soil demon hauls me under. *Shit*.

Almost immediately I'm up to my waist in wet, cold earth, kicking against the weight of the sodden soil. I can only watch as the Surari grabs Elodie by the arms and throws her off. She's up again in a second, her arms stretched out to take hold of the Surari again, but it's quicker than her. It has its hands on her hips and its mouth open to take a bite of her stomach.

I don't have a blade – my fingers will have to do. I lift my hands and start tracing, whispering the secret words, hoping they won't desert me when I need them most. I try to ignore the dragging at my heels. The exposed Surari moans and squirms for a moment, as if confused, then turns its face towards the source of the pain. I close my eyes and trace harder, whispering as fast as I can without jumbling the words. I can see a red light through my closed eyelids – it's just for an instant, but it's definitely red. A car's tail-lights? A farmer's tractor lights? I don't allow myself to open my eyes as my movements get faster and faster – the runes have taken over, carrying me with them. The soil demon growls – I stab and stab again without touching it, and the creatures howls in pain.

All of a sudden, I can't breathe anymore – my mouth is full of soil. Muffled sounds, my lungs exploding – there's no air, no air. It can't be. I can't die like this, buried alive. I can't.

"Elodie . . ." I try to say, but as I open my lips soil gets in my mouth and down my throat and I begin to suffocate. I cough. My chest is in agony.

Who's going to look after Sarah?

There's only darkness around me, and cold, and I can't even move a finger. A thought hits me, as clear as ice: *I'm dead. I'm dead.*

But there's another jerking movement, less hard this time – and different. Different because it pulls me up towards the surface and not down towards a wet, black tomb.

"Sean!"

The voice is muffled. Something is grabbing at my fingers, hard, and is yanking me upwards with a scream of rage and terror and a voice that belongs to Elodie.

I can make out the words. "*Niryana prati Surari!*" the voice is saying. "*Niryana!*" I recognize it as one of the battle cries of the Secret Families, in the ancient language. Whatever had been wrapped around my ankles suddenly lets go – and the blessed, blessed hand that pulls me upwards grabs my wrists – my lungs are bursting, exploding with pain – how long can a man survive without air? Not much longer. And then, with a final terrible effort, a million stars explode over my head and I'm staring at the night sky, and breathing, breathing deeply, painfully, like a baby who breathes for the first time.

"Sean! Sean!" Elodie's hands are brushing the soil away from my eyes.

I splutter and cough, and turn my head to throw up soil and bile. I gulp in fresh air at once, then spit some more and inhale some more, until my head stops splitting and my lungs stop screaming.

"Are you OK? Sean, are you OK?" Elodie says over and over again – she's terrified, I can hear it in her voice. So much to lose. So much more than when there were hundreds of us hunting – now every loss is a disaster to humanity.

"I'm fine. I'm fine." I wipe my mouth with my sleeve. I'm covered in mud, and wriggling little creatures fall out of my hair as I sit up.

"That was close," she whispers.

"Did you see someone? Did someone see us?"

"What do you mean?"

"I saw a red light. I thought maybe a car."

Elodie shakes her head. "There was no car. It was you. Your runes. There was a red light." She waves her slender fingers in the air. "Like a ribbon."

I have no idea what she's talking about, and no time to ponder. "The soil demons?"

"One is dead." She points to a lifeless bundle lying not far from us – it's curled up in a ball, its white skin gleaming feebly. Its lips are blue. Elodie has poisoned it. Black liquid is pouring from where I'd stabbed it with my runes.

"The other?"

"I don't—"

A hand spurts out of the soil like a monstrous root, and another, fumbling at her legs – and then a head, growling and sniffing the air for flesh. But this time I'm ready – I slip my *sgian-dubh* out of its strap and start tracing the runes once more.

The Surari lifts itself up in fury and leaps at me – I raise my dagger, placing an invisible barrier between us. The creature growls and holds its throat where I have slashed it open, black liquid spurting from the severed flesh.

"You buried me alive, you bastard!" I scream. *What am I doing? Speaking to the Surari, like Sarah?*

"Back soil . . . Me . . . back soil."

"*Niryana!*" yells Elodie again.

"Elodie! No!" But it's too late. She's thrown herself on the demon, as agile as a cat. But she is no match for it. The Surari grabs her hair, its mouth is open.

I have no choice. I launch myself towards the creature to stop it biting Elodie.

But there's no need. Before I can reach it I see Elodie's

lips, black as the night, touch the Surari's rotten, pale ones. Its arms, posed to claw the flesh off her bones, flail and fall to its sides. The demon clutches at its throat as its mouth darkens, a blue-black tinge slowly spreading over its face. It collapses, squirming on the ground, and I'm shocked, I'm speechless as I see something on its face.

A single tear, rolling down its cheek.

"It's OK," says Elodie. "I can handle this."

8
Makara

The seventh wave
Is the one that carries my heart

The Atlantic Ocean

Niall was clutching the rusty metal rail so that the wind wouldn't sweep him into the ocean. He wished he could jump off the cargo ship into the water and swim all the way back to Ireland, back home. But he knew that wasn't an option. He knew he had to save his own life. Going home was simply impossible. Not yet, anyway. Since the Enemy had risen and started the slaughter of the Secret heirs all over the world, all Niall was allowed to think of was survival.

"Planning a swim?" Mike was beside him suddenly, shivering in his bright red jacket, his arms wrapped around himself. He hated the cold. They could barely hear each other over the roar of the wind.

"Hopefully soon," Niall replied. There was a gust of wind so hard that he thought it might blow him into the sea –

and he would have loved that, he would have loved to feel the seawater on his face, around his body. But the cargo ship was too fast – he would lose them. It was only that thought that stopped him from jumping. It didn't worry him that the Atlantic is cold and deep and vast and that they were in the middle of it, because Niall didn't have reason to fear the cold, or the depth of water. He was a Flynn, and Flynns can't die in water.

"Only a few days to go before we arrive. Look at those clouds! Oh, man. If they come our way we're in for a choppy sea." Mike shuddered, imagining the worst.

"Those are not a problem."

"No?" Mike looked at Niall, puzzled.

Niall smiled, took a deep breath, and sang in the ancient language. He sang the clouds away. Slowly but surely they moved, the gale weakening ever so slightly, then more and more until it was just a breeze blowing softly their way. Mike stared at Niall, his eyes big and round.

"There you go," said Niall with a satisfied grin.

"Niall. How did you do that?" Mike asked, still stunned.

"That, my friend, was the power of Song."

"Seriously?"

Niall shrugged his shoulders. "All Flynns can do it. My little sister is great at it. She could sing the wind when she was in her pram!"

My sister, Bridin. And Cara, a year younger than Bridin. Hiding in Dublin. I don't even know if they're safe. I don't know if my parents are safe either. They would not leave Ireland. Niall would have gladly stayed too, but he couldn't. It was his duty as a firstborn Secret heir to survive and fight.

"You're full of surprises, Niall."

Niall shrugged. "I told you I had the power of Song."

57

"Yeah, to kill demons." Mike lowered his voice to an urgent whisper, swiftly looking left and right. "Not to change the damn weather!" He pointed at the corner of blue sky appearing where the black clouds had been only seconds earlier. His teeth were chattering.

"Yes, well . . ." Niall shrugged as if his powers weren't that big a deal. "Let's go inside. You're freezing."

"I am, yes. But I've spent forever on this boat, I have cabin fever!"

They walked down the narrow steps, and sat on the benches in the lounge where the crew went to chat and smoke and drink. Two crewmen were cradling a cup of coffee each, their waterproofs on. As soon as Mike and Niall came in, they got up and left, throwing them suspicious looks. *They probably think we're criminals on the run*, thought Niall.

"You alright there?" said one of the other men. Anders, a Dane, was the only one who occasionally spoke to the two strangers on board.

Mike nodded. "Fine, thanks," he replied briefly, as Anders too left the lounge. He took his woollen hat off and threw it grumpily on the table. "I can't wait to be off this boat," he muttered.

"Five days to Liverpool. We're nearly there."

"And then?"

"Another boat, I suppose."

"Over my dead body," growled Mike.

"Swim?"

"Ha ha."

"Ah well, we'll think of something. We always do," said Niall good-naturedly. But Mike didn't hear what Niall had said. His eyes were fixed on the waves out of the window, his coffee-coloured skin suddenly bleached with fear.

"Niall . . ."

Something in his friend's voice made Niall's heart quicken. "What is it?"

"I don't know. I think I saw something. Out there."

"Like what?"

"Like an eye." Mike pointed to the porthole.

"An . . . Shit! I saw it too!" Niall rushed to get a closer look.

A grey mound had risen from under the waves, and a black eye as big as a horse was staring at them. They barely had the time to register what they'd seen, when the eye disappeared under the water.

"It's not a whale," whispered Mike.

Niall's voice was shaking. "No. It's not a whale. It's a Makara."

Mike's eyes widened as he recognized the word from the ancient language: sea monster. "We can't do this on our own. We need to tell the captain," he said. His Gamekeeper training had kicked in. No time for panic.

"You go tell him. I'm going up on deck to try the Song."

He'll get killed, thought Mike despairingly. But he knew there was no choice.

They both knew they had no choice. There was no way they could fight the demon without Niall's power.

Mike ran up the steep steps and barged through the heavy door, into the bridge. "Captain. You need to listen to me now. There's something out there."

Captain Young was examining a map and didn't even turn around. He hadn't been entirely happy about taking these two lads on board for the crossing but until now they hadn't been much trouble. Still, he had no intention of making them feel welcome on board.

"I'm busy. Next time, knock," he said coldly.

"Captain Young. There's a *monster* out there," Mike repeated, trying to keep his tone even. He knew that if he started shouting he'd be dismissed.

"Are you drunk?" the captain growled, turning to face his visitor.

"No. You must call your men—" Mike couldn't finish the sentence. The boat made a sudden jump, as if something had hit it, and then kept rolling on the crest of subsequent waves.

"What was that?" yelled the captain. He moved across to hang onto the brass rail that ran along the inside of his cabin.

"It's a sea creature. A big one." Mike swallowed. He knew it must sound like something out of a children's fantasy novel.

Captain Young's eyes widened. "I knew you were trouble," he whispered, but as the ship pitched and rolled, he realized that whatever his feelings about the boy, the ship *was* in trouble. He strode towards a low cupboard. Inside were several guns. He threw one to Mike and kept one for himself. They made their way downstairs, struggling to stay upright on the swaying boat.

There was an eerie silence on deck, men standing in clusters, some of them armed, holding onto the rails and waiting for orders. And then Niall started singing, his head to the sky, his eyes closed, the words of his ancient song sounding soft and sweet like a lullaby. Mike blinked – was that a song of war? Because it didn't sound like it.

The boat was still undulating violently, but there was nothing to be seen, nothing emerging from the waves. The men were staring at Niall – what was the daft Irishman doing? Singing? At a time like this?

Suddenly something grey and vast burst out of the water,

soaking them all. "Shoot!" screamed the captain and his men let rip with a volley of bullets.

Niall opened his eyes at once, and the song nearly choked him. He had been trying to soothe and stun the Makara until they were ready, but the men had started shooting too soon. Now the Makara's tentacles, thick as cables and covered in suction pads, were flailing around in a terrible dance, as the Surari was hit over and over again. Sprays of seawater were everywhere, and screams echoed across the vessel – then those tentacles hit the boat blindly, smashing skulls and breaking bones. Crewmen were falling all around, and the guns were ripped out of their hands, rolling down the deck as the ship tossed in the water and then overboard into the sea.

Mike watched in horror as a man fell just beside him, hitting his head on the deck with such violence that something white and sticky began pouring out of his ears, immediately washed away by a spray of frothing seawater.

Mike was thrown backwards against the metal cargo containers piled up in the middle of the deck, his breath knocked out of him. Slowly, he dragged himself back onto his feet, holding onto the handle of a container, trying to remain upright in the chaos. A shout resounded in his ears, above the screams and moans of the hurt crewmen. "Help!"

It was Anders. He had fallen overboard and was desperately holding onto the handrail, his legs thrashing above the frozen waters – above the mass of tentacles. Mike let go of the handle and made his way, wavering and slipping, towards the rail. He knelt before it, holding onto the bars, and looked into Anders' terrified face. Mike tried to reach him with the hand that wasn't holding the gun, but he was just out of reach. Mike attempted once more to take hold of Anders' hand, as the crewman's body was thrown around by the roaring sea, but it was no use. In a split second, he made a decision: he let go of the gun.

The ship undulated again, hit by the waves born under the Makara's enormous flailing body, and Mike watched the weapon slipping away across the wet deck, away from his grasp and into the sea. Anders' face was contorted with terror.

"Don't let me go," he mouthed.

"Grab my hands!"

"I can't!"

"You have to!" Mike implored, desperately trying to close his freezing fingers around Anders' wrists. All around them there was panic, men shouting and bodies falling, but Mike couldn't hear a thing, he couldn't see a thing; he was hypnotized by Anders' frightened eyes, and he couldn't look away.

What happened next seemed surreal, like a bad horror film. In a massive effort the Makara lifted itself above the surface of the water and opened its body up in a fan, its tentacles like a huge, dripping crown around the black centre. In the middle of its body, just above the opening that was its mouth, there was a bony beak bigger than a human being.

The next few seconds were so horrific that Mike could never quite describe what happened. All he knew was that Anders was still holding onto the deck, even without a head. And then his decapitated body fell into the bloody waters and disappeared as the Makara closed its tentacles around him.

Mike felt his gorge rising as the full horror of what had just happened sank in. He looked around, just in time to see another crewman lifted by a flailing tentacle and thrown against the containers, his chest crushed and smeared against the metal boxes, suspended in the air in a strange crucifixion. And then the man fell in a heap, like a broken doll.

Mike looked towards Niall. Clearly, guns were nothing against this demon; their only weapon was his song. They had no other hope. Niall was still singing, standing with his arms open and his head thrown back. The tone of the chant had changed; it was cruel, hard, with words that spelled pain and hurt.

Mike winced as the Makara hit the deck to the left and right of his friend, in a desperate attempt to silence the sound that was hurting it so. By luck, or destiny, or simply because the creature was too damaged to fully control its movements, it kept missing.

Out of the corner of his eye, Mike saw Captain Young firing the last of his bullets into the creature, barely denting its thick, slippery skin, and then throwing the gun away in fury and despair. A tentacle hovered over him, ready to lower and crush him. Mike could hear a voice shouting.

"Captain! Move!"

That voice was his own. He ran, and his movements felt to him slow and frustrating, like trying to run in a dream, but he made it in time, throwing himself onto the captain just a second before the tentacle could crash down and put an end to the man's life. Mike and Captain Young lay one on top of the other on deck, and their eyes met. Mike saw hatred in the captain's gaze, and it wasn't for the Makara: it was directed towards him. The man flung Mike aside violently and stood up.

"Shut up! Shut up!" Captain Young screamed and leapt on Niall, holding him by the waist and throwing him onto the deck with a thud. The song had been brutally interrupted, and the ship fell instantly and eerily silent. No more screams. There was nobody left to scream. Just silence, but for a deep underwater moan: the Makara wailing in pain.

"Let him go!" Mike yelled, breaking the silence and throwing himself at the captain. Niall was lying nearly senseless, in shock from having had his song interrupted. His body started convulsing, as he came out of his trance.

"Niall's the only chance we have!" growled Mike as he grabbed Captain Young and flung him to the ground and into a puddle of blood and saltwater. Then he lifted Niall up by the shoulders and slapped him softly on the cheek. "Niall! Niall, wake up! Wake up!"

Niall groaned, his eyes unfocused. "I must . . . I must sing," he whispered.

"Yes. You sing or we're dead," said Mike calmly. His words were accompanied by another deep, otherworldly moan coming from the watery depths.

"Help me," replied Niall, leaning heavily on Mike. Mike supported him as Niall closed his eyes and started singing again. At first Mike was supporting most of Niall's weight, but as the song took flight it seemed to carry Niall's body with it, lifting him upright and throwing his head back once more.

As the song rose the Makara stirred again, agonized, its tentacles sweeping the deck blindly. Now its grey, thick skin was stained with black blood. With a terrible howl the Makara opened itself up again, its tentacles arranged around its centre like a crown – but now two of them were just stumps, and others were crumpled and bloody. Mike finally allowed himself to hope they had a chance.

But it took him just a few seconds to understand what the Makara was doing. It wasn't surrendering. It was trying to open itself up again, to do to them what it had done to Anders. The Surari opened its black mouth, and its deadly beak was ready to strike. Mike knew he had to make a decision, and make it fast. Try to move away and interrupt Niall's song, or stay put and hope the Makara would miss its target? As his mind struggled to choose, he felt a terrible pain cut through his head. Niall's song, resounding right beside him, was beginning to hurt him too. It was as if two blades had been inserted in his ears and they were twisting painfully, cutting him inside. He pressed his hands against his ears, and he was not surprised when he saw that his fingers were covered in blood.

Mike was determined to stand firm in spite of the pain, ready to help Niall if he needed it. There was no way he could interrupt him again. The Makara went to lower its beak to attack, desperate to put an end to the terrible sound that was ripping it apart – but its movements were slow and jerky now, and its huge body fell sideways, in a splash of foamy water and black blood.

Mike felt Niall swaying. "It's nearly finished. Niall, do you hear me? You can do this!" he whispered in Niall's ear. Niall seemed to hear, because his song rose even higher, roaring like the sea and the wind. Mike moaned in agony and fell on his knees, holding his bleeding ears, while the Makara thrashed and flailed and flung itself from side to side, until finally its movements juddered to a halt and the huge body was still.

And just in time, because Niall was spent. He doubled over and fell soaked and trembling onto the deck.

Mike shook his head, trying to get rid of the high-pitched sound that still resounded in his ears. He stood up slowly, slipping once on the wet deck and rising again, head spinning and every bone sore. He looked around him. Niall, drained but alive; Captain Young, standing frozen, leaning against the cargo; one, two . . . five men lying broken, senseless. The others had disappeared.

Mike forced his shaking limbs towards the parapet, panting in fear. He wasn't convinced that the Makara was dead, he expected a tentacle to rise from the waters at any second – followed by that bony beak, ready to take his head off as it had Anders'.

Step after step, in the surreal silence, Mike reached the rail and wrapped his shaking hands around it. He looked at the waters, now calm and black, with patches of red. The crewmen's blood.

And then the eye appeared above the waves, and the mound of its enormous, battered body. Mike let out a gasp and fell backwards, then scrambled to his feet quickly, sliding on the wet deck as he tried to make his way back to Niall as quickly as he could. He had to protect him at all costs.

"It's dead!" called a voice. It was Captain Young.

Mike stopped for a tenth of a second, but he still made his way to Niall, throwing himself over him, ready to take the coming blow.

"It's dead!" The captain repeated.

The blow wasn't coming. Mike let himself rise slowly and crawled to the rail again. His heartbeat was hammering in his ears.

The eye was still there – Mike breathed in sharply as he saw it, but stayed where he was. He noticed the white film over it, and how the grey mass rolled and floated, carried by the ebb and flow of the waves.

Captain Young was right. The Makara was dead.

And so were most of the crew.

Even without a crew, the cargo ship was still afloat, together with the giant squid's body. The waves, gentler again, cradled them both. Mike would have felt compassion, had he not just seen fourteen men being dragged down to their deaths, cut in two by the Makara's beak, or strangled by its tentacles.

Quickly he and Captain Young checked the men lying on the deck, looking for a pulse. Only one was still alive. Captain Young shook uncontrollably, his teeth chattering and his hands covered in the blood of his men.

He turned to Mike. "Why are you alive?" he whispered in the ghostly silence.

"You're in shock," said Mike kindly, but urgently. "You need to get this boat back to harbour. Any harbour. Now."

"I said, why are you – and your friend – still alive?"

"We have no time for this, understand me? Snap out of it, man! Take us ashore!"

"We need to get out of here," Niall reiterated. He was slumped against one of the doors, still white and weak, but recovering. Next to him was the only surviving crewman. A pained moan came from him.

"Did you hear that, Captain? Your man needs a doctor. Get your ass back inside. We need to go." Mike took a step towards the bridge.

"You're not going anywhere," the captain answered in a low voice, his face full of despair for his lost men. But there was something else there: fury. He pointed a shaking finger, first at Mike and then at Niall. "It was you who called that thing. With that weird song. I know it. I feel it in my bones."

"Captain Young," Niall began. His voice trailed away. The man was right. It had been them who had called the Makara to the cargo ship, in a way. But Niall couldn't explain that had it not been for people like them, the sea would be full of Makara – and other things – and there would be no ships sailing safely across any of the world's oceans.

"My men are all dead. Or as good as," he added, gesturing at the injured crewman. "You shouldn't be alive," he said calmly, and without warning picked up his gun and pointed it straight at Niall's chest. Without hesitation, Mike lunged forward, grappling for the firearm.

It was all so quick, as the sound of shots filled the air. There was blood on the deck and on Niall's hands as he crouched beside the captain, who lay with his eyes closed.

"Captain Young! No! Mike, what did you do!"

"What do you think I did? Look, it's just a graze." Mike pulled back the Captain's jacket to reveal a small wound.

"He's unconscious!"

"He knocked himself out. He'll be fine. Now, let's get these men downstairs. Shit, how do you steer a big-ass cargo ship?" Mike ran his hands through his cropped hair.

"I've steered motorboats before, but nothing as big as this. I can try."

"Take us ashore. Before another of those big-ass squids comes calling."

9
Listen

How can we speak
How can we listen
If there is no time and place
For us?

Sean and Elodie ran all the way to Sarah's house. They were covered in soil and still reeling from the terrible encounter. Sean kept taking deep breaths, relishing the feeling of air entering his lungs. He opened the wrought-iron gate with his *sgian-dubh*, and they stepped inside. No locks could keep Sean out. He had ways to get wherever he wanted, leaving no trace of himself.

Sarah's bare oak trees whispered a swaying welcome.

"Come inside," whispered Sean to Elodie. "I can't have you out here on your own."

"Defenceless?" Elodie finished for him, grinning.

Sean brushed a smudge of soil off her cheek. "Hardly!" he said, smirking at the thought of how black her lips had been, how painful the Surari's agony had looked as it died slowly.

"But I still don't want you to be alone."

Elodie nodded and followed Sean onto the gravelly path and up the stone steps. Shadow was sitting in front of the door, a still and silent sentry – it was as if she'd known someone was coming. Sean admired the way Shadow came up to him, circling him with her tail tapping the ground, as if she had to defend Sarah – she was infinitely loyal. Shame she wasn't able to tell friends and enemies apart.

She looked up at Sean with sheer hatred, refusing to let him by. Sean did what he had so often done before, quickly touching her between her eyes so fast that she couldn't run away – she was asleep on the stone steps at once. One of the skills he had learnt in Japan, sending any creature to sleep with one touch. Like invisibility, like his runes, one that seemed to come easily to him, almost as natural as breathing.

Sean and Elodie made their way past Shadow's still form and into the house. With a brief nod Sean went up the stairs, leaving Elodie standing sentinel against the front door in the darkness, silent and alert.

Sean stood in the doorway of Sarah's room, and for a moment the desire to see her was so strong he had to stop himself from barging in, picking her up and holding her in his arms as he used to do. He made himself stop and draw a breath before opening the door slowly.

Sarah was in a deep sleep. The air was full of her perfume – something between peaches and a darker note, richer. Sarah's own scent, the unique chemistry of her skin and her breath. Sean knew that scent from the many times she'd been close to him, from the many times he'd been in her room. He breathed it in – it was oxygen to him, the chance to fill his lungs with life again, to fill his heart with her presence.

He desperately wanted to hold her hands and keep her

close to him. He wanted to see her eyes fill with relief when she saw him, as they had when he used to go to her after one of her terrible dreams. But he knew that when she woke up and saw him standing in her room, it'd be fear, not relief she'd feel – and he braced himself for it.

He also knew that her eyes, and her hands too, could hurt him badly – which was why he couldn't wait a second longer, as much as he would have loved to have kept looking at Sarah's black hair spread on the pillow, a white hand uncurled beside her lovely face, the rhythm of her back rising and falling under the sheet as she breathed in and out, slowly. He couldn't risk for her to wake up, panic and use the Midnight gaze on him, or touch him with the Blackwater. He did what he had to do.

Sarah screamed as she felt someone grab both her wrists – she barely had an instant to see Sean's face over hers, before he covered her eyes. She was blind, and his knee was on her chest, stopping her from filling her lungs – she instinctively started thrashing, trying to free herself, but it was no use. Sean was reeling with the absurdity of it. He was scaring Sarah, he was hurting Sarah. It made no sense. It couldn't be happening.

It needs to be done. It needs to be done to save her life. But God, I wish there was another way.

"Sarah. Sarah, it's me. You're safe. It's Sean . . ."

"Let me go!" Sarah struggled, trying to free her hands – she growled, and Sean knew that given half a chance, she'd strike, she'd hurt him. No sign of the vagueness that gripped her when Nicholas was around.

"Please, Sarah. Please. I need to speak to you," he whispered.

"Let me go!"

"Just listen. Just give me the chance to explain."

"Go away!"

71

"Sarah, please." Sean begged again and again, but she wouldn't stop writhing. He saw no other way but to lean on her with all his weight, waiting for her to exhaust herself and stop. He heard something snapping, a thin, small ripping somewhere – was she hurt? Sarah's fingers felt hot already. *She's so much quicker in calling her power than she used to be*, thought Sean, and for a second he felt proud of her, in spite of the circumstances.

A new wave of self-hatred washed over him as she struggled against him. Finally, she lay still. She was blinded by Sean's hand, panting with the effort and with the weight on her chest.

"Sarah. Let me speak. Just for a moment." Sean tried again.

"What do you want from me?" she whispered, her voice dripping with fear and fury.

"Tell me I can let go of your hands."

"You can."

"Will you use the Blackwater against me?"

"No."

"Give me your word."

"You have my word."

Sean didn't really know whether to believe her, of course. But he needed to give her a chance. He needed to give them both a chance to change that terrible scenario – it was too awful, too painful, to be laying into her the way he was.

"What have I done to you? What did Harry ever do to you? Why are you doing this?" she whispered.

"To save your life—" He was desperate for her to understand. "I couldn't save Harry, but I can protect you."

"Let me look at you. Take your hands away."

"You'll use the Midnight gaze on me."

"No. No I won't."

"I don't believe you, Sarah."

Sarah tried to lift her knees in an attempt to kick him off her, but she couldn't. He was a lot stronger. Sean leaned even more heavily on her chest, his fingers burrowing into her wrists. She tried to inhale, panicked and whimpered in pain. Sean closed his eyes. How had it come to this? He couldn't believe it, he couldn't believe he was doing this to her. *I'm actually hurting her. Hurting my Sarah. In what crazy twist of my mind has this ever happened? None of them. Ever.*

He felt a teardrop rolling between his fingers. Her breathing was heavy and fast, but her body was growing weary. She knew there was no way out.

I can't do this, thought Sean. *I can't take it anymore. I can't hurt her anymore.*

In one swift, unexpected move, he lifted his hand from her eyes, freed her wrists and climbed off her to stand beside her bed. "There. You're free. You can do whatever you want now."

Sean waited for her to strike, praying she wouldn't. His own survival wasn't his first concern, though he certainly didn't want to die. *How many of us are left to fight? How many more can we afford to lose, before there are no Secret heirs, no Gamekeepers left?*

Sarah leapt to face him, and narrowed her eyes. The Midnight gaze. He folded into himself, beaten. It was over.

And when he was gone, who would she have beside her? Who would be loyal to her until the end? What an idiot he had been. He should have kept going. He should have held her down, and now it was too late. Her survival instinct had taken over – the Midnight instinct for the hunt, just like when she had slaughtered the demon-slave that had killed Leigh. She wasn't Sarah anymore. She was a Midnight huntress, and he didn't stand a chance.

But as he watched, Sarah blinked over and over again, until the deadly green light from her eyes finally dimmed, and she didn't strike, she didn't try to touch Sean with the Blackwater. She was standing in a pool of moonlight that seeped from the silvery curtains. *She's like the moon,* he thought, *white and pure and never quite within my reach.*

"Sarah. Sarah. Please listen to me. I didn't kill Harry. I'm sorry I lied to you," he said, the words tumbling over themselves as he tried to make her believe him.

I love you.

"I had no choice."

I love you.

"I wanted to tell you the truth, but there was never a right time."

I love you.

His voice trailed away. He sounded feeble and somehow weak, even to his own ears. It was as if the truth was too complicated to convey. As if the breach of trust could never be repaired.

Sarah looked at him the way she always did, in her own direct, fearless way. In her eyes, anger and disappointment. Sean could see it as clear as day, and it pained him so much.

She's disappointed in me, because I lied to her. How ironic. A Midnight is, by definition, a liar.

"Say your piece," she said in a low voice.

Sean took a deep breath. His one and only chance.

"Harry Midnight was my best friend. He was like a brother. I didn't kill him, the Secret Council did, the Sabha. It's been infiltrated, corrupted."

She didn't move. She didn't talk. She was full of that Sarah stillness he knew so well.

He tried again. "You're still in danger. And the danger is

closer than you realize. We were attacked by two soil demons on the way here, they nearly took me under."

Sarah's eyes widened, travelling up and down his body and taking in for the first time his muddy clothes, his wet hair.

"Sarah. The Valaya that was after you, Cathy's Valaya, it's just one of many. They want to destroy all the Secret Families. Someone is behind all this. We don't know who . . . or what. Yet."

She frowned slightly. "I know all this, Sean." The moonlight made her skin glow and gave her hair, tangled in the fight, a blue halo. She didn't look afraid anymore.

"You know?"

"Nicholas told me."

Sean grimaced at the mention of Nicholas's name. "You need to let me help you."

"In case you haven't noticed, I've got powers. And I'm not alone. I have Nicholas with me, and as you saw that day, he has incredible powers too. Unlike you."

Sean's heart sank. He was just a Gamekeeper, not a Secret heir like Nicholas Donal. *If he really is who he says he is.*

Sean decided against mentioning his fears about Nicholas now – it would only anger her more. "All right. Point taken. But Sarah, he's not enough."

"You've seen him in action, *Sean.*" She said his name as if it was an insult, another reminder of his deceit.

He tried to ignore the disdain in her voice. "Listen to me, Sarah. Harry was married to another Secret heir, Elodie Brun. Elodie Midnight. She's the last of your family, although not by blood. She's here, in Edinburgh."

"Ah, but is she really who she says she is?"

"She is Harry's wife. Harry's . . . widow. You must believe me."

Sean's shoulders hunched under the weight of the terrible, terrible mess he had made, believing he was doing what was right. How could he possibly know? Why had he ever accepted Harry's mission? Why had he not just followed his heart and gone to Sarah as himself, Sean Hannay?

But the answer to that was simple. Because she wouldn't have let him into her life.

A lose–lose situation. Trust him to be in one of those.

Sarah thrust her chin up defiantly. She knew that she had the power in this relationship. "Why should I believe you? After all the lies you've told me?"

"Because I'm telling you the truth now. All I did was for you, Sarah. And for Harry. It was he who asked me to take his place. Elodie can tell you that."

"Where has this Elodie been all this time?" She spat.

"In Italy. Harry knew he was dying. He'd been poisoned. The day before he died he called me to him. He sent Elodie to Italy to look after the last Japanese heir, Aiko Ayanami, and sent me to look after you. It seems as if he left a message for us. Elodie found it in a book Harry gave her. It's in Gaelic. We need you to translate it. We can't trust anyone else."

Sean's voice faded. *It's no use. No use. No need for more words.*

Sarah stood still and silent again. For a long time.

Another tear rolled down her cheek, shining feebly in the moonlight.

Sean took a step towards her. "Don't be frightened."

She dropped her head. "How?"

"How . . . what?"

"How do you do that? Not be frightened? I don't know how." She folded her arms around herself. "I've been frightened all my life, Sean. All the time. It's all that I know. Do you know how it feels, to be as scared as I am? To feel like you're drowning in terror all the time? I live on the edge of disaster, always *waiting*. When I was a little girl, any phone call, any letter, any day could spell my parents' death. My death. Any night could have been the night they didn't come back. And guess what? It happened. One night they didn't come back. And any day now it will be my turn."

"Welcome to the human condition, Sarah!" Sean cried in frustration. "It's like that for everybody, in case you haven't noticed! Every single person on this planet can say 'This might be the day I die. This might be the day my loved ones die.' You don't need to be an heir to be always afraid!" He took hold of her shoulders.

"Go away!" She tried to shake him off.

"Look around you, Sarah. This room, this house. Everything is spotless. Everything is so clean I could eat off your floors! Does it make you feel better? Does it help, for God's sake? Look at your hands!" Sean grabbed her – he was past caring about the Blackwater. "Look at them. Look at the way they are again." His fingers traced her raw, rough skin. "I don't see Nicholas making much difference to your obsessions! It had got better, remember? But you're just as fearful now. Worse, perhaps."

She nodded then met his eye. "You made it better, Sean. And then you went away. It was all a lie, even your name. Everything was a lie." Her voice hardened. "Don't come and tell me I'm not well. I know I'm not well. Don't preach to me when it's you who made me this way. Go."

"No." He suddenly felt strength return to his battered body.

"Go away!"

"Let me stay with you. You need me. You need us. Me, Elodie. Harry's wife. She's here to help us. Please let me stay with you. Let us stay with you." He spoke calmly, simply.

Sarah looked at him with eyes that wanted to be hard, but they were somehow pleading – Sean could see how much she wanted to believe him.

"You were everything to me. Do you know that?"

Sean couldn't help gasping in shock at her confession, a sharp intake of breath that sounded a bit like a strangled sob. He hadn't expected an admission like that. He was at a loss for words.

"You were all that was left of my family, but you were lying. And I can't let myself be hurt again."

"I won't hurt you again," he said.

She studied his face, as if she wanted to read his mind, read his soul. Sean held her gaze – he had nothing to hide anymore.

"Who are you?" she said finally.

"My name is Sean Hannay, I'm a Gamekeeper. I was born and raised in New Zealand. Before becoming a Gamekeeper, I studied medicine, like Harry. Harry Midnight was my brother in everything but blood. And you're all I have, do you hear me? You're all I have." *You're all I have* was their mantra, their special coded message that replaced the words they would have really wanted to say but couldn't.

Their bodies pulled towards each other. Towards comfort, respite and out of the lonely state they'd both found themselves in. It nearly happened – he nearly held her in his arms the way he used to. But all of a sudden Sarah steeled herself. They stood immobile, her hands in his, fighting the gravity that pulled them together like a planet and its moon.

"Where are you staying?"

"I'm renting somewhere near here. A farm cottage on the moorland."

Sarah nodded. "Come back tomorrow. I want to speak properly."

Sean nodded, giddy with relief.

"I want you to go now," she said in a soft voice, a voice that made it sound as if she actually wanted to say *stay with me*. And he wanted to stay, he wanted to hold her through the night. He remembered what it was like to kiss her, their one and only kiss. He remembered her lips on his, and he didn't want to be away from her, not then, not now, not ever.

But it was too soon. He would be patient. It was best if he went.

Just one last thing.

"Sarah?"

"Yes."

"Have you ever heard of forgiveness?"

Without waiting for her reply, Sean turned and walked out of the room, out of Sarah's house and into the darkness.

Soft footsteps followed him, and he turned and took Elodie's hand, a slight smile on his lips. There was a little glimmer of hope in his heart, because when he had looked at Sarah's face just before walking away, her eyes were still saying *stay with me*. So he did stay, with Elodie by his side, both of them still and cold – watching the soil anxiously, watching over Sarah for the rest of the night.

10
Days and Nights

To just do it
To dive from barren land
Into blue waters

While Sean and Elodie were still hidden and invisible among the oak trees, Sarah was sitting at the kitchen table, examining her wrists, lost in thought. Small purple bruises were appearing where Sean had held her down, like bracelets, or handcuffs, getting darker on her pale skin. In front of her, on the table, sat a little red pouch, the protection charm she'd made for the man she'd believed was Harry. It had snapped the night before when she'd tried to hit him with the Midnight gaze. Sean had been wearing it all that time.

Sarah took a sip of her cappuccino, feeling the soft red velvet of the charm with her fingers. She could make out the shape of the little pink quartz in it.

She believed Sean. For some weird reason – a hunch, a gut feeling, whatever you might call it – she believed him when he said he didn't kill Harry. He wasn't a murderer. Just a liar.

And then another Sean-thought, a bittersweet one, came fluttering into her mind: his blue eyes, so clear, the forbidden feeling of lips on lips, skin against skin, a girl who suddenly knew what to do and was unafraid.

She stood up quickly and started wiping the table. That thought she couldn't cope with – the memory of her feelings for him, and their one and only kiss. All that was over and gone forever. And Nicholas wasn't to know.

She'd asked Sean to come back. She should have told him when – she had deleted his number from her phone in a fit of anger when she'd discovered his betrayal, so she had no way to contact him now. How long would she have to wait? Maybe she shouldn't go to school, in case he turned up there. Or maybe he'd come in the evening. Or the night again, when she was in bed and helpless? The thought chilled her. It had been a terrifying experience, not least because of what she might have done to him.

She wasn't afraid of Sean hurting her anymore – had he wanted to, he would have done so already, but she still wanted to be in control. Not in the dark, unprepared and vulnerable way she'd been earlier. She wanted to be able to think clearly the next time they met. And if Nicholas was there . . . No. The thought of the two of them crossing paths in her home was just too strange.

What she wasn't admitting, not even to herself, was that she couldn't wait. She wanted to talk to Sean properly, sort it all out. Decide whether she could bear having him in her life again. Whether she could bear *not* having him in her life anymore. But could they sort it, after all that had happened? When she was still so angry, when she needed him so badly, when she was so confused she couldn't even begin to unravel her thoughts?

She walked over to the calendar on the wall, lifting the page to count the weeks until Christmas. Until Islay. She remembered her conversation the previous day with Aunt Juliet. *When is Harry coming back?* It would solve so many problems, if she could allow herself to contemplate Sean being back in her life. Maybe he could help her find a way to do more than just survive. Find a way to rise against the Surari once and for all. With Nicholas's help. They could look for other heirs, try and coordinate somehow, now that they knew the Sabha could not be trusted any longer.

Truth and lies were so mixed together, Sarah couldn't even begin to comprehend it all. *It all comes down to who I choose to believe*, she thought, a small flower of fear blossoming in her chest once more. Fear was second nature for her. That didn't mean she ever got used to it.

Her eye fell on the clock. Nearly time to go to school. She ran upstairs and put on her uniform. Her skirt was hanging ready, a freshly ironed shirt beside it.

Downstairs, Sarah wiped every surface of the kitchen, then stood in front of the hall mirror, checking her uniform again. She straightened her skirt, she smoothed down her shirt and ran her hands over her tights. She let her hair down from its ponytail, and did it up again, making sure it looked perfect. She noticed how thin her legs were, how pale her face was. She had lost weight, and she wasn't looking better for it.

Is love not supposed to make you bloom?

"He's not back, then?"

Sarah knew at once who Bryony was talking about.

They were sitting on one of the wooden tables dotted along the edges of the football pitches. Sarah had taken to having her lunch there alone, in spite of the harsh winter weather. From there she could see the exact place where she and Sean had killed Simon, and where Leigh's fate had been sealed. That memory haunted her, but still she couldn't stay away. It was like some absurd hope to turn back time and change things. Change Leigh's destiny.

Sarah, Bryony, Alice and Leigh, the four girls who were always together since their nursery years. Now Leigh was gone, the mystery of her murder still unsolved. She had been found strangled in the drama room. Only Sarah knew the truth, that she'd been a victim of the Scottish Valaya – and in Sarah's mind, a victim of the Midnights and their cursed, violent life. She knew, rationally, that Leigh's death hadn't been her fault, but she couldn't help feeling the way she did. Now she was so scared about anything happening to her other friends that she was avoiding them, keeping herself to herself. And Bryony and Alice wandered around the school grounds, the lost half of their close-knit group.

But today, Bryony had followed her and sat at her table, giving her no chance to walk away. Sarah's absence was breaking her heart.

"No. He's not back. Not yet, I mean."

Bryony was desperately trying not to look Sarah in the eye, not to put an arm around her shoulder and hold Sarah close to her, as she would have done only a short while ago. She was relishing the rare chance to speak to her and didn't want to scare Sarah away.

"Will he be back at all?"

"Of course he will." Sarah's tone was unconvincing. For once the Midnight talent for telling lies had failed her. Nobody would have believed her too-bright smile.

"Will he? Are you sure?"

"Bryony, please. I just don't want to talk about this now."

"Don't push me away, Sarah." Bryony sounded choked all of a sudden, and Sarah looked up in alarm.

"I don't mean to . . ." How could she explain? How could she tell Bryony that she was keeping away from her because she was terrified of putting her in danger? That she felt she was like a walking curse, a curse that had befallen Leigh already and might fall on her too?

"You might not mean to, but you are. I barely see you anymore. You're not answering my texts. I've given up calling you. What's going on?" Bryony's eyes were full of hurt. "Since Leigh . . . Since she . . ."

"I know. I know. It's just that . . ." Sarah wanted so badly to tell her friend the truth. The whole truth. But she couldn't.

Or could she, one day? Had she made Bryony part of her secrets, would she have believed her?

"I know it's been a terrible time. Your parents, and Leigh . . . but hey, it's still you and me, isn't it? Best friends?"

"Yes." Sarah smiled, a thin smile. *But better than nothing,* thought Bryony.

"Sarah . . . If you're on your own . . . if you're having to cope with all that family situation all over again, having to move in with Juliet . . . You can always come and stay with us, you know that."

"It's OK. Really. I'll find a way."

"The offer is always there, you know that." After a pause, she continued, "Why did Harry go? I can't believe he let you out of his sight. He seemed so . . . so attentive." *A bit too attentive,* Bryony thought. *More like possessive.*

"Work. Stuff to sort out down in London." Sarah smoothed down her hair, checking that her ponytail was still perfect, ran her hands down her skirt, straightening it. Bryony knew Sarah like the back of her hand – when she started straightening and checking and sorting, it was time to change the subject.

"By the way . . . Michael. I haven't had the chance to tell you. It's serious," she announced.

Sarah couldn't help smiling. Bryony changed her boyfriend every few months, moving on from one to the other in her sunny, cheerful way.

"Is it?" She couldn't keep a touch of amusement out of her voice.

"Yes, yes, laugh away! But it is," Bryony grinned conspiratorially.

"You mean . . . you and him . . ."

"Yes!" The girls grabbed each other's hands.

"Oh my God!" Sarah grinned. "So it *is* serious."

Bryony nodded. Sarah stroked her best friend's red, wavy hair gently, in a gesture that was unusually demonstrative for her. They looked each other in the eye, and Bryony took in how worried Sarah really looked.

"Are you happy?" Sarah asked, a strange look in her eyes, one that Bryony couldn't quite decipher. All she knew was that something was troubling her friend, and she wondered if it all came down to Leigh's death, or if there was something else. With Sarah it was always difficult to say.

"Yes, very. Very happy. Listen, why don't you come up to my house tonight? Michael will be there, but my sisters will be around too, so I promise you won't play gooseberry!" she laughed. "We'd love to see you."

"I can't."

Bryony's face fell and she tipped her head to one side. "Oh, come on. You and Michael can get to know each other better . . . My two favourite people in the world."

Sarah smiled at her friend's coaxing tone. "I really, really can't. I'm seeing my boyfriend."

85

"You *what*?"

"I'm seeing my boyfriend."

"Yes, I heard what you said! You have a boyfriend and you never told me? Who is he? When can I meet him? Did you . . . do you? Have you . . .? No, of course not," she added quickly, seeing Sarah's face. "Tell me all!"

Sarah looked away again.

Oh, God, she's not happy, thought Bryony.

"Well, his name is Nicholas."

"Nice. Is he from Edinburgh?" chirped Bryony, trying to be upbeat in spite of Sarah's vagueness.

"No, he's from Aberdeen."

"Cool. What does he do? How did you meet?"

"He's taking a gap year from Uni. He's doing law. We met . . ." *In my dreams? He saved my life, and killed Cathy, the Valaya leader, by having her pecked to death by ravens?* "We met in the Royal Mall. By chance. In Thornton's. We were both buying chocolates."

"Oh, romantic! But when? How long have you been together?"

"Just after my birthday. It's early days, really."

"Right." Bryony played with her bracelets for a while, stroking the beads with her fingers, pretending to be totally absorbed. "Sarah," she said then without looking up.

"Mmmm?"

"You asked me if I'm happy. But are *you*?"

"What? Of course I'm happy!"

Bryony raised her eyebrows and gave her a meaningful look.

Sarah sighed. "He's my first serious boyfriend, you know that."

"I know, I know. After years of being married to your cello!"

"Yeah, well, my cello is good to me!" Sarah laughed, in spite of herself. For a second she looked like the old Sarah, the girl she was before her life fell apart.

Bryony covered Sarah's hands with hers. "But . . .? Because there is a *but*, isn't there?"

"It's just that – I don't know." Sarah shrugged. "I don't know if I . . . love him."

"Love is a big word! Do you feel butterflies when you see him?"

Sarah looked at her friend, opening her mouth to reply, and then she closed it again. How could she explain what happened to her thoughts when Nicholas was around?

"Yes. Yes, of course."

"You don't seem convinced."

Sarah stood up suddenly. She'd said enough. "Well, I'll keep you posted. It's all good. And anyway, these days all I'm thinking of is that letter from the RCS."

"That'll take ages. I'm dying to hear from the art schools. So, when will I meet this Nicholas?" Bryony wasn't giving up.

"Soon. Promise." *As soon as I have the whole Sean mess sorted out. As soon as I can face it.*

"We can go out, the four of us. For chips, maybe?"

"Sure. Great idea," Sarah replied, aware of her stomach tightening at the weirdness of the whole set up.

Why should it be weird for us to go for chips all together? I don't know. But it would be. Nicholas hardly ever eats, for a start. There never seems to be the time, somehow.

In a rush of affection, Bryony threw her arms around Sarah, who closed her eyes for a brief moment, inhaling the distinctive scent of her friend's hair – bluebells, she would have recognized it anywhere.

"You know I'm here, don't you? Any time, day or night, you can phone me. Or come up to my house."

"I know, I know." *If only I could tell you.*

Bryony got up and started gathering her things. "Oh, wait! I completely forgot. I have to do a project for my photography class. Pictures of the full moon. I thought your garden would be the perfect place."

Sarah hesitated. Just because she hadn't been dreaming, just because they'd had some peace for a while, didn't mean they weren't still under threat. To have Bryony wandering around her garden at night . . .

She wracked her mind, trying to find an excuse. Couldn't think of anything.

"When?" she asked with a smile, pretending to love the idea.

"The full moon is tonight. Please, please, please, Sarah? Sorry about the short notice."

Oh, no.

"Okay," Sarah sighed, trying not to sound too anxious.

"Great, then! I'll see you around nine."

The girls turned their backs on the football pitch and all that had happened there, and walked, arms linked, towards the school building.

As soon as they were gone, Sean broke his glamour of invisibility, stretching his arms and legs.

I'll watch over you both, he thought.

"Yes?" whispered Sarah into her phone, gaining a few dark looks from the serious looking boy sitting across her. They weren't supposed to take calls in the library, but when Sarah saw it was Nicholas, she had to answer. She had to warn him that he was about to meet Bryony, the girl he'd heard so much about.

"It's me. I just called to say hi."

"I was about to phone you. Bryony is coming round to the house tonight. Around nine."

"Exciting. I'm about to meet the famous Bryony. I'll come and get you at school."

"No. I mean, I have so much homework ..." She scrambled. The boy sitting across Sarah stood up, glared irritably and strode out of the room. He was going to find Mrs McGough, the school librarian, to complain about Sarah.

"Would I ... inconvenience you, Sarah?"

"No, of course not. Honestly, Nicholas. Come up to the house later. I need ... I need some time alone, I have stuff to do."

"Right."

His voice was cold and Sarah's heart started beating faster. *Have I upset him? And why should I feel so guilty for wanting some time alone?*

"I'm in the library. I have to go."

"Fine."

She closed her eyes. "Please don't be angry," she began, but stopped at once. *This is not me. I shouldn't be apologizing for this.*

She heard the click that signalled the end of the conversation. Suddenly, she realized why she was feeling so nervous about Bryony's visit. It was because she felt in her bones that Bryony wouldn't like Nicholas.

What if Sean turns up tonight too?

Sarah stared out of the window onto the school car park. Nicholas, Sean and Bryony all there at the same time. The thought of it was like a firework going off in her head. She stood up and gathered her things quickly, so quickly that a few loose papers and a pencil fell out of her messenger bag, and she didn't even stop to gather them. On the doorstep she bumped into Mrs McGough, followed by the boy who'd been so annoyed by her talking on the phone in the library.

"Do I have to remind you that you can't take calls in here, Miss Midnight?" Mrs McGough began. "The school has a very strict policy about the use of mobile phones."

"Sorry," interrupted Sarah, and stepped out – but she hesitated and turned, her long hair brushing the boy's arm, her eyes searching his, finding them, locking him to her stare.

A hint of the Midnight gaze – just a hint.

I've never seen eyes as green as this, the boy had time to think, just as the pain hit him. He pressed his hands against the sides of his head, sudden agony exploding right in the middle of his forehead.

"Ouch!" he murmured, staggering slightly. The librarian took a step towards him, then turned to glare at Sarah, as if something told her where the boy's distress was coming from.

But Sarah was gone. The boy managed to open his eyes in time to see her striding down the corridor, her long black hair down her back. He blinked over and over again, as if he couldn't quite believe what he was seeing – there was a girl following her, a little girl with blonde hair, wearing a blue pinafore – a little girl who hadn't been there a second before. He blinked once more, and she was gone.

11
Crown of Thorns

Because I never thought
It could be different.

Sarah needs time alone. She needs time away from me.

Very calmly, very coolly, Nicholas slipped the phone back into his pocket and let a silent fury sweep through him. Certainly she must see that this was a mistake. There was no reason they should be apart that night, no reason at all. They could only be apart when he decided. There was no sense in Sarah being on her own, or with that girl, Bryony.

I'll start tonight. I'll start with Bryony.

Nicholas closed his eyes and prepared himself to speak to his father. He knew the King of Shadows would rejoice in his son's fury, his desire to kill.

The Surari heard their summoning from a long way away, deep within the Shadow World. One of Nicholas's favourite species, the ancestral predators – those who fill human beings with primitive terror and awake memories of being torn limb from limb. Sarah's house would be their target tonight.

Nicholas would be there to protect the girls, of course, and he would do his very best. But one of them would be beyond salvation, and Sarah's breaking would have properly begun.

12
Scrying

If I came close to you
Would it be the way
It used to be?
Or would I know at last
That what was there is gone?

Sarah was in the basement where her parents kept all their magical and hunting equipment, the door safely locked, kneeling on the duvet spread on the floor. Open in front of her, the wooden chest that held their precious maps, some new, some so old they looked as if they would crumble under her touch. Sarah chose a modern map of Edinburgh from the stack and spread it carefully in front of her. She'd also laid out Sean's protection charm, one of her mother's silver bowls and the *sgian-dubh* that used to belong to her aunt Mairead.

Sarah unclasped her silver bracelet and took off her earrings, one by one, slipping them inside her jeans pocket – her mother's diary had told her that metal interferes with magic. She sighed, summoning her courage. The scrying spell she was about to cast made her uneasy. Frightened, even.

The last time she'd tried one, she'd ended up being possessed by something that spoke through her, announcing the return of the King of Shadows – not to mention being thrown against the wall and getting badly bruised. It was unlikely that this attempt would go without incident. Which is why she had prepared for a soft landing – spreading two duvets and a few pillows on the basement floor.

She lit the white candle, signalling the beginning of the spell. The blade was cold against her skin. She flinched as her blood gushed red and copious into the silver bowl – she had sharpened Mairead's knife and the cut was deeper than she'd intended. Her arm hurt and trembled as she lifted the bowl over the map; her heartbeat was furious and her breathing shallow as she closed her eyes and waited. The little red pouch started vibrating softly.

The air shifted around Sarah, a strange, electric feeling – and she knew the spell was working. She opened her eyes in time to see the pouch float upwards and sideways, over the silver bowl. It dipped itself into Sarah's blood, and then floated up again above the map, as if deciding where to go. Suddenly, it dipped, marking a spot with its blood-soaked velvet and rising again at once.

Sarah swallowed, expecting something to happen at any moment, as it had happened with the last scrying spell she had performed.

But nothing happened.

Trying to breathe normally, Sarah allowed herself to lower her eyes to the map, the protection charm still hovering in mid-air, to check the place it had marked. It was a spot very close to her house, right where Edinburgh ended and the moorland began. That very moment the pouch fell, spraying thin drops of blood over the map. The candle flickered and went out. The spell was over, it seemed. Sarah waited another instant before she felt she could exhale at last. Yes, it was over.

She was about to place the bowl on the floor when something grabbed her, pulling her up and away from the floor. Incredulously, she saw her bent legs hovering a few inches from the duvet, as if she were floating on an invisible cloud. She closed her eyes and braced herself, because she knew what was coming. There was nothing she could do, nothing she could hold on to as she was lifted higher and higher, still holding the bowl. Suddenly, she was thrown against the wall with such force that multi-coloured spots exploded in front of her eyes before she landed with a thump and a soft cry, every bit of her body hurting. Lying on her back, she could see the room circling around her – the weapons' wardrobes, the desks, the oak table, the duvet – and something else. A face.

There was a girl kneeling beside her, bending over her, her face close to Sarah's. Sarah tried to focus, to take in the girl's features – *who was she?* – but a wave of nausea took her, and then everything went black.

After some time Sarah came to her senses, her eyes fluttering open. She felt sick, and her head was throbbing. She sat up slowly, holding her head, and felt a stab of pain in her back and in her side. She checked her ribs, her arms and legs, moving them slowly and carefully – nothing was broken.

And then she remembered – the girl. Was someone there, or had it been a vision? She looked around, braced for another attack – but there was nobody. The door was still closed. Sarah dragged herself to her feet – she had to lean on the wall for a second – and limped towards the door. She checked the handle – it was still locked. Nobody could have come in.

Who was that girl?

One thing was sure, she thought, contemplating the hideous mess that the spilled blood had made on her duvet and how she would need to clean the place up: if she could help it, it would be the last time she'd cast that spell.

13
The Watcher

Shining above me
A canopy of stars
And below me
The ancient domes

Soil demons. Sarah shuddered, remembering her friend Angela being dragged underground. A ghastly, lingering death, to be slowly suffocated by soil, never to see the light of day again. Angela's hands sticking out of the mud, desperately trying to hold on to something – and Sarah grabbing her fingers as they slowly disappeared. It was an image she'd never forget. Soil demons were too frightening for words. And yet, there she was, walking alone towards Sean's house, knowing that two of those creatures had attacked Sean and Harry's widow, Elodie.

Sarah looked across the street, over the blonde sandstone houses and further on towards the moorland. The shadows were closing, night was drawing in, and she'd have to walk there, on the soft earth in which the soil demons hid. Every step could be the one where a white, bloodless hand closed around her ankle.

Sarah breathed deeply. *I'm not turning back. After all, I haven't dreamt of soil demons at all,* she said to herself.

But I haven't dreamt of anything at all in weeks.

Sarah frowned. She'd cast the spell. She'd found where Sean was living. And now, to stop him coming to her, she'd go to him.

Sarah pulled her shoulders back to feel the comforting presence of her *sgian-dubh* slipped into her bra. A useful trick, one that Sean had taught her. Though the idea of carrying a knife in her bra was somewhere between horrible and funny, really.

Her steps echoed on the pavement and into the night. The street was quiet, the lights on in the terraced houses. Most people were home from work now and sitting with their families in peace, the curtains closed. Sarah wrapped her arms around herself and sped up, walking as quickly as she could without breaking into a run. A little park, and after the park – the moorland. Black, deserted. And somewhere about a mile from where she stood, Sean's house.

Sarah stepped onto the soft, mossy soil. She swallowed. Would a hand come out of the earth? Would a white face appear, mouth open to bite the air blindly, looking for flesh?

She slipped her hands under her jumper, and took out her *sgian-dubh.* Just in case.

She didn't feel it coming, she didn't hear it coming, and it didn't spring out of the ground. The creature stepped behind her and held her in a vice-like grip, scratching at her jacket, shaking her like a dog shakes a rabbit.

Sarah could feel the Surari's fur against her neck – but no, it wasn't fur – it felt different – were they feathers? She looked to the hands that had grabbed her waist – they were monstrous, with claws as long as little daggers, tearing at her jacket. Something began to burrow into the back of her neck – something pointed, sharp. Painful.

Because the demon had both her arms in a vicious grip, Sarah couldn't use the *sgian-dubh* in her defence. Instead, she writhed and struggled, trying to free herself, but getting nowhere. To her horror, she felt one of those clawed hands travelling up her arm and to her neck – the claws felt cold against the throbbing skin of her neck, so thin, with its watermark of veins and arteries just beneath, easily reached, easily torn.

But in moving its hand, the creature released its hold a fraction, giving Sarah just enough time to lift her arm and elbow her attacker in the chest. She used her advantage to turn, her aunt's *sgian-dubh* in her hands, and she was face to face with her assailant.

She let out a gasp of horror – in front of her there was something feathery and beaked, crowned with a mane of long, straight, lucid black hair. Two black, almond-shaped eyes glared at her from among the feathers – but the gloomy light made it impossible for Sarah to see more. Sarah shook herself and summoned her power. She stared into the Surari's eyes, expecting the thing to shake and wail under the Midnight gaze – but it didn't move, it didn't even flinch.

No demon is immune to the Midnight gaze! thought Sarah in anger and disbelief.

Sensing her hesitation, the Surari launched itself again towards Sarah. She went to push the *sgian-dubh* into its stomach but she missed, the feathered creature had turned at the last minute. Her hands were burning with the Blackwater – one touch, if held for long enough, would suffice. If only she could touch it, and at the same time avoid those claws.

Sarah and the Surari were face to face again now. It wasn't any bigger than she was, and it seemed just as slight as her – gaunt, even – had it not been for those claws, and that vicious pointed beak.

After a brief moment of sizing each other up, the demon went for her again. Sarah lifted her *sgian-dubh*, and this time she grazed its arm. Immediately, the creature stopped, holding its wounded arm against itself, frozen. Sarah was dumbfounded. It was just a graze – definitely not enough to kill it. And this was a Surari – one of the most terrifying forces in the world. Why was it standing there like a child crying over a scraped knee? It made no sense.

Sarah saw her chance. She jumped on it, her hands burning, ready to strike with the Blackwater.

And something completely unexpected happened.

The Surari lifted itself out from under Sarah's astounded gaze and slowly began to levitate away, its black, almond-shaped eyes never leaving Sarah, its arms extended and its legs curled beneath it like a hawk's legs. It rose further and further up until it was in line with the roofs of the terraced houses, then it did a backwards flip and disappeared towards the city. Sarah hadn't spoken a word, and the creature hadn't made a sound.

She was burning with shock and anger. *The Midnight gaze failed. This Surari must be immune to it . . . or is it me? Is the gaze failing me, like the dreams? Still, it worked on that boy in school – though it was just a touch, not a full attack.*

She turned and ran across the moorland, her eyes scanning the sky as she went, still watching her step for things that might come out of the soil – but now she was too furious to be afraid. Sooner or later, she knew she would destroy the demon-bird.

14

Night Deceives Us

Next time I see you
There will be walls

Elodie ran downstairs and burst into the kitchen. "Someone is here," she said urgently.

Sean was sharpening his *sgian-dubh* against a kitchen knife. Without missing a beat, he placed the other knife on the counter, the knife still in his hand. "Did you see something?"

"I felt them. Leave it to me," whispered Elodie. Her lips had taken on a bluish tinge already.

"Wait!" Sean took her by her arm. "Wait!"

Somebody had called his name from behind the closed door. And the voice beyond the door, the voice that spoke his name – that voice he knew.

He flung open the door and there she was, standing on the doorstep, eyes big with apprehension and cheeks red from the cold. Sean stood still, holding himself back.

"Sarah."

"Can I come in?" she said in a small voice.

"Of course. Of course. You must be freezing. Come and warm yourself," he said, ushering her into the hallway.

Sarah steeled herself. She hadn't risked the scrying spell and come all this way to show him how lost she was. She wasn't going to play straight into his hands.

But she'd missed him so much, and his parting words had haunted her since he had left her the previous night. She needed to find a way to forgive him.

The awkwardness of it all made Sarah blush. But she was determined to do what she had come to do, to say what needed to be said. She was just about to speak when a blonde woman stepped into the hallway.

Sean spoke without turning his eyes away from Sarah. "Just a minute, Elodie."

Elodie. Harry's wife, Sarah thought.

"I couldn't wait to see you," she blurted out, and immediately regretted her words. They didn't sound right. She didn't want him to know that she'd missed him.

Sean's eyes widened. He was fighting the urge to take her face in his hands and just look at her, look at her properly, the way he hadn't been able to do for so long.

"Where's Nicholas?" he said instead.

Sarah hadn't expected that. "Probably at my house right now. He's there every night." Her voice had an imperceptibly petulant undertone.

"Is he?" Sean shrugged. "What a great boyfriend."

"Yes, well I think who I go out with is not really the main issue here."

Sean sighed and lowered his eyes. "No. Of course not."

Sarah read his face: defeat. Her heart contracted painfully. "I need to speak to you. Alone." She added, glancing towards the living room where Elodie was waiting.

"Of course. Come upstairs. Just don't attack me, please." Sean attempted a smile, one of his dimpled smiles that never failed to stir her.

They walked up the musty stairs. "This place is falling down around your ears, Har—I mean Sean."

"It serves its purpose, I suppose."

Sarah looked around Sean's bedroom in dismay. Mould eating the ceiling, wallpaper peeling off in damp curls, a wintry draught from the window that chilled the whole place. Sean read her thoughts. "Like I said, it serves its purpose. And it's only temporary," he mumbled.

"It has to be, unless you want to die from the cold. And . . . mould poisoning, or something."

Only then Sean noticed the mark on Sarah's black jacket. "Sarah?" he asked, pointing at the torn material.

Sarah nodded. "It happened on the way here."

"Jesus, Sarah!" Sean placed his hands on her arms and looked into her face. Sarah was startled – his touch was sudden, unexpected. But she didn't move, and she held his gaze. She wanted to look away, but she couldn't. The name had changed – Harry Midnight had become Sean Hannay – but those clear blue eyes she had looked into when waking up from one of her terrifying dreams, when she thought she was about to be killed, when she'd found her mother's diary, when the world was full of threat and he had provided her only place of refuge – those eyes were still the same.

"I'm sorry," he said. "Please don't make me leave your side again."

I love you, he didn't say.

"I forgive you," she said.

Don't leave my side again, she didn't say.

"Elodie. This is Sarah."

Elodie looked from one to the other, and back again. The expression on Sean's face had taken her by surprise. *Sarah's presence makes him happy*, she realized, and the thought stung, for reasons she couldn't really understand.

"Harry's wife," said Sarah.

"Yes."

They looked at each other for a second, and Elodie's expression was harder than she intended. Sarah held her gaze, not giving anything away.

"Sit down, Sarah. Here, near the fire." Sean led her to the warmth. He was concerned by her frail appearance. "Coffee? Something to eat?" he offered.

Sarah half-smiled. Sean seemed to think caffeine was the answer to everything. She remembered once, after a terrible attack where they both nearly got strangled by a seven-foot tall demon and Sean had been hit over the head with such force that he'd passed out, after coming to he'd gone straight to the kitchen to make himself an espresso.

"Yes please," she said, surprising herself. "I'm starving."

And she was. It wasn't the time and place to explain to Sean how little she'd been eating, how every time she was around Nicholas she lost any interest in food. But now her stomach was rumbling. She was reminded of when Harry – *Sean* – had first arrived, how that night she had been able to eat properly for the first time since her parents' death.

"I'm on it," said Sean, and disappeared into the kitchen, leaving Sarah and Elodie in an awkward silence, studying each other from under their eyelashes. Thankfully, he was back in a few minutes with steaming coffee and some toast. Sarah tucked in, relishing every mouthful.

"Sarah was attacked," Sean explained to Elodie.

"You can't be left alone," the French girl remarked at once.

She sounded genuinely worried, but her implication that Sarah couldn't fend for herself annoyed her no end.

"I'm here, am I not?" she snapped.

Elodie lowered her head and Sarah felt strangely triumphant.

"What was it? Did you kill it?" asked Sean. He waited while she finished her toast, noticing how fast she ate it.

"I've never seen a Surari like that before," Sarah answered, cleaning her hands carefully on the napkin. "For real or in my dreams. It had a bird's face . . . and clawed hands. But the rest of it looked quite human – arms and legs in all the right places. It was dark, though, and I didn't kill it. It . . . flew away."

"Flew?"

Sarah nodded.

"This means it's still around," hissed Elodie.

Sarah ignored her again.

"How did you find the cottage?" asked Sean, apparently unaware of the tension between Sarah and Elodie.

"Guess." Sarah twisted to lift her jumper slightly. On her lower back there was a red, angry mark that was beginning to turn blue.

Sean winced. "The scrying spell," he guessed, remembering what had happened the time they'd cast that spell together.

"Oh, and this." Sarah brushed her hair away, revealing a blue bump on her forehead. "At least the demon-bird only shred my jacket and not my skin. By the way, this is yours." She buried her hand inside her jeans pocket and took out the red velvet pouch.

"My protection charm. I must have left it when . . . when I . . ." *When I pinned you down, trying to stop you from using the Midnight gaze.*

"Yes." Sarah knew exactly what he was thinking.

105

"Oh God, Sarah! There's your blood on it. I wish you had never cast that spell. You should have just asked me!"

"Well, I managed it *myself*, Sean. I'm here now," she said coolly, biting into a second slice of toast.

Elodie looked from one to the other again, trying to take it all in. There was something between them, something she was no part of. Her heart sank, and she didn't even know why.

"We have something to show you."

She took a book from the mantelpiece and sat beside Sarah at the fireplace. Sean joined them, and the two blonde heads and the black one bent over the book.

"Harry gave me this before I left. He wrote a message in it. It's in Gaelic," said Elodie, showing Sarah the scribbled sentence.

"*S ann an Ile a tha n fhreagairt. Cum faire air Morag, airson gur ise an iuchair*," murmured Sarah without hesitation. "The accents are missing."

"OK, but what does it mean?" said Elodie impatiently.

"Did Harry leave this message for you?"

"Yes."

"We think that Harry knew Elodie would need you to translate it. That's why he wrote it in Gaelic," explained Sean.

"So what does it mean?" Elodie repeated.

Sarah sat back in her chair. "It means I was right. I had a hunch I had to go to Islay, to Midnight Hall. That there I'd find out something more that I need to know, something about all this . . . and about my family as well. The message Harry sent us says: *The answer lies on Islay. Watch over Morag, she's the key.* Morag Midnight, my grandmother."

"Watch over Morag? As in, look after her? It doesn't make sense," pondered Sean. Sarah shrugged, as if to say *that's what it says*.

"We must all to go to Islay, then," Elodie said quickly.

"No need. Nicholas is coming with me."

"Can you trust him, Sarah? Can you?" he snapped.

"Can I trust *you*, Sean? Because you lied to me. Over and over again." Sarah's anger had seeped through once again.

"How many times do you want me to apologize?" yelled Sean.

"Fine. Come with me, then. But Nicholas is my boyfriend." Sarah crossed her arms. "He's coming too."

"You don't know him! I can't let you."

"You can't *let me*? Who are you to tell me what I can and can't do? *I* decide, Sean."

"No you don't, Sarah." Elodie's voice had a strange note to it. Her lips were ever so slightly blue. Sean tensed. "We decide together. Harry – my husband – lost his life because of this war. He trusted us to sort this mess after he was gone. I won't let him down."

"Someone else to tell me what to do, Elodie Midnight?"

The two girls glared at each other, their eyes flashing.

"Sarah." Sean reached out his hand. With Elodie's lips darkening and Sarah's eyes beginning to glimmer bright green, things could turn dangerous.

But Sarah blinked. "I need to go home now. I promised Bryony she could come up and take some pictures in the garden tonight." She put her jacket on and wrapped her scarf around her neck twice, the way she always did. Just seeing that familiar gesture broke Sean's heart in two.

"Bryony? Another heir?" gasped Elodie. "Did you know about this, Sean?"

"No, no. Bryony is not from a Secret Family."

"Your friend is not a Secret heir? How do you manage that?" asked Elodie, genuinely surprised.

"I don't. My life is chaos, as you can see." Sarah shrugged.

"At least Elodie and I will be around." Sean frowned.

"No need. Nicholas will be there."

Sean massaged his forehead. "Again! Sarah. Honestly. You have to make everything awkward! You and Bryony will be strolling around that enormous garden of yours in the middle of the night."

"We'll be fine. Thanks for the toast. I'm going."

"Jesus, Sarah! Why did you come here at all if you don't want me back in your life?" Sean looked stricken, and Sarah wavered.

"The thing is, Bryony and Nicholas never met."

"She's never met Nicholas? Your best friend never met your . . . boyfriend?" the last word was dripping with disdain.

"There's never been an opportunity." Sarah looked away.

A bitter sort of satisfaction filled Sean's heart. "You avoided them coming across each other, didn't you? You're worried about Bryony sensing something weird about Nicholas."

"Of course not. Why would I?"

Sean exploded. He couldn't keep it in anymore. "Because he *is* weird, and you know it. And you're weird when you're around him. And it was all awfully fast, wasn't it? The two of you getting together. What is he doing to you, Sarah?"

"Sean, please," whispered Sarah. Something pained, something frail in her voice made Sean ashamed of his outburst. She'd gone from strong to soft in the space of a few minutes, the way Sean knew so well.

"Look, I'm sorry," Sean said. "I'm sorry. I'll hide, OK? I'll do what I usually do. But I'll be there."

"Fine. Fine then." She held up her hands in defeat. "Come with me. But only so that we can be sure that Bryony is safe. And like I said, you can come to Islay with me . . . *and Nicholas.*"

Sarah's words resounded in the silence. Sean closed his eyes and breathed. Breathed deeply, for the first time in a long, long while. In spite of the mention of Nicholas, a dagger in Sean's side, she'd finally accepted him back.

"Thank you," he said simply.

Sarah stepped out into the hall, and Sean went to follow. But Elodie wasn't moving.

"I'll be there in a sec," he whispered to Sarah, and walked back into the living room. Elodie was leaning on the wall beside the window, her arms crossed.

"'You OK?"

"Yes. Yes, of course, sorry. Going to get my jacket now."

Sean took hold of her arm gently before she was out of the room. "Elodie. We've known each other for a long time. What's wrong?"

"Nothing." Another pretend smile.

And then, surprisingly, unexpectedly, she pushed herself into Sean's arms, all soft cream and white, hair like gold between his fingers, holding on to him – leaving him wondering why this good news, Sarah letting them into her life again, didn't feel good to her at all. He held her tighter, hiding his face in her neck, trying to make her feel safe. Elodie always had a faint vanilla scent, like a sweet shop, but there was a strange note to it now. Something too sweet, too ripe. Something that worried Sean.

Elodie wrapped her arms around his neck, and her mind was cast back to Marina Frison and her prediction for Elodie's life. Marina had fed her a pomegranate and then she'd placed it to burn into the wood stove. The pomegranate had come out intact.

It means you'll love again, she'd said.

Elodie held Sean tighter.

Sarah had walked into the cold, clear night and was looking up to the sky, waiting. The night was icy and the sky full of stars. But what was Sean doing? She turned around, blowing on her frozen fingers, and then she saw them. Silhouetted against the living room window were Sean and Elodie, in each other's arms.

Sarah brought a hand to her throat. She felt breathless again.

She forced herself to tear her eyes away from them. Nicholas was probably waiting for her on her doorstep, wondering where she was. She took her phone out of her pocket and switched it back on.

Fourteen missed calls and a message, all from Nicholas. The text chilled her blood, when it should have made her heart beat in anticipation.

I'm waiting for you.

15

Torn

Tainted sometimes
Shines like gold

Sean

When we arrived, Nicholas was standing beside the fire in Sarah's living room. He'd clearly lit it himself, given it was blue. Those freaky blue flames that spurt from his hands give me the creeps. And Nicholas gives me the creeps even more. How is he in her house already? Has she given him a set of keys? Or does he have ways to open doors, like me?

Or is he living with her now?

His eyes narrow briefly as he sees me following Sarah through the door. For a moment I rejoice in his bewilderment, but he regains his composure almost immediately.

"Sean." He nods. His eyes are just as black as his ravens', wide and lucid, with a disturbing hint of slow-burning embers. And he's huge. I'd almost forgotten. I'm not short myself, but he must be well over six foot five. Broad, too.

Freaky.

"Nicholas Donal," I say without offering him my hand.

"So. Sarah forgave your lies then," he replies immediately. What he's really saying is: she made a mistake.

"Yes. Nicholas. She did. And I realize that I never thanked you for saving her life. Our lives."

Sarah turns to look at me, incredulous. I know what she's thinking. *Is this really Sean talking? Sean showing Nicholas Donal gratitude?* Thing is, it's the only way. I can hardly assault him, as much as I'd like to. He'd toast me with those finger flames of his, for a start. I'm under no illusions as to how powerful this guy is.

Sarah sits down heavily in one of the chairs. She looks drained all of a sudden, and a strange, hazy expression has fallen on her features. Or is it my imagination? It can't be. I know it isn't.

"That's what we're meant to do, us Secret heirs. Help each other. But of course, I forgot – you're not an heir, are you?" Nicholas says, a slight smile playing on his lips.

I will my temper to stay in check. *You're right. I'm not an heir. But who are* you*, really? You look as if you've just walked out of a bloody grave.*

"Sean's a Gamekeeper," Sarah intervenes, the slightest hint of annoyance in her voice. Trouble in paradise?

"Impressive," he replies, and I allow myself to fantasize about my *sgian-dubh* making its way into his throat.

"Nicholas Donal." Elodie's silvery voice breaks the tension, but only momentarily.

Nicholas looks at her, and he freezes – just for the millionth part of an instant, but I notice. His eyes grow even blacker, shinier, like a kestrel that's spotted a mouse.

But Elodie doesn't waver. "I'm Elodie Midnight," she says.

"Elodie. Of course. I'm sorry . . . I'm sorry to hear about Harry." Nicholas lowers his head.

Elodie frowns and looks away. My eyes dart between them, and it's like seeing the two halves of the Tao – Elodie, all cream and white, blonde and fair, and Nicholas, dressed in black, raven hair, eyes like coal.

"Thank you," she whispers, and turns towards Sarah. "Your friend is here."

"Bryony? At the door? I didn't hear the bell," Sarah replies, still unaware of Elodie's psychic abilities.

"She's at the gate. She's walking up the path now."

I catch Nicholas looking at Elodie again, studying her face – as if she has something he wants.

As if she *is* something he wants.

16
Full Moon

The letter that came
From the second star to the right
The day of sorrow
That tore us apart

"Just remember, everyone," said Sarah icily from the doorway, her eyes moving between Elodie, Nicholas and Sean, "Bryony knows Sean as Harry. We must keep up the pretence."

"Sure, we'll remember," replied Nicholas as Sarah left the room. "*Harry*," he added, spitting the word out.

The doorbell rang. At the sight of her friend, Sarah had no choice but to smile. Bryony looked so . . . Bryony. She was like a walking painter's palette, shining against the night. Her coat was bright yellow, the collar tucked around her ears, and she had pulled a purple beanie over her bright red hair. Her cheeks were flushed pink from the cold, and her camera hung ready around her neck.

"Hello! I can't believe I invited myself here like that! Sorry,

Sarah, I know it's super short notice, it's just that there'll be no full moon for another month."

"There won't be, no!" laughed Sarah, and stepped aside to let Bryony come in.

"Exactly, I knew you'd understand, and your park is just perfect."

"It's a *garden*! Park sounds a bit grand!" Sarah hugged her friend affectionately, surprising Bryony with her uncharacteristic expansiveness. It didn't happen often. It hadn't happened in a long time.

"You've lost weight, you lucky person," said Bryony as she hung up her coat. "Come round to our's for dinner one evening – Mum would love to fatten you up."

"Bryony." Sarah interrupted her friend. "I have a few people over," she told her in a low voice.

"Oh, I'm sorry, you have guests." Bryony's eye's widened.

"I mean . . . Nicholas," Sarah whispered.

Bryony gave a tiny whoop. "Oh, cool! I'm about to meet your new boyfriend!"

Sarah put a hand over Bryony's mouth, jokingly. "Shhhh! Don't embarrass me!"

"Promise I won't!" squealed Bryony.

"Come on." Sarah led her friend into the living room. "Everyone, this is Bryony." Her voice was taut with nerves.

Nicholas stepped up first. "Hello. I'm Nicholas."

Sarah looked from one to the other, holding her breath. *Please like each other.*

Bryony stared at the tall, dark-haired man for a second. "Hello." She smiled. Sarah was her best friend. And if she thought that her boyfriend looked scary, she would not be telling her.

"Nice to meet you. You're just as Sarah described you," said Nicholas.

"Oh, am I? Hope that's a compliment!" Bryony could hear herself wittering. *Jesus, this guy's skin. And those eyes!* Everything about him unnerved her.

"And . . ." Sarah began.

Bryony turned, eager to avoid any further conversation with Nicholas for the moment. "And Harry is back!" Bryony anticipated Sarah's announcement. "You didn't tell me! Hi!"

"Hi. Yes. Here I am." Sean smiled broadly, his "everything is normal" smile.

"How was London?"

"Great," he replied brightly. "It was great. But I missed Scotland. I missed Sarah."

Sarah blushed, and cursed herself for it. She cleared her throat. "And this is Elodie. A friend of Harry's."

Elodie's expression was mildly reproachful as the two girls shook hands. Thankfully Bryony didn't notice, but Sarah did, and wished she could give Elodie a piece of her mind.

"It's freezing outside," said Bryony, crossing the room to stand beside the fireplace and stooping slightly to warm her hands. "Oh, this fire looks weird. Is it driftwood?" Bryony pointed at the blue flames.

"No, it's a new kind of briquette thing. They're much less messy than wood or coal, far less to clear up in the morning. They even burn in different colours," Sarah replied coolly.

"Wow, I've never seen anything like that." Bryony turned and stood with her back to the warmth, about to continue the conversation. But Sean was not in the mood for small talk.

"Right then," he cut her short. "It seems we're all coming with you."

"Are you?"

He nodded. "We love stargazing, and as you can tell, tonight's perfect for it. Right, Elodie?" They shared a knowing smile.

"I'll get the torches." Sarah led them all into the hall and opened the cupboard under the stairs. She handed a torch to Sean and Nicholas, and kept one for herself. They put on their coats and headed out into the night, followed by Shadow, gliding on silent paws.

A full, pure moon was high in the sky above the Midnight garden by now, delighting Bryony, if not the others.

"It's so beautiful," she said, over and over, snapping away.

Elodie and Sean materialized at Sarah's side. "This is crazy! What were you thinking?" she hissed. "It's dangerous for her to be here. Who knows what's out here, waiting?"

"Elodie . . ." Sean tried to smooth things over, to no avail.

"I didn't know what else to say, Elodie," Sarah explained. "She was so insistent."

"'No' would have been a good choice."

Sarah's tone was hard. "Well, too late now. She won't stay long."

Nicholas had overheard their conversation, in spite of their whispers. "Hey, hey. It's good for Sarah to invite friends round," he intervened, wrapping a protective arm around Sarah's shoulders.

Sean gaped at him. *He's so condescending! Like he's pandering to the whim of a small child. Sarah would never take this tone from anyone.*

Would she?

But Sarah was not saying anything.

"Even if their lives are in danger?" Sean said in a low voice, and immediately regretted it. Silent memories of what happened to Leigh rose between them.

"Nobody will be killed here tonight," said Nicholas, looking straight into Sean's eyes.

"What a chilly night!" exclaimed Bryony, striding across

the grass and slipping her arm into Sarah's. "I think I'm nearly done now. I took some lovely shots. Just a few more . . . Are you OK? Are you cold? You look like you've seen a ghost!"

Sarah and Bryony walked on under the clear and cloudless sky. A frosted halo shone around the moon like a crown of ice. The moonlight was bright but they used their torches, just in case. Not a whisper of wind moved through the trees and the bushes, not a noise was to be heard except for footsteps on the frosty grass. Sarah tucked her arm into Bryony's.

"Harry is back! You didn't tell me!" whispered Bryony. "Oh, hello, Shadow!" she added as the cat darted between them.

"He just . . . appeared," answered Sarah, bending to stroke Shadow's fur before the cat disappeared silently towards the back of the garden. "You know what he's like."

"You're always full of mysteries, Sarah. I can't keep up."

Sarah sighed. "Yes, it sort of works out that way."

"And is that his girlfriend? Elodie?"

Sarah stiffened. "No. No, she isn't. Just a friend."

Or is she? She recalled the sight of Sean and Elodie through the cottage window earlier that evening. Everything was so complicated.

"This place is incredible, really." Bryony looked around. "It's like a little castle."

"Yes. It's beautiful. I love my house." Sarah's words were full of meaning.

Bryony understood at once. "With Harry back, you won't have to leave. Your aunt Juliet can't argue with that, can she?"

"No. Well, she's tried, but . . . no. By the way, we're going to Islay for Christmas. You know, to my grandparents' house."

"House? Mansion, more like! I've seen the pictures!"

"Well, yes."

"Are your aunt and uncle going with you? And your cousins?"

"No. Just us. And Harry." She decided to forget about Elodie.

"Wow, you and Nicholas spending Christmas together. It's a big step!" Bryony's eyes widened.

"Not in our situation. His mum and dad are abroad, mine are dead . . ." Sarah faltered and shrugged.

"Yes, of course. Sorry. It's just very grown up, I suppose."

"It's OK."

"He seems . . . nice. Nicholas, I mean." She chose her words carefully. "He reminds me a little of your dad, in a way." *Your dad scared me too,* Bryony thought.

"He is. He really is. I never thought of that before." Sarah seemed quite pleased with the idea.

Bryony sighed. "It's about time you had a boyfriend, Sarah!" She teased her. The sound of the girls' laughter broke through the perfect silence.

Sean and Elodie were walking behind the girls, keeping an eye on them.

"This is crazy," Elodie repeated once again.

"I know. It's the way it is, in Sarah's world."

"Doesn't make it less crazy."

"You've been brought up as a Secret heir. Properly, I mean. Nearly everybody around you knew what you knew. But Sarah has always lived in the real world, hidden from what her family does. It's not easy, for her, to accept the Secret world."

"It's not easy for any of us," snapped Elodie.

Sean rested a hand on her arm for a second, and a silent understanding passed between them. Elodie's hair glowed golden in the light of Sean's torch, and her face was full of shadows.

"I know things are taking a strange turn, but you've got to trust me. I'll keep everyone alive. And we'll find a way to end all this."

Elodie nodded. "I know. I know we will. We must."

Sean squeezed her hand, and Elodie held onto his fingers, reluctant to let go.

Nicholas walked alone. His face was a mask, expressionless. He was quietly seething. Sean wasn't supposed to be there. And that other heir. The girls were supposed to be alone. Alone with him. So that he could be Sarah's saviour. So that Bryony would die. His plans had been spoiled. But it wasn't too late. There was still a chance of success.

"Look!" called Bryony dreamily. From where she stood the moon was reflected in the still waters of the pond, a perfectly white, round twin to the one in the sky. She took hold of her camera. "I've just got to get that . . ."

Sarah took advantage of Bryony's distraction to reach Sean. "Everything OK, it seems," she murmured.

Elodie crossed her arms. Her face was stern. "Hopefully it'll stay that way."

"Stop this, Elodie. What else could I do?" hissed Sarah. She'd had enough.

"Find friends of your own kind," replied Elodie, her delicate face set hard.

Sarah breathed deeply. *I've only known her five minutes and I already want to slap her.*

Bryony kept taking pictures around the pond, from different angles. The torchlight made a circle of yellow around each of them. The moon, the pond, the circle of torches, the people inside it; circles within circles, in the centre of the

Midnight garden. A cold breeze began to rise all of a sudden, twirling around them.

And then the breeze seemed to whisper, a ripple of sound that swept everything – the tops of the trees, the black bushes, breaking the glassy surface of the pond into ripples – imperceptible movements, imperceptible sounds that Bryony didn't notice, but the Secret people did. A shiver took them all.

"Sean . . . Harry," whispered Elodie.

"Ready. Sarah?"

"What's happening?" Sarah looked left and right.

"I don't know yet." Sean took a step towards her, ready to shield her.

Taking picture after picture, Bryony was oblivious to the sudden tension and to the whispers passing between the others. She kept snapping, dotting the *snap-snap-snap* with little comments. "That's beautiful – another one. Can you just move that torch a little bit, Harry?"

"Sarah!" Nicholas called.

"I'm ready," she murmured, flexing her hands.

Instinctively, they had all gathered around Bryony in a circle, looking outwards. The wind was even stronger now, twirling and whirling around them. *The sky? The soil? The water? Where will it come from?* Sarah's heart was pounding, her hands scalding hot already.

Sean jerked his head towards the house. "We need to go."

"Bryony. We need to get inside, now." Sarah's voice sounded strong, controlled, in spite of her terror.

"What? But I haven't finished."

"Now, Bryony." Sean walked over and grabbed her arm.

"Hey!" Bryony looked shocked.

"I saw someone on the wall, there," Sarah explained

quickly. "Somebody tried to burgle me last week – didn't I tell you? We need to get inside."

"I don't understand . . ."

A sudden noise, a thud, a growl. Then nothing. The torchlight started moving frantically, illuminating sections of the pond, of the trees, of the ground around them.

"Everyone! See to Bryony!" Sean commanded.

In a second Bryony found herself surrounded – Sarah, the man she knew as Harry, Nicholas and Elodie crowding her, shielding her. Harry and Elodie each carried a torch in one hand, and, to her horror, what looked like a knife in the other.

A *knife*?

"What are you doing?" Bryony whispered. The camera in her hands was trembling.

"Be quiet!" Sean said.

The torches continued their dance.

"Nothing," said Sarah.

"Then what was that noise?" Elodie retorted.

Sarah swung round to glare at her. But Elodie spoke before Sarah could snap at her. The French girl's voice was small now, all anger gone. "Sarah."

Elodie's torch was pointing at the ground. In its beam, a furry shape, still and crumpled.

A black cat with a white paw, lying lifeless in a pool of blood.

17
Goodbye

Had I known the days were numbered
I would have said goodbye

"Shadow!"

Sarah threw herself on the ground. She lifted the cat's bloodied little body, cradling her. It was soft and limp, every bone broken. She felt the heat of the Blackwater leave her hands and flow away. A lump of tears formed in her throat, but there was no time to cry.

"Oh my God," whispered Bryony. "Shadow. What's going—"

Before she could finish the sentence, she was thrown flat on her face with bone-shattering force. Some kind of beast had jumped over the protective circle around Bryony and landed straight on her.

"Bryony!" yelled Sarah.

The torches swung down to illuminate the terrible scene. Bryony was smothered by something between a tiger and a hyena, with an enormous muscular body and clawed paws.

Already the creature's fur had started turning yellow, the same yellow as Bryony's coat.

Camouflage, thought Sean. "Nobody move!" he commanded, and began tracing deadly runes with his *sgian-dubh*. The Surari was hit at once, but barely shuddered. It growled in rage, leapt off Bryony and turned towards Sean. Finally he could see its muzzle – an impossibly wide mouth, full of row after row of yellow teeth, and black slits for eyes. Its fur was changing colour again, turning black when standing on dark ground.

Sarah grabbed Elodie's torch and shone it against her own face. "Look at me. Look at me," she called to the beast, calmly, coldly. Her eyes were greener than ever, shining in the bright light. "Look at me!" She repeated. *Will it work? Will the Midnight gaze work this time?* But she had no chance to find out. The beast turned its eyes away, as if it knew what Sarah was trying to do. It shook its head, growling again, and looked at the others, one by one, everyone but Sarah – Sean, Elodie . . . Bryony.

And it chose.

Bryony wasn't moving, lying prone on the ground. The Surari raised a clawed paw, ready to slash the back of her neck – but Sean was faster, and he threw himself against the beast, rolling on the grass with it. The *sgian-dubh* fell from Sean's hand, and the creature's claws dug into his chest. As soon as it touched Sean's jacket, its fur turned blue. It was ripping and slashing the fabric, and through it, to Sean's skin.

Elodie jumped on the demon's back with a scream, stabbing it repeatedly with her knife – but to no avail.

Sarah stood by with her arms raised and the torch at her feet, calling the Blackwater, praying for her hands to heat up again, having gone cold from the shock of Shadow's death.

Sean screamed helplessly under the beast's claws, blood seeping through his jacket, and Sarah shuddered, losing concentration.

"Nicholas!" she called desperately. "Where are you!"

"There are two of them!" Nicholas called back from somewhere in the darkness.

Sarah grabbed the torch and pointed it towards Nicholas's voice. He was standing in front of another demon-tiger, camouflaged black against the dark backdrop of the bushes. She was horrified to see that Nicholas's face was red with blood. *Whose blood? The beast's, or Nicholas's?*

Sarah's face changed all of a sudden, setting in a hard, furious expression. She let the torch fall and closed her eyes, then raised her hands to her chest and lowered her head.

Concentrate, concentrate.

Shadow. Shadow is gone.

Fury rose within her, and it happened – the Blackwater flew into her hands, at last. They burned, ready to strike. Sarah had to choose quickly – Nicholas was bloodied but still standing, while Sean was about to get his head bitten off. She threw herself on the Surari that had Sean in its grasp and dug her hands into its fur with a growl that nearly matched the beast's. Sarah felt the demon tremble under her touch – it started shuddering violently in an attempt to shake her off, but Sarah's hands were holding on to its black, hard fur, and she wouldn't let go. The Surari growled in pain and brought its bloody paws over its head, freeing Sean from its grasp. Blackwater had started to sprout from the beast's ears and nostrils. Sarah kept digging her hands into the demon, mercilessly, until she felt its skin moistening. At last it was beginning to weep and melt away.

Released, Sean lifted himself up from where he'd fallen, supporting himself with one bleeding hand, the other feeling around the ground for his *sgian-dubh*. By now, the Surari was contorting in agony, black blood and the black liquid from its weeping skin mixing and soaking the ground.

It seemed to take an eternity, but eventually, with one last convulsion, one last growl, the Surari dissolved in a foul-smelling gush under Sarah's deadly touch. She rolled away, soaked and spent.

But she had no time to rest. She turned towards Nicholas at once. The second Surari's tail was twitching in a menacing rhythm. It hadn't attacked yet. *Why? What is it waiting for?*

"Sean!" Sarah implored as she staggered to her feet. Sean heard her call and followed her gaze. He saw Nicholas and the beast face to face and raised his *sgian-dubh* again, his face a mask of anger.

Nicholas turned to him, wide-eyed. *He's barely standing, and he wants to come to my rescue?*

"Hey! Beast!" shouted Sean.

The Surari turned its monstrous head, its mouth open wide, its teeth yellow in the moonlight.

"Yes, you!"

Once again, Sean began tracing his runes, his hands moving impossibly quickly, sweat and blood pouring down his face. The demon roared and sat back, preparing to pounce – but this time Sean's runes were too strong to resist. It stopped and tried to snarl, a snarl that turned into a yelp. Black blood started pouring from its throat, the flow becoming greater and greater the longer Sean's hands kept weaving his deadly spell.

"Nicholas!" called Sarah. "Help him! Help Sean!"

Nicholas was standing, paralyzed. Then, as if waking himself from a trance, he raised his hands, commanding the blue flames from his fingers.

"Nicholas." A dark, strong voice. Sean. "It's . . . not . . . necessary." Each word was accompanied by a stab of his *sgian-dubh*, each stab drawing more blood from the Surari's throat. The demon staggered then fell. One last shiver, a deep, painful howl, and it was still.

Sean fell to his knees, holding his wounded chest, and Elodie was at his side at once.

"I'm OK. I'm OK. See to Bryony." But Elodie wouldn't leave his side.

Bryony was lying face down on the ground, very still. Beside her, Sarah placed two fingers against her friend's neck. "She's breathing. She's alive. Thank God. Thank God."

"Sarah," Bryony mewed, shifting slightly, painfully, and Sarah gently helped her turn until she could cradle her friend's head on her lap. A blue bruise was slowly appearing above Bryony's left eye and she had a split lip. She was shaking from the shock.

"What . . .?"

"Shhhh. It's OK. It was the burglar. He jumped on you," Sarah began.

"It wasn't a burglar. Sarah, I promise you, it wasn't." Bryony pushed herself up slowly until she was sitting. She turned from Sarah to Sean, and back. "That wasn't a human being. It was like a . . . tiger. Or a panther."

Sean laughed a hollow laugh. "A panther? In an Edinburgh garden?"

Sarah turned away.

Bryony shook her head. "I could have sworn . . ." She stopped suddenly at the sight of her friend gathering the cat's lifeless body against her chest, kissing her fur softly, inhaling the scent she knew so well, tears finally flowing down her cheeks.

"Oh no, Sarah." Bryony stood up and threw her arms around Sarah, Shadow's little body between them. The others stood awkwardly.

After a few moments, Elodie took Sean's arm. "Sean. Listen," she said, and whispered something into his ear.

"Sean? Who's Sean?" Bryony murmured to Sarah. But Sarah's mind was too clouded with grief to make up an excuse.

A rustling of leaves, a sudden noise.

"Shhhh!" Sean lifted a finger towards Bryony. She gasped as she noticed the knife in Sean's hand.

"Quiet!" Sean grabbed her arm, harder than he'd meant to. Bryony whimpered softly.

More rustling.

So it wasn't over. Sarah glanced at her friend, wondering how much she had seen. Elodie stood alert, her lips blue. Everyone was poised, ready to fight.

A gust of wind, a low bark.

And then, a pair of shiny little eyes appeared among the leaves, followed by a red head with two pointy ears, and a magnificent tail. A fox, looking at the strange gathering in alarm before vanishing again into the undergrowth.

They all let out a deep breath, hunching in relief.

"It's over," whispered Sean, and offered his hand to Bryony.

She didn't take it. "I don't know what it was that attacked me, but it was not a man," she repeated, looking around her with bewildered eyes.

18
The Worst Kind of Fear

The day we bargained our lives
For a lie
That was
The day of the choice

Sean

Had Bryony been killed, I don't know what would have happened to Sarah's state of mind. It's bad enough that Shadow ended up mangled like that. Poor little Shadow, she didn't stand a chance.

If I were a cynical man, I'd say it's good that this strike took place. It's good that Sarah saw once more how the danger is not over, and how Nicholas is not enough to protect her. She needs us as well. She needs *me*.

I'm as sore as hell. Elodie has washed and dressed my wounds – the damn thing clawed at my chest and my arms. I bet these scars will stay – but hey, what's another scar?

We're all in shock, crowded around the kitchen table,

sipping hot tea. Bryony is holding a wet towel to her lip, and she's as white as a sheet.

"We need to call the police," she keeps telling us.

"We can't do that. Bryony, please," Sarah begs her. She's sitting holding Nicholas's hand, and her eyes are red raw.

"We have to! There was a . . . tiger thing in your garden! Whatever it was! And it's still out there!"

"It was a burglar, Bryony," I repeat, hoping that she will eventually believe me. Thank goodness she was unconscious until we were finished with the bloody things.

Bryony sighs in frustration and studies my face. "What's going on here?" She looks at all of us, one by one. "Why do you carry a knife, Harry? Isn't it illegal to carry knives? And what did this . . . 'burglar' use to hurt you like that?" She points at my chest. "Because those look like claw marks to me. And why on earth is everybody calling you Sean?" Her voice is rising with the beginnings of hysteria.

"Bryony, please." Sarah is in no mood to explain.

"No! Sarah, I know what I saw!"

"But you didn't see anything, did you? You were out of it." I dismiss her.

"Look at the bruising on my head! I want an explanation!"

"You can have no explanation!" My tone silences everyone, leaving no room for discussion. This is not the time to be delicate. "Do you want Sarah's life to be in even more danger?"

Bryony shakes her head feebly, confusion on her pale face.

"Sean." Sarah puts a protective hand on Bryony's arm.

"Do you want Sarah to get killed, like Shadow?" My voice is steely.

Bryony shakes her head again, a frightened look in her eyes. She's afraid. Afraid of me.

"Then don't speak about this to anyone. Do you hear me?"

Bryony nods.

"Do you hear me?"

"Yes!"

"This," I point to her bloodied lip, "happened when you fell while taking pictures. OK?"

"OK." She looks to Sarah, and their eyes meet for a moment.

"Please trust me," Sarah whispers.

"I trust you."

I know what she's thinking: *I trust you, but not him.*

"Good. I'm taking you home," I say, softer this time.

Bryony stands, so keen to leave that she doesn't even mind that I'll be the one taking her. But she still has a question. "Who are you? Who is Sean?"

I haven't the strength to lie. "I am Sean. My name is Sean Hannay. Sarah will explain later." Sarah nods wearily. "But not tonight. Let's go."

On my return I find Sarah, Elodie and Nicholas back in the garden, well away from the area of the attack, gathered around a little body wrapped in a blanket. Elodie is standing guard, her lips blue already, in case of another ambush.

"I wanted to wait for you. To bury her," says Sarah in a broken voice, without looking up.

And here we are, under a moon that's as beautiful as it's merciless, putting little Shadow to rest at the foot of the thyme bush where Sarah found her mother's diary.

"If only I'd dreamt of this," Sarah whispers. "If only I'd known, I could have prevented it."

Yes, why did she not dream of this? Is she not dreaming anymore?

"Just be thankful it's a cat, and not one of us," Elodie says sharply – cruelly, even. Not like her.

It feels unreal. Only a few weeks ago Sarah and I were here in each other's arms, the night she'd unearthed Anne's diary. It seems a lifetime ago. It was another full moon, and we were so close, the two of us in a dangerous, chaotic world. But tonight, under this moon, it's another man that Sarah turns to. When the last fistful of earth falls on the grave, it's Nicholas's arms that comfort her.

Still, at least she waited for me to come back before burying Shadow, and as we walk back into the house, I catch of glimpse of her looking at me in a way that warms my heart for a second. It's as if she's making sure I'm still there.

I'm here, Sarah, I tell her in my heart.

19

The Boy Who Disappeared

Wherever she goes
She'll find shadows and withered flowers

Nicholas was stroking Sarah's hair slowly, rhythmically. She was soft and weak in his arms, the way he liked it – more proof that picking her friends off one by one, like petals off a flower, was the sensible thing to do.

Sure, it hadn't worked out the way it was supposed to. It was Bryony who should have been lying dead that night, her throat slit open and every bone in her body smashed.

Nicholas wouldn't forget that night for a long time. Nothing had turned out quite as he'd anticipated. It would have been so easy for Sean to wait just a split second before intervening – more than enough time for the Surari to finish Nicholas off. It wouldn't have happened, of course – but Sean didn't know that. As far as he knew, the Surari was going to kill Nicholas, so he intervened, even though he was barely standing. Quite the hero.

Sean was in love with Sarah, and he was desperately jealous;

Nicholas knew that well. So why did Sean not just stand by and let Nicholas fight alone? Die alone? The whole thing was surreal. Sarah had been so powerful, so strong – not the way he needed her to be if her destiny was to remain in his hands. Still, it had been amazing to see. Her face when the tiger-demon pounced on Bryony, and again when the girls were holding hands, once it was all over. The intensity of Sarah's feelings for Bryony amazed him.

Friendship. It wasn't something Nicholas had ever experienced. There had never been any need for friendship in his life, a life among Elementals and Surari. With a pang, Nicholas wondered if it could have been different for him. Had he grown up around people as she had, would he be able to feel the way Sarah felt? The way Sarah and Bryony seemed to feel about each other?

When he realized that Bryony had survived the attack he'd felt a hint of something unsettling. Something unexpected. It was a while before he could identify the feeling – and then he'd realized that it was relief. Relief on Sarah's behalf that her friend had survived.

Odd.

Memories from long ago rose in his mind. Another girl, another Nicholas, even. Those absurd, forbidden feelings swept Nicholas while he gently entangled his fingers in Sarah's hair.

What was happening to him? Was this a sign that he might not be the person his father had raised him to be?

There used to be a boy called Nicholas, long ago – someone real and truthful, someone with a soul – but he was gone. One lie after another, to his mother, to himself – to the black-haired girl all those years ago. Each lie had taken him another step away from that boy.

Now he was lost.

"Are you OK, Nicholas?" whispered Sarah, shifting so that she could look at him. Nicholas realized he must have moaned in pain.

"Yes. Yes. Sorry, just a headache. Lie back."

Of course. His father must be displeased. He would know about the thoughts he'd had, the relief he'd felt at Bryony's survival, the memories of the time he had loved and lost. He should not be putting these feelings into thoughts – he should not have these feelings at all. A member of a Valaya would die for less. The King of Shadows might not kill his son, but that didn't mean he wouldn't punish him. And his punishments could be so painful, so excruciating, that people would rather throw themselves to the Surari than face his wrath.

He stopped stroking Sarah's hair and she opened her eyes and studied him again. There was a question in her eyes. A question Nicholas couldn't answer.

"I love you," he said. The only truth he knew.

20
Slaughter

If I die today
Will you be there to hold my hand?

Juliet opened the boot of her BMW and started taking out the grocery bags piled on top of each other. They were full of Christmas food and decorations, a cheery tangle of tinsel and mince pies and chocolate boxes. It was going to be a small celebration – just the four of them and Trevor's parents. Still, Juliet felt Christmas had to be marked. If anything, for her daughters.

It was the first Christmas since Anne had gone.

But she wouldn't think about that now, she decided. She slammed the boot of the car as if she were slamming her sad thoughts away. If only Sarah had agreed to be with them. No, that thought wouldn't do either. She had to concentrate on good things, happy things. Stop worrying about things she couldn't control. Like her niece. Instead, she'd think about the outfit she had planned for the Christmas celebrations, a black silken dress; the presents for the girls, a new iPod each, with pink cases; the weekend away she and Trevor had planned for January – maybe a short skiing trip? Yes, a skiing trip would be just the thing, she said to herself, sweeping her golden hair from her eyes.

But Anne was gone.

Her sister was gone.

And what kind of mince pies would she buy, lattice or shortcrust? What colour of tinsel would the girls like this year? What would they to give to the girls' head teacher?

Nothing *really* mattered. Except that Anne was gone.

But would it really be much different? For the last eighteen years, the sisters had spent Christmas apart. Juliet had tried to convince Anne to be with them, at least alternate years. She'd done her utmost to try and get their families together. But Anne had always said no, settling for a hurried phone call instead. Juliet knew it was James who'd decided, who'd kept their conversations short, even on holidays. But in the last few years, Anne seemed to be warming to the possibility of confronting James and celebrating Christmas with her side of the family, for once.

But now Anne was dead, and they'd never get the chance to spend a Christmas together again.

Would these terrible thoughts go away? Or were they going to stay with her for the rest of the day, give her yet another sleepless night?

Juliet grabbed the first few bags, clutching the car keys, her handbag strap slipping down her arm. Trevor smiled and waved at her from the window. Her spirits lifted at once. Trevor was home for a rare few days – it was a treat. Her husband's face disappeared from the window. He was coming to help her with the bags. He'd park the car in the garage for her and make her a cup of tea. They would have a chat, probably centred around their daughters, while putting the groceries away. Maybe she could ask him again if he'd help her talk Sarah round.

Juliet took a step towards the front door. An orange rolled down the path in front of her feet. What was her fruit doing on the ground? She turned around, irritated, towards the bags piled beside the car. She was aware of Trevor yelling.

Juliet turned back towards the house, puzzled.

The pain was so sudden and unbearable, so unlike anything she'd ever experienced. It was as if the skin was being ripped from her face. As she lost consciousness, she screamed at the agony, the sheer impossibility of what was happening to her. A single word seared through her mind, then everything went black. She was mercifully unaware of the wildcat's claws tearing her apart, tearing at her eyes and ripping into her cheeks with its searing teeth, until she was totally unrecognizable.

She did, though, have time for one last thought: that she'd never see her family again. And she also had time to hear the voices screaming in her head, screaming that one word over and over again – the word that really explained it all, all that had happened in the last few years, all the mysteries and secrets and finally, her sister's death.

The word she heard before the wildcat sunk its teeth into her neck: *Midnight*.

21
Seawater

Words between us
From the impossible planet to earth
And every time you and I speak
My heart finds peace

"I'll never take another boat again," groaned Mike, wiping his face with his hand as he walked. "I've been on land for days and I'm still seasick. All that time we had to stay on the ship after the attack, I never stopped wondering whether the next wave might throw up another demon."

A soft drizzle was falling over the city of Edinburgh, and white, thin mist shrouded the streets. Mike and Niall were walking towards Sarah's house, and Sean's dead drop in her garden, hoping to find news of him. The plan was to tell Sean that the signal they'd intercepted in Louisiana the night they were attacked had come from somewhere in eastern Europe. After that, there was no clear path. Hiding, going to look for the Enemy, maybe searching for more surviving heirs – it was difficult to decide what to do. All Mike wanted, for now, was to find Sean alive and well. And to stay on dry land.

Niall shrugged. "I wasn't a bit worried."

"Bull. You were, I saw you."

"Maybe a wee bit. For you, mainly. I really didn't want to face another big calamari. Anyway, here we are. We made it," he said with a sigh.

The journey on the cargo ship after the Makara's attack had been a ghastly affair. They had seen to the injured as best they could, using the Med kits on board. Captain Young's wound had been just a graze – Mike was a good shot – but he was in shock, and his distress was horrible to see. He was so sure that Mike and Niall were somehow to blame. His babbling sent shivers down Mike's spine, and they had to guard him night and day to make sure he wouldn't attack them again.

They'd come as near to the coast as they could. Then, they sent an SOS for the captain and the crewman to be rescued and left the cargo ship aboard a small lifeboat with a modicum of food and water. Had it not been for Niall's powers they would have got lost, unable to control the raft, but Niall used the song to force the wind and the waves to take them up the east coast to Edinburgh, where they moored in great secret. Mike struggled to believe that he was still alive, after days and days on a boat that looked and felt as if it might capsize at any moment.

They never knew what became of Captain Young and the wounded crewman, and whether anyone believed their story about a giant squid attacking the ship.

"A few more minutes and we'll be at Sarah's house," said Mike, checking the map he was holding. "Niall, I was thinking ..."

"Yes, I wonder about that too."

Mike stopped suddenly. "What? You know what I was thinking? Can you read minds, is it a power of yours?" he asked, horrified.

"No, I can't read minds!" Niall laughed. "I just know you so well by now that I know what you're about to say."

Mike frowned. "Are you saying I'm predictable?"

"Very."

"As in, boring?"

"Yes, that too. I know what you're going to say next: shut up Niall."

"Shut u . . . Oh, for heaven's sake!"

Niall patted his friend's shoulder as they walked. "Just messing with you, Mike. It was written all over your face – you're wondering if Sarah has found out that Sean is not Harry. If you know what I mean."

"Just as well you don't read minds, you'd know what I really think of you."

"You fancy me."

Mike laughed. "In your dreams. Anyway, yes, I was wondering about just that. I remember that Harry warned Sean about Sarah's diffidence. But you'd think she'd understand the whole situation by now."

"The unforgiving Midnights."

"What do you mean by that?"

"My mum knew someone who knew Morag Midnight. A distant cousin of ours, Amelia Campbell. She ended up somewhere in Australia or New Zealand, I think. Isn't that where Sean is from?"

"Yes."

"Anyway, Amelia was in awe of the Midnights, and not always in a good way. That's what she called them, 'the unforgiving Midnights'."

"Harry was a Midnight, and he was the kindest person I've ever met."

"No wonder he didn't speak to the rest of them, then."

Mike nodded and shrugged. "You have a point." He pulled his collar up as high as he could. "Jesus, I'm done in, man. This weather is brutal."

"You need to eat something. Come on, I'll go and get breakfast for us. With our last—" Niall counted the coins in his pocket, "—five pounds and forty-four pence. You wait here."

"You can be useful, sometimes." Mike let himself down onto a bench, heavily, his rucksack tipping horizontal on the pavement.

"I was sent to you by the angels, Mike."

"Ha 'bloody' ha."

Niall crossed the road to the first coffee shop he saw. It was uncommonly busy for that time of the morning, somewhere between breakfast and lunch hour – overflowing with mums and prams, students with no lectures or bunking off school, and office workers on their tea breaks. Niall stood in the queue, looking left and right, watching for possible threats.

There were some suspicious looks. He'd slept in the same clothes for days, had the straggly beginnings of a red beard and smelled of some foul Himalayan Pine deodorant they had bought in the chemist's to cover the fact they hadn't showered since they got off the boat.

After twenty minutes of queuing, Niall finally got his hands on two bacon rolls and two white coffees. That meant they had twenty-four pence left, unless they found Sean soon. They couldn't use any of their cards, of course, they'd be easily traceable.

Mike bit into his roll at once. "Oh man, this is good. What took you so long?"

"The world and his granny are having a coffee this morning."

"The world and who?"

"His granny."

"Can you please make sense when you speak to me?"

Niall laughed. "Right-o. By the way, this is our last meal. After this, it's pickpocketing for me."

"Fine. Just don't get caught."

"That's not like you, Mr we-can't-do-this-it's-wrong!"

"What's the alternative? Find a job, with no documents?"

Niall nodded, chewing. "We should have taken those."

"They had tentacles all over them, I'd like to remind you! Now get a move on."

They swung their rucksacks over their shoulders and set off once more. Finally, they entered a long, tree-lined road, with gated villas at both sides.

"I think this must be her street," said Mike finally. "We're looking for an wrought-iron gate marked by two red pillars. Let's go."

Not even a mile on, they spotted the red pillars, and on top of a small hill, the grey sandstone villa that Sean had described: Sarah's home. A stone wall ran around the property, high but conquerable.

"Fancy," commented Niall with a low whistle.

They looked around, making sure no one would see them, and threw their rucksacks over the stone wall. Then they climbed over, letting themselves fall on the grass.

"What are we looking for exactly?" asked Niall, taking in the beautiful grounds around the house, the oak trees at the sides of it, the still water of the pond marked by a fountain in the middle.

"A painted S. On the north wall. Let me see, north . . . that one should be it," said Mike, and started walking.

Niall followed suit. He briefly turned his head towards the house. "All the shutters are closed."

Mike followed his gaze. "Yes. Just as well. I'm not approaching Sarah until I know."

They walked the length of Sarah's garden, past Anne's vegetable patch, now wintry bare, past the pond, towards a small copse of beeches, ashes and hawthorns at the back, their black, naked branches jutting out against the sky. The northern wall ran behind the trees, covered in ivy and moss. Mike and Niall began inspecting the stones, looking for Sean's sign.

"There!" Mike called finally, pointing at a small, spray-painted S. He started feeling every inch of the stones around the sign with stiff, frozen fingers.

"Ergh . . . slug." Mike grimaced. "And random wiggling creatures."

"Same here." Niall muttered, kneeling on the carpet of rotten leaves to inspect the bottom section of the wall, and shivering in the chill wind.

After another few minutes of swearing and searching, Niall uttered a small cry of joy.

"And here we are!" Scrunched inside a tiny fissure in the stone was a square of transparent plastic sealed with sellotape. He passed it to Mike.

"Bingo!" Mike ripped the small package open. Inside was a piece of paper torn from a lined notebook, and on it, a series of numbers.

"What's that?" asked Niall.

"Gamekeepers' code. Give me a minute." Mike took a pen from the depths of his rucksack and started scribbling.

"Can you not do it in your head? Bet Sean can do it in his head." Niall loved irritating his friend and grinned, satisfied, when Mike gave him the usual exasperated look. Niall put his hands up in surrender. "Sorry, I'll be quiet now."

"That'd be a first. Right, there, I've got it. 'Not at the Heron's house anymore. Midnight Hall. Eesley.' Eesley? Where on earth . . .?"

"Let me see. It's Islay – Aye-lah, my American friend! In the Hebrides, islands off the west coast of Scotland. Gorgeous place, lots of great music," Niall explained enthusiastically. Niall was a keen fiddle player, and he could play just about anything he put his hands on. "There are some great sessions to be found there, I'm told."

"An island? Oh God . . . not another boat," groaned Mike.

"Come on, Mike, you're in Scotland now, you need to get used to the choppy seas!" said Niall, smiling.

"Shut up, Niall."

22
Banished

There was you, and me and them
Over a birthday cake
And a photograph, it seems
It's all that's left

Sarah leaned over her bed and folded her white jumper. Then she unfolded it, and folded it again. She moved it onto the chair, carefully, and smoothed her bed where the woollen jumper had left an invisible indentation.

But by then the jumper was crumpled, lying on her dressing table chair at an angle. Sarah sighed in frustration. At this rate, the packing for Islay would take the whole day.

Sean and Elodie were downstairs, spending time together in the easy way old friends do. They'd been chatting about old times, with a couple of mentions of Mary Anne, Sean's old girlfriend. Sarah had decided then that her room was altogether a better place to be.

Once more Sarah folded the jumper and smoothed it

down in the suitcase that was lying open on the floor. This time it worked. She could move on.

"Sarah! Somebody for you!" Elodie's voice drifted upstairs.

Sarah turned away from the pile of clothes on her bed. Elodie was at the bottom of the stairs.

"Who is it? Where?"

"A man. About to knock at the door."

"But the gate was locked! It must be Nicholas, only he can open it."

Elodie shook her head. "It's not Nicholas," she said assuredly.

Sarah raised her eyebrows; she couldn't help being impressed with Elodie's gift.

Sean was already up and behind the door, his *sgian-dubh* in his hand. Elodie's lips started turning blue, and Sarah stood, rigid and waiting in front of the living room window. Then she saw who it was, and all alarm left her.

"It's OK," she muttered to the others as she ran towards the door. "This I can handle." She pulled the door open. "Uncle Trevor!" She wasn't overly fond of him, but at least it wasn't a demon.

"Sarah."

Sarah frowned. She'd never seen her uncle so dishevelled in her whole life. His eyes were circled blue and red-rimmed.

"You stupid, selfish girl. You thought you could get away with it, didn't you? Cut us out of your life forever. Well, you certainly accomplished that! With your witchcraft, or whatever it is you and your parents get up to. You've got what you wanted. And now you are dead to me. To us. You and your despicable family. Do you understand?"

His lips barely moved, but the venom in his words was crystal clear.

"I *don't* understand. What happened?" Sarah asked, shocked.

Her voice was trembling and already full of grief. Because she knew. She felt it.

"Playing dumb, are you? Well, that's all you need to know. Never, never come near us again, do you hear me? You, or any of your insane family or little friends. Do you hear me, Sarah bloody Midnight?"

"Hey! Trevor!" Sean came out from behind the door. His dagger was behind his back, but he looked no less intimidating.

Trevor didn't budge, didn't change his expression. Grief had made him fearless.

"Is it Aunt Juliet?" Sarah whispered, a world of grief in her words.

That's what it was, the weird feeling after I said goodbye to her the other day.

"You're dead to us, Sarah," Uncle Trevor snarled, and threw a bundle of keys — Sarah's house keys — and a book at her feet. The book lay with its spine broken and open, its pages crumpled under their own weight.

Trevor turned and walked away. Sarah watched his broad back and his uncertain step down the gravelly path. He brought a hand to his face — Sarah guessed he was drying his eyes. That was the man with a swagger, who was always dressed in perfectly pressed designer clothes, who had the salesman's smile perpetually painted on his face.

Sarah bent to retrieve the book. It was a photo album. She flicked through the pages in silence, shaking Sean's hand off as he tried to touch her shoulder. The album was full of pictures of Sarah as a child, and of her mum.

"He didn't tell me how," she whispered desolately. "Oh my God, was it the demon-bird?" She clasped her hand on her mouth. "It got away. I should have killed it!"

Stricken, Sean took a step towards her once more, and again she stepped back.

"Aunt Juliet is dead," she said aloud, like she couldn't quite believe it.

Like my parents, like Leigh. And little Shadow. And it's always my fault.

"Sarah! What happened?" Nicholas was walking up the path towards them.

Perfect timing, thought Sean.

"Who was that weird-looking guy coming out of here just now? Just barged past me. Sarah?" Nicholas had seen her face.

"Something happened to my aunt. I think she was attacked. I think she's dead."

Nicholas took the steps three at a time and enveloped her – such was Sean's impression, that he'd swallowed her whole with his huge frame.

"Shhhh," Nicholas soothed. "It's OK. It's OK. I'm here now. I'm here." He stroked Sarah's hair with his pale fingers.

From where he was standing, Sean could see a sliver of Sarah's face. To his horror, he watched her expression change from stricken to dazed in the space of a few seconds.

She allowed Nicholas to take the photo album from her, allowed him to lead her upstairs, murmuring in her ear, as Sean and Elodie watched, stunned.

"Everything will be alright," he was saying. "I'm here."

They heard Sarah's bedroom door close and Elodie turned and walked slowly towards the kitchen. But Sean stood as if immobilised. Sarah had told Nicholas that Juliet had been killed. And Nicholas didn't seem surprised. He didn't seem surprised at all.

★

Nicholas and Sarah lay on her bed, entwined. Sarah had curled herself up in the nest of Nicholas's body. She felt warm and safe, and had no desire to move. She was sure that if she moved just an inch away from him, the terrifying grief that had been brought to her front door would overwhelm her and she'd suffocate.

A blue light started flickering on her bedside table, emitting a little *beep*. Sarah extended her hand and wrapped her fingers around her phone.

Bryony's name flashed on the screen. Suddenly, Sarah wanted to speak to her friend so badly, tell her all. See her, her familiar face, her family – people she'd known and loved since she was a wee girl.

She switched the phone off.

She wouldn't put Bryony and her family in danger. She would never go near them again. Just as she would never go near Trevor and her cousins again.

She made herself as small as she could, as small as a child, in the shelter of Nicholas's arms.

In the darkness, he was smiling.

23
Islay

Every scent a memory
Sea and grass
Peat and salt
Where we came from
And what we left behind

The journey to Islay was like a dream of beauty, wind and rain and sea shaping a landscape unchanged for millions of years. It was like a balm on Sarah's wounds, in spite of her grief for Aunt Juliet and Shadow, and in spite of the fear of another demon strike.

There were still no dreams. She'd always hoped for the dreams to disappear, she had fantasized about how peaceful, how free her life would be without them. But now that they didn't come, it wasn't like that at all. Being dreamless left her lost and uncertain and added to her terror.

She didn't know what she was going to find at Midnight Hall. She suspected that the demon-tigers and the attack on Aunt Juliet were just the beginning of another wave – another

Valaya? But she couldn't count on the dreams to warn her. There was a constant sense of anxiety with every movement, every change of light, every unexpected noise.

Still, even with the black cloud hanging over her, Sarah couldn't help feel a huge relief to be on the ferry to Islay – because everything around her spoke of freedom. Even in her sadness and fear, she could hear the call of home.

Nicholas stood beside her on deck, unable to keep his eyes from her. Sarah's black hair was blowing in the wind, and she looked at one with the landscape, as if she'd been born from it – a Celtic goddess, going back where she belonged.

"It's beautiful, isn't it?" she said over the roar of the wind.

"Yes," he answered simply.

Something in his voice made Sarah do a double take. She studied his face. He was carrying a weight on his shoulders. Sarah could sometimes feel it so intensely that she could nearly see it, an invisible, malevolent incubus encroaching on his back, refusing to give him peace. The uncertainty in his eyes wasn't like him – he was usually so confident, even arrogant with it. As if he ruled the world, as if nothing could ever worry him or break his composure.

"Are you OK?"

"Yes, yes. I'm fine," he smiled thinly. He couldn't confide in her, of course. He couldn't speak about what tortured him, and what he had on his mind. He couldn't tell her that the attack on Juliet hadn't been his idea at all, but his father's. That he hadn't known it was going to happen, not so fast, so cruel.

His eyes roamed over her face, blue shadows under her eyes, cheekbones jutting out. He could see how much the attack on Juliet and Shadow's death had taken out of her.

"You'll love it on Islay," she said and smiled at him, willing him to experience the same feelings she had as the ferry made its way across the sound.

"I'm sure." He wrapped an arm around her shoulders and brought her closer. She breathed in his scent of earth and smoke, still persistent in spite of the wind and the smell of the sea. Nicholas took a quick look around. Sean and Elodie were on the other side of the boat. It was a good moment to speak.

"I'm so sorry about what happened to your aunt." He cupped her cheek, turning her to face him, his black eyes holding her gaze. It was too good a chance to remind her how much she needed him. How much she depended on him. "They're everywhere. The demons, I mean. Nowhere is safe. Except when you're with me."

Sarah gave him a wan smile and leant into him, feeling suddenly weakened. "I know. I'm very lucky to have you. We'll be just fine," she said.

"Yes. As long as we're together, we'll be just fine."

They stood in silence for a minute, Sarah's head on his shoulder, then he spoke again.

"Sarah."

"Yes?"

"Do you ever dream of going away? Somewhere far away from all this? Somewhere entirely different. A new life."

"What brought this on?" she asked softly.

"I'm not sure. Just . . . thinking."

"Away from my home, no. I love Scotland. Away from being a Midnight . . ." She sighed. "Yes. Yes, of course I would. It's not an option, but I wish I could. Why, are you planning to run away with me?" She smiled.

"I'd love to. You and me. Some place where nobody could find us." His voice trailed away.

Sarah slipped her arm around his waist. She could feel his

sadness and didn't know what to do about it. "We can't run from what we are."

"I don't know. Maybe there's a way. Maybe together things can be different for us."

Sarah didn't know what to say. She couldn't think of the future now, she couldn't think of going anywhere, being anywhere but Islay. They stood entwined, taking in the beauty around them, heavy burdens on both their minds.

Suddenly, Nicholas interrupted Sarah's thoughts. "Look!" he pointed to a group of seaweed-covered rocks shining with rain and seawater. A lone seal was sitting there, watching the ferry with its round, black eyes. Sarah met the seal's gaze and they looked at each other for a few moments before the seal slipped into the water and out of sight.

"A spirit of the water?" asked Sarah dreamily.

"Maybe. Not one of mine. If they were near, I'd know."

"A free one, then."

"Lucky for them," whispered Nicholas, and Sarah was left wondering what he meant.

24
Midnight Hall

The shape of my eyes,
The shape of my arms
The way my hair flows
And the way I stand –
All this from you, and still
I don't know who you are

"We need food, and peat for the fire," said Sean. They were just off the ferry, standing beside the cars – Sean's black Bravo and Nicholas's huge monster of a Jeep that reminded Sarah of her parents' car, and not in a good way.

"No need. Mrs McArthur has everything ready for us," replied Sarah.

Sean's eyes narrowed. "Is she a Gamekeeper?"

"No, but my parents trusted her just as if she'd been one," Sarah reassured him.

Sean nodded. "Let's avoid drawing attention to ourselves as much as we can, anyway."

Elodie turned her face to the sky. She was wearing a white

jacket that swamped her slender frame. She looked deceptively delicate in it. "Do we have far to go? I think it's going to snow."

"It won't take more than an hour." Sarah pointed along the coast, beyond the heathery hills. "Hopefully we'll be there before it starts snowing. Follow us."

She's acting like herself again, thought Sean, watching her climb into Nicholas's Jeep. *If this is the Islay effect, long may it last.*

Sarah leaned back in the seat and let her eyes and mind wander. She took it all in with a sense of hunger, wanting to swallow it all, the sea and the soft, moist hills and the sky above, so wide, so free.

"Did you come to Islay often when you were a child?" asked Nicholas after a while.

Sarah blinked, coming back to herself.

"Yes. A lot. Then . . . we stopped coming all of a sudden. That was when my parents started going hunting every single night. It was relentless. Looking back, I knew there was something wrong, I could feel it. I just didn't want to admit it. And they never explained."

"Never mind. It's all in the past now."

Sarah sighed. "Thing is, my past won't really go away."

"Yes." *Mine won't go either. My mother is still with me*, thought Nicholas, his mind suddenly whirring with memories. *And so is—no. Don't think of her. It will just break you.*

"That's why I'm here," Sarah continued. "To find some answers about the past. My parents hardly told me anything, my grandmother was a mystery. There's an aunt I never knew I had. I just don't know . . ."

". . . Who you are," Nicholas finished for her.

"Yes. You read my mind." Sarah turned to him and her heart leapt. His profile was so handsome, flawless against the wet car window, and beyond it, the stormy sea. His eyes were like obsidian, and his hair blue-black against his ghostly white skin. He looked like some forgotten god of a lost civilization, or someone out of a vision.

And he is, thought Sarah. *After all, he did come to me in a dream. And he doesn't look quite . . . human,* she couldn't help thinking.

No. She rejected the thought with all her might. *He's a Secret heir, like me – we're supposed to be a bit unusual.*

"It happens to me too," said Nicholas. "Not knowing who I am." *More than you can imagine.*

"You are Nicholas Donal, and you're my boyfriend," smiled Sarah. She hated seeing Nicholas so upset.

"That much is sure!" Nicholas smiled back, but his eyes remained solemn. *That much is a lie,* he thought helplessly, and the bit of his heart that still belonged to him, and not to his father, throbbed painfully once more.

Sarah sat up suddenly. "There it is! That is Midnight Hall, see? Up on the hill! Turn left, just past this bend."

Sarah rolled down the car window and waved to Sean, who was following them. Her cheeks were flushed with excitement, and her eyes were shining.

Have I ever felt this way before? Ever in my life? Nicholas asked himself.

They drove along a little winding road that climbed down towards the sea and drew up right in front of Midnight Hall. It was a red sandstone building, with slate-covered roofs and turrets, and a multitude of windows. Right at the back of it was the open beach, and the sea.

"Here we are!" exclaimed Sarah, jumping out of the car the moment it stopped.

"Looks a bit like a haunted house, *n'est-ce pas?*" whispered Elodie as she lifted her suitcase from the boot of Sean's car.

"That's likely. That it's haunted, I mean – knowing the Midnights," said Sean matter-of-factly.

"Sarah! Welcome!" A grey-haired woman hurried down the grand stony steps.

"Mrs McArthur!" They hugged briefly.

"I haven't seen you for so long. I'm so sorry about your parents, Sarah." She shook her head, twisting her fingers nervously, and Sarah nodded, her eyes downcast, unable to speak, before dashing up the steps. "So, you must be Sarah's friends? Here for Christmas?"

"Yes. Always up for a party, these Midnights, huh?" said Sean, deadpan, locking the boot of his car.

"Ehm, yes. Aren't they?" Mrs McArthur laughed feebly. That wasn't her memory of James Midnight, let alone Morag and Hamish. But it seemed impossible to disagree with this hard-looking, authoritative young man. Was he Sarah Midnight's boyfriend?

"Thank you, Mrs McArthur. We'll take it from here," he told her. Mrs McArthur looked confused.

"Sorry," intervened Sarah. "I should have introduced you! This is my cousin, Harry Midnight."

Silence fell for a second, while everybody froze. Everybody but Sean. "Nice to meet you. I've always wanted to visit Midnight Hall," he replied coolly.

"Harry Midnight! Stewart's son! What a pleasure to meet you! If your poor dad could see you here . . ."

Elodie drew a breath at the mention of Harry's name, and Sean noticed her distress.

"Yes. Yes. Lovely to meet you too. Anyway, no reason to

158

come and check on us in the next few days. Enjoy a Christmas break. We'll come and say goodbye when we leave."

"Oh. Sure."

"Thank you so much for all your help, Mrs McArthur. Really, thank you." Sarah softened Sean's harsh words.

"A pleasure. If only this house was lived in again," she sighed. "But sure, you have your own life there in Edinburgh, don't you? The city is more exciting than this island, I suppose!"

Exciting is one way of putting it, thought Sarah.

"Well, call me if you need anything. Bye, Sarah dear. Bye, Harry." Mrs McArthur climbed into her car, turning back to wave a couple of times.

"Why did you tell her I was Harry?" whispered Sean as they watched Mrs McArthur's car trundling down the road.

"Because if something happens to me here, I want you to take over."

"Me? What about . . . Nicholas?" He winced, as if saying Nicholas's name reminded him of the bond between him and Sarah. But he couldn't help asking.

"Nicholas has a family. A home. You're free to take over any role you need to. And there's nobody left if I go. No Midnights left. Except for Elodie, I suppose, and in a way, you." Sarah's face wanted to be hard, but there was a tenderness in her eyes that surprised Sean, and confused him. It didn't last long. Sarah clammed up again, and the warmth was gone.

Sean opened his mouth to reply, but nothing came out. He couldn't find the words.

"It's freezing out here," complained Elodie. Sean turned in surprise. Elodie never complained. He noticed, and not for the first time, how pale she looked, and how her eyes were shadowed with blue.

"Let's go," he said, taking her by her cold hand. "Let's get you warm."

The majestic wooden door creaked as Sarah opened it. They tip-toed in as quietly as they could into the vast, stoned-paved vestibule, without even being aware that they were doing so – as if they were scared to disturb somebody. There was nobody, of course, but the space didn't feel empty.

"This is a psychic's paradise," said Elodie in a low voice.

The high ceilings, the grey stone floors, the walls full of portraits of long-dead people. The soft, low creaks of an old building forever settling, forever whispering. The chill, musty air, which, Sarah remembered suddenly, would stay chill despite the fireplaces, because of the thickness of the walls and the height of the ceilings. One of those houses that has been ancient forever, since the day it was built.

Sarah shivered as they stood in the hallway, taking it all in. Memories flooded her, of the many times she'd stepped into the Hall with her parents. It was as if she could see the little girl she used to be, walking onto the stone floor with her satchel and the cello case strapped to her back, following her tall, strong-framed father and her graceful, lithe mother, with her black hair spilling down her back – the hair Sarah had inherited. Her Grandfather Hamish had died soon after Sarah's birth, so she didn't remember him at all – but the image of Morag Midnight walking down the grand staircase to meet them was burnt into her memory. Her grandmother had been nearly as tall as her father, always dressed in dark colours, standing proud and straight-backed.

"Hello, Sarah," she always said, without ever giving her a hug or a kiss. Morag wasn't that kind of person. But Sarah could feel that her grandmother was happy to see them, all three of them.

"I'm back," she whispered to the empty space where her family had been. Everyone stood still.

It was Elodie who broke the spell. She jerked her head towards the door. "Sean. There's someone outside."

"Demons?"

"I don't know." She closed her eyes briefly. "Two of them."

Not yet, prayed Sarah silently. *Give us just a few hours of peace . . .*

They all turned to face the door, readying themselves. Sarah's hands were burning, Sean's *sgian-dubh* was poised, Elodie's lips were darkening. As Sean pulled the heavy wooden door open they saw Nicholas's ravens swooping across the sky and twirling over and around Midnight Hall, as if they were of one mind. Two men stood at the foot of the entrance steps.

Sean squinted in the dusk, trying to make out who – or what – they were. But before he could decide, Elodie screamed, "*Niryana!*" and shot out, fast and agile. She threw her full weight towards the mysterious figures, and in seconds, one of the men was lying there, unconscious.

25

Deadly Princess

To meet your eyes and see
We're on the same side
To feel for once that we
Are not alone

Mike had driven from Edinburgh to Oban in a stolen Mini – borrowed, Mike insisted. They had abandoned the car on a double yellow line near Oban harbour with a note on the front seat: *I come from Edinburgh, take me back. Thank you.*

They had no money left to rent a boat, so Niall went to the pub and came out with somebody's wallet.

"I'd better watch my pockets while you're around, Niall," Mike commented.

"No point. There's nothing in them."

"Very funny. Now, where's our transport?" asked Mike, a nauseous feeling growing in the pit of his stomach. Just thinking of more sailing made him want to be sick. They managed to convince a German couple that they were going to surprise some friends camping on Islay. The generous fee helped, and the couple sailed them over in no time. All they had to do now was find Midnight Hall.

They walked under a milk-coloured blanket of clouds in silence. The sky was heavy with snow, and the wind blew bitter, showing no sign of relenting. There were cottages and little farms dotted here and there on the rolling hills, few and far apart, and they walked on, heads bent against the wind, freezing and exhausted. They tortured themselves with talk of a warm bed, and of food as they walked. Finally, they saw a red sandstone mansion – the first house they'd seen that looked grand enough to be Midnight Hall.

"Hopefully, that will be it," said Mike wearily. "But even if it's not, I'm counting on a warm welcome."

"Even just a cup of tea will do me," said Niall feebly.

They approached the house with trepidation, Mike with his hand in his pocket, ready to take out the gun he'd kept from the attack on the ship, if needed. They could see through the windows that the fires were lit; somebody was inside. Mike gestured to follow him. In silence, they walked round the back of the house where they spotted a little red Punto.

Through an upstairs window, Niall made out the shape of an old lady with a duster in her hand, and beside her, a little blonde girl. He took Mike's arm and pointed upwards. "Someone is clearly here. What do we do?" muttered Niall.

Mike surveyed the space around them with his eyes. He spotted a few outhouses, ivy-covered and – most likely – locked.

"We wait until Sean comes in or out," whispered Mike, pointing to the outhouse closest to them.

"And if he doesn't? If this isn't the right place?"

"We need to start walking again," Mike replied darkly, making his way towards the small stony buildings. They walked across a small stretch of what used to be a garden but was now growing wild, stepping over some gorse bushes and jumping over mossy tree stumps. They tucked themselves behind an ivy-covered wall that protected them from the worst of the wind, and sat with their backs against the stones, hugging their knees for warmth. Time stretches when you haven't slept properly for days, the cold seeps in your bones, and shelter is only a few yards away and yet unreachable.

"I'm so hungry I'm going to pass out," Niall complained.

Mike didn't reply. He had fallen asleep. Niall closed his eyes and let himself nod off too, wondering if that was really Midnight Hall, who were the old woman and the blonde girl? Finally sleep caught up with him too, and he nodded off. They slept huddled together, lullabied by the sound of the sea a few hundred yards away.

"Niall! Niall! Wake up. Somebody is here!" Mike shook Niall out of his slumber. They could hear car doors slamming, and voices.

The world spun around Niall as he got up and followed Mike out of their hiding place. An unkindness of ravens was settling in front of the house, their heads jerking left and right, as if examining their surroundings. *That's a lot of birds*, thought Niall, rubbing his frozen hands together.

"They're going inside. Oh my God, that girl!" Mike yanked on Niall's rucksack. "That's the Heron! That's Sarah!" he cried, pointing to the slender young woman with the waterfall of black hair. "It is! Come on!"

They scurried on, clambering over the tree trunks and scrambling to avoid the gorse bushes. Eventually they found themselves at the foot of the steps, with the ravens eyeing them warily. Niall barely had time to exhale in relief – *It's them, we found them* – when something slight and blonde blew out of the house as if carried by the wind, threw him onto the ground, and sat on him. Neither he nor Mike had the time or the energy to scream.

Flat on his back, Niall was frozen, and then with a flip of his left leg he was on top of the girl. It was her turn, now, to be lying on the gravel with someone sitting on her chest. She flailed for a moment then pushed her hair out of her face and glared at him. Chocolate eyes, rosebud lips, lovely long blonde hair. She was like a princess in a fairy tale. He blinked. *She's perfect.*

He looked at her face for a little longer than he should have and the blonde girl took advantage of it at once. She lifted herself up and took his face in her hands. *Too late*, Niall saw that her lips had turned blue. She blew gently in his mouth, and instantly he was out cold.

When Niall woke up, the first thing he saw was a high ceiling, crisscrossed by wooden beams. The second thing he saw was Mike sitting on a rigid sofa beside him. And then, he spotted his deadly fairy-tale princess kneeling beside a lit fire. The smell of peat filled Niall's nostrils and made him think of home for the first time in a long while.

"Oh, there you are, man," smiled Mike. "Welcome back."

Niall tried to sit up, but everything twirled and danced around him, and he had to lie back down.

"What did you do to me?" he managed to ask the blonde girl.

"Poisonous breath." She had a slight accent, but Niall couldn't quite place it.

"Don't worry, she's one of us. Elodie Midnight," said Mike.

"Jesus, another Midnight," Niall blurted out, and everything went black once more.

26
Together We

There's always more to things than meets the eye
Look closely and try
To read between the lines

When Niall woke again shadows were gathering in the sky and over the sea. The hall was softly lit from the stone fireplace in the middle of the main room, and by many little lamps scattered around. Sarah, Sean, Elodie and Mike were scattered on sofas and armchairs around him.

"I'm having some of that," was the first thing Niall said, blinking and pointing at the whisky bottle on the low table in front of him.

"Sure!" Sean grinned, and grabbed the bottle to pour the Irishman a glass of the golden-coloured liquid. He had a very young face, Sean noticed, but lined, like someone who'd been through a lot. Niall sat up. It worked, this time. He managed to stay conscious and looked around him, groggy.

"Sorry about earlier, Niall," said Elodie. Her eyes were mischievous. She didn't look sorry at all.

"No worries. It's nice to meet you. And a bit painful." Niall rubbed his brow.

"It was just a small, tiny dose. You jumped on me." She shrugged.

"You jumped on me first!"

"I didn't recognize you. Sorry," she repeated without a hint of regret, and she tipped her head back, smiling at him from beneath her eyelashes.

"Ah, well. Fair play to you. It was a good hit," Niall admitted, and turned to look at Sean. "So, Sean Hannay. It's a privilege to meet you at last, sir."

"And you," Sean exclaimed. He opened his arms, struggling for words, his gaze darting from Mike to Niall and back. "You're *alive*. Jesus. I didn't think . . . I kept hoping . . ." He was surprised at the wave of emotion he was feeling.

"Niall *did* die, actually," Mike remarked. The light of the fire danced on his coffee-coloured skin, the terrible memory casting a shadow on his features.

"Well, sort of," specified Niall. "I did drown, I'll give you that, but Flynns can't die in water, so here I am. You look terrible, Sean."

Sean had paled hearing of Niall's brush with death. He took hold of himself. "Now – introductions. Niall," he said, "meet Sarah Midnight."

"At last, Sarah!" Niall rose to his feet. To Sarah's horror, he wrapped his arms around her. Her cheeks flamed scarlet.

"Hello," she muttered, stiff, but after a few seconds she put her arms around him too. "So, the two of you are the mysterious friends Sean used to speak to all the time."

"It's us, yes," said Mike, smiling kindly.

"What happened in Louisiana? Did they find you? Did they attack you?" asked Sean, leaning forward, impatient for details.

167

"We intercepted members of the Sabha talking to each other," said Mike, shaking his head. "Harry was right. The Sabha *is* corrupted, Sean, there isn't a shadow of a doubt. They were talking to each other about . . . about slaughter." He shuddered. "About all the heirs they'd killed, and where, and the places they were still to hit. When we intercepted them, they sort of . . . *saw* us. A map of Grand Isle appeared on the screen, and then it zoomed in on our shack. We disconnected everything, but it was too late. They sent demons. From the sea."

"Sort of jellyfish creatures I'd never seen before," Niall intervened, "and I've seen a few sea demons. Prehistoric stuff." He shuddered. "I hope I never cross paths with them again."

"The Sabha are using Surari to do their bidding," whispered Sean, horrified. "This is what it's come to."

"They were nasty things, I'm telling you. Had Niall not distracted them . . ."

"Mike would have gone the same way as me. Except he wouldn't have come back." Niall looked down in dismay. Sean read in his face the deep bond between them. *Good. That's what we need: loyalty. Harry was the best at creating ties between his people and nourishing them, that's how we're still here, his friends, still gathering around his memory.*

Right at that moment, like a cold wind, Nicholas strode in. He'd gone for a walk while waiting for Niall to come to. He took in Mike and Niall's presence and didn't flinch, didn't move a muscle. Sean studied his face, but he couldn't figure out what he was thinking.

"I'm glad to see you're awake," he said to Niall. "Sarah told me about you," Nicholas said. His tone was as expressionless as his face and belied the concern in his words.

"Thank you. You must be . . ." Mike began. *Leaf. The guy with the ravens. That explains why there are so many of them out there.*

"I'm Nicholas Donal."

"Donal? There are no more Donals," said Niall curtly. Sean's heart skipped a beat. "At least, that's what I was led to believe. I thought the last of the Donals died years ago, in the war. My grandfather used to know them."

Nicholas shrugged. "Clearly, there are still some of us around. Me, and my parents. A lot of Families prefer not to advertise their existence. I'm sure you understand why."

Sarah shifted uncomfortably. The atmosphere in the room was suddenly charged. "How did you get here, guys?" she asked quickly. She didn't like Nicholas being subjected to the third degree.

"We managed to find a passage on a cargo ship," replied Niall. "Thought we were the luckiest fellas alive, until a Makara attacked us."

"A Makara?" said Sean, astonished. "Really? Oh my God! Was it as deadly as they say?"

Mike nodded. "Worse. Fifteen guys in the crew, plus us. Only one crewman survived — just. And the captain. It's a miracle we're alive."

Sean shook his head in horror.

"By the way, Sarah. There was someone here when we arrived. An old lady," said Niall.

"Oh yes, the housekeeper. Don't worry, she's on our side."

"And a little girl. With blonde hair," he added, gesturing to his own reddish-brown hair.

"I didn't see any little girl. Just an old woman," Mike intervened.

Sarah stared at him. *A blonde girl? The same girl I saw after the scrying spell?* Her lips went to form an answer – though she wasn't sure what she was going to say – when a sudden noise silenced her. Something slamming, deep inside the house.

27

Blood and Paper

Words will reach you
From the depths of time
Hidden in the prayer book
She left behind

"Stay here, Sarah," said Nicholas at once. *Another attack, without my knowledge?*

"No. I'm coming with you." She stood and faced him, the tilt of her chin making it clear that she would not be told what to do. Not in Midnight Hall.

Sean smiled inwardly. *The old Sarah, shining through.* "Everyone ready?" he whispered, his *sgian-dubh* in his hand once more.

"Ready." Elodie's lips had already turned blue.

"You look freaky," whispered Niall.

"Shut up," Elodie growled.

Mike grinned. "Amen!"

The sound had come from the end of the corridor. They stepped out of the room warily, leaving the vestibule and staircase behind them, and advanced towards the heart of the house. Nicholas and Sean were on either side of Sarah at the front of the group, and Niall and Elodie at the back, with Mike behind them, walking backwards, his gun ready.

"I think it came from here," whispered Sean, and stepped into a room whose walls were lined floor to ceiling with bookshelves brimming with books, and a stone fireplace against the far wall.

"This used to be my grandmother's study," Sarah whispered back. The fire had been lit by Mrs McArthur, and Sean noticed at once that it was flickering and hissing, its flames veering towards the windows.

A *draught*, he thought immediately, and looked towards the heavy velvet curtains drawn over them. Three sets of curtains were still, but one was blowing ever so gently, and from the gap between the two sheets of fabric a fine drizzle was being sprayed in by the wind.

"Over there," whispered Sean, gesturing to the windows.

"I'm on it." Nicholas walked over, slow and careful. He threw the curtains open, jumping to the side at once.

A collective intake of breath.

Nothing. Just the open window, and the empty beach beyond it.

"Look." Elodie pointed to a track of wet footsteps that led to the heavy, dark wooden desk in the corner. "Someone got in. And out again."

Sarah walked slowly over to the desk. A parcel was sitting on it, wrapped in brown paper and fastened with . . . stringy seaweed? Her eyes widened. She brushed some sand from the parcel. Sean, Nicholas, Mike and Niall had formed a semicircle around her, all standing on guard.

"There's a note as well. There." Elodie gestured to a small, square piece of paper, with a little white-blue Venus shell sitting on top to stop it from blowing away.

Sarah opened it: *For Sarah*, it read simply.

"Be careful," Sean reminded her.

She nodded, and gently untied the string of seaweed, opening the parcel with care. Inside was a stack of creamy paper covered in small, old-fashioned writing in black ink. Sarah lifted the first sheet.

Dear Amelia,

It began. Sarah turned the page to look at the signature:

Morag Midnight

"My grandmother's letters," she said, wide-eyed.

At that moment, a gust of wind blew through the open window, and with it a shower of rain. She shivered. Long lost voices from the past were calling her. She clutched the stack of letters to her chest.

Sean kept looking around, checking all the dark corners in the room. "Someone left them here. That is pretty obvious. The question is, human or demon?"

"Whoever it was, *why* did they leave my grandmother's letters? Why did they have them in the first place?"

"Maybe they'd taken them from the house, and now they've returned them," guessed Elodie.

Sean shrugged his shoulders. "Why? And why now?"

"Because they knew I was coming," said Sarah, and looked at him, eyes large with fear.

"Watch Sarah. I won't be long," Nicholas said suddenly, and before his words could register, he had raced across the room and jumped out of the window.

"Not on your own! Nicholas!" shouted Sarah. But he was already running down the grassy slope that led to the beach.

"I'll go with him," said Sean, and poised himself to jump.

"Stay with Sarah," Elodie overtook him and easily coaxed her agile, supple body out of the window and onto the grass below, giving Sean no time to stop her.

28

An Infinite Horizon

Dark and light
In an infinite dance
Blessing all the shadows
That come my way

The sand was wet under Nicholas's feet as he ran. He needed to call to his Elementals, to his father, and he didn't dare do so from the house, in case someone picked up on it – particularly Elodie. She puzzled him. It was as if she could read some kind of subtext in everything that happened, a hidden story that no one else could sense.

Who could have left those letters? Was it a demon's doing, once again without his knowledge?

The beach was vast, endless, a stretch of pale sand, damp with rain, and a whirl of sky and sea and wind all mixed together. Nicholas could barely see as dusk spread into the sky, slowly turning the short December day into night.

When Nicholas felt far enough from the house to open his mind to his father he stopped and stood, eyes closed, calling

– letting his thoughts calm and then dissolve, to make room for the invocation.

And then he felt it.

A vague, shapeless form inside his head, weak in comparison to the shadow voices and yet strong enough to enter his mind. He stopped the invocation at once, forcing himself to come back to the here and now, frozen by the intrusion. Who was it? He turned round, his eyes narrowed, searching, until finally he saw her, standing on a grassy dune. Elodie was a spot of white against the stormy sky, her long, blonde hair blowing in the wind. She was completely still, her arms at her sides, looking back at him, silent.

She must know enough, he thought. Enough to harm him. He had to show her that nothing good could come from spying on him. He had to show her what happened to the Secret heirs in the new world created by him and his father.

Nicholas's ravens started dancing above their heads, endlessly circling the skies.

Ignoring Sean's protests, Elodie had run as fast as she could. Nicholas's long strides were hard to keep up with, but she was fast and kept pace – at a distance. It felt strange to go against Sean's will. He was a Gamekeeper, and she a Secret heir, but he'd always taken the lead in their small group – Harry was so often busy with the Sabha or on solo missions, and she and Mary Anne, Sean's former girlfriend and fellow Gamekeeper, respected his authority. That wasn't the natural order of things. It was uncommon for a Secret heir to defer as she did to Sean – but it seemed to have worked out that way between them.

Since Harry had died, though, since their whole world had changed, she had felt a new strength, a new self-belief. Italy had made her tougher, she would make her own choices. Also,

Sean's judgement about Nicholas was clouded by his feelings for Sarah – of that Elodie was certain. But perhaps there was some truth in them too. She had to figure it out for herself.

She kept to the dunes, out of sight, trying to let her mind reach out to the lone figure as he ran through the gathering gloom, trying to make out where he was going, and why. And where he had come from.

Elodie ran on, keeping Nicholas in her sights, her face and hands moist with drizzle and sea mist. Suddenly, Nicholas stopped, as if he'd hit an invisible wall and looked round, frantic. *Why? What is he doing?*

Elodie stopped too, and waited. Suddenly, her eyes widened, and then she blinked as a voice made its way into her mind – a voice calling. Nicholas's voice. It had a strange resonance, an echo that disquieted her and filled her with fear. It called and called with an intensity that made her tremble, and then it was gone.

Silence.

But not for long.

A distant cawing rose above the wailing of the wind and the sound of the waves. She lifted her head, wiping the soft drizzle from her eyes, trying to make out what was happening. A crow—no, something bigger. A raven. Two, three, four . . . a whole flight of them, circling above her head. She could hear the beat of their wings, the relentless cries.

Nicholas's ravens.

Elodie felt a chill run down her spine. She looked across to Nicholas and saw that he was looking straight at her. The ravens made one last circuit over their heads. Then they landed, scattered in front of Elodie. Their beady eyes watched her as they hopped, their feathers ruffled by the wind.

Elodie's hand went to her throat, her fingers curling around her silver star. Sean had told her how the ravens had saved his life, but there was something about the way these birds were watching her, tipping their heads first to one side and then the other. Their beaks looked very hard, very sharp. They could peck somebody's eyes out in a second.

Elodie tried to pull her thoughts under control. *They're only birds. It makes no sense to be afraid of birds, does it?*

She started walking down the grassy slope, making her way towards Nicholas. She expected the ravens to fly off, as birds do when someone approaches. But these ones didn't. They stayed put, and watched her.

She froze, her lips instinctively turning blue. *Something is going to happen. Something is going to happen this very moment.* She could feel it.

"Nicholas!" she called, and her voice sounded feeble in the roaring wind.

Immediately, the ravens took flight as if of one mind, swarming over her, swiping her face with their wings, circling her like a feathery whirlpool. Elodie covered her face and screamed as she threw herself on the grass, curling herself into a ball. But the birds began to push their way under her arms, trying to reach her face, thrashing their way over her, submerging her. Any moment now she'd feel her flesh being ripped from her bones.

And then, the voice again, speaking the ancient language, shouting it over the noise of the cawing ravens, of the wind, of her own blood flowing too fast and thundering in her ears. It was Nicholas, and he wasn't just in her head. His calls resounded over the soft noise of the rain and the ebbing and flowing of the waves.

The whirlpool gradually stopped and reluctantly the birds hopped off her body. Elodie lay shaking for a moment, peering between her fingers, barely able to raise her head from the shelter of her arms. At the foot of the dune stood Nicholas with his hands raised, still calling in the ancient language.

The ravens were circling, circling over her head.

"They won't harm you, Elodie. You can get up."

Still, she didn't dare move.

"They're going now. It's safe."

"They're still here!" Elodie yelled, a touch of hysteria in her voice.

"They're going . . . now!" Nicholas repeated, blue flames spurting from his raised arms, not high enough to reach the ravens, but enough to scare them. They flew away of one will, disappearing beyond the clouds.

Slowly Elodie got up, still trembling, but her legs buckled under her and she fell again onto the soft sand.

"Come on," said Nicholas and ran up the dune to offer her a hand. But Elodie ignored it and once again rose to her feet, trying to steady herself and stop the world from spinning.

"I'm sorry. The ravens, they misunderstood me. They can be quite . . . aggressive."

Elodie swept her hair away from her face. Was he warning her? Demonstrating his powers?

"Did you order them to attack me, Nicholas Donal?" she challenged.

Nicholas frowned. "I . . . I stopped them," he replied simply. He wasn't lying. He couldn't quite believe it himself, but he had, in fact, stopped them from shredding Elodie's skin to ribbons.

Elodie took a deep breath – her heart was still racing, and she was trying to calm her ragged breathing. She studied his face. *He looks . . . he looks surprised. Yes, surprised. Bewildered by what just happened.*

"Why did they—" Elodie began, but she never finished.

It happened in a split second – cawing, flapping wings, talons dancing in front of their faces, and Nicholas, his expression one of utter horror, raising his arms to protect himself. Elodie dropped to her knees, covered her face instinctively and shut her eyes.

Silence replaced the noise of the ravens as suddenly as they had attacked. As fast as they'd come, the birds were gone again.

Elodie turned to find Nicholas on his knees, his hands covering his face, blood dripping from between his fingers. She helped him up, and instinctively looked to the sky to make sure the ravens had flown away for good. But it was something else she saw – a strange figure twirling in the clouds, enormous leathery wings extended in the wind, like a monstrous glider.

"Nicholas," she whispered. "Look up."

Nicholas peered into the drizzly rain, his fingers feeling the slash in his cheek. *My father must have been informed that I spared Elodie! He sent a Surari to kill her.* "It's a Surari I've never seen before. We need to run!" he said, grabbing her arm.

"What? I'm not running! It's a demon, I'm fighting it!" she insisted.

Nicholas's hold on her tightened. "Listen to me. I don't know what that is." *And believe me, I know all species of Surari.* "We need to run. Now!" He sprinted off, dragging her with such force she had no choice but to follow. She nearly fell in his impetus, but he held her up by the waist. They ran all the way back, catching glimpses of the sky, but the hideous bird was gone.

29
Turning Tide

Red as blood
White as snow
Black as black is
The wing of the crow

"She'll be fine." Mike reassured Sarah, and a look passed between him and Sean. Sarah intercepted that look, and it told her all she needed to know. Her gaze went from Sean to Mike and back, her temper rising.

"You're worried about Nicholas harming Elodie! You still don't trust him!"

"Sarah. I never made a secret of not trusting him, did I?" his tone was hard.

"You're just—you're just—" *Jealous*, she finished in her mind, but she couldn't say. "Spiteful!"

Mike intervened – the peacemaker, as ever. "Hey, Sarah. Listen." Sarah shook her head, arms crossed. "No, no, listen to me now, girl.

Elodie going with Nicholas kills two birds with one stone.

We keep an eye on him, and Elodie helps him if there's an emergency. Cool?"

"Whatever!" said Sarah sullenly. "I'll carry our stuff upstairs."

"I'll help you." Sean followed her into the hall where they'd left the rucksacks piled at the top of the grand staircase.

"No need."

"What if whoever left the letters is hiding upstairs, Sarah? This is not the time to sulk!" snapped Sean.

"Don't dare tell me off! I'm not a child!"

"Hey! Everyone! Guess what I found!" Niall emerged from the depths of the corridor.

"Where did you disappear to, on your own?" Mike scolded him.

"There's a hundred rooms in this house. Seriously, it's crazy. Anyway, I found a music room! With a piano and a harp in it!" Niall was beaming.

"Yes. They were my grandmother's," said Sarah with a bout of regret for not having brought her cello with her. "Can you play?"

"I can play anything, Sarah of mine!"

"Brilliant. Let's have a dinner dance," muttered Mike, taking hold of a bag.

Sarah threw Sean one final, scathing look, and lifted her suitcase. She stomped upstairs.

"I'll play for you," whispered Niall, brushing past her on the stairs. Sarah rewarded him with a smile.

They made their way onto the staircase, with its polished wood banister and carved stone steps. The wall beside it was full of portraits of long-gone members of the Midnight family, including the formidable Morag and Hamish, and on the landing, a huge stained-glass window coloured the light like a rainbow, tiny particles of dust dancing in it. An elaborate M in dazzling blue glass was at the centre of the window.

"That's beautiful," breathed Niall. "We have a fine house in Skerry, but this is just amazing."

"Thank you," said Sarah. "I always loved coming here."

Another corridor lined with wooden doors, parallel to the one downstairs, led to the depths of the second floor.

"We have lots of bedrooms, as you can see. Share, or take a room each, it's fine by me," said Sarah. "I'll be sleeping in my parents' room," she added in a small voice. She was daunted at the idea of seeing her parents' things – at the same time, she couldn't wait.

Mike opened a random door and disappeared inside.

"We should probably share. It's safer," said Sean.

"What? I'm not sharing, man!" Mike called from the depths of the corridor. When Sean and Sarah reached him, he had thrown himself onto a giant four-poster bed. "Aaaah, paradise. Paradise!"

"You've got to share with Niall. Keep an eye on him." Sean's piercing blue eyes were twinkling.

"What? No way! I've been sharing with him for weeks! Give me a break! He's always damn *singing* in his sleep!"

"You love me, really, Mike. Oh look, one bed only! Oh well. Move over." Niall sat beside him.

"No way."

"You just hurt my feelings. Badly. I'll take myself somewhere I can be alone."

"Shut up, Niall."

"Right, boys, enough!" Sarah interrupted them, a smile playing on her lips, in spite of herself. "There's peat and briquettes in the kitchen. Feel free to light the fires Mrs McArthur hasn't lit already. Sean, the room next door . . ."

"I'm sharing with Elodie. Just in case."

Sarah froze. *Sharing with Elodie?* She glanced at him. *He's not joking!*

"Right. Sure, of course," she said with what she hoped was a nonchalant tone. She strode into the room across from Mike's. "This one, then," she called to Sean, trying not to look at the lovely four-poster bed, covered in brocade covers and a multitude of pillows. "My parents' old bedroom is the last one. Nicholas and I can share this one." She swallowed. She didn't really want to sleep in the same room as Nicholas, but she wanted to spite Sean.

"Good for you." Sean spoke in a staccato tone, and followed her into what was to be his room.

"Yes. Well."

Behind Sarah, Mike sighed and rolled his eyes.

"Will you be needing another bed in there, Sean? For Elodie?" said Sarah, a too-casual edge to her voice as she gestured to the bed-sit. "We have plenty. Of beds. Only if you want to, of course. Unless one is enough." Sarah jabbered on, cursing herself with every word. Her cheeks were bright pink.

"Yes, please. Lads, help me carry?" he said, his eyes glinting with mischief. *Had he been winding me up?* thought Sarah, furious.

"Sure," said Mike, a mocking smile on his lips.

"Oh, actually," Sean added, feigning innocence, "maybe I should check with Elodie if she's OK to share with me. She's a light sleeper. I'll tell you what, we'll take adjoining rooms."

Sarah breathed a sigh of relief that she hastened to hide. Mike chuckled quietly, straightening his face at once when he met Sarah's frosty gaze.

"We're back!" a voice called from downstairs. Elodie.

Sarah, Sean, Mike and Niall leant on the banister, looking down to the hall. Elodie and Nicholas were standing in front of the door, their hair wet and windswept, their jackets shiny with a million little droplets.

And then Sarah noticed the bright red stain on Nicholas's face.

"Nicholas!" She ran downstairs, and gasped at the sight of Nicholas's bloodied cheek. "You're hurt!" She touched his face softly and looked into his eyes, waiting for him to tell her what happened.

"Just an accident. I'm fine." The look in his eyes contradicted his words. He didn't look fine. He seemed spooked.

"The ravens attacked me," Elodie began. "Had it not been for Nicholas . . . I wouldn't have come back."

Sean bristled. "What? The ravens attacked you? But it's Nicholas who controls them in the first place!"

"Not this time, Sean," said Elodie quietly.

"What happened?" Sarah asked Nicholas.

"I don't know. They attacked Elodie, and I stopped them. So they . . ." He touched his cheek. Sarah covered his hand with one of her own. "Elementals can be . . . difficult," he shrugged.

Sean snorted.

"Sean," Elodie admonished him. "Nicholas saved my life. Do you understand that? Look at the facts!"

"Better keep our eyes open from now on," intervened Mike.

Sean was looking at Nicholas. "I'm keeping mine well open."

"Any trace of whoever left the letters?" asked Sarah, holding Nicholas's hand in hers.

"No. We didn't see anyone. Apart from a demon," Elodie said darkly.

"A what?" Sean barked.

"A sort of bird. Huge. It was flying above us. We couldn't see properly because of the rain. And then it disappeared."

"The demon-bird!" said Sarah. "The one that—that—" Words failed her, remembering Uncle Trevor's words: *You're dead to us.* Aunt Juliet had been killed by something – possibly that demon – and it was all her fault. And now the demon was back for more, to destroy more people she loved.

"You've seen that demon before?" Nicholas seemed deeply interested all of a sudden.

Sarah's voice was shaking. "It got me on the way to Sean's cottage."

Nicholas winced.

"I wounded it but I couldn't kill it. The Midnight gaze didn't work on it."

"It can't be!" Sean exclaimed. "The Midnight gaze works on all demons!"

"It didn't seem like it worked on this one." Sarah said bitterly. "I need to find it. And kill it," she continued, her eyes hard.

"That's what I wanted to do, but you stopped me," said Elodie to Nicholas.

"I'd never seen anything like that. I just didn't know what we were facing. I couldn't let it kill you," he replied. His words had a strange echo to his own ears. *Like I really don't want her dead.*

"I'll do this. I think it's the demon that killed my aunt," said Sarah.

"Sarah," Sean began.

"Don't worry, I won't be stupid with it. I'll take care, wait for the right moment. Come upstairs, Nicholas. I'll get you cleaned up and show you your room."

Your room? No sharing, then? thought Sean. The knot in his stomach loosened a little.

Sarah brushed past him on her way upstairs but wouldn't bring her eyes to meet his.

30
Ghosts

I remember the little wall,
And the hazelnut trees
And how your paintbrush
Captured the scene.
Were you the woman they said,
Or someone we have forgotten?

Sarah was sitting in front of the fire in what had been her parents' room, and before that, her grandparents'. She had gathered her legs to her chest, her chin resting on her knees. The stack of brittle, yellowed letters was laid carefully on the rug in front of her. The faint sound of Niall playing the piano was drifting up from downstairs, a beautiful, wistful melody that fit perfectly with the island. Everyone else was in the music room, listening to him. But Sarah needed some time by herself.

She had gone through her parents' things. She'd found her mother's clothes in the wardrobe, her father's books in the bedside table. There were framed photographs of them on the mantelpiece, and Anne's perfumes on the dressing table. It had been torture, and comfort, all mixed together.

She'd gone through the drawers too, looking for a picture of Mairead, but there was no sign. It was as if her memory had been utterly deleted from her parents' lives, from their minds. But why? In the many years she'd visited Islay with her parents, she'd never seen anything belonging to Mairead, or even hinting at her existence, and now she'd searched her parents' room as she couldn't have done when they were alive. Still nothing.

Instead, Sarah had found a mother-of-pearl framed picture of Stewart and Fiona, Harry's parents, and between them, Harry. Fair hair, serious eyes, a thoughtful, solemn look on his young face. In that picture he must have been no older than five. She'd run downstairs to give Elodie the picture for her to keep, and Elodie had accepted it gratefully, her eyes welling up.

"I wish I'd known him," Sarah had said.

"You had so much in common, Sarah," Elodie had whispered.

"Really?"

"Oh yes. He was very stubborn too."

Sarah couldn't help laughing.

Back upstairs, Sarah knew that now the time had come. She was going to go through her grandmother's letters. She felt full of trepidation as she fingered the creamy paper. Something told her these letters weren't going to be full of quaint memories and the kind of family stories that get repeated with a smile through the generations. Not many of those for the Midnights.

Sarah was afraid. After what Cathy had said about her father that terrible day – that he'd left Cathy, his wife, because she couldn't provide an heir – and how Morag Midnight had been involved in her repudiation, Sarah feared discovering anything more about the blood that flowed in her own veins. Still, she had to know. She took a deep breath and lifted the first page, only to put it down again at once, all determination deserting her.

The fire was dancing in the hearth, and the earlier drizzle had turned to rain, tapping gently on the windows. Sarah could hear her own breathing, her own heartbeat, both getting faster. Anxiety was overwhelming her.

She laid the first letter back on top of the stack then got up and straightened her bed, trying to make the covers as smooth as possible. Next she sorted her mother's perfumes on the dressing table, aligned the picture frames on the mantelpiece with military precision, though they were already perfectly placed. She threw all of the clothes she'd brought out of the chest of drawers and folded them again, one by one, setting them back in the drawers in perfect order. Finally she sat at the dressing table and brushed her hair, looking at her reflection in the stained antique mirror.

Exasperated with herself, she got up and stood in the centre of the room, scanning desperately for something else to tidy. She found nothing. She hid her face in her hands.

I've got to read these letters. Someone left them for me for a reason.

Sarah breathed deeply and sat down by the fire again. She lifted the letters into her lap. She couldn't look away now. Her family was her history, no matter what. She tucked her hair behind her ears and started reading.

That's it, she thought. *Now there's no turning back.*

Islay, July 1971
Dear Amelia,
I hope all is well with you. You've ended up so far away!

You've been gone three months now, and I miss you, as you can imagine. I'm not one to judge, and your family will not divulge what happened, but I'm sure it was Angus who made a mess of your engagement. A weakling, I've always said. And now it's you having to be sent away. What a loss for us all. How short-sighted are Angus and his family!

Anyway, nobody will say a word about what happened. As long as you know that, like I told you many times, I don't blame you. I know Angus Fitzgerald is not the easiest of men. Much better to have broken the engagement now than to spend a lifetime of misery. I pray every day for you to find a suitable husband, so you can fulfil your duty: produce more Secret heirs. I know that there are quite a few Secret Families in New Zealand. I have no doubt you'll be settled there soon, and everything will be as it should be.

As for my news: it's finished, at last. Mairead was born yesterday. She's lying in her little cot and I can't get enough of looking at her. She has soft, fine, baby blonde hair – will she remain blonde, like her brothers and me? She's tiny – but all the Midnight women are, small and very, very strong. And strong she will be.

When she started kicking inside me, I knew it was a girl – remember I told you that night you came down from Kirkwall? It had to be, with all the potions and herbs I took to have a baby girl. My boys are extraordinary, as you know – James, carrying the Blackwater, and Stewart, with his Midnight gaze. I'm very proud of them. James in particular is the one who takes after me the most. But it was time I had a daughter I could train in witchcraft and relinquish the power of dreams to at last.

I've been carrying the power of dreams for seventeen years already. I want to pass on the burden. Only girls can be Dreamers in the Midnight family – so I did all that was in my power to have one.

Labour took forever, which I was prepared for – what I wasn't prepared for was dreaming through it, though I was awake. That never happened to me before. To have a vision of a sea demon while giving birth was . . . well, you know what it can be like, don't you.

I survived. I'm not one to complain.

But there was something strange, and I can't tell anybody else. Mairead was screaming as she was born, and I know that's what babies are supposed to do, but there was something in her cry that chilled me. She didn't stop for hours.

I worry she's seen something too, something from my dream.

She exhausted herself crying and barely took any milk from me. She's still so unsettled, sleeping in fits of an hour or two before waking again. In a way perhaps it's good she was broken in so early – barely born, and she knows already what it's like for us. On the other hand, I fear that the dream hurt her somehow. Damaged her.

I hope I can undo the damage, if there is any – but if she has to live with it, well, that will be one of the many things she has to endure as a Midnight woman and as a Secret heir. You know yourself how strong we have to be, Amelia.

When Mairead comes into her dreams, I'll be able to go hunting with Hamish and my sons. I can't wait for that day! It's too dangerous now. I'm the only Dreamer in the west of Scotland, so we can't risk my life. My mother left me to go hunting when I was barely three days old. That same night she was killed. I can't remember her at all, but like her, I'm longing to do more than dreaming and witchcraft. I want to be the one holding the blade, I want to watch Hamish and James dissolving the Surari into Blackwater. Nothing can compare to that moment – the moment Hamish's face changes as he disappears into that trance, the supreme joy of the Blackwater coming, and the way the bodies dissolve gradually, not at once – so we can see the terror in their eyes as they melt. I've hardly ever seen that – I have always been sheltered, ever since my sister died and I became the precious Dreamer – but I was trained anyway, for the day I could finally pass on the gift to the next Dreamer. And that day will come in thirteen years' time.

I know you don't carry the dreams. It's difficult to explain what it's like. Dreaming is like nothing else. You must be strong. Yes, you must be strong and whatever you do, never complain. Because complaining doesn't get you anywhere. I live with it. So will Mairead. It has its compensations.

It's sad that there's nobody left of my family to meet Mairead. My parents and my sister are long gone. I watch Mairead sleeping, and I smile to myself thinking of what she'll grow up to be. My blood is pure, that's why my sons are so powerful, and why my daughter will be too. My sister Elizabeth – Eliza – was always weak, not like my mother and me. And she hated being the Dreamer.

She took to going on long walks wearing silly summer dresses, or even her nightdress, come rain or shine – and being Argyll, it was more often rain – until she got what she wanted. She caught pneumonia, and even when my father and the doctors did their utmost to keep her alive, she defied them. I remember one night sneaking into her room and finding that she'd removed her drip and that it was hanging, drip-drip-dripping onto the floor, little drops of blood on the sheets where she'd yanked it out of her arm. I told my father of course, and they put it back in and employed a nurse to watch she didn't spit her pills and choke up her food or pull out her drip again.

No use. Two weeks later she died. I heard my father whispering with the doctors – the nurse had fallen asleep and my sister had dragged herself to the window, opened it and stood there, breathing the freezing night air, though she was burning with fever. After that, she burnt up for days, wheezing, her lungs full of fluid, and she died without waking again.

I was relieved for Eliza because I knew that's what she wanted, but I resented her for being so weak. Who was she to decide she could give up?

I wasn't frightened to be the Dreamer of the family now, not for a minute. I knew that unlike my sister I could take it. Yes, I tried to make them stop a few times when they were really terrible. I tried to stay awake day after day and ended up falling asleep during dinner, just like that, with my face on the table, or outside on the beach by the house, where I'd go hoping the cold would keep me awake. My father would carry me to bed so that I could fall properly asleep, and the dreams could come the way they're supposed to. So there was no way out really.

All this built my character and I'm grateful for it. Mairead will go through it the same way, and come out a true fighter like me. I know she will.

I suppose it's not that bad, really. Dreaming. One mostly gets used to it. It's only when the demons kill me — I haven't got used to that yet. To think that in my dreams I've died so many times, in so many different ways, and still I'm not used to it. The pain can be a bit much, even for me.

Yes, it's only when the Surari actually kill me that I see why my sister kept ripping that drip from her arm. But then, she gave up, and I won't.

In thirteen years' time I'll be free, and it'll be Mairead's turn. Perhaps it's just as well she got a taste of it so early in life — the sooner you start toughening up the better it is for the Midnight women.

Midnight Hall is silent and empty with Hamish gone. The boys are sleeping in their beds. From my room I can see the black, black sky over the cliffs . . .

Sarah looked out of the window to the scene that Morag described. The sky was darkening slowly – winter was wrapping Islay in an eternal night, it seemed. Sarah could picture Morag at the window, her proud, straight back, her blonde, wavy hair gathered in a knot at the nape of her neck.

. . . I'm listening to the wind coming off the sea. It howls all around Midnight Hall. Mairead has woken again. What a restless baby! Not like her brothers. They slept peacefully, hour after hour. I nearly had to wake them to feed them, they were so mellow. Mairead just won't settle, she won't stop crying – I have no choice but to leave her to it.

I must stop now and go to my bed, in case a dream comes. She will stop crying, sooner or later.

I shall write again soon. And remember, I don't blame you for what happened with Angus.

Yours,

Morag Midnight

Sarah laid the letter down and put a hand to her mouth. *So Eliza wanted to die. She couldn't take the dreaming. And poor Mairead, to suffer like that from the moment she was born!* The full horror of the legacy swept over Sarah like a cold wave.

Right at that moment she contemplated the idea of thrusting the letters into the fire, one by one, as she'd done with her dream diary. She didn't want to know how the story unfolded. She didn't want to be part of it. She didn't want to be part of that line of women with such a burden. But she was, and there was no choice to be made.

A knock at the door made her jump.

"Sarah?"

It was Nicholas. "Come in," she called, trying in vain to erase the shock from her face.

"Hey, what's wrong?"

"Nothing. Just . . . reading about my family."

Nicholas wrapped his arms around her, his woodsmoke scent enveloping her once more. "Oh, family. Yes. Families can mess you up big time." *Wait until you meet my father.*

Sarah waited for the wave of dizziness to come, the one she

195

so often felt when Nicholas was around – that sense of her thoughts disappearing and strength leaving her.

It didn't happen. It hadn't happened for a while, she realized.

"Do you want to be alone?"

Sarah thought about it for a moment. "No. Stay. I want you to know." She freed herself gently and handed him the letter she'd just read.

Nicholas sat at the fire and read while Sarah studied the flames.

"Poor girl," he commented finally. "Elizabeth, I mean. She was broken."

I've seen a broken girl before, he thought. *I broke her.*

"I just hope the same doesn't happen to me," said Sarah.

Nicholas felt cold. "Why do you say that?"

"I don't know." Sarah shrugged. "Just a feeling I've always had. That one day I won't be able to take it anymore. That all this," she gestured at the room around her, full of photographs of her family, "will end up destroying me. And you know," she leaned her head on his shoulder, "I really want to live. Have a proper life, I mean. Like everyone else. Play my music . . ."

"Yes. I understand." *Believe me, I do.* Nicholas leant towards her and placed a soft kiss on the top of her head. *And I'm going to take it all away from you.* He felt ill, ill with the cruelty of it all. With the inevitability of it all. He held her tight once more. Too tight.

"Nicholas, you're hurting me."

"Oh, sorry," he whispered, and loosened his grip.

"Hey, you're shaking," said Sarah softly, looking into his face.

"Am I? Well, it's quite cold in here." Nicholas avoided meeting her eyes.

A sense of foreboding crept over Sarah, covered her like a black shroud. She sensed that the story about to unfold would be a terrible one, and that the ghosts of Midnight Hall were not going to leave her alone until she'd heard it all. Nicholas felt her anxiety rising and tried to distract her.

"Look," he whispered, and pointed at the fire. From red, the flames started turning blue, yellow, green and then all black, and red again. "Like your stained-glass window."

Sarah smiled. "It's beautiful." She touched Nicholas's wounded cheek gently. "Does is still hurt?"

"No. Don't worry about that. Don't worry about anything."

"Why did the ravens attack you, Nicholas?"

"I don't know."

You do. But you're not telling. "Don't keep secrets from me."

"Sarah," Nicholas replied wearily.

She waited for him to tell her he wasn't hiding anything from her. But he didn't.

"Can I stay with you tonight?" he asked instead.

Sarah drew in breath, softly. She wasn't expecting that.

"Nicholas . . ."

He put his hands up. "It's not like that, not if you're not ready."

Sarah shook her head and looked down. She wasn't.

"I just don't want to be alone tonight. And maybe you don't want it either," he whispered, lifting her chin tenderly with his hand.

All of a sudden, a name crossed Sarah's mind: *Sean.* It was like a stab in her heart, a loss too painful to bear.

She looked Nicholas in the eye. "Yes. You can stay."

They fell asleep in each other's arms, but it wasn't long before Sarah woke. Nicholas was tossing and turning, moaning in his sleep. Repeating the same word over and over again, a word Sarah couldn't quite make out.

"Nicholas! Wake up! It's fine, it's just a nightmare." It was the first time in her life that she had to comfort someone who was having a bad dream, and not the other way round.

"Martyna!" he called.

Martyna?

Sarah frowned, and took hold of his hand. "Nicholas. Shhhh. It's OK. I'm here. Wake up, you're safe."

Nicholas's black eyes opened in the darkness, and he sat up with a jolt. Sarah embraced him at once, stroking his hair, caressing his back, cradling him gently. She felt something wet against her cheek, and scalding hot. His burning tears.

"Nicholas."

"I'm sorry. I'm sorry." He clung to her in a way he'd never done before.

"Hey, it's OK. It's OK."

"Sarah. I'm sorry."

"It was just a bad dream. Go back to sleep."

It wasn't a bad dream. It was my life. It is my life. "I can't. I can't go back to sleep."

Sarah nodded. She knew very well what this felt like, not wanting to close your eyes again. "I'll light the fire and I'll make you some tea, OK?" She swung her legs over the side of the bed. "I'll be back in a minute."

She tiptoed out of the room, closing the door behind her, made her way towards the stairs, but just as she reached the top step she stopped in her tracks. There was a figure standing on the landing, shrouded in shadows.

Sean.

"I heard a noise. I thought I would come and check on you," he said.

"It was Nicholas. He was having a bad dream."

"Right." He didn't move.

"It's not what you think. We aren't—we didn't—" Words failed Sarah. She just couldn't explain. And why did it feel like a betrayal?

She turned and walked away without looking back.

31

Chrysalis

Seasons have tempered us
Like water to a burning sword

Nicholas was finally asleep, but Sarah was wide awake.

She couldn't lie in bed any longer. The house was calling her. Since they'd arrived she'd barely had time to walk from room to room, to hear Midnight Hall's whispered welcome to its rightful owner.

She got up and slipped her white jumper around her shoulders. Quietly, she opened a drawer of her mother's dressing table; of course, they were still there. Every room was equipped with an emergency kit of candles, matches and a torch, as there were often power cuts on Islay. The torch would have been more practical, but Sarah preferred the golden, soft light of candles. She took hold of one of the two silver candlesticks sitting on either side of the mantelpiece and stood in front of the dressing table. The match sizzled feebly as she lit it, and she turned towards Nicholas to make sure he was still asleep. He didn't stir.

The candle's small, warm light flickered and danced, revealing the draughts in the room. It lit up Sarah's face with a honeyed glow, and she was surprised as she caught her reflection in the dressing table mirror to see how much her face had changed. There was a strength in her eyes that hadn't been there before. Her eyes widened as she realized how much she looked like her mother.

Sarah's footsteps were too light to make a sound as she walked out of the room, protecting the flickering flame with her cupped hand. To walk with a candle in her hand made her think of her ancestors, her grandmother, before electricity came, and their nightly walks through the house, guided only by the light of this tiny fire between their fingers. The whole house was asleep and there was no noise to be heard.

She wasn't sure where to go, but her feet took her down the corridor, past the stained-glass window and down the stairs. She was shivering in spite of her jumper, and her feet felt cold on the steps. Still, in a strange way, she enjoyed feeling the stone against her bare skin, as if she were feeling the house itself, settling and creaking and breathing like a living thing. She put her right arm out, her fingers brushing the wall lightly. Step after step, the light of the candle illuminating her naked feet, and then the vast, high-ceilinged vestibule. She stopped for a second and breathed in. The house smelled of peat, of damp and of something else, something she recognized but couldn't quite place.

Lilies?

She closed her eyes and inhaled again. *Yes, lilies.*

Sarah smiled to herself. She knew now where she wanted to go. Past the small living room where Niall had been taken when unconscious, past the library whose walls were covered floor to ceiling with bookshelves, past her grandmother's study. The grand hall opened dark and cavernous to her left, but she turned right instead.

She entered the music room, where she'd spent so many peaceful hours listening to her grandmother and her parents playing, and practising the cello herself. She stepped into the darkened room, illuminating in turn a piano, a harpsichord and the shape of a covered harp, taller than her, resembling a bulky hunchbacked figure. Her fingers lingered on the piano. Carefully she opened its lid and played a few notes, balancing the candle with her other hand. The sound echoed in the silence of the night. Her mother Anne had been an extraordinary pianist, she remembered sadly.

Sarah closed the piano lid as the notes reverberated. She didn't want to wake anybody, and she didn't want to be disturbed in her journey through memory and time.

She walked on, towards the wall opposite, and fingered the soft, aqua and gold wallpaper. Under her touch, an invisible door hidden by the wallpaper opened. Sarah smiled, her secret hideout, the cosy, protected place where she went to read and daydream, was still there. It hadn't been secret at all, of course – everyone knew of its existence – but it felt like that to her, as a child.

It was a tiny room – more of a cupboard – whose purpose had been unknown even to Morag and Hamish. They had no idea why whoever built the house many generations before had decided to carve that small chamber just off the music room. There was no rhyme or reason to it.

Sarah stepped in, the light of the candle illuminating the small space. It was covered in the same aqua and gold wallpaper as the music room, and along the back wall ran a small wooden ottoman. Knowing that Sarah loved sitting in there with a book, Morag had had the ottoman covered in blue velvet cushions. Sarah smiled to herself again, remembering her grandmother's act of kindness. She placed the candlestick on the wooden floor carefully and kneeled in front of the ottoman, opening its velvet-covered lid.

It was full of treasures, intact from the last time she'd been in the room. As a teenager she hadn't used the hideaway as much; the prized possessions she had placed in the ottoman must have been there for at least five years. Inside, there was a pink fabric bag, embroidered with little pink sequins. Sarah opened it, and gasped in delight to uncover the treasure it hid. It was a tiny wooden box painted with blue and green flowers – she had forgotten all about it. She lifted the lid, and smiled upon seeing a pair of blue butterfly-shaped earrings that her father had given her on his return from a trip to London when she was ten years old. Those earrings had been her very first piece of jewellery. She slipped the box in the pocket of her jumper.

Next, she took out an address book, with a white kitten on the cover. It was full of phone numbers of former classmates.

Mary Elizabeth McGregor

Sophie Singh

Patrick Thomson

Patrick Thomson! Her first crush. How she'd sighed because of him. And still, when he'd finally noticed her and asked her to go for chips, she'd chickened out of it. The poor guy had waited for an hour and a half in front of the chip shop. She felt a pang of guilt at the memory. Poor Patrick. One of the many boys who'd fallen for her shy, prickly charm and her lovely dark looks, only to be bitterly disappointed. Nobody had ever come close to her, not even remotely.

Nobody, that is, until Sean arrived.

Her eye fell on a book with a green cover and the image

of a red-haired girl in a dress and straw hat sitting on a rope swing staring up at her. She took the book in her hand: *Anne of Green Gables*. How much she'd loved that book. She'd read it endless times. She opened the first page.

Happy Birthday, Sarah! From Aunt Juliet to Sarah, October 2005.

She'd been eleven years old.

The feelings of joy and tenderness gave way to a wave of sorrow. Aunt Juliet was gone and would never come back. She recalled their last day together, when she'd been so hard on her, so impatient. Like she'd always been, really. Only now Sarah was beginning to realize how present Aunt Juliet had been throughout her life, and how often she had rebuffed her for it, instead of being thankful. Now Aunt Juliet was gone – and her Uncle Trevor, and surely her cousins, didn't want anything to do with her anymore. She'd been severed from the last of her family.

Maybe that's what happens to all Midnights, sooner or later. One by one the people we love are picked apart and destroyed.

Something cold and steely blossomed in her heart. She would not let all this loss annihilate her. It would be easy to give in to the pain, but she wouldn't – she'd turn the grief into strength. She would be tempered, like metal in water. From the day she'd been told about her parents' death, to her first hunt, to Sean's appearance in her life and throughout the destruction of Cathy's Valaya, during those terrible times a new Sarah had emerged. The little girl lying alone in an empty house had grown into a resilient young woman who had learnt to face her destiny. Even the way she walked had changed, the way she held her body straight and proud.

Like Morag.

A small, soft nugget of the old Sarah was still nesting in her heart – the girl who longed to be loved – but it was hidden from sight. The new Sarah stood by herself.

Except when Nicholas was around. That's when her strength ebbed away somehow, albeit temporarily. Why did he have that effect on her?

And most of all, where were her dreams? Were they lost forever?

She shook her head at those uncomfortable thoughts and opened the wooden box again. She slipped the butterfly earrings into her ears. That's what she was, a chrysalis that had turned into a butterfly. And she wouldn't let anyone steal her newfound strength.

Sarah took hold of the candlestick again and closed the door on her former hideaway. She'd leave the little memories where they were. She felt they belonged there.

She wasn't ready to go back to bed, to share her space with Nicholas. He was fast asleep anyway, with no sign of nightmares anymore.

Who is Martyna? she asked herself as she closed the heavy wooden door of the music room.

She hesitated for a moment, then crossed the corridor and pushed the heavy, two-panelled door of the grand hall open. The light of the candle, flickering with the omnipresent draughts, seemed very small in the vast room. The ceiling was crisscrossed with black wooden beams, and the polished floor was covered in precious, exotic-looking rugs. Beams of golden light glimmered against the ceiling, the candlelight reflected in the crystal chandelier.

Sarah walked on slowly, turning around to illuminate the whole room – a stag head hanging on the far wall, together with tapestries and paintings. Suddenly, Sarah remembered her grandfather, Hamish, saying how much he would have loved to have demon spoils hanging on the walls – but he'd never been able to have them, because the Surari ended up dissolved in the Blackwater. Sarah shuddered, thinking of severed demon heads hanging on the walls of this place, watching them as they ate around the huge oak table.

She contemplated the velvet curtains drawn over the windows, a colour somewhere between crimson and burgundy, and then she moved the fabric aside slightly, to get a view of the beach. The sea and the sky were fused in blackness, pale clouds moving slowly like frayed, ghostly sails. Something stirred in Sarah's mind, the hint of a memory, something important, something she had forgotten, dancing at the edge of her consciousness.

In her mind's eye, Sarah saw herself as a small girl standing on the watermark, wrapped in her red coat and scarf, holding her grandmother's hand. It had been the day before Morag died, when they'd walked on the beach together.

Sarah shook her head slightly, trying to clear her thoughts, but the feeble memory was gone, too insubstantial to be held long enough to know what it meant. Sarah frowned.

The candle swayed violently from the draught that seeped through the window and threatened to engulf the curtain. Sarah jerked the flame away from the fabric as quickly as she could. When her eyes moved from the candle to the room again, she gasped. The hall had somehow turned into a blackened shell, covered in debris and ashes. Her feet felt wet, and she looked down to see that she was standing ankle-deep in Blackwater. The curtains beside her were now threadbare and frayed, crumbling to ash. Sarah panted, breathless and dizzy from the sudden vision. She blinked hard several times, and the vision was gone.

She stood under the impossibly high ceiling, the stag head looking on with its glassy, indifferent eyes, trying to steady her heart – she'd seen the whole place burnt down and destroyed. Was that a vision of what would have happened had she not moved the candle as quickly as she had? Or was it of something still to happen? It wouldn't be the first time a vision came to her when she was awake, and with her dreams having disappeared, maybe her gift had found a way to tell her what she needed to know.

What she needed now, for sure, was some tea to steady her nerves. She looked at her watch, twenty past three in the morning. She turned her back to the stag head and its staring eyes, and stepped out of the grand hall, pulling the thick door closed behind her. She stopped for a moment, trying to catch her still ragged breath.

She turned left on her way to the kitchen, considering how frozen her feet were, but something made her stop in front of her grandmother's study. She hesitated for a second, and lifted her free hand to feel her butterfly earring dreamily – then, on impulse, she opened the door and stepped in.

She inhaled the scent of old books and damp that had always been the signature of that room. The candlelight illuminated the enormous bookshelves and the dark wooden desk at the farthest corner, where Sarah had found the letters. A painting of wild horses hung over the desk. Sarah's eyes lingered on it. She walked on slowly, holding the candle so that its light would fall on the painting. The elusive memory that had visited her in the grand hall came back, shimmering faintly and disappearing, then reappearing for a second and fading again.

It's important. Remember.

Sarah jumped out of her skin. The words had resounded in

her mind as clearly as if they'd been spoken aloud. The hand holding the candle was trembling now.

"Can't sleep?"

Sarah jumped again, turning around with a gasp. Nicholas's tall, muscular body was framed in the doorway.

"Sorry, I didn't mean to startle you," he said, advancing towards her. He slipped his hands under her jumper, feeling the skin on her shoulders. Sarah fixed her eyes on his obsidian ones.

"I woke up and you were gone," he said.

"Sorry. I just wanted to have some time alone . . . with the house. If that makes sense." She smiled apologetically.

"Am I interfering? Ruining your moment with the house?" He smiled back, his voice soft and dark.

"No, of course not," she began, but his lips were on hers and she couldn't speak anymore.

Remember. It's important.

But her thoughts were unravelling already.

32
Runes

Take all I have
And when there's nothing left for me to give
I'll give you more
Because
He isn't you

Sean

So this is the day after the night before. After realizing that Nicholas was sleeping in Sarah's room, I wasted the rest of last night feeling sorry for myself.

Today Elodie asked me to teach her to trace the runes, and to my surprise, Sarah joined us. We spent all afternoon practising in the living room, with Sarah and I resolutely avoided meeting each other's gaze. And with Nicholas looking on. Awkward doesn't even begin to describe the atmosphere in the room. But the runes may serve Sarah and Elodie well. We can't be distracted by our feelings.

However, it doesn't help that Sarah's hair is loose down her back and she's wearing the blue top I love, the one that shows her shoulders. She might as well be carving the runes into my heart.

"Right. Try this. It's the most basic one." I guide Elodie's hand, tracing a simple rune.

They're eager learners, especially Sarah – Elodie takes a little longer. Still, it doesn't come easily to either of the girls. It's strange for me to see, really. I never found the runes that difficult. I'm surprised to see how slow, how weak other people can be when they trace them. Even two powerful heirs like Sarah and Elodie. Maybe it's because they just started and they need practice. Still, even the most basic ones seem challenging.

"No. Look. That won't work. You need to be more focused."

Elodie is getting frustrated. "You make it seem so easy!"

"It *is* easy! It is to me, at least."

"To you, yes. Harry always said your use of the runes was incredible."

I shrug. "Maybe. But you can learn, too, like I did."

Elodie crosses her arms. "We're useless, let's face it."

"Hey, speak for yourself. Look." Sarah repeats the basic rune. The knife flies out of her hand, making a graceful arc across the room and wedging itself into the wooden floor.

"Duck!" laughs Nicholas.

"Ha ha." Sarah walks over to where the knife fell, her heels clacking on the floor.

"Useless, like I said. How do you do it, Sean?" says Elodie.

"I don't know. All you need to do is learn the different signs, really. Harry taught me, I can teach you."

"Harry wasn't as good as you, though. Remember Takeo Ayanami? He was so in awe of you when he saw you sending people to sleep with your runes."

"Nonsense. It's like playing an instrument. You have to practise, that's all," I insist.

"I play an instrument," Sarah says. "I know what practice can do. But I still don't get this. It's as if I asked you to use the Blackwater. It won't work."

"It's not like the Blackwater. The Blackwater is a power, like Niall's song or Elodie's poison. This is a *skill*." I stress the word.

"So you keep telling us!" laughs Elodie.

"Maybe if you say 'skill' often enough, we'll get it!" echoes Sarah.

"And what about the red ribbons?" Elodie waves her fingers in the air. "The ones that appeared when the soil demons attacked us?"

"That's not supposed to happen. No idea what it was, or whether it'll happen again. Right, lesson over, pupils dismissed."

Niall has come into the living room and is leaning against the fireplace, his arms crossed. I see him look at me in a way that unnerves me, with eyes that see all the way into my soul. I've watched him and he does it with everybody. It's disquieting.

"Did your parents have any powers, Sean?" he asks me in his thick Irish accent.

"No. Well, not that I know of." I shrug.

"Right," he says, looking at me with that strange, watery gaze he has, as if he were looking straight into the sea.

33
Adrift

If we pretend, it's good enough for me
The illusion we create
Instead of what it is

"I don't know what half of this stuff is. Chestnuts?" Sean shrugged.

Sean, Mike and Niall were in the kitchen helping Sarah survey the food Mrs McArthur had provided. She needed to make sure they had everything for a proper Christmas dinner, with a turkey and all the trimmings. They had tried to argue with her that it was surreal to go to all the trouble of making a traditional Christmas meal when they could be attacked any minute, but Sarah put her foot down. This was her house. She was going to cook, and she was going to have a proper festive celebration.

There was something desperate about her determination. Sean knew how upset she was, how she was trying to cling to a semblance of normal life. Her first Christmas without her parents. Maybe this would help her think of her aunt Juliet a bit less . . . and of her cousins, Sally and Siobhan, left motherless. All because Anne had married a Midnight. And because Sarah couldn't defend her.

They had been over the same ground again and again, and Sarah was adamant. They would celebrate Christmas. They were alive, and together. In some warped way, it made sense.

"You don't know what chestnuts are?" laughed Mike, looking up at Sean from the potatoes he was stacking.

"I do know what chestnuts are. I just don't know what you do with them!" Sean protested.

"You make stuffing. For the turkey. Oh, thank goodness – chipolatas! She hasn't forgotten." Sarah had her head in the freezer, little icy clouds wafting from its drawers.

"Thank goodness!" echoed Niall.

"I know! It just wouldn't be the same without chipolatas wrapped in bacon," Sarah continued, pulling the icy package from the open freezer.

"I meant thank goodness for this!" Niall was standing by an open cupboard door with an amber-honey bottle of whisky grasped in one hand. Laphroaig, one of the Islay whiskies. He gestured to shelves full of similar bottles. "Bless Mrs McArthur. She knows her whisky."

Sarah rolled her eyes. "Oh, yes. Of course. We have a few of those. Just try not to drink yourself asleep. In case they attack and we can't wake you up."

"Me? I can hold my drink, young lady. You'll never see me passed out."

"True. I can vouch for that!" said Mike. "Hey."

Elodie had walked into the kitchen, her golden hair tied in a knot, her lithe body clad in a long, white woollen top and jeans.

"Sarah. Where can I find more peat for my fire, please? I've run out. And it's so cold." She was pale and shivery.

213

Niall smiled at her. "Oh, it's the deadly princess. Hello," he said. "I'll get your briquettes. Care to share a coffee with me? I was just making one." He spooned some granules into a mug.

"And what's this?" Sean, still wearing a puzzled expression, held up something he'd found in the fruit bowl. "Do you know, Elodie?" He reached out his hand to offer her the fruit.

Elodie turned to look, and all the blood drained from her face. Gingerly she took the red fruit from Sean's hand, locking her eyes on his and brushing his fingers with hers as she did so. Then she turned and ran out of the kitchen without a word.

Mike shrugged his shoulders. "What was that all about?"

"No idea," replied Sean, disconcerted, and ran after Elodie at once.

Sarah's gaze followed Sean as he left the room. She bit her lip, then turned back to her list. "Right. Where was I?" she said resolutely.

"What was it? The fruit?" asked Niall.

"A pomegranate," said Sarah. She opened the freezer door, sighed deeply, then closed it again. She untied her apron.

"You OK?" asked Mike.

"Of course. I'm just going to look for Nicholas."

"Sarah." Mike had a gentle smile on his lips as he put a hand on her arm.

"What?"

"Listen to your heart."

Sarah winced and looked away. "I'm trying. But there's always too much noise."

Sean

I have no idea what I've done to upset Elodie. I'm halfway to her room when she runs past me in the opposite direction, and out the front door. I follow her outside, determined to make amends. It's another windy, rainy day, as it's been since we arrived. Twilight is nearly upon us, though it's barely afternoon. Days last a heartbeat on this island.

Elodie is running towards the beach, towards the sea. I look up at the sky as I follow her; I fear another appearance of the demon-bird. I reach Elodie just as she stops in front of the watermark, the waves lapping at her feet.

"Elodie."

She turns around, and I'm astonished – she's crying, but she's smiling as well.

"What's the matter? Did you see something? Did you have a vision?"

Elodie shakes her head, and she fixes her brown eyes on mine. "I can't explain. You would laugh."

"Try me."

She opens her mouth, then closes it again and shakes her head softly. She's not going to tell me. I feel a wave of tenderness for her, my old friend, Harry's wife. Harry's widow. She's all eyes, having lost so much weight, and her hair shines golden in the dusky light. I stroke her cheek. She takes my hand and pulls it to her chest, over her heart. She keeps it there, and I can feel her heartbeat, so steady and regular and yet, so fragile.

"Sean."

And then something strange happens. Something that should not have happened, and that I didn't see coming.

She puts her lips on mine, and she kisses me, tenderly, for a moment only. And for a moment only I want to kiss her back, feel her hands on me, lose myself in her. I want to take her behind those rocks where a group of seals are dozing, out of sight, and be with her. Just once. Just long enough to feel alive again. I'm only human, and I've been alone for so long – and she's so, so beautiful.

But I can't, because my heart belongs to Sarah. It's as simple as that.

Elodie looks into my eyes, and she reads my thoughts. She gives me a heartbreaking smile and walks away without a word, without looking back, along the water's edge. I watch her walk slowly, her head turned towards the sea. Her hair has come undone, and it's blowing behind her. She's so slight against the backdrop of the ocean. I can't leave her alone, as much as I know she needs solitude. Not with the demon-bird around the house, and who knows what else. I'm as certain as I can possibly be that we are not safe. I look up at the sky again, anxious.

But it's empty.

They don't come from the air this time, they come from the water. Just as my gaze returns to Elodie, I see long, thin jelly-like tentacles bursting out of the water, wrapping themselves around Elodie's waist and dragging her under so fast that she doesn't even have time to scream.

34
From the Water

The depths of the sea
Are home to me
I'm one of those beings
Who should not be

Sean

I can only call her name, over and over again, as Elodie is thrown into the air and then pulled underwater with splashes and sprays of liquid grey. I take out my *sgian-dubh*, but do runes work underwater? I've never tried. How far has the demon gone? Is it swimming away from the shore? For a second, I feel there is no hope. I'm sure that Elodie is going to die there and then, just after our ill-fated kiss.

"Elodie! No! Elodie!" I hear a voice calling in despair, broken, full of terror, and the voice is mine.

And then a thought makes its way through the panic. If I stand on the shore, the demon will get me too. I have to turn away. I have to run. I have to leave Elodie to her fate because there's no way I can save her and save myself too. And I *must* save myself. For the fight.

I know that it's what I should do. But I can't. To turn my back on Elodie and run is just impossible. I can't.

That leaves only one option. To run into the sea and take the one-in-a-million chance that one of us, or both of us, might survive. Though my head is telling me that what will really happen, of course, is that we'll both die.

"Sean! Don't!"

I turn around just as I'm about to dive, and see Niall running towards the water. He stops right on the shoreline, closes his eyes, takes a deep breath and throws his head back. A long, powerful, chilling wail comes out of his mouth. I throw myself on the sand, my hands on my ears – but even that is not enough to block out the terrible sound. I can feel the sand lifting up in a whirlpool around us – it's stinging my cheeks and blinding me. I barely manage to make out the surface of the sea rising, and the water starting to turn into itself over and over again, until it becomes a colossal waterspout, a sea tornado, rising high in the sky.

I'm drenched and half blind, and my ears are in agony. The sound of Niall's song is still audible over the noise of the swirling water, and of the unnatural wind born from Niall's power. I try to drag myself up, but I'm flogged down again – once, twice – grains of sand lashing my face like steely whips. I open my mouth to call for Elodie, but it fills with wet sand, and I choke. The pain in my ears is so unbearable I think I'm going to pass out. I don't know how long I can bear this.

I half-open my eyes and try to peer over to where Niall is standing. He's a few inches off the ground by now, his arms thrown open, as if he's being crucified. His head is tilted back at an impossible angle, his features twisted in pain. A few more seconds of torture for both of us, and then out of the spinning waters soars a huge, light-pink mass, its tentacles flailing and whipping the waves. The demon is propelled out of the water and lands on the sand with a thud. Niall's song finally stops, and he falls to the sand, empty, unmoving.

I cough and splutter, my mouth and nose and lungs full of sand. I realize that my hands are covered in blood – am I wounded? No time to worry about that. Niall is lying on the ground, senseless, and there's no trace of Elodie. A split-second choice between the two, and I go for the one who's in the most danger.

"Elodie!" I call, and run into the freezing waves until I'm waist-deep. I'm about to dive under when a strange call resounds from the rocks. A seal is standing upright, barking. I don't know what forces me to look again, but something in the seal's call makes me do a double take. And that's how I spot something beside the seal, something golden against the grey skin of the animal.

"Elodie! Oh my God, Elodie." I look around wildly, trying to work out the quickest way to reach her, and without any further thought I dive into the freezing sea and swim as strongly as I'm able towards the rocks. When I emerge, the seal is gone, and a girl is sitting in its place. She's cradling Elodie's head in her lap, brushing away Elodie's soaking hair from her face.

"Elodie!" I call, sputtering water. The girl looks at me. I realize she's naked, but for her long, dripping hair, a strange shade of silvery-lilac.

Is she human?

I lift myself onto the rocks and place my hands over Elodie's chest. She's breathing. She's alive!

"Thank you," I whisper to the girl.

"You're welcome," she replies, and her voice has a light Scottish lilt to it. She's not embarrassed in the slightest by her nudity.

"Sean." Elodie's eyes open and she starts coughing up water. I help her sit up.

"I'm here. It's OK, it's over. Niall killed the demon."

She looks utterly stunned. "Who . . . who are you?" murmurs Elodie, turning to the silver-haired girl.

"I'm Winter Shaw."

"Of course." Elodie looks at Winter's face intently. "I dreamt of you once. Remember, Sean?" She shivers violently. She's soaking, and the cold wind is cutting us to the quick. Strangely, the naked young woman is not showing any signs of being cold. I'd like to ask her a few questions, but first I need to make sure that Niall is OK.

"Can you walk?" I ask Elodie.

"I think so."

I turn to the mysterious girl. "Will you come with us?"

"Yes. I think it's time."

There isn't time to wonder what she means. Niall is doubled over some way away across the beach, and he's holding himself as if in excruciating pain. We make our way across the rocks, hopping from stone to stone until we reach him.

"Elodie?" he murmurs. Relief shines from his grimacing face.

"I'm OK. Niall, you saved my life – you, and Winter."

"Winter?" whispers Niall.

The silver-haired girl kneels next to him. "It's me. I am Winter."

Niall picks himself up with exertion and looks at the silver-haired girl. I see his eyes widen. "Elemental," he whispers.

"Half Elemental, half human. The best of both," smiles Winter, innocent in her nakedness.

"Er, here." Elodie takes off her soaking jacket and hands it to Winter.

But she shrugs. "I'm not cold."

"It's more for us, really," I mumble, and look away.

She laughs. "Oh, sorry. I forget the way things are for people. I haven't often been in my human form in the last few years."

"Lucky you," says Niall gently.

Winter looks at Niall as if she sees him for the first time. "You're of the sea," she states, wrapping Elodie's jacket around herself. "A Secret heir?"

"Yes." Niall's voice is very, very soft. I expect him to make a joke, or pay Winter some kind of naff compliment, but he doesn't. He's deadly serious, and staring at her, unable to look away.

"Ow," he says suddenly, and folds himself in two again, holding his stomach.

"Are you hurt?" I put my arm around his shoulders.

"No. It's just that . . . it was all so sudden. No time to take the song slowly. It can be overwhelming when it happens like that. The pain'll pass soon, though. Where's the demon?"

"Over there, on the shore." I look over to the huge pink mass, as big as a car, quivering on the sand. Some of its tentacles are tangled under and around it, some are stretched for hundreds of yards across the sand.

"Sean!" gasps Elodie suddenly. "You're bleeding!"

I touch my ears, then look at the blood on my fingers. "Niall, you were supposed to kill the demon, not me!"

"Sorry. I can't help it. The song takes on its own momentum. You'll be OK, anyway. The noise didn't last long enough to kill you."

"Just as well," I growl, while Elodie touches my face lightly,

221

checking for bruising. "Let's go back to the house and get dried up. You can tell us all about yourself, Winter. And meet Sarah."

"Oh, I know all about Sarah Midnight. I used to play with her aunt Mairead," Winter says simply.

"You what? How old are you?" asks Elodie.

"I'll tell you all once we're back at the—Watch out!" Winter yells suddenly, pointing over our shoulders. Before I have time to turn around, a long, slippery tentacle lands with a thump between me and Elodie, missing us by a few inches. Niall is clutching an angry red mark on the side of his face, where the flailing tentacle swept him.

"It's not dead!" screams Elodie.

"No. But this time it's on land," I reply. My *sgian-dubh* is in my hand in a second, and I start tracing the runes with all the fury I felt when I thought Elodie had drowned.

The Surari launches its tentacles towards us – once, twice, and again. Elodie, Niall and Winter duck and avoid it the first time, and the second – but the third time it takes a grip of Niall's arm and throws him down on the sand. It's beginning to drag him towards the water, and I see Niall opening his mouth and trying to sing but no noise is coming out, he has given all there was to give saving Elodie. He's spent. Fear is painted all over his face as the demon tightens its grip, enveloping Niall's arms, his chest. Flynns can't die in water, but having their ribs crushed *will* kill them.

At last, my runes start working. Every trace in the air makes a cut in the creature's skin, black demon blood spurting from the wounds. The wind is roaring in my ears, and I see red. I can't stop cutting and stabbing and slicing the air, and with it, the demon – until its tentacles stop flailing at last and it lies still, with Niall still wrapped in its loosened grip.

A pause, a heartbeat, while everyone makes sure they're still alive.

"That was close," croaks Niall in the silence that follows, freeing himself from the dead weight of the tentacle and throwing it heavily on the wet sand. His face is scratched and bloodied where the tentacle hit him and where he'd been dragged across the beach. He's sitting with his head in his hands, and I can see he's shaking. "Now can we get out of here?" he asks.

"We better drag the demon into the sea first," I point out as soon as I can catch my breath. "We don't want any hill walkers spotting a prehistoric jellyfish on the beach."

"It would boost tourism. Like the Loch Ness Monster," says Winter with her Scottish lilt – and surprisingly, unexpectedly, we laugh.

35
Winter

The day we met,
The day our lives
Changed forever
And time did pass, but we're still there

"Sean, you're bleeding! An attack, and I haven't dreamt of it! Again!" Sarah clasped a hand over her mouth.

"I'm fine. It wasn't the demon who did this, it was Niall's singing." Sean had an arm around Niall's waist as he was so weak he could barely walk.

"Jesus, Niall. Come here." Mike took Niall's arm, and Niall leaned heavily on him. "Come and sit down."

"Niall," Sarah began, but she froze as she saw Winter emerge from behind Elodie. "And who are you?"

"I'm Winter Shaw."

"Winter? Mrs Shaw's daughter? It can't be! You should be . . . you should be – fifty years old, at least!"

"I'm fifty-three, yes."

"You—oh, never mind! What happened?"

"Sean and I were on the beach," Elodie began, and she blushed, remembering the kiss. "A demon came out of the water. It was one of those jellyfish things. It pulled me in and dragged me down." She shivered at the memory. "I'm not a good swimmer at all. I would have died, but Niall sang the demon out of the water, and it was Winter who brought me onto the rocks."

"The seal," said Sean, looking at Winter with awe. "It was you!"

Winter smiled. Her hair was shimmering silver and mother-of-pearl against the stained-glass window. "Yes. Seal is my usual shape, this is just for special occasions!" She laughed, gesturing to her human body. "My father was a spirit of the water, which is why I grow old so slowly, Sarah."

"Mr Shaw was a spirit of the water?" asked Sarah, incredulous. She'd seen pictures of him, a short, bearded man in a tweed cap, always with a shotgun strapped across his chest. He'd been the Midnight estate gamekeeper for forty years.

"No," laughed Winter. "Hugh Shaw wasn't my father. My father was my mother's lover. He left his human shape forever just after I was born and went back to the sea. Hugh, my stepfather, came after. He knew all about me, how I came to be."

Sarah was wide-eyed. "Mrs Shaw had a lover?" She thought of the black-clad, stern-looking old woman she had known as a child.

"I know it's hard to imagine. She was very reserved, wasn't she? But she and my father were very much in love. She loved life, in every way. And so do I." And with that, Winter looked straight at Niall, and through him, inside him. His face turned crimson.

"Was it you who left the letters?" asked Nicholas suddenly.

His tone towards Winter was harsh, almost accusing. Everybody tensed.

She nodded. "It was me, yes. Before you all arrived. My mother had taken them away from this house. She died three years ago, and when I found the letters among her things, I thought I'd wait for you to come back and hand them over."

"That's funny, man. This people-of-the-sea thing!" Mike chipped in. He wasn't very interested in the mechanics of delivering letters. "Being able to turn into an animal, or something. I wish I had some really cool powers like all of you."

"Well, in a way, we all belong to an Element," Winter remarked. "Human beings too. I mean, Lays. Non-Secret people."

"Do we? So what Element am I? Out of curiosity," asked Mike.

"You're . . ." Winter tipped her head to one side, studying Mike's face. "You're earth. Yes, earth. And so is Sean, with a touch of fire. Elodie is air and water. Sarah is air and fire." Winter smiled at her. "And you, Nicholas . . ." Nicholas had been looking down, lost in thought. Upon hearing his name, he raised his head with a quick, jerky movement. "You are fire." They held each other's gaze for a moment, and it was Winter who looked away first.

"I'm freezing," said Elodie. "I'll go get changed. Come, Winter, I'll get you some clothes."

Niall and Mike watched in awe as the silver-haired girl walked slowly upstairs, the light from the stained-glass window making her hair shimmer like the inside of a shell.

36

Don't Let Me Sleep

A child who asks, "What's happening?"
And then silence begins

Islay, May 1985
Dear Amelia,

Life has been quite complicated around here. I'm sure you know what I'm talking about. The time has come. Mairead's dreams have started. She screams throughout the night until she's exhausted, and everybody else with her. She's refusing to tell me anything of what she sees, or to write anything down in the dream diary we gave her, which means we can't use her dreams at all. She's worse than my sister was. Hamish says she'll grow into herself. I have to believe she will.

She does all she can to stay awake. Last night she went for a walk down to the beach, hoping the cold would prevent her from falling asleep. I know that trick, my sister and I used it too. Her brothers followed her from a distance to make sure she was safe. She walked up and down that beach until the small hours of the morning, until she couldn't stay upright anymore. Stewart carried her home and laid her on her bed, but she kept trying to get up, and when she realized she couldn't stand, that her legs couldn't carry her any longer, she started throwing herself off the bed, hoping that hitting the floor would keep her awake. We couldn't have that. I asked Stewart to hold her down, and she struggled and thrashed, with Stewart begging her to stop, to let herself go and surrender to sleep. He hated every minute of it, my poor son. What that girl puts us through!

In the end, she couldn't resist anymore. She's still a child, after all. She started nodding off and waking up with a jolt, over and over again, until sleep finally took her just as dawn was breaking. I stayed in her room. I knew I had to watch her, lest she tried to throw herself out of the window, like my sister tried to do when her dreams started. Mairead woke again two hours later, screaming and crying, begging me to make it stop. But how can I? What am I supposed to do? There is no way to stop the dreams, and we need her to dream. The family requires her to dream. But will she listen? Of course not.

So here I am, writing to you while she plays the piano downstairs, a terrible, haunting song she wrote herself. At least she has her music to keep her busy.

This morning, as she was washing, I caught a glimpse of her arms. They're purple with little bruises. She's even been pinching herself in the effort to stay awake.

Sarah couldn't read any more. She walked to the window, her arms folded, and looked out to the sea. It seemed to her that the salty waters were the tears that Mairead must have cried in that very room.

Low, ghostly music had started seeping up from downstairs. Sarah knew it was Niall playing, but to Sarah those were Mairead's trembling fingers touching the keys in a song of sorrow.

"What happened to you, Mairead?" she whispered, closing her eyes.

And then she gasped, forcing herself not to jump, not to move, not to scream, as she felt a hand run down her hair, lift a lock of it, gently, and then another, and small, cold fingertips caressing her cheeks with infinite tenderness.

As quickly as she appeared, she was gone, leaving Sarah wondering if she'd dreamt it after all.

A short while later, Nicholas came looking for her. "I think Mairead was in my room," Sarah whispered in his ear as they lay entangled on her bed.

"Was she?"

Sarah raised her eyebrows. "You don't seem surprised."

"Of course not. When the body goes, the spirit remains. For a while."

"She touched my cheeks, and my hair," murmured Sarah.

"Oh yes, I can see it. Look. She braided it." Nicholas lifted a plaited lock from the back of Sarah's head.

Sarah held the loose black braid in her hand, bewildered.

Come back, Mairead. Come back and speak to me.

"Who's Martyna?" Sarah asked suddenly. The question had been whirling in her mind since Nicholas's nightmare. She had to know. But she hadn't planned to ask him quite so abruptly.

Nicholas's face fell, and she could see a host of painful memories shaping his features into a mask of regret. "How do you know about her?"

"You said her name in your dreams last night. Is it . . . another girl?"

Nicholas resumed his usual calm demeanour, stroking Sarah's cheek, and then her hair. He was back in control. "Yes. A girl I loved once. But she died."

"She died? Oh, I'm so sorry." Then a lingering question.

She had to ask. "Was it the Surari?"

"Yes." He looked at her intently. "It was the Surari."

It was me.

"I'm so sorry," repeated Sarah.

I'm so sorry, Martyna.

37
Darkness

In death is freedom

Alone in his room, his eyes once more on the sea and the sky, Nicholas listened to the whispers and screams in his mind. He knew another attack was imminent, and he knew it would be the deadliest yet. He couldn't even trust his ravens anymore. The Elementals didn't show him any loyalty now. He knew that any decision about the fate of Sarah's friends was out of his hands, and that it was only a matter of time before the King of Shadows demonstrated the terrible extent of his powers. Juliet had been just the beginning – only Nicholas and Sarah were supposed to come back from Islay.

Even though everything he knew and understood was shifting, Nicholas was sure about what would happen in the next few days – he knew how his father worked. The Surari would be instructed to spare him and Sarah, and to kill everyone else, as was the original plan. Then he would be punished for having strayed, a punishment much worse than having his face pecked and scratched by his Elementals. So much worse – his thundering headache told him that. A taste of the brain fury. Enough of a warning.

But he would not be killed.

Not unless he betrayed his father's trust.

Nicholas had never believed that there could be any other option for him but to obey his father. But after all that had happened, he could see it now. There had been a choice all along. He could decide that he didn't want to be his father's puppet anymore. He could lift the fog that was still blocking Sarah's gift and allow her and the other Dreamers with her to dream again. Then they'd all know what was about to happen.

Nicholas put his head in his hands. The King of Shadows had terrible ways to kill his enemies. Would he be pecked to death by Spirits of the Air, drowned by Spirits of the Water, suffocated by Spirits of the Earth, consumed by Spirits of Fire? If all those failed – and they might because Nicholas was, after all, very powerful, and he would fight for his life – the Surari would intervene. And if by some weird occurrence the Surari failed to kill him, his father would simply use the full force of the brain fury. There was no escape from that; nobody ever survived once his father decided to unleash the whole of the brain fury.

If he did his father's bidding, though, he would survive, and live the life he was meant to. Fulfil his destiny as the heir of Shadows, and come the time when finally his father's life force faded, he would take his place.

When a spirit dissolves, there's nothing left; the body has gone long before, the soul is all that survives. And then the soul is gone too, leaving nothing but a memory.

Sometimes death seemed a better option.

Death was the way Martyna had chosen. Another black-haired girl ensnared in the King of the Shadows' plans, chewed up and spat out. *Martyna*. The name was like a curse in Nicholas's memory, the curse of the woman he had loved and helped destroy.

Martyna had been beautiful in a strong, insolent way, the kind of girl who would always get noticed wherever she went. It seemed as if light shone from inside her. She was a Dreamer, of course, and a powerful one. Over the years Nicholas had found ways to prevent himself from remembering, but memories have a way of ambushing you when you least expect it.

Nicholas was the one who'd chosen Martyna, not his father – and his biggest mistake, as the King of Shadows was so fond of reminding him, was falling in love with her. Nicholas asked his father not to start working on her mind straight away, to give him a chance to do things differently. And his father agreed.

Things went well, for a time. Or at least Nicholas thought they did. He succeeded in pretending there would be no mind-moulding needed, no deceit, that they could step out like any other man and woman in love. It was the best time of his life.

It didn't last long. The King of Shadows ended up taking control, as he always did in every matter concerning his son. Nicholas's mother cried and begged Nicholas to stop, to leave Martyna alone. Not to do to Martyna what had been done to her. But Nicholas was resigned. Deep down, he'd always known that their enchanted time, their time to love freely, had to stop sooner or later. It was fantasy, a useless masquerade, to pretend to be a mortal man with the chance to live a normal life. Martyna would never accept shedding her body and entering the Shadows forever, not unless they mind-moulded her. And slowly but surely his father made Nicholas see reason.

He proved to him that to destroy a woman in body and mind was the only way she could ever be convinced to come and live in the Shadow World. Nicholas was made to see that his pretence that things for Martyna and him could be different was just a pathetic dream.

The King of Shadows decimated Martyna's whole family in the space of one night. Between sunset and sunrise her parents and her sisters died, one by one, leaving only the ashes of burnt bodies. The sun rose on a world she couldn't recognize, a world she couldn't live in. It was too sudden and too traumatizing for her to accept. And she never did.

The day Martyna died was the worst day of Nicholas's life. He found her trapped among the reeds, her body floating face up, her hair covering her face, a face that used to be beautiful and that was now a blue mask of pain.

For a while after Nicholas wished he'd been with her when she drowned herself, and that he'd done the same. Her life was over because of him. She wasn't going to be anybody's wife now. Nicholas hadn't given a second thought to her parents or her sisters, just as he hadn't given a second thought to anyone they had caused death or despair to, but Martyna's destruction stayed with him, haunted him. He couldn't stop thinking about what had been done.

Maybe it was also because his mother had watched him do to Martyna what his father had done to her.

After that, Nicholas's mother was never the same. She refused to be kept prisoner anymore, and she took the only way she knew to be free again. Spirits live a long time, but they aren't eternal; they will, in time, fade away. Ekaterina let go of her will to live, and allowed herself to fade slowly, leaving nothing but a memory. She had only lived a few hundred years in the Shadows, a heartbeat from their point of view.

Martyna's fate had sealed his mother's desire for freedom, and in a way, Martyna's death set her free.

The love of his life and his mother. The two women he had loved and lost.

Nicholas went to visit their graves whenever he could. Ekaterina's grave had been built by her human family; they thought that she'd died of heartache because of her newborn son's death. They couldn't know, of course, that although her body was in that grave, her spirit was alive, imprisoned and bound to the Shadows. Martyna was buried in the same graveyard. Because she'd taken her own life, she shouldn't have been allowed to be entombed there, but the priest took pity on her and arranged for her to be buried against the stone wall, at the very edge of the cemetery, a few yards from her parents and sisters. Nobody except Nicholas ever visited Martyna, because her entire family were killed at their hands; there was nobody left. He was the only one who tended to her grave – and every time he went back it looked more abandoned, more forgotten.

Nicholas forbade himself from thinking that Sarah might follow the same path as his mother and Martyna. Sarah was stronger, wiser. More used to being alone, more used to suffering. Sarah would survive her destiny, he had to tell himself that.

Before she died, his mother had whispered her last wish, that when the time came for the King of Shadows to fade and leave his son to rule the Shadows, Nicholas would refuse. He had looked at her, desperately wanting to reassure her, but he'd said nothing.

38
Andromeda

Beneath the waves
What kills me
Is what saves me

It was nearly a relief to be in that place again. The place of
dreams, with the purple sky and the endless waves of swaying
grass, the heightened colours and the wind. Sarah sighed in
her sleep. At last the dreams were talking to her.

She was standing alone on soft, mossy ground, shivering
in her T-shirt and leggings. A salty smell invaded her nostrils,
and the muted sounds of the sea came from behind her. She
turned towards the sounds, and saw that she was standing on
the edge of a white sandy beach dotted with Venus shells. The
wind was making the sea dance, frothy and white-topped.
Sarah took in the beauty of it all, the near-emerald colour
of the waters, the translucent shells – a scene so enchanting
it could not be real, it could only be born in a dream. Such a
place was nowhere on earth.

But she didn't let the beauty deceive her. She knew what

that dreamy landscape hid. She knew what would happen, as always in her dreams. Her heart tightened in fear and anticipated rage.

Too much had happened for Sarah to be the trembling lost girl she had once been whenever a vision took her, resigned to another ordeal, frightened to her very core. Inexperienced, clueless, able only to yield to whatever came upon her.

The forces that she had encountered, and that she had survived, meant that she had now grown into herself. She was still frightened, but she had learnt how to handle it. She had embraced her Midnight blood at last. After having been deliberately shielded from her rightful inheritance of power throughout her childhood, her parents' death meant that she had finally reclaimed it, been forced to reclaim it. All that Sarah was meant to be, she was, at last. It was a conquest made of pain and loss, like most conquests, and it gave her strength, and a belief in herself she had never felt before. Only now, standing by the seashore, drawn there by her dreams, could she fully grasp how far she'd come. Her hands were burning, her senses were awake and alert. She stood on that beach flexing her hands, waiting to find out what was in store for her.

She didn't have to wait long.

It was Mermen who emerged from the sea, their scaly skin shimmering in an opaque rainbow, pale green and mother-of-pearl, their gills faintly throbbing in the transition between water and air, webbed hands at their side and wide mouths open to reveal row after row of thin, needle-like teeth. Two, four, six, ten of them, walking unhurriedly towards Sarah, waddling slightly from side to side, the sound of their gurgling breath coming nearer. They were close enough now for Sarah to see the barnacles attached to their skin, the sea anemones that had made a home on their chests, on their hips, on their legs, and the seaweed dangling from their arms like ripped clothes. Little creatures slithered over them, newborn eels and many-legged things that resembled woodlice. A slimy trail shimmered faintly behind them on the wet sand.

Sarah tried to calm her pounding heart – there were too many of them. They were going to kill her. The best course of action was at least to try and get as much information as she could out of the dream – when it would happen, and where – before they slaughtered her.

She drew a deep breath, her eyes glinting with the Midnight gaze. "Who sent you?" she screamed into the sea wind, her voice determined but coloured with the terror of what was soon to come.

The Mermen neither acknowledged her question nor replied. Instead they continued their silent march across the shore towards her. They resembled fish gasping for air, their mouths opening and closing intermittently, their gills pulsating in rhythm with their heartbeat. A nauseous smell of things decaying underwater wafted off them, carried towards Sarah on the wind.

"Answer me! Who sent you?" she repeated, and a bittersweet memory came back to her – how Sean used to get so impatient with her whenever she tried to communicate with the Surari. She used to try and communicate with them to avoid fighting, and it angered Sean no end, but this time she was on her own, and she was demanding the truth.

The Mermen were now a few yards away and coming closer, closer. There was no point in turning around and running. She could have outrun them, but she would have learnt nothing. She raised her hands, now scalding, and readied herself. Suddenly she felt something brushing her elbow and she jumped in alarm, but it was only Nicholas, having materialized beside her in perfect silence.

"Oh no," she whispered.

"I'm glad to see you too." He grinned sarcastically.

"I don't want you in this dream. You'll die too."

"No. I won't. And neither will you." And with that, Nicholas started shouting to the creatures at the top of his voice, with such fury that his fingers were sparkling blue and crackling with fire. Sarah could recognize only a few words as they were spoken in the ancient language, the one used by the human tribes during the Time of Demons.

Immediately the Mermen stopped in their tracks, and one of them replied in a gurgling, watery series of sounds that vaguely resembled the ancient language, but sounded alien as well, alien to this earth and all its creatures.

A dialogue followed that was fevered and full of anger on Nicholas's part, and calm and steady from the Merman. He kept repeating the same things, on and on, over and over.

Sarah turned and smiled sadly at him. "Nicholas, I don't think you can help me here," she said gently.

"Sarah . . ."

She turned back to the Mermen. "Come on! Come and get me!" she screamed, and as one, they starting moving up the beach towards them again.

Sarah could feel Nicholas tense at her side. Now that the sea creatures were right in front of them Sarah estimated that they were twice her size, their arms thick with sleek muscles. There must have been at least twenty of them. She'd never seen so many Surari in one place at the same time.

Another gust of wind, and Sarah gagged at the rotten smell that swept over her. Recovering quickly and ignoring Nicholas's muted pleas, she crouched slightly before leaping with a growl, her hands thrust forward, trying to grab at least one of the Mermen before they bit her, or drowned her, or whatever they were planning to do to put an end to her life. But the Merman she attacked didn't react by retaliating. He simply put one arm around her waist, lifted her off her feet and threw her aside effortlessly.

Sarah landed on the sand, her breath knocked out by the fall. For a few hazy seconds she watched as the slimy, wet fins of the Mermen moved towards her, then around her, marching over the dunes, leaving her behind. They weren't interested in Sarah. She wasn't the target.

Where are they heading?

Sarah sat upright and looked ahead of her. The landscape had changed; the sea and land had swapped places, so that the water was now in front of her. The Mermen were marching towards a formation of rocks that jutted out of the waves like rotten teeth.

Sarah stared aghast and peered into the gloom. She could see something tied onto each of the rocks – some*one*.

It was Niall, Elodie, Mike, and a bit further away, Sean. Her Sean. Their feet were dangling over the water, their hands bound behind them, and she could see now that their eyes were pools of horror and despair. They knew what was ahead of them. They were waiting for the sea to take them – they were like Andromeda, waiting for the sea monster.

Nicholas scrambled along the shoreline, shouting warnings one moment and threats the next, but the Mermen took no notice, continuing their march into the water, towards the rocks. It was as if they were being controlled by some other power. Sarah watched, frozen with horror. She couldn't speak, couldn't move, and worst of all, she couldn't close her eyes as, one by one, the Mermen climbed over her friends and tore their bodies limb from limb, ripping flesh from bone, leaving only trailing, reddened ropes of sinew behind.

Unable to take any more, Sarah threw herself on the sand, staring in silent despair. Why couldn't she have stopped them? Why couldn't Nicholas have stopped them? Eventually she found the strength to raise her eyes towards the scene of devastation. She felt her world spinning as she contemplated a lock of blonde hair strewn with blood floating on the incoming tide. All that was left of Elodie.

Sarah woke up panting, her eyes open wide in the pure, unbroken Islay darkness. The horror of the dream had been burnt into the back of her mind – she'd never get rid of it for as long as she lived. Her skin was covered in freezing sweat, her heart would not stop pounding, and the room was so dark, so silent that she couldn't even make out the shape of the furniture. All she could hear was the beating of her heart and the rush of blood in her ears.

Why? Why had the sea demons devoured her friends but not her and Nicholas?

Sarah felt the edge of her bedside table with a trembling hand and eventually found the lamp switch. Soft, yellow light illuminated the room. She sat up, and breathed deeply – once, twice, three times – trying to calm her heart. There was no doubting the dream. But despite its cruel clarity, there were things she didn't know or understand.

I've got to warn them. Now. She swung her legs over the side of the bed, bare feet on the ice-cold stone floor, and tiptoed out of the room. Nicholas slept at one end of the corridor, Sean's room was at the other. She stood for a long, long moment, hesitating – *which way to go?*

Finally, she made her choice.

★

He was awake, of course. When he'd heard the footsteps outside his room, he had got up instantly, weapon in hand. He was standing by the bed as Sarah pushed her way in.

Ready for anything, she thought, and felt better for knowing that. "It's me. Were you not sleeping?"

"You know me, I never sleep. Are you OK?" he whispered as she closed the door behind her.

"Yes. I dreamt again tonight. It's the first time since . . ." She shook her head, puzzled.

Their eyes met, and lingered for a moment. And then it happened – they were drawn towards each other like a planet and its moon.

Sean's body smelled just the same as it used to, of soap and of the sea, with a soft, lingering scent of coffee. She didn't want to let go, and he clung to her with all his might – it was as if they had come home to each other. But eventually they forced themselves to break their embrace and take a step back. Sarah's cheeks were scarlet in the darkness.

"Come here. Here, have this." Sean switched the table lamp on and took a blanket from his bed, wrapping it around Sarah's frozen shoulders as he sat her down in an armchair. Then he knelt in front of the fireplace and lit the fire. It didn't take long before she saw the soft, warm light reflected in his face, dancing over the old white scars on his arms and the more recent ones on his chest. He was wearing only a pair of sweatpants, and the glow of his skin, the strong contours of his body made Sarah want to run her hands over him, made her want to be close to him.

The horror of her dream followed so quickly by the

sudden rush of desire made Sarah's mind go blank and she sat immobile, rigid, unsure of what to do or say.

"What did you see?" Sean asked. He sat at her feet, looking up at her.

Sarah's emerald-green eyes widened at the memories as she pulled the blanket tighter around her shoulders. "Sea demons. Mermen. They were huge." She flinched, thinking of their wide, fish-like mouths and their razor-sharp teeth. "They came out of the sea, and I thought they were coming for me. But they ignored me. Just cast me aside. They . . ." She took a deep breath. The last thing she wanted was to recall the terrifying images.

Sean found her hand under the blanket and held it tight. Once more Sarah considered how big, how strong his hand was, and she clung to it, drawing strength from him. She braced herself to tell the last part of the story.

"You were there, tied to a sea rock. Niall, Mike and Elodie, too. The Mermen," she shuddered, "tore you all to pieces."

Sean grimaced, then recovered himself. "Was Nicholas not there?" he asked carefully.

Sarah nodded, frowning. "He was with me on the shore, trying to help me. He kept shouting and calling to the Mermen in the ancient language, trying to convince them to stop."

"Are you sure? You don't understand much of the ancient language. How would you know what he was saying?"

Sarah rubbed her forehead. "No, I don't, but the meaning was clear. He was begging them. Honestly, Sean, *begging* them. But they wouldn't stop."

Sean nodded, his manner almost businesslike. "Any indication of when this would happen?"

Sarah shook her head.

He stood up. "We must be ready then."

"Sean. They killed you." An abyss was opening slowly in her heart. All her strength, all her courage leaked away in the face of a world without Sean, and she was horrified to realize how much she needed him, how much she . . . *loved* him.

He stood there, looking at her, then once again knelt in front of her and took her hand. His striking blue eyes were full of longing, his face open and strong, his hair shone golden in the light of the fire. Sarah reached forward slowly and took hold of the red velvet pouch around his neck, the protection charm she'd made for him.

"I never took it off."

"I know."

They both felt at once what was to follow. Arms and lips looking for each other, irresistible as gravity, but almost immediately the sinking feeling in Sarah's stomach that she was betraying Nicholas, betraying her boyfriend, that she really ought to stop it now . . .

"Sean! Can I come in?" A voice at the door. Elodie.

Sean and Sarah looked at each other, shocked, the moment shattered.

"Come in," answered Sean, jumping to open the door. "Come in."

Elodie entered, pale and troubled. "Sean. I dreamt."

"You too."

"Oh," she gasped, her face tightening when she saw a pale-faced Sarah standing beside Sean's fireplace. "I didn't realize."

Sarah took in Elodie's graceful figure in her white cotton slip trimmed with lace, her slender legs, her arms like willow branches, her silky blonde hair cascading down her back. She was delicate, and perfect, and Sarah's heart sank. "I dreamt tonight too," she said quietly.

"Mermen?" Sean asked Elodie.

"Yes. It was horrible," Elodie replied, her accent made thicker by distress. "So what are we going to do? Wait until they come to get us?"

"All we can do is prepare ourselves as best we can. Elodie."

"Mmmm?" she replied, biting her lip.

"In Sarah's dream we were all killed, except Nicholas and Sarah."

"Yes. In mine too." Elodie's face was hard as she glanced over at Sarah. "What can this mean?"

"Nicholas was trying to stop them." Sarah assured her. "Trying to halt the attack. You must have heard that."

"Yes, I heard that too. And saw him. Just like he tried to stop the ravens from attacking me on the beach yesterday," pondered Elodie.

There was a gentle knock at the door and before they could answer, it swung open. "Hello. A pyjama party, and nobody told me?" Niall walked in, pushing a hand through his hair, his eyes sleepy and his feet bare.

"You dreamt too?" asked Sean.

"Yes. And judging by the colour of your faces, it was the same dream. I dreamt we were fish food. It wasn't pretty."

"The revenge of the clam?" chipped in Mike, appearing from behind Niall now. "After all the shellfish we ate in Louisiana?"

"More than likely," teased Sean briefly, but his face became deadly serious and a silence fell over the room.

Suddenly, Elodie gasped.

"You OK?" asked Sean.

"Yes, yes. It was just a shadow."

Sarah noticed that Sean's eyes rested on Elodie for a long

time after that, but the French girl didn't offer any further explanation. Sean brought his hands to his temples, massaging them. "I need to think this through."

"When's the first ferry?" asked Mike hopefully.

"To go where? They'd just follow us," Sarah replied. "At least here we're on familiar territory."

Sarah was interrupted by Elodie in a voice so frail yet firm that they all turned to her with concern. "No more running away," she whispered.

Sean nodded his agreement. "Elodie's right," he said.

"I think we need a drink," Mike concluded after a short pause.

The whole house instantly came alive with lights and footsteps and conversations as Mike and Niall took Elodie downstairs to steady their nerves. Sarah and Sean stayed behind.

"I don't want to be alone," Sarah whispered.

"Go to Nicholas then," replied Sean immediately, his voice harsh.

Sarah wasn't expecting that. It was as if she'd just been punched in the stomach, the air knocked out of her. Sean had turned away from her.

"OK. I will. Yes." She walked towards the door, reeling from Sean's response.

At the doorway, he took her arm and turned her until he was looking straight into her eyes. "Nicholas is your boyfriend, after all."

"Yes."

"Because if he weren't, I'd ask you to stay here with me."

Sarah froze.

Too much.

Too much, too confusing. Too complicated.

The dreams coming back, the choices she was faced with. The danger. The one choice she didn't know how to make.

"You can't ask me to choose now, Sean. Can you not see?" she whispered, her mind somewhere between being angry and imploring him for a reprieve.

"If not now, when, Sarah? It's not likely to get better, is it?" He took her by the shoulders firmly. "Do you love Nicholas?"

There was nothing she could do but to tell Sean the truth for once — to reveal herself, and reveal her heart.

"I don't know what love is," she said, with a clear, steady gaze.

Sean's eyes were solemn, unsmiling, when he replied. "Yes you do. And when you decide to admit it, I'll be there."

It's a promise, Sarah.

39
Be Ready

Rules of the heart
Before rules of the mind
Be ready then to face
The time to fall

Nicholas had been in his room, standing in front of the open window. All he could see was darkness, except for the intermittent lighthouse beam shining from beyond the hill. His whole body was alert, and a film of sweat coated his forehead. His nails sank into the palms of his hands.

Earlier that evening he had lifted the fog that had enveloped Sarah and the other Dreamers for weeks. Now he would wait for her to dream and for her to tell the others what she had seen, what she'd been finally allowed to discover. Nicholas knew what would happen next and he had stood there waiting for them to come and challenge him. Or hunt him down, probably. He was ready to defend himself.

To be human is to be afraid. Tonight, I'm wholly human.
Any time now.

When Nicholas felt Sarah's dream starting, he had forced his mind into hers. He made himself witness it, and he couldn't believe what he saw. He was still shattered by what had happened.

In Sarah's dream, he had seen himself trying to stop the Mermen, trying to protect Elodie, Mike, Niall. Even Sean. Sarah had read his heart before he could read it properly himself. In her dream, for the first time in a long time, his mind and his heart had acted in harmony.

The cold air crept over his moist skin, making him shiver. He couldn't bring himself to move. For some time his gaze remained fixed on the black sea, as waves of shock at his own behaviour swept over him.

I have chosen. Or destiny has chosen for me.

Suddenly there were noises and lights going on in the house, shining out into the garden, and people coming and going outside his door. *They must know by now.*

Nicholas closed the window and let himself fall backwards onto his bed, his eyes staring up towards the ceiling. He didn't have long to wait. The brain fury hit him almost immediately – his father's wrath was merciless. Right at that moment he heard rapid tapping at the glass. Turning as best he could within the pain, he caught a glimpse of sharp beaks and beady black eyes, and then came the voices from the Shadow World screaming, screaming, using every possible argument and threat to get him back.

It was worse than he could have possibly imagined. He lay in agony, knowing that finally the die was cast and that there would be no salvation. Not for him. He felt Sarah coming into the room, but he wasn't ready for her. He lay still, calm, pretending to be in a deep sleep, using the last of his self-control not to cry out with the pain that exploded in his head.

He was aware of her standing by his bed for a few seconds, then walking out as quietly as she had come in – a ray of moonshine sweeping the room and disappearing.

No salvation for me, but I'll keep you safe. And I'll keep you with me, Sarah Midnight.

40
Comet

Is it written, is it chance?
The way we move and the way we go
The way it will all end

Something is not right. Everything is not right.

All Niall's radars were roused in alarm, but he couldn't figure out where the threat was coming from, he couldn't figure out who was with them and who was against. He was just relieved that Winter hadn't been in his dream, that she wasn't among those killed. It didn't mean she'd come to no harm at all, but he clung to the little hope he had that she'd survive.

He'd heard Elodie gasp in the gloom, and somehow he knew, as surely as he knew his own name, that she'd had a vision. As they were making their way slowly downstairs for a drink, he caught her elbow and gently made her stop.

"Tell me," he whispered.

"What?" Immediately she looked away, defensive.

"What did you see?"

"In my dream? We all had the same dream. You know what I saw."

"No." Niall shook his head. "Afterwards. In Sean's room. You saw something there, I'm sure of it. And you were horrified. I saw the look on your face. What did you see?"

Elodie pleaded with him. "Don't make me tell you, Niall. Please."

"I need to know."

"I . . ." She turned away.

Niall grabbed Elodie's wrist, a gesture so weird for him, so out of character, that Elodie was alarmed. "I need to know," he told her in a measured staccato.

Elodie took a deep breath. "I saw one of us . . ."

Niall's eyes narrowed. "One of us?"

"It's difficult to explain. One of us . . . wasn't there. There were five of us in that room. And then suddenly, there were four."

"Which one of us?" asked Niall calmly.

"I don't know."

"If it was me you can tell me, Elodie. I'm not afraid."

Elodie looked him straight in the eyes. "Believe me. I don't know! The vision only lasted a second. I didn't see who it was. I swear to you. Now let's go downstairs."

Niall studied her face. She was telling the truth. He eased his grasp on her wrist, and Elodie continued down the stairs, flushed with anger.

Which one of us?

41
The Last Letter

Your voice across the years
Told me why they said
You never smiled

Sarah waited until she heard Sean's rapid footsteps on the stairs. Then she crept along the hall and let herself into Nicholas's room. He was fast asleep, immobile, his breathing heavy and regular. *Strange*, she thought. *How can he sleep when the whole house is awake?*

A tapping at the window made her jump. Through the glass she saw a beak tapping, and a confusion of wings and black, shiny bodies – the ravens, crowding Nicholas's windowsill. The sight of them pressing and pushing against the glass as if they wanted to come in made her shiver.

She tiptoed back to her room. There she was alone once more in a daze of sleeplessness, still reeling from the horror of the dream, but also from Sean's words.

If these are the last days of my life, who do I want to spend them with?

She took a moment to steady herself. Her entire body and soul screamed for her to be back in Sean's embrace.

She lit the fire – the room was so cold that she could see her breath coming out in little white clouds – and opened the box she'd stored the letters in. All that was left, as far as she could see, was one last letter in the same creamy paper as the others, and a few loose pages torn from notebooks, lists and receipts and various bits of paperwork. One last letter left to read, and the dreams had started again. She felt the chill breeze from the storm to come, and she was suddenly sure that her time to leave Islay would be soon.

One last letter.

She wrapped herself in her duvet and started reading.

Midnight Hall, Islay
November 1987
Dear Amelia,
I have to tell someone. It all weighs in my heart so. I need to take it out before it rips me inside. I just don't know how it happened. It feels as if someone else had planned it, and I carried it out. But it was me who planned it, though I struggle to believe it. I always believed that we are all here for a reason – us Secrets, I mean. If we don't fulfil our purpose, what's the point of our existence? I never thought I, out of all of us, could give birth to a useless heir, someone who doesn't rise to her mission. Someone like my sister could have given birth to a failure, but not me. Not me.

The letter continued along the same lines. Sarah frowned. The tone was all wrong. Was this Morag? So emotional. Out of control, even. But yes, the handwriting was the same. Sarah's eyes travelled to the bottom of the page to check the signature, but there was none. The letter finished abruptly in the middle of a sentence:

I know it's all over now, and it's for the best, but

That was it. No more. Sarah checked the box again. No more creamy paper, no more letters. Just a bunch of crinkled scraps remained.

She tidied the letters away, and sat looking at the flames, losing herself in the dancing shapes. She ended up falling asleep in the armchair in front of the fire as a grey winter dawn broke over the sea.

No dreams came to haunt her sleep, but when she woke up and went to the bathroom, she saw that her hair was dotted with tiny braids again, made by fingers so light that she hadn't felt a thing.

Where's the rest of the letter, Mairead? Sarah asked her reflection, stroking the braids softly, as if it had been Mairead's hair she was caressing.

Winter was brushing her hair in front of the open window, unaffected by the cold wind, when she saw Sarah running up the hill towards her.

"Winter!" Sarah called when she saw the silver-haired girl.

"Sarah!" she waved, and ran to greet her.

By the time Winter appeared at the top of the stairs Sarah was standing on the doorstep, panting after the run, her cheeks very pink, her hair blowing dark and silky behind her. The door of the cottage was wide open, and the wind was blowing in – the whole house was freezing, and it smelled of the sea. Winter didn't much care for the difference between "outside" and "inside".

"Winter. There's a page missing from this letter. Look." She showed her the final page she'd read.

"I know."

"You *know*?"

"Yes. I kept it from you."

Sarah was astonished, and angry at how easily Winter admitted that.

"Why?"

Winter said nothing. She was less sure of herself now, looking for the right words, but in vain. How could she explain?

I just don't want her to know, Winter thought. *I don't want her to suffer. Can I tell her? Can I tell her that I don't want her to suffer? Would she understand?*

"Come outside. I feel stifled in the house, I need to feel the wind," she said.

Sarah rolled her eyes. *Fine, feel the wind. As long as you give me an explanation.*

They stood just outside the house, facing the grassy patch that sloped towards the sea, turning into sand mid-way down the hill. Neither of them spoke. There was a fine drizzle falling from the wintry sky, blown around by the wind. The ocean was foaming with menace, and a herd of clouds was galloping in from the west. Soon, very soon, the drizzle would turn into a downpour, and the rough sea would turn into a stormy one.

"Look at the sky, Winter," said Sarah impatiently. "It's going to pour in a minute." The clouds were taking on a sinister look. "Tell me about the letter. Where is it?"

"Yes. This is all so complicated."

Sarah was ready to scream with the combination of frustration and cold. "What's complicated? Do you have it or not? The missing letter?" Her hair was blowing over her face.

She swept it away and tried in vain to stop it from getting tangled.

Winter studied Sarah's face. Sarah Midnight was all she imagined her to be, and more. *The power in her heart and soul is so strong that I feel it vibrating under my skin every time she's around. She's very much like her grandmother, Morag – only Sarah is kind. I can see it in her eyes.*

"I have it," Winter admitted finally. "I just don't want you to read it."

Sarah frowned, but tried to remain calm. "It's not up to you. It belongs to my grandmother. It's mine. I have all the right to read it."

"You have the right to read it, yes. It's just that . . ."

Sarah scrutinized Winter's face. "I can tell you this, Winter. I'm fed up with people hiding things from me because they want to protect me, OK? My parents did it, Sean did it, and look where it took me! Up until a few months ago I didn't even know how to use my own powers, and it almost killed me. Enough secrets. I don't need protecting. I want that letter, Winter. Now."

"Sarah."

"Have you destroyed it?" Sarah demanded, anger flashing in her eyes.

"I wanted to, but I knew it wasn't my place to do that. I just couldn't destroy that memory. It wasn't up to me."

"No, it's not up to you." A roar of thunder rattled through the skies. Winter could see Sarah's lips moving, but the final part of her sentence was carried away by the noise. The waves were getting bigger, and a thin, jagged string of lightning cut through the sky in the west. The light turned suddenly livid, eerie.

As she looked into Sarah's face, Winter saw her, Morag

Midnight, playing in her features like blood memories do.

"Sarah," she blurted out. "There's more to your family than you imagine. The Midnights wanted me dead. And they nearly succeeded."

"What? Why?" Sarah cried out, then her features rearranged themselves into suspicion. "I can only think of one reason they would want you dead. You are—" Instinctively she flexed her hands and her Midnight eyes began to shimmer.

For a second, Winter was afraid. "A *demon*? No. I told you the truth. I'm half human, half Elemental."

"Then why—"

"Your grandmother didn't really approve of mixing species, so to speak." Winter shuddered, remembering the catalogue of ghastly words Morag had used for her mother – whore, among many others. And for her: half-breed, bastard child. Monster.

"I still don't understand." Sarah flung out her arms in frustration. "Explain, please!"

"Your family . . . they never cared much for Elementals. Mainly because they can't be controlled easily. The Midnights could never control them, anyway. And they certainly didn't approve of new breeds. That was considered totally unacceptable. Secret people marrying Lays was bad enough, but a human and an Elemental having a child with potentially unknown powers? Surely you were aware of this?"

"I told you, my parents hid things from me. I didn't even know there were other Secret heirs in the world. I thought it was just us."

Winter had to assume that James and Anne Midnight had their reasons for keeping their daughter in the dark as they'd done, but to leave Sarah ignorant was to leave her unarmed. "You see, Secret men can marry Lay women and the powers are passed on, but not the other way round. The children of Secret women and Lay men won't inherit any Secret power, no Blackwater, in your case."

Sarah shrugged. "My parents never told me. I suppose if they had, they would have had to explain that there were other Secret Families, and from there . . ."

"I think they would have had to tell you sooner or later, because I can't imagine James letting you marry a Lay."

"I can't imagine my dad letting me marry anyone he didn't choose for me," said Sarah quietly, a chill running down her spine as she realized what that implied about her father.

"Yes, your father could be quite . . . controlling. He did, after all, try to kill me."

Sarah stared at Winter. Winter read the horror in her eyes, and a sense of compassion invaded her. Sarah really didn't know her father. At all.

"I don't understand." Sarah's voice became small. "So they disapproved of what your mother did, and of you." She gave a little laugh. "Fair enough, I suppose. As far as I know my grandmother disapproved of the whole world, really. But trying to kill you . . ."

"As I said, Sarah, you really don't know much about them."

"Then you need to tell me. I want to know."

"I'm sorry," whispered Winter, taking Sarah's hands in hers. "I wish I didn't have to be the one. Listen. Whatever happens, I want you to remember one thing, Sarah. You're not like them. Do you hear me? I can see it in your eyes. I saw it all along, since the first time I met you. You're not like your parents."

Sarah felt sick. "What did they do to you, Winter?" she asked.

"It doesn't matter what they did or didn't do to me. Not

now. I'll give you the last letter. Then you'll know what happened to Mairead."

As she watched Sarah's baffled expression she suddenly recalled a quote from the Bible, one that her mother had been very fond of: The truth will set you free.

Would the truth set Sarah free, or would it destroy her?

I have to have faith in the last of the Midnights, I have to believe that Sarah will survive, and that she'll be different, thought Winter.

"Winter!" called Sarah suddenly, bringing her back to the present.

Something in her voice made Winter's heart jump. Sarah's face was turned skyward, and when Winter followed her gaze she saw something moving amongst the livid clouds. Something black, skeletal, gliding slowly towards them.

"It's the demon-bird," whispered Sarah, flexing her hands.

Winter breathed in sharply. She'd seen demons before, but she'd never been attacked by one. "What shall we do?"

"You go inside. I'll see to it."

"I'm not leaving you on your own, Sarah!"

"Don't be stupid! You weren't made for this. Apparently I was." She laughed mirthlessly. "Go inside! I can't have your death on my conscience."

"Sarah!"

Sarah had no choice. She turned her gaze on Winter's and the silver-haired girl whimpered in pain. "If you don't go inside right now, I'll keep going. If you think that's painful, I can do worse."

Winter had no choice but to obey. She ran inside and upstairs, watching from the window of her bedroom as the horrific bird swooped slowly towards Sarah. The storm had made its way round the bay and was moving back towards them, the swollen clouds had opened up, and a shower of rain, tossed around by the wind, began falling on the beach.

"Come on, come on," Sarah murmured to herself, her hands scalding already. "Come on!" Sarah shouted again over the sound of the storm, wiping her face with her hands. The rain didn't seem to affect the flight of the creature at all, but the wind was buffeting it, making it glide from left to right, forcing it to turn into itself with a flap of its leathery wings as it made its slow progress towards Sarah.

She was breathing heavily, ready for the fight, furious and frightened and ready to kill. "Come and get me!" she taunted the demon once more.

A blade of lightning cut the sky, illuminating the creature for a moment. Sarah could make out the beaked head, the enormous black wings, and the emaciated shape of its body, tiny in comparison to the wings. And the claws, silhouetted against the leather of the demons' wings – long and sharp enough to eviscerate a human being.

Mum, Dad, protect me, thought Sarah as a bout of fear swept through her. The demon-bird was circling now, closer and closer – soon it would land.

"Sarah!" A voice came from above her. It was Winter calling from the window, but whatever she was saying was drowned by a new clap of thunder, and by the time the noise was over, the creature had landed. It was standing a hundred yards away on its own two feet despite the wind, its wings folded and resting at its sides.

And it started striding towards her.

Sarah was ready, hands raised, eyes flashing. The Midnight gaze hadn't worked on the demon-bird the night it had attacked her, and it wasn't working now. Unperturbed, the Surari walked on, nearer and nearer. Sarah's chest tightened once she could see its face, the almond eyes, dark as coal, the black mane falling over its shoulder, and the long, bony beak.

Suddenly the demon-bird took flight, rising with its wings outstretched, readying itself to pounce on Sarah from above. Sarah raised her hands, her eyes wide with terror and flashing green. In a single bound the creature landed on her and threw her to the ground, its beak inches from her face.

Sarah's eyes were deadly green, but the creature was still unaffected. Furious, Sarah grabbed its wings with her burning hands, but again, the demon didn't flinch.

Her heart missed a beat.

Is the Blackwater not working either?

She fumbled, trying to take hold of the demon's flesh. Its almond eyes were fixed on hers, its beak poised to strike. Finally, Sarah managed to grab its shoulders, and the demon froze just as its beak readied to pierce Sarah's face. It groaned, a muffled sound that to Sarah's ears sounded too human for comfort. But she would show no mercy. She tightened her grip on the demon-bird and watched it squirm while the Blackwater dissolved its skin.

"Sarah!"

Sean?

Sarah's concentration wavered for a split second, and the demon took its chance, slashing at her with its claws, wounding her bare throat. She screamed in pain and fury. She knew exactly what it was aiming at – her jugular. In a haze of pain, Sarah grabbed at its shoulders again, digging her fingers into its flesh. When she dared to turn her head slightly towards Sean's voice, there he was, tracing the runes with his *sgian-dubh*, slashing the air.

The demon-bird began thrashing, pummelled by Sean's runes. With enormous effort it freed itself from Sarah's grip and leapt up, staggering between Sarah and Sean, watching them with eyes full of pain.

Pain. Sadness. What is this demon about? How can a demon look . . . sorrowful?

Sarah shook herself. She saw Niall, Elodie and Mike rushing up the slope towards Sean, Niall already humming his song. Frantic now, the demon swept around to face them all, then turned back to Sarah. It was her blood that was on its claws.

Then, as if a brake had been put on the world, they heard the creature say, loud and clear, "Sarah Midnight." Everybody froze.

Sarah's heart stopped for a second. Stars danced before her eyes as she clutched her bleeding skin. Strange. She felt no pain. She looked at her friends, but they stood stunned in the rain. Niall's song was rising higher and higher, and a subtle pain was beginning to make its way into their ears, but the Surari seemed unaffected, just like he'd been by Sarah's gaze.

"What are you? What do you want from me?" demanded Sarah, trying to disguise the panic she was feeling.

"You're talking to demons. Again!" yelled Sean, punctuating each word with a hit of his blade. The Surari brought a clawed hand to its chest, mirroring Sarah's gesture, and it came away bloodied, its blood mixed with Sarah's. With one last look, the creature spread its wings and lifted itself without effort, despite the blood pouring from its chest.

Sarah growled in anger as she watched it fly upwards. "Running away again? Scared to face us, you coward?"

The demon rose up to the height of Winter's window, and they watched in horror as the Surari and Winter, frozen in fear, looked at each other.

"Winter!" Niall called frantically.

But the demon wasn't interested in attacking her, and instead continued its ascent, gliding on the wind. It rose towards the clouds and disappeared into the stormy sky.

Sean wrapped his arm around Sarah's waist. "Are you OK?"

Sarah nodded. "I'm fine," she said. "I'm just fine." And then she fell unconscious into Sean's arms.

42
Wounds of the Body

Wounds of the soul
The ones you don't see
Will never heal

"It was worse than we thought." A voice, coming from afar.

And another voice. "Pretty deep wound. Shit, it nearly got her."

Sarah opened her eyes and blinked repeatedly, letting the world fall into focus. Her throat was dry, and her entire body ached.

"You're awake." The first voice again.

Sarah turned towards the sound. It was Elodie. Yes, Elodie. Sitting on her bed, holding her hand.

"What happened?" her voice came out weak and croaky. Her lips were parched.

"That bird thing hurt you. Quite badly. You lost a lot of blood."

"Oh."

"Don't worry, Sarah, you'll be fine soon," Elodie said

gently, stroking her face. Sarah closed her eyes, relishing in that unexpected tenderness. Gradually, memories began to answer some of the questions hurtling round her head.

"The demon-bird. Did we kill it?"

Elodie shook her head. "No. Not yet."

Sarah winced.

"Don't think of that now. We'll find it, I promise you," Elodie reassured her.

"Sarah!" It was Nicholas, barging into the room.

"Where were you?" said Elodie, getting up to make room for him on the edge of Sarah's bed. Nicholas ignored her.

"Sarah, what did they do to you?" he murmured.

"Really, I'm OK. Please stop fussing," she repeated with as much irritation as she could muster. She felt so weak. "Help me sit up."

It took a while, and it hurt, but once Nicholas had propped her up with all the pillows he could find, Sarah could see, out of the corner of her eye, that there was someone else sitting in the armchair beside the fireplace. Once her eyes had become accustomed to the light she saw that it was Sean, mute and pale, watching her.

"I'm *fine*," she called to him, anticipating the question.

He nodded, still silent.

Sarah could sense his fear. An invisible hand squeezed her heart. "Really, Sean. I am," she said, softer this time.

Sean rose slowly and walked towards the bed. Nicholas, his head bowed, didn't move an inch. Sarah stretched out her hand to Sean, and when he took it, she drew him closer. Nicholas was forced to step aside as Sean sank onto the bed.

He looked ghastly. "I thought I'd lost you."

"No way. Not for a stupid bird, anyway." She laughed briefly, her breath catching at the pain in her side.

Sean smiled wanly.

"How did you know what was happening? Was it Winter who called you? Some sort of sea call or something? A power she didn't tell us about?"

Sean smiled, more broadly this time. "Sort of," he said. "It was a mobile phone. She called me."

Sarah laughed weakly despite herself.

"Winter asked me to give you this," Sean added, handing her a rolled up piece of paper he was holding. "She said that you had been looking for it."

It was the missing letter. Sarah clutched it as a thought darted through her mind: *Where had Nicholas been when she'd needed him?*

43

A Child in the Water

In between two worlds
In between two bodies
One whole me

Winter saw her hair floating on the waves: the Midnight child, the blonde, quiet little girl she had played with so many times. She dived at once and swam towards her as quickly as she could. The water was freezing. In her human form Winter felt the cold on her skin, a million tiny needles piercing her. It was unbearable, but she knew that if she changed, she wouldn't have arms to hold Mairead with, so she tried to endure it. The cold took her breath away. She thought her heart would stop. After a few seconds she just couldn't take it anymore, she couldn't breathe, she couldn't move. She willed herself to keep going, and she did, though pain ripped through her chest and black sparks danced before her eyes.

Winter had no time to ask herself what had happened for Mairead to be floating in the frozen sea, but she knew that whatever tragedy had befallen the little girl, it was a long time coming. She had sat beside Mairead on the beach many times, basking in the moonlight the way her father used to do. She had heard Mairead crying and calling in despair after her dreams, and nobody comforting her.

At last Winter was there, so close to Mairead that she could entangle her fingers in her hair, pale strands twisted around her human hands. She tried holding the little girl in every way she could – by the arms, by the chest, by the head – but she was just a little girl herself.

Finally the cold and distress had the best of Winter. Her breath faltered and her body started turning by itself. She had no way to stop the transformation. She kept swimming around Mairead in a circle, begging her with her seal eyes to hold onto her. Winter had no more power of speech, no arms, and her skin was slippery, but she could have helped her. Mairead could have held on, had she wanted to.

She didn't.

Winter caught her eyes for a second, those green eyes, her wet eyelashes – from tears or seawater, Winter couldn't tell – and they were far gone, somewhere else already. She watched the girl sinking slowly. She watched the black sky, the black waters, the faint glow of the lighthouse beam moving slowly on their stretch of sea, from east to west, from west to east, until there was no more blonde hair left to illuminate. When it was finished, Winter pushed her body back to shore for her mother and father to find. Then she looked for a lonely place among the sea rocks, to cry and mourn in peace the girl she couldn't save.

Winter's mother had always told her, since she was a little girl, to keep her real nature a secret. Nobody would understand, she'd said. The other children from the island would be scared, even if stories about creatures like her have been told here since the beginning of time. *Selkies*.

But most of all, she had to keep her nature a secret from the Midnights, her mother always admonished her. And Winter managed to do that, even though she used to play with Mairead all the time, and even though she was at Midnight Hall a lot when her mum was working there.

For years, it was easy to hide her true nature. From babies to young men and women, people with Elemental blood grow at a normal pace, like everybody else. It's only once they reach young adulthood that they start growing older slowly, so slowly as to give the illusion they stayed young forever. Winter always knew that when she reached the age of eighteen or so, she would have to isolate herself from the community on the island, and live somewhere truly wild where nobody knew her, or they would notice that she wasn't growing old.

But before that time came, the Midnights found out about her in an entirely different way.

Mairead had been dead two years. Winter was seventeen. It was a perfect sunny day, and she was on the beach with the seals, sitting among them. They were lying in the sunshine, basking in the light and the fresh wind. Winter was happy and relaxed, and for the first time in her life – the first and last time – she took to her seal form without first making sure that she could not be seen. It was a mistake.

When she clambered back on the rock, she saw him watching her.

For a second Winter thought it was Stewart. Stewart and Winter had played together as children, though he was three years older than her, and as they grew up, he'd started looking at her with different eyes. Winter knew he liked her, and he was gentle and kind. Not like the rest of the family. Had it really been Stewart, Winter could have explained, she could have begged him to keep it a secret.

But it was James.

Winter, having changed back into her human form, was frozen to the spot, horribly, painfully aware that she was naked, though it had never bothered her before. He strode towards her, an avenging angel with a black soul.

"How could you, Winter? I don't even want to look at you."

"James . . ."

"You're not even an animal! You're a monster!"

Winter thought she'd never forget his eyes as he was shouting at her, so intensely green. And his hair so golden. He looked like the prince from a fairy tale, like a knight in shining armour, and yet she'd always known that beyond his appearance there was a soul as hard and as cruel as a blade.

"Your mother is a whore, and so are you. Cover up." He averted his eyes, as if Winter's body disgusted him. "Come to the house. Now. We'll have to decide what to do."

She didn't go up to the house, of course. She ran home and cried with her mother. Murdina Shaw was beside herself with worry. The man everybody thought was Winter's father, Hugh Shaw, had died the year before, and her real father had left long ago. Winter and Murdina were alone, and they had no idea what to do.

They were summoned. Hamish himself went to their cottage – something never seen before, the laird walking into the little house – and asked them to go and speak to him and Morag, that they would sort it all out, that Murdina could keep her job and her home and everything would be fine.

Winter and Murdina stood in the grand hall, ready to take judgement. Murdina had her head low, though she'd done

271

nothing wrong, while Winter felt James's eyes burning into her, travelling over her body in a way that made her cringe. When he'd seen her on the rocks there was something in his eyes that wasn't loathing, or righteous indignation. His gaze had lingered on Winter a little longer than it should have had he been so thoroughly disgusted by her as he'd said he was. Fear blossomed in Winter's chest. She knew then that she had a place somewhere in James's black heart, the place where he kept cruelty and desire.

Morag and Hamish reassured Murdina that she could keep her position as housekeeper and that there was no need to leave the cottage. They told her that they knew she'd been deceived, and misled, and it wasn't her fault she'd ended up having a child out of wedlock, and with a … spirit, Morag said, spitting out the word. They said they could accept Winter's presence on Islay as long as she kept herself hidden, and as long as they were happy with her behaviour. Things would change if she were to *mate* with another Elemental. That's the word they used, as if Winter were a beast.

"If we get the slightest hint that you're conniving with demons, Winter, we'll crush you," Morag said calmly.

"Why would I?" Winter replied, aghast. "Why would I ever do that?"

"Some Elementals end up serving the Surari, Winter. They become their minions, or even their slaves. If that happens to you, I'll make sure I'll rip that seal skin off your body myself."

As Morag said that, Murdina sobbed and brought her hands to her face. The sound of her fear and horror echoing in high-ceilinged room was burnt forever in Winter's memory – and the sight of Morag, with Hamish and James on either side, sitting in judgement of them like a heartless queen.

They were dismissed with a wave of her hand.

Stewart met them on the way back to the cottage. Murdina held onto Winter's arm, gasping as she saw him.

"It's fine, Mrs Shaw. I'm here to help."

Murdina breathed out, relaxing ever so slightly, but Winter didn't allow herself to hope.

Stewart continued, "Winter, listen. They're not going to harm you. They just want to keep an eye on you, that's all. I'm sorry."

Winter looked into his face, so similar to James's and yet so different – gentler, with dark green eyes, mellower than the harsh emerald of his brother's. "You *knew*, Stewart. Didn't you?"

"I've seen you a few times," he said, blushing. "I never told anyone, I promise you."

"Of course. I believe you. So, do you think it'll be OK? Do you think I can stay?"

"I'm sure. They just wanted to scare you. They've made their point now. Just . . . don't step out of line and you'll be fine. Mrs Shaw?"

"Yes, my lad?" Murdina put a grateful hand on his arm.

"I'm sorry," he said softly.

Since that moment, Winter often wondered what would have happened between Stewart and her had she not left. She doubted he would have gone against his family, but she'd never know.

Stewart was wrong, of course. They didn't leave Winter alone. James didn't. She kept well away, trying to melt into the landscape, spending most of her time in the sea on the other side of the island. She hoped that would be enough, that she wouldn't have to leave.

But one afternoon, James came looking for her. He wasn't

angry. He wasn't out of control. It wasn't rage that had taken hold of him and brought him there to Machir Bay, looking for silver-haired Winter. She saw him from afar, striding on the sand, a young man of nineteen with cold eyes and something in his hand: a silver dagger, engraved with Celtic patterns. She stood from where she was sitting on the rocks overlooking the sea.

Rage burnt inside her. With all her heart and soul, she hated him. And she hated Morag Midnight. They had destroyed Mairead, and they had sat in judgement of her mother. They'd called her a monster, an abomination. She hated them both, and Hamish too.

James stopped at the feet of the sea rocks and looked at Winter with cool, calm eyes.

"I'm getting married soon. To Cathy."

She was taken aback. What was he expecting her to say, congratulations?

"Poor Cathy," she replied.

"Very funny. By the time I get married, I want this island to be *clean*."

Winter understood at once what he meant. She knew that the blade he was carrying was for her.

"I won't use the Blackwater, Winter. It'd be too painful for you. I'll use this," he raised his *sgian-dubh*, "and I'll make it quick. You might as well let me do it, because sooner or later, I'll get you."

Winter was terrified, but anger had the best of her fear. She saw red, and threw herself on him. He was too strong for her, Winter's only real strength was in the water. He held her down, and his hands were burning her skin already.

"Not the Blackwater," she implored, hating herself for begging, but to have her skin and flesh and bones melt away like she was some demon . . . She didn't want to die that way, she couldn't.

"No. Don't worry, Winter," he said, and his voice became strangely soft. "It won't take long." He looked her straight in the eye as he pushed the *sgian-dubh* into her side, slowly, tenderly even. When he took it out Winter thought she'd die from the pain, but he stroked her hair and held her.

"Shhhh. It'll be over soon," he whispered.

But it wasn't over soon at all. He had pierced her so that she would lose blood slowly, and her agony would last a long time.

James walked away as if nothing had happened, leaving Winter on the sand.

She implored him to come back. "Please don't leave me," she said, hating herself for having begged him twice, but she wanted to live. She was too young, too full of life never to swim again, never to lie in the sun again.

He didn't come back, of course. Winter watched James Midnight walk away, feeling the whole world spin as the little patch of bloody sand beside her became bigger and bigger. She crawled into the sea, dragging herself inch by inch, and let the water enfold her. Her despair eased at once, because at least she was going to die in the water – given the circumstances, she felt she couldn't ask for more.

But it wasn't her time.

Her sight was blurred, she was weak, she knew she was lost, and then she heard a high-pitched, whale-like sound, and a whisper. "*Hemalla, putri . . .*"

It was her father in his Elemental form. He was a whirlpool of water, a bit darker, a bit denser than the sea, vaguely seal–shaped. He cradled Winter to him and swirled around her until everything went black and she was sure she'd died.

★

Winter woke to find herself on a rock in the middle of the sea, so far from the shore that she couldn't see land anywhere. She was surrounded by a pack of seals, their black noses nudging her legs, a fin resting on her arm, as close as they could get, to make her strong again. Her wound was agony, but it wasn't bleeding anymore. Her father had healed her.

She swam ashore and slipped into her mother's cottage – Murdina cried as she heard what had happened, but she promised to pretend Winter was dead. It was the only way.

Winter swam to Jura, and up to Colonsay, and there she lived, mostly alone with the seals. She didn't return to Islay until her mother got ill. By then Hamish and Morag had died, Cathy's destiny was a mystery – she had been sent away – and James was in Edinburgh. Winter couldn't leave her mother to die alone, and she couldn't take her away from the island, it would have broken her heart. She had no choice but to return.

Not long after her return to Islay word came through that James and his second wife, Anne, had died too. The family was finished, but for Sarah Midnight and for Stewart's son, Harry, in London. Winter knew already that Stewart had ended up rejecting the Midnights, and that he'd moved to New Zealand and died young. Winter never set eyes on a Midnight again, until Sarah arrived. She felt no hate for her. Stewart was a kind man, and Mairead was as innocent as a seal pup – Winter couldn't hate the whole family.

And Sarah? Would she be like her father, like her grandmother?

Maybe Sarah would be the one who saved the Midnights, who restored them to their old power, to the way they were always meant to be – protectors, guardians of them all.

44

A Child Ashamed

She was told they knew
She was one of them
A child ashamed,
Already sure
Her blood was black

. . . I wish I could ask for forgiveness. I wish I could say I did it because she asked me. She asked me by trying to do it herself, over and over again.

But in here I only write the truth, and here it is: she was about to jump into the cold waters, to be drowned like an unwanted kitten. But at the last minute, she turned around.

She said, "Mum, I want to go home."

And I thought of her screaming, I thought of the hours spent trying to get some sense out of her, of her precious diary full of scribbles and little drawings and stupid poems when she should have done her job, for all of us. And I didn't mean to, of course, but before I knew it, all the disappointment, the sheer embarrassment of having such a coward for a child came back — and yes, that's what she was, a coward – and I pushed her into the water.

She looked at me, surprised. That was the last thing she'd ever expect. Of course. Who would think that their mother is going to put an end to their life?

She fell into the water and she didn't struggle. No splashing, no writhing. She just floated there for a minute, and then she looked at me again. As if she had accepted what I just did.

She looked so scared, though. And her little hand went up towards me, once, but without much spirit, as if she knew I wasn't going to take it.

Without spirit, yes. Even in death she was spineless.

Our eyes met and she was without reproach. Her gaze was sweet, resigned, which made me despise her even more – and still, those eyes will stay with me as long as I live. I watched Mairead throw herself back to float with her face skywards. Her little face was quite blue already, and I knew she'd die from the cold before she'd die drowning.

I am quite dead myself now. But I have to find a daughter for the family. She won't have the dreams, but at least she'll have witchcraft. Proper witchcraft, not Mairead's little gentle games.

How was she ever born into our family?

When I walked in and I told them all – when I told them how I tried to save her – they looked at my dress, and they saw it was dry. Hamish accepted it. He couldn't entirely blame me, anyway. Mairead was half his. Probably all his, given the way she had turned out. James, even at his young age, understood. But Stewart. Stewart hates me now, even more than before.

I foresee that this will dissolve our family. Another consequence of Mairead's uselessness, I suppose. All I can do is wait until James is old enough to marry and see that he and his wife have the daughter I was supposed to have.

★

Slowly, deliberately, Sarah tore the letter to pieces, and piece by piece she put it into the fire.

The last memory of Mairead's murder had been destroyed.

45
Broken Destiny

What they turned you into
Black embers

It was well after midnight when Nicholas came to find Sarah in her room, sitting beside the cold, black remains of the fire. She looked very small and very lost in the big, shadowy room. Then she turned her face to him, revealing her tear-streaked cheeks.

"What happened? A dream? Oh, Sarah."

She let him put his arms around her, inhaling woodsmoke and soil, the Nicholas scent she'd come to know so well.

"It wasn't a dream," she told him quietly. "I read the last letter. Morag Midnight was a monster. And so was my father. And so am I!"

"What? Slow down! What letter?"

"The final letter. Yes. She . . . my grandmother . . ." Sarah covered her face with her hands.

"It's OK. It's OK."

"It's not OK! She murdered Mairead! It was she who killed her! And my father knew! They all knew!"

"She killed her own daughter? Why?"

"Because Mairead couldn't cope with the dreams. She wasn't strong enough. She took her to the sea and threw her in. And Mairead was . . . resigned. She accepted it, in a way, if you believe what Morag wrote. She wanted it!"

"You told me she was only thirteen. A thirteen-year-old child doesn't want to die!"

"She must have been made to feel that way. Can you imagine? She knew she was a disappointment." Sarah's voice broke.

Nicholas held her close. Was this a chance he needed to take? He didn't want to use the mind-moulding on her again, but he wanted to make her feel better, and he didn't know how. In desperation, he cast his numbing fog around her again, cradling her in his arms, watching as it took the edge off her thoughts, softening her pain.

"Shhhh. It was long ago. It was so long ago, and you can forget it now," he soothed.

Sarah closed her eyes. "I can't. I'm just like them."

"No, you aren't. It ends here, Sarah. The misery that was handed down to you. You don't need to hand it down to your children. Although their blood is in your veins, you're your own person. You can choose who you are."

Nicholas's hypnotic voice was calming her, bit by bit, as it had done so often. She felt the familiar dizziness taking her, weakening her.

"Do you hear me, Sarah? You don't need to be like them."

"That's what Winter told me," Sarah murmured into his chest, confused. She wrapped her arms round him.

"You can choose who you want to be." Nicholas repeated his mantra over and over, his hold on her strengthening.

You need me too, she thought suddenly, the notion piercing the blanket of sleepiness that he brought with him. She frowned, surprised. He was comforting her, not the opposite, so why was she feeling this way, that she was somehow supporting him, that for once he was the vulnerable one?

Sarah disentwined herself from Nicholas and looked into his face. She gasped at what she saw. His eyes were as red-rimmed as hers, and just as troubled. He looked as if he was on the verge of breaking.

"Don't be upset, Nicholas. I'll be fine. We'll be fine," she whispered, but the blurriness was returning. "I'm so tired. I can't speak. I can't think. Why are you doing this to me? What are you doing to me?" She wasn't sure whether she was making any sense now.

"I'm sorry," he murmured into her hair. "I'm sorry."

"I don't want this anymore, Nicholas. Please stop," she muttered, leaning against him, unable to move.

"I'm sorry," he said again, but he didn't lift the fog – he wanted to hold her in his arms for as long as he could, and never let her go.

It was late the next morning when Sarah walked into the kitchen.

"Are you feeling OK?" Sean asked her when he saw her pale face and tousled hair. He put down *his sgian-dubh* – he and Elodie had been practising the runes again. "You look terrible."

Sarah stretched and turned slowly around, taking in the scene. "I'm fine. I fell asleep."

"Come and sit down," Sean interrupted. He didn't want to know the details. "I'll make you a cup of coffee."

Sarah smiled wanly at the offer. *Caffeine man*, she used to call him, because he thought that everything could be fixed with coffee.

"There might be biscuits to go with that," Niall began, pulling a tin out of one of the cupboards.

Elodie chipped in. "Oh, me too, thanks!"

Mike stood up. "Here, take my chair."

"I read the last letter. My grandmother murdered her daughter," said Sarah suddenly. Her words fell like stones, and the room was silenced. "She wasn't good enough. My aunt Mairead, I mean. She was frightened, she couldn't take the dreams. They were too much for her. So Morag drowned her. Just there." Sarah pointed out the window, towards the beach. She spoke as if she couldn't quite believe what she was telling them.

"Jesus," whispered Niall.

"So anyway. I'm going for a walk. Alone," said Sarah before anybody could suggest otherwise.

"No you aren't. Unless you have a death wish," replied Elodie. "The demon-bird is still out there."

Sarah shrugged. "I need to be alone."

"I'll walk ten steps behind you, OK? But I won't leave you." Sarah looked at Elodie, surprised. There was warmth in her voice, something she wasn't expecting.

But Sarah misunderstood. *I hate to be pitied*. She lifted her chin. "No thanks."

Elodie took a step back, biting her lip. Sean was about to speak, but too late.

"I'll come with you," said Nicholas, appearing as if from nowhere.

Sarah swung round. "No. I need to *think*," she whispered, a tight note in her voice.

Nicholas's face darkened. "Of course. I'll leave you be." He stood back to let her pass.

"You're not going anywhere on your own." Sean strode over and took Sarah's arm, turning his back on Nicholas.

Finally, Sarah exploded, shaking him off in a single violent movement. "Will everybody let me be! I'm a curse! I'm a walking curse! And I want to be alone!"

Sean and Elodie exchanged a quick look, and unspoken words passed between them. Sarah would not go alone.

Nicholas frowned as he watched Sean storm out after her, but he didn't stop him. Sean's form blurred and vanished as he walked onto the beach.

Sarah sat on the rocks at the far side of the bay, lashed by the wind and rain, looking out to sea, eyes dark with sorrow. *Let the demons come. If the last of the Midnights dies, it might not be entirely a bad thing.*

Sean sat not far from her, invisible to her, so immobile, so still that he was sand and water, part of the landscape, watching over Sarah, keeping her safe.

46

Death Written in Blood

Our end is coded
In the spark of our beginning

The demon-bird sat panting, his back resting against the stony cliff. *I failed again*, he kept telling himself, choked with fear and fury. His hands were clutching his chest, where blood oozed from his wounds. *Please stop*, he begged. *Please heal. Please let me have enough strength to complete my mission.*

With huge effort he removed the mask from his face, loosened his beak and mane and laid them on the sand beside him. Relieved of the disguise, he closed his eyes and breathed deeply. Next, he removed his leather cloak, which he used to catch the wind as he flew, and the claws.

Tancredi Falco grabbed some rags from a bag beside him and held them tightly to his chest, willing with all his might for the bleeding to subside. He didn't have long. And he had accepted that. He'd go the same way as his brother Ranieri, and soon he'd see him again. But first, he had to do what he'd come to Islay for. He ran his bloodied hand through his long, straight brown hair, leaving a smudge of red on his forehead.

How long will it be, before I'm strong enough to strike again? Because if I don't kill Sarah Midnight, it'll be the end of us all.

47

Poison

Ceilings heavy with memories
Walls thick with years
Never silent, always whispering
The births and deaths of generations gone.
Listen when I beg the old house
Let your children go

Sean

This house is poisoned, if you ask me. I know Sarah has been fantasizing about living here, but it is so full of sorrow, so full of ghosts. If it was me, I'd knock it down and let nothing but weeds grow on its foundations. I'm still reeling from Sarah's revelations about her aunt's murder. The Midnights are even worse than Harry let on. I wonder if he knew – his father certainly did.

It's Christmas Eve. Sarah is in the kitchen now, cooking away. In a crisis, Sarah cooks – that's what she does. We decided to stay on Islay for a little while longer.

"What would be the point of going?" Sarah had said.

"Wherever we go, the Surari will follow us. We might as well face them."

I looked to Elodie, who, unexpectedly, echoed Sarah's words. "No more running away," she whispered as she turned away from me.

Ever since our kiss on the beach, there has been an awkwardness between Elodie and me. I can't help thinking that she's not really longing for me, but for Harry's ghost, Harry's memory. When I catch her looking at me I am afraid, because I can never feel that way for her. She doesn't deserve any more heartache after all she's been through. I don't want to hurt her, but I can't help being in love with Sarah.

There, I said it. It was no secret, after all. I'm in love with Sarah, and that's never going to change.

I can feel this house humming, vibrating with what's to come. We're all jumpy, nerves taut under the skin, waiting. The Midnight ghosts are all around us, and sometimes I think they're closing in on us; and so, we have to presume, are the Surari. Any time now, they will strike.

So here the rest of us are, counting the hours trickling slowly one after the other, with Sarah sorting cutlery and polishing silver obsessively. As Niall whispered to me, while we prepared the vegetables exactly the way Sarah instructed us, we are like the orchestra on the Titanic, playing on as the ship is about to sink.

Sarah brushes past me on some errand, running upstairs. The light of the multi-coloured window plays in her hair, and the hand she leans on the banister is raw and bleeding.

48

The Blood Is Strong

A mother's call
To keep you safe in times to come

Sarah knelt in front of the fire in her bedroom again, as if in front of an altar, and the box of letters clutched to her chest was the sacrificial offering.

The wood flamed wildly in the grate. This was the second time in her life she was burning something her family had inflicted on her. First her dream diary, the black-bound book where she had recorded her first four years of dreaming, and now her grandmother's letters.

One by one they went into the fire to be engulfed in flames. And then it was the turn of the loose pieces of paper scattered in the bottom of the box. She was determined that there would be nothing left. Sarah started scrunching them up and placing them into the fire too, but before she completed the task, one of them caught her eye.

Amelia,

I have to ask you to stop writing. You disgust me. I will do nothing to help you. You are one of those irresponsible, foolish people who one day will cause the demise of the Secret Families. To think I've defended you over and over again. To think I've taken your side over Angus, and all along you were having a relationship with a Lay. All your powers will go to waste. You won't be able to pass them on to your children, the little bastards you'll have with that Lay. You knew what you were doing. We all know that we female heirs can only ever marry Secret men or our children will be worthless Lays. You knew that. And still, you did it, you deceived your fiancé, which was bad enough – and me, believing it had been him who did you wrong! And you betrayed him with a disgusting little Lay. A servant, moreover.

Amelia, you're dead to me. Never, never look to me again for friendship. I hope you, your Lay and the bastard you've had with him burn with the Surari.

Morag Elspeth McGregor Midnight
Midnight Hall

Sarah trembled in anger. It was just as Winter had said. So much cruelty, so much grief inflicted on everyone around Morag. The irony of all ironies: her grandmother passing judgement on Amelia for having fallen in love with a Lay when she herself had committed the unforgivable crime of murder. Murder of her own daughter.

She checked through the rest of the papers in the box, wondering why Morag had the letters she had sent to Amelia. She could only find one explanation: her uncle Stewart. He must have received the letters from Amelia and then given them to Winter's mother after Morag's death, knowing that she would keep them safe. Mrs Shaw would never have dreamt of taking anything from the house. Her job was much too important to take a risk like that.

Stewart Midnight. I wish I'd known you.

Other memories flooded back. Sarah thought of her dad, James, of how inflexible, how hard he could be. How her mum would never disagree with him, how Bryony and her other friends had always been a little scared of him. *James is the one who takes after me the most,* Morag had written.

I wonder if I take after her. Am I like my father? How quick, how merciless she'd been in sending Sean away when she'd found out about his deceit. She closed her eyes, remembering how close she had come to using the Blackwater on him. And the rage she'd been feeling inside for so long, the desire to burn and kill and destroy. Especially since Leigh had been murdered. *Does that make me like them?*

Sarah was shaking with the strength of her emotions. Unshed tears were prickling behind her eyes, but she knew they couldn't find release.

There was no time. She and her friends would have their Christmas, their bizarre celebration, holding the future at bay a little longer. And then eventually she would pack, and leave. She would do what she was meant to do, and not look back.

She grabbed the rest of the papers with both hands and went to thrust them into the fire. But something colourful among the scraps of paper caught her eye. It was a stamp. A New Zealand stamp, on a scrunched-up blue envelope. Something – a feeling, a hunch – made her place it on the rug and smooth it out.

There was a name on it, written in faded blue ink: Stewart Midnight.

Sarah took a deep breath. *More discoveries?*

She shook her head, and crinkled the letter again. *I can't take this anymore. It's too much.* She raised her hand to throw it into the fireplace.

And then she stopped. *It's to Stewart, though, not Amelia. Winter said she trusted him. This letter might be different than the others.*

On impulse, she took the letter out of the envelope, smoothed it the best she could, and read. And her life once again changed forever.

Dear Stewart,

I'm begging you to help me. Your mother won't have anything to do with me, and I don't know what to do. Allan died last year, and I'm very ill. Our son, Sean, is going to be raised by Allan's parents, whose hatred for me is only matched by the indifference they feel for Sean. For the long friendship between our Families, the friendship that your mother wants to end because of what I did, I'm begging you to find Sean one day, and help him to become a Gamekeeper. I never want him to know that he's half-Lay, half-Secret – I can't bear to inflict this shame on him, and to have him exiled, stigmatized, tormented as I was, as his father was. I want his life to be happy and without shadows. I want him to be proud of himself in a way I couldn't be, having betrayed my family. Don't get me wrong, I'd do it all again for love of Allan. I'd do it again a million times over.

Please find Sean for me one day. He is my precious son, and I know that he can play his part in our battles. Make sure he's alright, make sure he finds his place in the world. And never, never tell him of my shame.

You're my only hope.

Yours,

Amelia Campbell Hannay.

"Oh, God."

"What's up? All OK?" Hearing her curse, Niall had poked his head in from the hall. Sarah shook her head, putting a hand up to silence him. She read the letter again, and once more.

Sean. Amelia's son. In New Zealand.

Sean's parents died when he was a child. He was raised by his grandparents.

Allan Hannay's son.

Sean Hannay.

"Sarah?"

"Yes. Yes." She took a deep breath and clutched the letter to her chest. "I've found a very special letter, Niall."

"And important it looks too," he mocked half-heartedly, sensing her mood.

Sarah nodded. "Yes. Very important. Have you seen Sean?" she added in a trembling voice.

"I think he's in the kitchen."

Sarah looked at him, wide-eyed. "I can't explain now. I'll tell you later," she whispered, and ran off.

Sean was lost in thought, looking out of the kitchen window into the lilac sky, nursing a cup of steaming coffee. He smiled when Sarah came to stand beside him, but his smile faded when he saw her serious expression.

"Sean," she said. "I need to speak to you."

49
Look Behind You

There's more than one way to forget
Whether it's you or myself that I hurt
Every drop of blood
Is a memory gone

"Nicholas," whispered Elodie. They watched as Sean and Sarah emerged from the kitchen and stood together at the edge of the garden, where the grass ended and the sand began, out on their own to speak in private. The bond between Sean and Sarah, the pull between them, was so strong that it was nearly visible, a silver chain tying them together. Elodie and Nicholas watched as Sean stepped back and put his head in his hands, and Sarah reached out to him.

When Sean and Sarah were finally in each other's arms, Elodie grew pale, and at first Nicholas didn't show any visible emotion. He stood still and silent, looking on as if it didn't matter. But inside him it was like old times, like the Nicholas he used to be. He had an irresistible urge to destroy something, anything. To kill and maim, to inflict on someone else the pain he was feeling. Suddenly he raised his hand, and the ravens were with him once more. At once, there was a symphony of whispers in his head – calls, and greetings, and congratulations. The speed of the reaction stunned him. *Nicholas is back*, they said.

Startled, Elodie watched the ravens circle above their heads with dark, liquid eyes. Then she turned to him, as if something fundamental had changed in her life too. "Do this for me," she said, and rolled up her sleeve, exposing her white, delicate arm. "Ask the ravens to help me forget."

Nicholas stared at her. What was she thinking? "I don't understand," he whispered. *I don't want to understand.*

Her arm was tiny, her skin was too thin, and still there were no veins to be seen, as if she'd been bled already. *Her blood isn't flowing properly*, thought Nicholas. Once more, he had seen something in Elodie's eyes that he wished wasn't there.

"Ask them to hurt me, to make me forget."

Nicholas was horrified. "Don't ask me to do that, Elodie."

"Why? It wouldn't be the first time you make your ravens hurt someone."

Nicholas continued to stare at her. *What does she know? What has she guessed?* "Demons. Not Secret heirs."

"I'm not asking you to kill me. Just help me take the pain away," she pleaded, fixing her eyes on his. Her look reminded Nicholas of someone. Someone spent, tired of living.

Then he remembered. His mother.

At that moment, the fury he'd felt watching Sarah and Sean holding each other faded as quickly as it had come. If he hated anyone, it was himself. He closed his eyes. What was happening to him? His thoughts whirled, rearranging themselves in his head, contradicting each other, making no sense. He wouldn't kill anymore, he wouldn't hurt again. He needed to get away.

"They can see us," he whispered, and led Elodie round the side of the house, across a little dirt road and up onto a grassy mound. They stood overlooking the ocean, screaming seagulls in the grey sky above.

"What happened to you, Elodie?" he asked, taking her by the shoulders.

"Harry died," she answered simply.

She's as soft, as white as a dove – but she's black inside, I can feel it. Too much pain, too much anger.

"Sean won't bring him back. Look, Elodie. Don't go trying to get hurt, because believe me, we'll all get hurt soon enough."

"I don't really care if I live or die. I want to do what Harry asked of me. Of us. I want to destroy the Enemy." The chorus of screams and whispers in Nicholas's head got louder all of a sudden. "And then I won't have anything left to live for." She gave him a bleak smile.

The ravens had caught them up. They had chased away the seagulls and were flying in circles over their heads, cawing. A few of them landed and hopped beside them, their little heads tipping from left to right, awaiting instructions. Nicholas felt his fingertips tingle. Suddenly, he knew exactly what was about to happen.

Let us taste her.

"Let's go back. Now." He took Elodie by the arm and began pulling her down the path. The terrible chorus in his head kept calling. *Let us finish what we started on the beach. Let us taste her. Let us.*

More ravens landed in front of Nicholas and Elodie, blocking their way down the path – a sea of feathery black, dotted with hungry eyes. *No!* Nicholas protested silently. But it was too late. He barely had time to call Elodie's name, when the ravens took to the air, and, quicker than the eye could see, they were on her. Elodie screamed and fell to her knees, a moving blanket of black, oily feathers smothering her. In seconds drops of her blood began to stain the ground.

Stop!

Why? Why do you want them to stop, Nicholas?

It was his father's voice.

Nicholas clutched his head in his hands, the blinding pain of the brain fury ravaging him all of a sudden – just a hint, not its full force, but painful enough.

"Nicholas!" Elodie called desperately, trying to beat the ravens away from her eyes with her arms. Her body was crawling with birds, black and crimson mixing in a terrible kaleidoscope on the ground.

You need to stop, now.

But the ravens wouldn't listen. They were ruled by a higher power now, one they had no choice but to obey.

"Nicholas!" she implored again, her strangled voice muffled in the grass.

Leave her. Leave her! Nicholas looked around in desperation as blast after blast of pain shot through his head. And then he thought of something, the only argument he could use. *They will find out who I really am!*

They will know soon anyway, came the reply.

Despair filled Nicholas's heart. There was nothing else he could do. The ravens were going to peck Elodie to death, just as they'd done to Cathy, as they'd tried to do to Elodie once before.

His moans of pain as the brain fury burnt in his head echoed Elodie's.

But not yet.

A sudden gust of air hit Nicholas, followed by the sound of beating wings far too close. When he opened his eyes, he was astonished to see the ravens flying back into the sky. His father must have called them back.

He threw himself beside Elodie's bloodied body, ignoring the agonizing pain in his head.

"Oh, Elodie," he murmured.

She couldn't hear him. She was lying curled up, unconscious. Quickly he gathered her in his arms and ran towards the house, bracing himself for attack every time he heard a distant cawing, his head still sore from his father's punishment.

Only Niall was in the kitchen when Nicholas pushed the door open and staggered in, and he paled at what he saw. Nicholas's voice was croaky, broken. "The ravens again."

Quickly Niall took Elodie from him, horrified as her blood began to stain his chest and arms. "The ravens? *Your* ravens?" He sat down on the settle next to the range, careful not to jostle her.

"It was me who saved her," Nicholas said brusquely. *You'll know the truth soon, Niall, but not yet.*

And then Elodie opened her eyes, and from the shelter of Niall's arms, she called a name. But it wasn't Niall's, and it wasn't Sean's.

"Nicholas."

Disbelief showed on Nicholas's face. *She called me. Me.* He looked at Niall, then into Elodie's battered face. "I'm here," he said hoarsely.

"Have the ravens gone?" she whispered.

"Yes. They've gone. You're safe."

"I shouldn't have asked you."

"Shhhh. Don't speak now," he said, resting a hand on her head. The look between them was so intense that Niall frowned, sensing something unspoken in the air. He was about to speak when Sarah stepped into the kitchen. Her eyes were red-rimmed, but they widened when she saw the strange scene – Niall with a bleeding Elodie in his arms, Nicholas's hands covered in blood, his hair matted with it.

"What happened? Was it the demon-bird again?"

"No. No. Elodie and I . . . We went for a walk. It was the ravens."

"The . . . ravens? I don't understand." And then Sarah saw Elodie's ravaged skin. "Oh my God." She took the girl's bloodied hand.

Nicholas's words tumbled over each other as he struggled to find a way to explain. "Sarah. The ravens have turned. The Surari control them now. They don't do my bidding anymore. If you see ravens or wildcats, you must be very careful."

"What are you talking about?"

"Why?" said Niall. His eyes narrowed in suspicion.

"What do you mean?" asked Nicholas.

"Why have the ravens turned against you, Nicholas?"

"How should I know? I don't know anything more than you, Niall!" he growled.

"Nicholas." Sarah walked over to where he was standing and put a soothing hand on his arm.

I know. You don't need to tell me. You've made your decision. You're leaving me. You and Sean are together now. "Where is Sean?" he asked, bracing himself for the answer.

But it wasn't the one he'd expected.

"I don't know. I have no idea," Sarah replied, avoiding his gaze, her voice strained.

Nicholas looked at her, surprised, but she would not meet his eyes. *Something must have happened between them, it's not what Elodie and I thought we saw.*

A huge wave of relief swept over him— and at the same time he realized that the pain in his head had vanished. There was no more screaming in his mind, no more reproaches, and no more brain fury. He staggered slightly, overwhelmed by the sense of escape. Somehow, by some miracle, his father and the Shadow voices must have believed him when he said he needed the ravens to protect his secret by letting Elodie survive the attack. They couldn't have known that Nicholas genuinely wanted to save Elodie's life. They must have sensed Nicholas's rage and despair when Sean and Sarah embraced, the rush of blood thirst. They must have believed that his doubts about his place in the Shadow World had vanished, that the old Nicholas was back. But he wasn't out of danger yet.

In an instant, Nicholas closed his mind to his true feelings and replaced any hint of relief with images of Elodie in pain, prostrated on the grass, screaming. He invoked memories of hatred, of darkness, of the people he had hurt and killed over the years – he filled his mind with all that his father wanted him to be. The Shadow World needed to believe that he was still on their side. This would buy him a bit more time.

"I'm going to take Elodie to her room," said Niall, gently lifting her into his arms again. "Sarah?"

"I'll get the med stuff," Sarah replied, and hurried out.

Nicholas went to follow, but Niall gave him a withering look. "No need for you to come," he said firmly. But before he had left the kitchen, the injured girl spoke.

"Nicholas," called Elodie softly.

"I'm here," he said. "I'm coming."

And there's nothing Niall can do about it.

*

Niall laid Elodie on her bed and Sarah saw to her wounds. They both flinched when they saw what the ravens had done to her back, pierced with tiny lacerations, her flesh shredded, the skin hanging loose in little bloody flaps.

"Tell me exactly what happened, Elodie," Sarah asked gently as she bathed the wounds.

Elodie struggled to speak, such was the pain. Her breathing was shallow. "We were walking. They attacked me. Like they did on the beach that day. Maybe I'm marked. A mark that only they can see." She shivered, thinking back to the swan she'd seen many years before, in her childhood.

She had gone for a walk on a lakeshore with her parents; before her father could lead her away, before her mother could shield her eyes, she'd seen a dead swan, its chest torn open, lying bloodied on the pebbles. And right there and then, she'd had a premonition – that one day, she'd be the swan. One day she'd be the one lying there.

"Nonsense. You're not any more marked than the rest of us," Niall said, stroking her hair with a gentleness that made Nicholas's heart tighten. "I used to dream of ravens when I was a boy. They weren't nice dreams. I hate ravens," Niall continued.

Elodie yelped as Sarah dabbed at her wounds. "Is everybody else safe?" she asked. "Where is Mike? Where is Sean?"

Sarah flinched. "I don't know," she murmured. "Try and lie still."

Niall walked to the window and looked at the sky. "The ravens are still out there," he said in a low voice, "and so is that bloody demon-bird, and who knows what else. Sean can't go wandering off on his own like this. I'll find Mike and we'll go and bring him back." He placed a kiss on Elodie's forehead and strode out of the room.

"Take care!" Sarah called after him.

"Will do!" His footsteps faded into the distance, and then they heard him calling Mike's name.

"Sarah. What happened between you and Sean?" whispered Elodie after a few moments, her voice muffled by her pillow.

Nicholas's heart skipped a beat. He waited.

Sarah shook her head, concentrating on the task at hand. "Nothing happened. And nothing ever will." She kept her eyes solely on Elodie's wounds, then she pulled the bedclothes carefully up to the nape of her friend's neck. "Rest now, Elodie. If you need me, just shout and I'll be straight up. Thank God you're safe," she added, and a rare look of affection passed between the two girls.

"Are you OK?" She then asked Nicholas, unable to read the look in his eyes.

He nodded. "Yes. I'll sit here with Elodie for a bit. If that's OK with you."

"Yes. Stay," murmured Elodie. She lay as white as a sheet, her eyes feverish with pain.

We have done this to her, thought Nicholas in despair.

He made a promise to himself. Never again would he be part of the King of Shadows' world of pain.

50
Threshold

Same planet, two dimensions
The love that wasn't meant to be

Sarah

Just when I was about to make my choice, just when I was about to tell Sean that I was ready, that I knew what love was at last, he told me that he'd abide by the rules.

Secret women cannot marry Lay men.

Sean and I can never be together.

But none of those rules make any sense to me now. Everything has changed, the old order of things has crumbled. None of us is who we thought we were, and still, Sean is clinging to the old world as if its laws still stand.

I tried to tell him that it makes no difference to me whether he is a Lay, or half-Secret, or even an Elemental, for all that matters. I don't care whose blood runs through his veins – he is Sean. My Sean.

But in the garden today, once I'd explained what I'd

discovered in the letter, he told me that he believes in the rigid structure on which the Secret Families base their existence. He told me he agrees with Morag that the powers Secret Families hold should be nourished and protected, and that we should breed among ourselves and not dilute our powers. Yes, *breed*, like pedigree dogs, or prized cattle. When I protested that I didn't care about my powers, he said that he couldn't bear to be responsible for the loss of the Blackwater. That I should marry Nicholas, or Niall, or any other surviving Secret heir, but that it could never, ever be him. Never anyone with Lay blood in them.

He held me one last time, and then he walked away.

Nicholas came into my room as I was trying to gather my thoughts.

"Sarah." He took my hands in his, and without warning he tried to kiss me.

I turned away. "I'm sorry," I heard myself saying.

I think he understood at once.

To see the devastation in his face broke my heart, but at least I wasn't living a lie anymore. If Sean and I could never be together, I didn't believe I could ever love anyone else. I couldn't deceive Nicholas any longer. I couldn't deceive myself any longer.

"I'll wait. I'll wait for you to change your mind," he said, clutching my hand.

I had never seen him like this. "Nicholas, I'm sorry, but I won't."

"Sean," he growled.

"No. There's no one. There can never be anyone, Nicholas. I'm a Midnight, and believe me, it's a lot better for everyone if the Midnight line stops here with me."

51
And Then I Found You

Watch while what was in the dark
Is cast into the light
Watch while the secrets we kept
Don't choke us anymore

While Elodie rested and Sarah and Nicholas talked upstairs, the others were gathered in the living room. Sean and Mike were chatting quietly by the fireplace; Niall was lying on one of the sofas, his arms crossed behind his head; Winter, having entered while Niall and Nicholas moved Elodie upstairs, was sitting in an armchair near the window, as if she wanted to be halfway between inside and outside, near the freedom of the windy beach. She had tucked her legs under herself, and her silver hair was flowing freely down to her waist. With the moonlight shining on her, her eyes gleamed silver too. She'd been spending a lot of time at Midnight Hall – just like when her mother was the housekeeper there, and she had played with Mairead every day.

Niall was trying to catch glimpses of her when he thought

nobody noticed, but Winter knew, of course. She was quite aware of the effect she had on the opposite sex. There was something wild and beautiful about her that never failed to entrance.

"Will you come and explore with me, Niall?" she said suddenly, her clear gaze on him and a smile playing on her lips. Mike stifled a smile, his eyes darting from one to the other. What was happening, what had been slowly happening since Winter had arrived on the scene, was clear for everyone to see. Unlike Sarah, Winter was an open book, her feelings and desires always plain for everyone to see.

"I haven't been in the grand hall for years. I want to see what it looks like now," she continued.

Niall rose at once. "Sure thing!"

Upon seeing him so eager, Mike couldn't suppress his smile any longer.

"Let's go, then," said Winter sweetly, and Niall's cheeks flamed scarlet.

"Have fun," called Mike mock-seriously. Niall ignored him.

"This place is huge," Niall murmured as they stepped out into the corridor. "It's at least double the size of our family home in Skerry."

"It's at least fifty times bigger than my cottage!" laughed Winter.

"But a lot smaller than the sea," said Niall.

"True," Winter replied softly. "When I was little Mairead and I used to roam around this place for days on end," she continued as they walked. "Playing hide and seek here was just brilliant, we wouldn't find each other for hours!" Winter laughed her lyrical laugh. "Come. I want to show you something."

She took his hand, entwining her fingers with his – Niall felt something warm stirring in his chest, and held onto her. She led him down the corridor to a wooden door, and pushed it open.

"The library," said Niall.

"How did you guess?" she laughed, gesturing at the floor-to-ceiling bookshelves full of leather-bound volumes of all shapes and sizes.

"I'm very observant!" He winked.

Niall scoured the shelves. "I've never seen such a collection before. Botany, astronomy. Oh."

"What do you see?"

Niall laughed. "A modern book. *Yoga Workouts*. Do you think Morag Midnight did yoga?" He grinned, holding up a pink-and-yellow-covered book with a woman sitting in the lotus position.

Winter laughed too. "Maybe Hamish." Her eyes danced. "What is it doing here?"

"It probably belonged to Sarah's mum." Niall fingered the soft covers, walking slowly from shelf to shelf. "Some of these are five hundred years old," he said in awe.

"Look," said Winter, pointing to a thick black volume. "*The History of the Midnight Family* by Lord Gregor Midnight. One for Sarah."

"Ideal bedtime reading," smirked Niall. "Oh," he said, crossing his arms and looking up.

"What's the matter?"

"That book up there, see?" Winter raised her chin, flicking her hair away from her neck. A gust of her seawater scent wafted towards Niall's face and he breathed her in deeply, glancing at her white throat as she looked up. "*Between Two Worlds*," he said, trying to regain composure. "I want to have a look at that."

Winter looked around. "There should be a ladder somewhere, or at least there used to be."

"There!" Spying the wooden ladder, Niall positioned it and started to climb, stretching himself until his fingers brushed the book he wanted.

He wiped the dust off the cover with his sleeve and opened the first page. An intricate label had been glued on it. *Midnight*, it said in Gothic fonts. He climbed down and handed the book to Winter. She traced the deeply engraved letters on the cover with a finger.

"Come," said Niall, and took her hand. He led her to the sofa by the window. "Ouch! The Midnights' idea of comfort was quite . . . different," he complained as he sat on the rigid leather surface, hitting the backrest.

"I'll tell you a secret," whispered Winter as she sat beside him. "When my mum was housekeeper here they had no hot water. At all. Ever. They all took cold showers and baths. They bathed the babies in water from the stove, but as soon as they were toddlers, cold baths for them too! It wouldn't bother us, of course, but if you're not of the sea like us . . ."

Niall whistled. "Tough people."

"Mmmm. You can say that again. So. *Between Two Worlds*," said Winter, resting the book on her lap. She shuffled a bit until her leg was touching Niall's.

She couldn't be any closer if she sat on my lap, thought Niall, a bit panicky. But Winter seemed not to notice his embarrassment.

Get a grip, man, Niall scolded himself.

He leafed through the pages. "This is about demons." He paled. "Do you know anything about demons and the Secret history?"

"Not much. I saw a few demons, and Stewart told me things once in a while, but I'm mostly ignorant. I never hung out with Secret people, apart from Mairead and Stewart. And when I went away, I was mainly among seals, really."

"Were you not lonely?"

"Well, there were a few friends, a few boyfriends," she said matter-of-factly.

"Of course." Niall scowled.

"Why 'of course'?" asked Winter.

"Because you're beautiful," he said simply. *You really are beautiful*, he thought, taking in her silver hair, her strong, warm body in a slightly faded blue cotton dress with little white flowers – her pink cheeks and shiny eyes, a face that spoke of easy joy and laughter, unlike Sarah's and Elodie's.

"Well, thank you," she said, and gave him a little peck on the cheek.

Niall swallowed.

"So yes. Anyway. This book . . ." He continued skimming through it, his eyes scanning the words. Suddenly he froze.

Winter looked at him curiously. "What's wrong?"

"This mentions the Time of Demons," he breathed. "The gate between the worlds." He started to read more frantically. "Have you heard about the Shadow World, or the Underworld?"

"The *underworld*, as in under ground?"

"Not exactly, no. According to this, the Shadow World is . . . a *different dimension*. A different universe." He stopped briefly then began to read aloud. "*The demons that seep into our world cross over to our own dimension*. Apparently, it's not easy for them to do so. *Only the strongest survive the passage.*"

"But why do they do that?"

"The earth belonged to them, thousands of years ago. That was the Time of Demons. We humans were the endangered species, if you like."

Winter smiled. "*You*, humans. I'm half Elemental."

"So you are," replied Niall, resting a hand briefly on her arm. Though it only lasted a moment, he loved touching her, feeling her warm skin. And he loved her smell – the sea was his favourite scent in the world.

Niall steadied himself and continued reading. "*Then the ancestors of the Secret Families, the Secret children, appeared. They claimed the planet and banished the demons to the Shadow World. But the Secret Families knew that they had to keep guard, and that the demons would try and overcome them again.*" He paused. "That's happening now."

"Who is the King of Shadows?" asked Winter suddenly. She'd skimmed over his shoulder while he spoke, and now pointed to a passage farther down the page.

Niall frowned, his eyes following her finger. A sudden chill swept over him, despite the proximity of Winter's warm body. "*The King of Shadows, the King of the Underworld. He has many names,*" he read. "*The most powerful demon of all. The one who rules the Shadow World.*"

Winter continued, "*The King of Shadows is a Surari, but unlike any other. Legend has it that he is a spirit who rules over a world of spirits. He is bound to the Shadow World but his will and power reaches into our own. It is rumoured that a gate to the Shadow World exists and can be entered through an ancient location, though no one has yet succeeded in finding it.*"

Winter trailed off. For a moment they sat in silence. Then Niall shook his head, gathering his thoughts and taking it all in. "We have to tell the others." He took a shaky breath.

Winter got up and stood very, very close to him.

Niall blushed. She just came up to his shoulder, and Niall wasn't a tall man. Only then did he seem to notice how small she was.

"We need to—"

But he didn't get a chance to finish the sentence, because suddenly Winter was kissing him, and everything else, for a moment, didn't matter.

52

Between Two Worlds

We worship the moon and our herds
Our home is the plains
Our roof is the sky
We rise, we are
The Secret children

With pots boiling on the stove, and a lovely smell coming from the oven, it was like any other kitchen at Christmas. And Sarah was hoping to keep it that way, at least for one day. She was arranging a centrepiece made of red candles and holly as Niall and Winter barged in. The moment she saw their faces, she knew something had happened. The Christmas decoration seemed so absurd all of a sudden, like a little raft in a stormy sea, a desperate attempt to hold on to some normality.

"Hey, man. Are you OK?" called Mike, noticing how pale Niall was.

"Not really," said Niall, and lifted the book for everyone to see.

"*Between Two Worlds*," read Sean, taking the leather-bound volume from him. "What's this?"

"We found it in the library," Winter intervened.

"Look here," said Niall, opening to the page he and Winter had read.

Sean and Sarah crowded around him.

Niall read the relevant parts aloud, and the kitchen fell silent.

"The King of Shadows. That is what you said during the scrying spell, remember, Sarah? *The King of Shadows is coming,*" said Sean.

Sarah's face was white. She nodded. "The Enemy is the King of Shadows."

"There's more," said Niall. "Listen. *It is rumoured that a gate to the Shadow World exists and can be entered, though no one has yet succeeded in finding it.* A gate. A gate to the Shadow World."

"So we know who he is, and where he is! What's stopping us?" Mike exclaimed.

"We need to go and find him. It's as simple as that," stated Sean, lost in thought.

Sarah was silent.

"Sarah," Niall said gently. She was standing still, the certain stillness that descended on her sometimes.

"Yes," she said finally. "Yes. We need to go, but how will we know where to find him? Shouldn't we think this through?"

"I agree with Sarah," came Nicholas's voice from the corner of the room. "We need to think about this, calmly. In the morning. We'll leave when we know more about what we're dealing with." He hadn't moved, hadn't spoken as Niall and Winter spoke. They had forgotten all about his presence. But he'd been standing there all along, hands curled into fists to stop them from shaking, trying to quell the fear racing through him.

"Nicholas is right, we can't leave till we know where we're

going. Might as well enjoy the evening, and all this." She swept her arm towards the boiling pots and pans, the gently glowing oven roasting the sweet-smelling turkey.

Sarah looked to Sean, her face solemn, pleading.

"Tomorrow," he said.

Mike put his hands up. "But—"

"Mike," said Nicholas in a low voice. "We need to figure out what's happening."

"I suppose so," Mike agreed reluctantly.

A look passed between Sarah and Sean, a look laden with meaning. *The storm is coming*, were their unspoken words.

Nicholas stepped out into the frozen afternoon air. He'd muttered something about needing a walk – he often did that, and nobody questioned it. He stood on the watermark, the wind whipping against him. He was shaking badly, anxiety was sweeping through him and devouring his thoughts, leaving a black knot of fear growing in his stomach.

They'll know soon. They'll know who I am.

But now, I know who I am. It doesn't matter. Not to them, anyway.

A strange elation took him, easing his anxiety. He turned back towards the house – he could see the lights of the kitchen, and the silhouettes of Sarah and her friends moving within. One of the windows upstairs was lit too: Elodie's room. She'd gone back there to lie down for a while.

The waves ebbed and flowed, the water winter-dark, hiding what lay in wait beneath its surface.

53

Christmas at Sea

The untold stories
And how they end

A vast oak table stood in the middle of an ancient hall, covered in red silk and as many flickering candles as Sarah could find. Seven chairs, seven people and seven sets of secrets and hopes and fears.

On one side, a black-haired man burning with fear, white-as-snow hands clutching the napkin on his lap in terrible anticipation, and beside him a tall, fair woman with bandaged arms and weary eyes.

At the opposite side, a girl with silver hair, placid and beautiful and brimming with kindness, beside a man whose grey eyes always smiled, and a dark-skinned man between them, his desires and hopes well hidden away, buried beneath selflessness and duty, strong and loyal as the roots of a tree.

At either end of the table, the ones with the invisible chain between them – Sarah's hair flowed down her back in a sweet-scented stream, the scars on Sean's arms shone white in the light of the candles against his bronzed skin. Unspoken words went back and forth between them, hands that longed to meet and a story interrupted.

And then, in a shower of glass, the Mermen came.

At last, thought Nicholas, and rose slowly, readying himself to fight. Because he, like Sarah, had finally made his choice.

54
Things That Come Ashore

Teeth and bones and flesh
Fragile like glass
Soft as clay
The million different ways
To break a human body

The windows exploded in a shower of glass, shards falling all around them and darting across the polished floor. A foul, rotting smell filled the air, and through the broken windows the Mermen made their inexorable way inside the Hall, waddling, arms outstretched to grab, teeth bared to bite. There were too many to count, shuffling along the floor under the golden light of the chandelier.

They prepared themselves in a heartbeat. Sarah was poised to leap, her eyes shimmering with the Midnight gaze, hands ready. Sean had his *sgian-dubh* in his hand faster than the eye could see; Mike drew his gun. Niall stepped back slightly, and started humming softly; Elodie's lips began to take on a deadly shade of blue, quickly turning to black.

Only Winter remained sitting, momentarily frozen, her whole body, every bit of her screaming for the water. Out of the sea she was just like any other human being, no powers, no Gamekeeper's training – just the instinct to survive and an innate, animal courage. And that's what kicked in. A split second later she was standing too, ready to fight with all she had.

After the shattering of the windows, there were no sounds but the Surari's gurgling breath, their fins dragging over the floor as they spread across the room, and Niall's soft humming. The Islay night enveloped them in darkness and silence.

And then it began. It was relentless, and bloody, and painful. The Mermen were thumping and breaking and biting soft flesh, moans of agony and exertion and fear exploded into the air like thousands of fireworks. It didn't take long for Sarah and her friends to realize what was really happening: the sea's power itself had been unleashed, and they were about to be overwhelmed. It didn't take long for Niall's song to be interrupted, for Elodie to be trapped in a fight she couldn't win, for Mike's gun to be knocked out of his hand, and for Winter, the weakest of the pack, to be isolated and cornered. A wave of despair swept the room, and for a moment, the end looked near, the fight as short as it'd been savage.

But suddenly red ribbons began to fly about the room, spurting from Sean's runes like bloody streams, and soon his power was clear for all to see. Mermen fell all around, cut by an invisible blade, as Sean's movements got faster and sharper, the ribbons dancing and slicing. The Surari were taken aback for a moment, and Niall had the time to jump to the table, raising himself above the battle long enough to resume his humming. Elodie, agile and quick as a cat despite the pain she was in, twisted out of one of the Merman's grasp and started working with Sean so that every time he floored one of their attackers, she would jump on it and give it her deadly kiss. The creatures writhed and contorted for a few instants, gasping for air, their mother-of-pearl skin turning darker, their eyeballs bulging and their gills pulsating frantically in their death throes.

By now Sarah was everywhere, her eyes shining emerald and lethal – Elodie could actually *see* a flash of green wherever Sarah went. The instant she felt that the Midnight gaze had paralyzed a weakened Surari, she grasped it with her toxic hands, dissolving the hideous creatures one by one. A thin film of Blackwater began to cover the floor, engulfing and suffocating the little sea creatures – the eels and crabs and unnamed slimy things that came from the deep, carried on land by the Mermen, were thrashing in it, suffocating slowly. It was as if the sea had turned black and poisonous, flooding Midnight Hall.

Niall's song strengthened, rising in volume and power. He flinched as he watched a Merman throw Mike to the floor and bite a chunk out of his leg. But nothing stopped the song. It was all Niall could do. His voice became increasingly high-pitched and painful and deadly, reaching Mike's attacker just as the Merman was preparing to bite Mike's face off. It folded into itself, holding its head, while Mike crawled across the room to grab his gun and fire it, once, twice.

To his dismay, the bullets lodged into the Surari's translucent skin but didn't reach its insides. Its skin might have looked deceivingly thin and scaly, but it was as thick as an elephant's hide. The discovery made Mike moan in despair. All he could do was aim at their eyes, and so he did. One Merman fell, its face blown off, but before he could fire again, another

Merman grabbed him with all its strength and threw Mike to the wet, blackened floor.

A Surari climbed over the table and grabbed Niall's legs, throwing him down on the hard wooden surface. His song came to an abrupt halt as his mouth filled with blood and he fell in a sea of broken crockery and splattered food, the Merman still holding onto his legs. Niall braced himself for the bite: and it came, excruciating, as the Surari sank his teeth into his thigh.

"Niall!" As the song was interrupted, Elodie had instinctively looked at the table to check on him. She threw herself on the Surari holding Niall down and stabbed it repeatedly. She grabbed its head and placed a poisonous kiss on its lips, the Merman's sharp teeth cutting Elodie's mouth, and her blue lips were smeared with red.

"Are you OK?" she asked Niall when the demon had fallen, wiping her mouth and wincing in pain.

Niall nodded and spat out two teeth. Then he saw something out of the corner of his eye, and gasped. Winter had been holding her own in every way she could. Her arms were lined with deep cuts and her hair was dripping with Blackwater, but she didn't seem mortally wounded. A Surari was standing in front of her, and they were looking at each other – the Merman baring its teeth, anticipating the taste of her flesh, Winter trying to stop herself from shaking, trying to stop her legs from buckling, trying to pretend she was unafraid. Suddenly, with newfound courage she leapt on the Surari, a strange sound coming from the back of her throat. It was a call the Merman recognized – a seal call.

Infuriated, it grabbed her by the shoulders and sank its teeth into her chest. Winter screamed in pain and terror, but Niall was already on the Surari, the magic song streaming from his mouth, the notes spurting into the air like blood from an open wound. Elodie was close behind.

Agonized, the Merman let Winter go, and both covered their ears, hit by the full force of the song. Elodie took her chance and, with a graceful leap, bent over the Merman, kissing it and killing it in seconds.

The sounds of battle were retreating.

Niall stopped singing and took Winter in his arms. They clung to each other, breathless, surveying the horrific scene. A Merman had just dissolved under Sarah's touch, another one was writhing on the floor in its final moments, Sean standing over it, panting in fury. Another one lay dead, a bullet hole between its eyes. Mermen corpses lay everywhere, lapped by the mixture of blood and Blackwater on the floor. The last of the dying Surari became still, one after the other.

For a few seconds Sarah and her friends allowed themselves to breathe, looking around in the sudden calm.

Could it be?

Could they have made it? Could they have survived such a merciless attack?

And then gurgling, shuffling, and what was left of the windows shattered. Another deadly wave of Mermen erupted into the hall. Icy panic shot through Sean's veins as only one thought filled his mind: *This is the night we die.*

55
One Soul

Like many before me
Beneath the waves, beneath the crosses:
I'll never see my home again

A merman ripped Winter from Niall's arms, ready to bite. A suffocated sound came out of Niall's throat. He was faced with a terrible choice, with Mike on one side and Winter on the other, and him in the middle, scrambling to get the song going again, and failing.

In the terrible instant before the Surari crowded in on him, Mike saw Winter's predicament. There was no doubt in his mind as to what to do. He pinned his eyes onto the Merman's.

"Hey, you! Damn bastard fish! And you!" he screamed at another Merman making its way through the wrecked window. "Come and get me!"

"Mike! No!" Niall yelled, surging forward to help his friend.

But Mike's words stopped him. "Don't you dare, man. Go help Winter. Now!"

Niall knew his friend was right. He threw himself on the Merman that was pinning Winter to the floor, and stabbed him over and over again with the knife he'd grabbed from the table.

With a howl of pure fury, Winter grabbed the Merman's head and pushed her fingers into its eyes, scooping out its eyeballs with a shudder of revulsion. The Merman jerked backwards, convulsing on the floor, scraping at its head with its hands, dark, foul-smelling liquid pouring out of its empty eye sockets.

Niall had barely got his bearings before two Mermen threw him aside. One of them grabbed Winter's leg and took a bite out of her calf, then threw her face first into a puddle of Blackwater. The other ripped into Niall's back, lifting him off the floor by his shoulders. Niall roared in fury, until finally he swept into the song again, every bit as deafening as before. The Mermen fell to the ground, rolling in agony, covering their ears with their hands. Niall fell heavily, released by his captor, still screaming and singing and howling the deadliest sound that had ever come out of his mouth.

Elodie lost no time, kneeling beside the fallen Mermen, delivering her deadly kisses – two, four, six Mermen fell unconscious and died, touched by Elodie's poisonous lips. But soon Niall's song got too much even for her. She slid underneath the table and covered her ears with her hands, blood dripping through her fingers.

Sean pulled her out of the other side with one hand, while the other was still tracing the runes with the last of his energy, sending deadly ribbons hurtling through the air. Niall's song was hurting him too. "God, Niall, stop!" he shouted, though he knew that their lives depended on it.

The only one who seemed unaffected by the song was

Sarah, who kept placing her hands on fallen Mermen, her eyes closed, pressing their bodies until their skin starting to weep and ooze away. One after the other, Sarah dissolved them, utterly focused on what she needed to do.

Elodie and Sean huddled by the wall, unable to move, grimacing with the pain. Sean's ears were now bleeding heavily too. But Niall would not give up. They had been caught out once, he would not let that happen again. He kept going as long as he could, slowly folding into himself as his body weakened and the spell drained the last of his strength.

The song turned into a final terrible wail, and then silence. Niall lay mute and panting on the ground. For a few seconds there was no movement in the room except terrified eyes darting, trying to work out where the danger would come from next. The only noise was heavy breathing. In the sudden calm, two uninjured Mermen moved swiftly towards where Mike was lying. One of them bent over him, grabbed him by the hair, and then dropped him, in full view of the others.

Mike lay lifeless, his throat ripped open.

Niall let out a shout of grief and anger. He crawled towards the fallen body and shook Mike's shoulders, trying not to acknowledge the terrible thought that kept forcing itself into his mind.

Mike is dead.

No.

Mike is dead.

No, no!

"Look out! Niall!" yelled Sarah.

A Surari grabbed him from behind, shaking him and squeezing him so hard he couldn't breathe. He had no energy and no breath left to sing, and the knife was out of reach, stuck into a dead Merman. In his head he was already dead, alongside Mike. But then Nicholas was standing there, his hands raised, blue flames flowing from his fingers and enveloping the Merman. The Surari caught fire immediately, as if it'd been doused in fuel, blackening and curling up at once. Niall was astonished to see the look on Nicholas's face as he looked down at Mike's dead body. The sparks from his fingers faded. He dropped his head into his hands.

This is it. It has started, Nicholas told himself.

The brain fury in all its might – not the headaches that had been tormenting him. This was the real thing.

"No! Stop! Please, stop!" he begged in a daze of blinding pain, clawing at his scalp. It was as if acid were being poured through his eyes, burning through his skin, his bones, and the soft tissue of his brain. Every breath was crippling, every blink like dying a thousand deaths, until he shut his eyes and curled up into a ball, unable to do anything but wail.

And then when he thought that the pain could not get worse, the King of Shadows – his father – unleashed the full force of his power on his own son, driving him through acute pain into near madness. Nicholas shuddered and screamed, a scream that chilled everyone's blood, drawing their attention from the remaining Mermen.

"Nicholas!" Sarah was facing a hideous Merman whose hands were woven with seaweed, and whose face was encrusted with sea anemones. She too wondered where he had been all this time. She shook her head briefly – she had to concentrate, summon the Midnight gaze, and quickly – but her eyes couldn't focus, not with Nicholas screaming like that. She had never heard anything like it.

Summoning all her remaining strength she finally looked at the Surari with all the force of her Midnight eyes, and incredibly the Merman faltered, scrambling blindly at her with its slippery hands. Sarah took hold of both its hands at once, and for a second it looked almost as if they were dancing – and then the Merman's skin began to weep and blacken, until its arms dissolved with a splash, and its head, its body, its legs followed, gushing across the wooden floor in a black puddle.

Breathing heavily, Sarah surveyed the scene. Many Mermen were dead, but there were many others still standing, waiting for the humans to fall. Sean was badly wounded, Elodie looked utterly exhausted. Nicholas, to her horror, had begun to bang his head against the wall, and Niall . . . Niall was crying. Her eyes met his across the room and she raised herself to go to him. But Nicholas needed her first. She had to stop him injuring himself, splitting his head open against the wall. What had happened to him?

She was sure that the way across the room to reach him was clear – but almost immediately a Merman halted her in her tracks, punching the air out of her lungs, and throwing her to the floor. As she landed, she felt something breaking – the ribs she'd cracked only a few weeks before, probably. The pain was so intense she almost fainted. She braced herself for a kick or another vicious punch. But instead of the ghastly face of one of her attackers she saw the innocent little girl with long blonde hair. The girl she'd seen the night of her scrying spell. Everything fell silent.

"Mairead," she mouthed.

"Remember," said the little girl, and her voice resounded clear and composed in the sudden silence.

Not a second passed before Sarah found herself standing on the beach. She was a child again, eight years old, the wind blowing on her face, and someone holding her hand. She looked up. It was her grandmother, Morag Midnight. The scene twirled and danced around her, and suddenly the beach vanished and they were in her grandmother's room. She was showing Sarah something. A book.

"A storm is coming, and it will hit before long. If you have no other choice left, and you have to read this book, death might not be far away."

"Gran," she murmured, troubled at what she had been told.

And then the scene dissolved.

She was back in the hellish mess of Midnight Hall and Mairead was in front of her again, caressing her face. Somebody was screaming. Nicholas was screaming. Sarah fixed her eyes on Mairead, silently pleading for help, and then the world ebbed away.

Nicholas had seen Sarah falling, and with impossible effort he'd steadied himself. He moved away from the wall, yelling in the ancient language, ordering the Mermen to take hold of Sarah, to lay her in a corner of the room where she would be unharmed, to guard her. She was his chosen bride, she must be saved.

The Mermen heard him, but they showed no sign of obeying his orders.

And then, the voice in his head.

You're going to die, and so is Sarah. You sealed her fate with your choice.

"No! Sarah!" Nicholas clutched at his head again, fighting the fire that was consuming him.

Had you not betrayed me, she would have been spared.

"Sarah!" Nicholas's brain was burning, scorching. He could no longer see anything but painful bursts of lightning piercing deep darkness. His forehead was bruised and bloody from where he'd banged it against the wall.

The effort to keep conscious was draining him. He must not give into it. He knew that soon he wouldn't be able to stand, but still he called and pleaded in the ancient language, desperately hoping that the Mermen would listen, though by now he knew in his heart that all hope was gone.

It seemed as if the Surari were pausing. Hearing Nicholas's crazed screaming, Sean turned his back on the Merman nearest him and followed the black-eyed man's gaze. Sarah was unconscious on the floor, and he started running towards her, tracing flailing symbols in the air. Immediately the Surari mobilized. Sean knew that it was the wrong decision to run, and he knew that he couldn't run fast enough, but he had to try. The nearest Surari reached him in two long strides, took hold of him and sank its teeth into his arm, keeping them there and sucking, savouring the taste. Sean collapsed from the pain of it, unable to reach Sarah.

The pain in his head was so strong that Nicholas could see nothing – but he forced himself to raise his arms, and it worked. He felt the blue sparks flickering from the tops of his fingers again. Relieved, he opened his eyes, and although he was looking at where he knew his hands were, he still saw nothing but darkness.

Panicked, he began spinning, flicking his hands at random, directing the flames at the curtains, the rugs, the tablecloth, until the whole room was ablaze. A terrible cry passed his lips, a cry of pain and rage and despair, and made every creature in the room, human or Surari, stop and listen in horror.

The slight pause was enough, and one by one the Mermen went up in flames – they seemed to burn as fast as kindling, melting and crackling, pouring into liquid fat and disappearing into ashes.

Finally free, Sean limped to Sarah, wading through the puddles of Blackwater mixed with ash, and squatted beside her. With great effort, and despite all his bruises, he gathered her in his arms. She was slowly coming back to her senses.

"Sarah. We need to get out. It's all on fire!"

"Nicholas?"

A flaming curtain fell from the window in front of Sean's feet, nearly setting them both alight. Sean jumped back with a scream. "We need to go, Sarah. Now. I'm sorry."

"No!"

"Sarah! We'll all die!" Sean took her by the shoulders and looked straight into her eyes. "Look around you! We have to save ourselves." Blue flames danced around them, enveloping everything they touched.

Sarah nodded miserably.

Nicholas. Forgive me.

Sean and Sarah started their slow progress towards the window, towards safety and fresh air. "Elodie! Niall! Niall! Winter! Out now!" Sean yelled over and over again.

On hearing Sean's voice over the last of the incinerated Mermen's screams, Niall shook himself. He took hold of Mike's body – he wouldn't let him burn, he wouldn't leave his friend – and lifted him over his shoulder.

"Winter!" he called. "Elodie!"

He looked behind him, but the smoke was now so thick that he couldn't breathe, and he could barely see. Suddenly, Elodie appeared in front of him, choking, her body wracked with coughs. To his horror, he saw that the bandages on her arms were on fire. He pushed her roughly through the broken windows before negotiating the jagged shards of glass around the window frames, Mike's weight throwing him off balance.

Through the smoke billowing into the night sky, he saw Elodie rolling on the grass, trying to put the fires all over her body out. She lay on the grass for a moment, panting, holding her blackened arms.

"Elodie! Help!"

Niall was struggling to push Mike's heavy body through the jagged holes in the window. He was coughing violently, and his eyes were streaming with tears. She jumped to her feet, taking hold of Mike and helping Niall to lay him on the grass a safe distance from the house.

"Are you OK? Your arms," croaked Niall, wiping his eyes on his sleeves.

"I'm fine. It didn't burn the skin. Oh my God." She knelt by Mike's body, lowering her ear to his mouth, calling his name.

Niall shook his head. "He isn't unconscious. He's dead."

"It was him. It was him, then," she murmured. Her eyes met Niall's, and they mirrored each other's pain.

But Elodie shook herself. "Winter, Sean and Sarah are still inside, I'm going to get them." She stood up, facing the inferno that was now the dining room in which they had started their Christmas dinner not long before.

"I'm coming with you."

With a final look at Mike's body, they prepared themselves to race inside again, but a wall of toxic smoke and the blast of terrible heat forced them back. Niall and Elodie looked at each other again. There was no way they could return inside.

"They're gone," Elodie cried, and clasped her hands to her mouth.

"Elodie! Look!" Niall was pointing at something pale moving carefully out of one of the far windows. They ran closer. It was a white hand, clutching the broken glass.

"I'm coming!" called Niall. He grabbed the fingers, holding them firmly as they groped along the glass. It was a woman's hand. Sarah's? Winter's? He couldn't make it out. Another hand appeared, and a pair of bleeding arms, and finally, a silvery head covered in ashes.

It was Winter, her hair blackened and singed, her skin red raw where the flames had burnt her.

"Niall?"

"I'm here. I'm here. Come on." Niall helped her up and out, not caring about whether he cut his own arms or not.

Winter staggered free and lay down on the grass, panting and coughing up black blood.

"Thank God," murmured Elodie. But she couldn't rest. "Sean! Sarah!" she kept calling, to no avail.

Once he was sure that Winter's breathing was steady and that she could stand – and run if need be – Niall joined Elodie once more, as close to the house as they could get in the face of the scorching heat. They called frantically. No reply. Just licks of blue flame darting out of the windows.

"They're gone. Sean and Sarah are gone," Niall whispered in disbelief. He pushed his hands through his filthy hair and turned away.

Mike. Sean. Sarah. Nicholas.

Dead.

Niall felt a wave of despair sweep him. It was all over.

Elodie appeared by his side and took his hand. Instinctively, he took her in his arms, gesturing to Winter to join them. The three of them stood close together, clinging to each other, watching the house being reduced to ash and rubble.

And then there was the sound of shattering glass and, in disbelief, they watched as two blackened shapes threw themselves out of the farthest window, followed by hungry blue tongues of flame. They lay on the ground a few yards from the house, skin cut, eyes weeping, coughing, heaving, snatching ragged, short, painful breaths. But alive.

It was Sean and Sarah.

As soon as she could draw enough breath to speak, Sarah tried to scramble to her feet. "Nicholas!" she screamed. "Nicholas is still inside!"

"There's nothing we can do!" Sean restrained her, but she struggled to be let go until he encircled her in his arms, pinning her to him, refusing to let her re-enter the building. Finally she stopped struggling and turned away, weeping with frustration.

And then she saw the body.

One of them hadn't made it.

Sean walked over and knelt, taking in the frozen, livid features of his friend. Mike, lying terribly, terribly still, his body broken and his soul gone. Sean whispered his name over and over, louder with each call, and then he screamed, all his fury pouring into the terrible sound.

Sean's cry of rage was joined by sounds of sadness from the others as they all began to take in the enormity of what had happened. And as they stood there, a million little flakes started falling on and around them all, resting delicately on their stricken faces and their bloodied hands. They stood there, in shock, the heat of the burning house coming against the frozen December air.

And then, as the fire in the house consumed itself, as the snow kept falling, a black figure appeared silhouetted against the white sky – black hair, black face, eyes crazed with pain.

"Nicholas!" cried Sarah. She ran to him and held him, but he was too heavy. They fell together on the grass. "You're alive!"

"I can't die in fire," whispered Nicholas through parched, charred lips. "Because I. Am. Fire," he added slowly, as if to remind himself of his identity. He fell supine on the slowly growing mantle of snow.

Sarah bent over him and touched his face, his hair, feeling his features with her fingers and sweeping the ash from his skin. Something was wrong, she knew it. Something was very wrong, and it would never be right again.

Nicholas kept blinking, his eyes streaming from the ash and the smoke, but he wasn't focusing. His eyes were sweeping all around, darting towards the sky, the ground, not quite resting anywhere or on anything. Sarah's heart missed a beat.

She looked into his eyes, and that's when she realized what had happened to him.

Nicholas was blind.

56

Like a River to the Sea

The last words I said to you
Weren't even words at all

Sean

He was the best Gamekeeper I knew. But before being a Gamekeeper, he was my friend. Mike had sacrificed everything for our mission, as if he'd had no other life at all, nothing but the fight alongside the Secret Families. We all toss and turn under our burdens, we all complain and pity ourselves – every second thought of ours starts with *I*. I want, I need, I wish. Mike had forgotten all about his needs and desires. He was the one among us who lived for the world, not for himself.

And now, he is the one who lies wrapped in a white sheet on the snowy ground.

Sarah and Elodie have prepared him, washed him, dressed him. All his wounds are nearly invisible. He seems asleep, peaceful.

Niall is quiet now, calm, but his eyes are red, and his hands curled into fists. I can sense the anger rolling off him, an acidic, half-burnt scent that is completely out of place on Niall, who's usually so mellow. I think he has changed forever, like Sarah did when Leigh died.

Elodie has her hand in mine, our hair getting damp under the snowfall; Winter is standing beside Niall, her arms and legs bare in her cotton dress. Sarah is not with us. She's with Nicholas, who's been hurt in the fight in a way we can't quite understand. They're in Nicholas's room, curtains closed.

We're all bruised, wounded, limping – a band of survivors still bleeding from the battle. I can't quite believe it all happened just a few hours ago. The flames extinguished themselves as quickly as they had started, sparing the rest of Midnight Hall. Only the grand hall was destroyed, a blackened shell coated with foul-smelling grease and melted glass.

I say a few words to try and steady us, but my voice sounds feeble and distant in this dreamy white landscape. Not loud enough to tell the world what a tragedy it is to have lost Mike, how cold, how black everything is now. Or maybe words aren't necessary.

And then Niall starts singing, the Irish Gaelic words running off his tongue like a waterfall. He sings the saddest song I've ever heard. Once the song has died away, Niall recites the words in English so that we can all understand his last tribute to Mike. His words are punctuated by our soft sobbing:

Many a night both wet and dry
Weather of the seven elements
He would find for me a rocky shelter
Where I would take refuge
They let your blood yesterday
Great is my sorrow, great

Our tears mix with falling snowflakes as we gently lift Mike up and place him in the cradle we have dug for him in the soft, not yet frozen soil of Islay.

"So far from home," whispers Winter.

Everyone is silent and shivering as we walk back inside. Everything is covered in ash and debris, and the windows on one side of the house are empty and black like blind eyes. Sarah is walking slowly down the stairs, a smudge of ash on her cheek.

"How is he?" whispers Elodie.

Sarah shakes her head. It's enough of an answer. Right on cue, a half-cry comes from upstairs. It's Nicholas. "Leave him," says Sarah. "There is nothing – nothing – you can do to help him."

I rake my fingers through my hair. "We need to go back to the mainland, but it's too early to leave now. We will wait until morning, as planned. Niall has arranged a lift with the trawlermen."

Sarah nods.

"We need to get Nicholas on his feet and out of here. I'll go see him." My voice is still hoarse and broken.

"Be gentle, please, Sean. He's in agony." Sarah begs me. But she doesn't stop me.

"He might be in agony, but worse may be to come, so we still need to go, Sarah." I don't have kinder words for Nicholas now. All I can think of is that, unlike Mike, he's not six feet under.

Sarah and Elodie follow me upstairs. Quietly, I make my way into Nicholas's room. His body is shuddering with the intensity of his sobs, his face hidden in a pillow.

"I can't take this anymore, Sean. Please kill me," he slurs, without showing his face. I'm horrified. The powerful, arrogant Nicholas is begging like a little boy. *What's going on?* I look to Sarah, who has her hands clasped over her mouth.

"Nicholas, what's happening?" I ask.

He cradles his head in his hands and moans softly.

Sarah kneels beside his bed. "There must be a way for us to help you. Please, Nicholas. You must know something."

He sits up suddenly, still holding his head. "I made my choice! I made my choice!" he yells, as if he's hallucinating.

"What choice? What choice did you make?" I take him by the shoulders, and he strikes out at random, catching my nose. A warm gush of blood flows over my hands, but I signal Sarah to leave me be. I was already in pretty bad shape after tonight's attack. One more ache won't change the score much.

"You're all dead!" he screams. "And so am I!"

I can see now that he's delirious with pain. There's no making sense out of him.

Sarah is distraught. "Nicholas, please."

"My father is coming!"

"Who is it, Nicholas? Who is your father?" I press him.

"The King of Shadows!" he screams, issuing a heartbreaking wail.

We still, remembering Niall and Winter's words from only a few hours earlier. *But what can he mean? There was no mention of a son of the King of Shadows?*

He looks up for a long instant, his blind eyes open and staring, and then he shudders. Blood is flowing from his nostrils and his mouth, and, horribly, out of his eyes – it's as if he's exploding from the inside. In perfect silence, as if drowned in his own blood, he falls against the pillow, unconscious.

"Nicholas! No!" Sarah kneels on the floorboards beside the bed, clinging to him. "Oh my God, he's dead! Nicholas! No!"

337

Elodie is shivering so violently that her teeth are chattering. "Nicholas," she calls despairingly.

My hand is on his neck at once, checking his pulse. "He's not dead."

Sarah sobs in relief.

"Help me."

We prop him up, peeling the drenched sheets from his body, wiping him clean, remaking the bed with fresh linen Sarah's found in the cupboard.

"What's happening to him? Sean, please help him," Sarah begs.

"I don't know what's going on. This started during the battle, didn't it? He was in pain while fighting the Mermen. I thought it was the attack, but maybe it's something else?"

Sarah is wringing her fingers. "He kept shouting. He kept saying 'I made my choice,' as if he was talking to someone."

"Sean." There's an edge to Elodie's voice that makes me look up at once. "He might not be delirious."

"What do you mean?"

"He told us the King of Shadows is his father."

"Clearly he doesn't know what he's saying!" protests Sarah, an arm across Nicholas's chest as if to defend him.

But Elodie is adamant. "This pain he's suffering. This . . . burning up in his head. Where else have we seen it, Sean?"

I feel ill. "Members of the Valaya."

Elodie nods.

"This makes no sense. *You* make no sense!" Sarah yells. "Get out! You always wanted him dead!" she screams at me, her face smeared with blood and tears.

"Sarah," I begin, but all of a sudden Nicholas's voice – the one we're familiar with – interrupts me.

"Why am I alive?"

He has opened his eyes. They're blacker than night, his face whiter than the sheets Sarah's arranging around him. He looks like a man who has come back from the dead.

"Nicholas," whispers Sarah, a hint of fear in her voice.

"The pain is gone. Why did he not kill me?"

"Who? Who are you talking about?"

"My father. The King of Shadows," he murmurs.

Sarah's face seems to crumple in despair, and then it turns expressionless, blank. She lifts her arm and stands back.

"Now or never, Nicholas Donal, if that is your name. Who are you?" I force the words out, almost scared to hear the response.

But Nicholas is beaten to the truth by Elodie.

"You *are* the Enemy's son," she says, anger seething from her voice.

"Yes." Nicholas barely has the energy to speak. His battered, bloodied face could have been through the Apocalypse.

My hand is on my *sgian-dubh* at once. "You betrayed us. You just sat there while Niall and Winter told us all about the book they found in the library, and you said nothing! You let the demons come!" I spat.

"No. I saved you," he whispers, barely audible. "And my father will kill me because of that. I thought he would have done so already, but I'm still alive," he whispers, as if the fact surprises him.

"Why did you do it?" Elodie's voice is as cold as the snow outside.

"Because I made a choice. You helped me make it, Elodie. I won't help my father kill anymore."

I fight the impulse to bury my *sgian-dubh* straight into his heart. This liar killed Mike as surely as if he'd shot him in the head.

"I know what you're thinking, Sean. But I'm the only chance you have."

I laugh. "How selfless you are. You want to be kept alive for our good! You pathetic bastard." But I know he's telling the truth. I know he's not imploring us to keep him alive. He's imploring us to keep *ourselves* alive.

Elodie's eyes are fixed on Nicholas's. "You saved me. Twice. It was your father, wasn't it, who ordered the ravens on me?"

"Yes."

"But you stopped them."

"Yes."

My anger is all-consuming, I'm sure I could burst into flames at any minute. "Your father started all this. Your father killed them all. Harry, Mike, all the Secret heirs around the world."

"I want to stop him. I'm going to take you to him. The gate the book described is in an ancient forest, hundreds of miles from here. We need to head east."

Elodie and I look at each other. I'm chilled at the cold fury in her eyes.

"How do we know you're not lying? That you can be trusted? That you won't turn on us? What is your word to us after all this?" I ask bitterly.

"Do you have a choice, Sean? You want this destruction to end, don't you?"

"Shut up. Now."

Elodie and I turn at Sarah's biting words. We've been so absorbed in what was happening that we've forgotten all about her. She's been standing there, at a distance from us. Her eyes are shining bright green, sharp as two blades, cutting whoever looks into them, and I see that her hands are raised, ready to hit.

"You lied to me all this time."

"I'm sorry, Sarah," Nicholas begins. His face crumples.

"You lied to me, you pretended you loved me! Why did you not just kill me straight away? Why did you not kill us all! Did you want to play with us a little bit longer?" she hisses through gritted teeth.

"You were never supposed to die, Sarah. You were chosen as my bride."

An icy shudder runs down my spine and I hear myself unleash a deep growl. *Over my dead body!*

Then Sarah strides over to the bed. "As your *what*? Are you insane? The bride of the . . . Prince of Shadows, or whoever you are? What is this, some crazy fairy tale?"

Nicholas is gripped by a coughing fit so hard he might choke. And it wouldn't be such a bad thing if he did. There's a bluish tinge to his cheeks, and his breathing is fast and shallow.

"Stay awake, Nicholas. Don't you close your eyes!" Sarah's tone is deadly. Nicholas shivers. He's losing consciousness again.

"Look at me!" Sarah shouts, and then she pounces on him, her hands in front of her. Elodie and I grab her at once, holding her back. In the scuffle Elodie cries out in pain.

"You can't kill him, Sarah. As much as you want to – and believe me, so do I – we need him alive!" We're holding Sarah from behind, trying to avoid her deadly eyes.

"His father killed my parents! And Harry! He's killing us all!"

"We need him to take us to the Enemy. Think, Sarah, *think*! Don't let your rage win, Sarah. Think of what's best. Don't let your rage win." I repeat, like a mantra. Eventually Sarah's body softens in our grip.

Elodie unwraps her arms from round her waist, letting me hold her alone.

"You're not a man. And you're not a demon. You're a monster," Sarah whispers. Nicholas has his eyes closed, too weak to reply, too weak to move. "You can let me go, Sean. I won't touch him," she adds, composed.

I free Sarah from my hold, and Elodie takes her other arm, keeping her face turned away from Sarah's. "Come on. Come with me."

Sarah allows Elodie to lead her away, but at the threshold she turns around. "Why me, Nicholas? Why?" Her voice is laden with fury, and hurt.

"My father chose you among the heirs. You are the most powerful Dreamer of your generation. And your blood is still strong."

"Still" strong? What does that mean?

Nicholas looks like a wax mannequin, white but for the blood that stains his face, still, nearly lifeless. I wish I could strangle him with my own hands.

"Get up and get dressed," I say instead. "We're leaving this place, and soon."

Sarah is standing at the bottom of the stairs, her hands over her face. It's so surreal to see the lovely, pristine stone floors strewn with ash and debris, and where the great hall used to be – the room that Sarah always modestly called the living room – is a blackened, gaping hole.

"Sarah."

"I just can't believe it, Sean. I can't believe it."

"I know. I know."

"I thought you were just jealous of him."

I nodded. "I was. But there was something else as well.

342

I often thought he could be corrupt, I wondered whether he was collaborating with the Sabha. That maybe he was a member of a Valaya himself. I knew there was something about him that didn't quite add up. But I could never, ever have suspected that."

"The King of Shadows is his father," Sarah hisses. "How is this even possible?"

"I have no idea, Sarah."

She abruptly turns on her heels. "I need to get out."

"I'm coming with you." I'm expecting her to protest, but she doesn't. I grab coats for both of us and follow her outside. We stand together in the snow that has covered the grass at the back of the house. The snow is still falling. Sarah is looking towards the beach and the water, a million dancing snowflakes falling silently on the sand and the sea. Dawn is seeping through the clouds, turning the sky a light purple.

"I've been close to him all this time, Sean. I never suspected ..."

"It's not your fault. He deceived you."

"I feel sick."

"Seriously?"

"Yes. Oh." She takes a few steps, and starts retching. She falls to her knees, her black hair even blacker against the snow.

I brush her hair away from her face, holding it clear until she's finished. She's very pale, and a film of cold sweat covers her forehead.

"I left him," she tells me quietly.

"What?"

"It was after you said we could never be together. Because of all that genetic crap."

"That wasn't crap. That's the way things are," I whisper. My heart is in pieces.

"Great. Just great. First I fall for you . . ."

I hold my breath. *I wasn't just imagining it, then.* "But I couldn't have you, and then I found out you betrayed me," she continued. "Then I end up with Nicholas, and it turns out that he's a monster. What else now?"

"Did you . . ."

"What?"

"Did you love Nicholas? Really?"

She frowns and sighs heavily. "I thought I did, but there was always something. I don't know, something *wrong*. Whenever he was around I felt . . . I couldn't think clearly. It was as if he controlled my thoughts."

"And I wasn't there to kick his face in." Anger is making my hands shake.

"I had sent you away."

That was true. "I should have done something, though." I raise my head as we speak. I see Niall in the kitchen, looking out of the big glass windows. Winter is standing beside him, her silver hair strewn over his arm, her head resting on his shoulder. For a second, Niall looks like an old man. My heart skips a beat. Now that Mike is gone, nothing will ever be the same.

"Things had changed, though," Sarah continues. "Since we'd come to Islay he didn't seem to have the same effect on me, confusing my thoughts, I mean."

The snow is falling thick and fast around us, resting on Sarah's face, on her black coat. A sliver of sunlight is shining on the sea. "He was much more worried about things, always seemed to be upset about something. Not as confident as he used to be. Not as arrogant." She shrugs. "I wonder what brought all this on. This . . . repenting thing. Deciding to turn against his father to help us. Who knows?" Sarah shivers, wrapping her arms around herself.

"We'd better go. You're freezing. I'll make Nicholas coffee – that should wake him up fast. And then I suppose we have to trust him to take us to where his father is. At least we know now what we're up against."

I can't even begin to think about all that now. I'm set to go, and I turn to head for the house, but Sarah puts a hand on my arm, stopping me. "Sean? He said my blood is still strong. What did he mean?"

"Maybe he was talking about your powers. The Blackwater?"

"Yes. That must be it. The most powerful Dreamer, he said. Some good it does me."

Before I can stop myself, I take her hand in mine. "Why did you leave Nicholas?" I ask, hoping and praying for the answer I want.

"Because I love someone else," she whispers. Our eyes meet for a second, and what I wouldn't give to put my lips on hers.

"I thought about the message Harry left in the fairy-tale book." She interrupts my thoughts.

"Yes?"

"It occurred to me, 'Morag' in Gaelic means Sarah. The message is about me, not about my grandmother. *Watch over Sarah, she's the key.* That's what it meant," she whispers, and walks away, letting go of my hand. Our fingers hold on for a second. Her soft scent lingers in the air, and as she goes, I feel like a part of me has just been cut off.

But my heart is beating wildly. *Sarah doesn't love Nicholas. She loves somebody else.*

And I know it's me.

It's the answer I've dreamt of, but not an answer on which I can act.

I watch her walk through the falling snow towards the broken house. There's a cold, hard splinter in my heart. It's her absence. I feel it when I breathe, when I walk, when I speak. It's lodged in there and shows no sign of vanishing. But I'm right about us not being able to be together, I know I'm right. However painful and unbearable that might feel.

I curse the Secret Families for never having told me I couldn't be with a Secret. I curse my own blood for being all wrong. Everything is wrong. While Sarah and I were falling for each other life has been mocking us.

I stand in the snow for a little longer, going over the conversation earlier between Sarah and me, when she told me what she'd discovered about my parents.

The truth about my parents, Amelia Campbell and Allan Hannay, has blown me apart. Would it have been better if I hadn't ever known? Sarah thought she was doing the right thing by telling me. But I'm not sure. Should I say I'm bitter for what was denied to me, my rightful inheritance, my place in the world?

My parents, a proper family.

The truth is, I never knew, and I never suspected. I thought it'd been the Gamekeeper training that taught me how to use the runes, how to move under a mantle of invisibility. I suppose I should have noticed that no other Gamekeeper I knew had talents as special as mine. I would have noticed had I not been so busy doing my bloody job. Harry did say a couple of times that the way I used the runes was special, but he never made a big deal of it. Now I know why. I was never to know of my half-Secret, bastard blood.

They lived in a different world, Stewart Midnight, Morag, and Amelia. My mother. A world of old prejudice and suspicion, set in ways as ancient as this rugged rock they call

Islay. They exiled my mother, and for what? So she fell in love with someone who wasn't of her kind. She failed the Secret Family, she failed them all. And because of this, they destroyed her.

The irony is, she ended up having no more children, so their plan didn't work. Her powers weren't passed on anyway, not to any proper Secret heir, I mean. Just me, the mongrel.

And because of my parentage, I can never be with the woman I love.

Before I head inside I turn around one last time to look at the little snowy mound where we've buried Mike, shimmering faintly in the lilac light of morning. I bet he never thought he, a man from Louisiana, would end up buried on a Scottish island. An unmarked grave, for now. Just for now.

I'll come back and see that you get a proper burial, Mike. I'll come back and see you.

57

Alone With You

That night you said our souls
Are made of the same thing

Niall couldn't cry, he just couldn't – even if the lump of tears
he had in his throat was suffocating him. He needed to be at
sea, but he couldn't do that either. They had to stay together.
All of them.

As the thought formed in his head, Niall felt a stab of pain
in his heart. *No, not all of us*, he remembered. Just those who
are left.

He watched the waves ebbing and flowing from the
window in his room. Every wave called to him. Only the
water could have healed his raw soul, but the water was
forbidden to him for now. Only Winter, who was standing
beside him, the same longing in her eyes, could understand
how he was feeling. She'd held his hand throughout the burial
and never left his side since. Winter's hand in his, her warm
body beside him, reminded Niall that he was still alive, that
he wasn't lying in that grave with Mike. Though it felt like it.

Niall couldn't get Mike's face out of his head. His voice, his jokes, his mannerisms. In the short time they'd spent together Mike had won Niall's friendship, his admiration, his complete and utter loyalty.

And now he's gone, killed by those bloody bastards we've been hunting all our lives.

"We must go and look for the King of Shadows. We must at least try and destroy him. Or we'll be picked off one by one," he murmured.

Winter touched Niall's face. "I know."

"I might not be back."

"I'm coming with you."

He turned to her in shock. "You can't, it's too dangerous! Please, Winter, stay on Islay. Wait for me."

"Do you really think I'd be safe here? After what happened in this house? We're all in danger, wherever we are. On land or in the water. There are no heirs left here, Niall. The nearest Families, as far as I know, are further north or down south in England, and I have no idea if they're still alive. Islay is not safe anymore."

"Probably, but it's certainly safer than coming with us."

"I'm not going to leave you," she said. She wrapped her arms around his neck, and pressed her warm lips to his. They tasted salty, and there was the usual scent of fresh air and seawater coming off her skin.

Kissing her is like kissing a wave, Niall had time to think before all thoughts ebbed away. With her hands on him, and her lips on his there was no time to think, no time for anything but to wrap himself around her and dive into her warmth. He let his sorrow melt into her, he let his tears flow away, a river of sadness dissolving into the sea.

★

Dawn found them entwined, Winter's silver hair on his chest, her soft breath in his ear. He opened his eyes to see her lovely face resting on his shoulder, her body against his. The sorrow for Mike's loss invaded him again, but there was a little light of hope nesting in his heart now, that he would drink from her again and again, and that if night had to close on them forever, at least it would happen when they were together.

58
Blind

Pain is a secret society
That makes those who feel it
Kin

Elodie sat quietly, her hands in her lap. A frozen, still sky was pressing against her window, dotted with a million swirling snowflakes.

So that's what it was. My hair standing on end every time Nicholas was around, those whispers that crawled in my ears and I couldn't get rid of – that sense of unease, of danger – fighting with the evidence, the fact that Nicholas had saved my life. The fact that he could have killed me, twice, and he didn't.

There he was, in flesh and blood, the man ultimately responsible for Harry's death. The man who destroyed her life.

He was lying sleeping, curled up, as harmless as a child. He'd tried to get up, but had fallen on the floor, his legs giving way. He lay so still, so white, that for a moment Elodie thought he was dead – then she realized he had fallen asleep suddenly, like babies do. The torture he had suffered for hours, that terrible thing he'd called brain fury in his delirium, had left him half-dead and spent. And blind.

So this is the man who killed me.

There was nothing Elodie would have wanted more than to give Nicholas her poisonous kiss. It would have been an immensely stupid thing to do, of course – it didn't take Elodie long to see that clearly, to turn her rage into a plan. The final plan. The time when everything would come together, and Nicholas would take them straight to the lair of the beast.

Elodie wetted a towel and washed the blood off his face, calmly. She'd never seen anyone bleed from their eyes before. She'd never seen anyone in so much pain. He had clawed at his own cheeks and bit his lips until they were shredded and bleeding. He'd bear the scars for as long as he lived.

Elodie had no sympathy for him, not even now, lying here a broken man. He hadn't chosen to be born a monster, but he had chosen to do his father's bidding, to kill and destroy for a long, long time. Until life had taken him to Sarah.

What is it about Sarah that enchants them all?

"Elodie?"

She jumped out of her skin. Nicholas was looking at her with black, shiny, unseeing eyes, so dark that the pupil fused with the iris. Elodie felt a wave of hatred, but didn't betray any emotion. "You need to get up. We must go."

He groaned. Immediately, he was sick by the side of the bed. "I'm sorry," he whispered.

For what? Killing my husband? Planning to destroy humanity? I have nothing to say to that. Nothing to say in the face of his apology.

Without saying a word, Elodie cleaned up his mess using some of the discarded bloodied sheets Sarah had removed. It was as if someone had been cut to pieces there.

"Come on. Let's get you ready," she said, bringing him to a sitting position. He couldn't even sit upright. He whimpered as she lifted his T-shirt over his head, then fell back down as she removed his torn trousers.

So human, so vulnerable. Just a boy, really. The heir to the Underworld, half naked, wounded, helpless.

She led him to the bathroom, slowly, faltering step after faltering step – he wasn't used to walking in darkness yet – and helped him sit in the bathtub. He closed his eyes as she ran the shower over him, washing the blood and pain away. An unwelcome voice was worming its way into her ear. A voice of compassion that she didn't want to listen to.

You can't hate someone as broken as this. You can't hate someone while you run a wet cloth over their wounds, while you wash encrusted blood out of their hair, and they squeeze your hand when the pain is too much to bear.

Elodie hardened her face. She wouldn't listen.

She helped him out of the bathtub and wrapped a towel around him, drying him as gently as she could. They walked out of the bathroom, and Elodie caught her breath in fright, which transferred itself to Nicholas. She felt his hand squeezing hers, heard his soft gasp of fear.

"It's OK," she reassured him. "It's Sean."

Sean was standing in the room with a steaming mug and a dark look in his eyes.

"All well, Elodie?"

Elodie nodded, faltering under Nicholas's weight. Sean took a step towards them, but she raised a hand to stop him.

"Make him drink this, I need him awake."

"Yes," she replied tersely.

Then Sean left, with one last hateful look towards Nicholas.

"Is he gone?" Nicholas asked.

"Yes. He's gone. I'm going to find you some clothes," she said.

"Don't go away," he replied, an edge of panic to his voice. "Everything is dark. I don't know where I am."

"I'm here," she said, echoing the words he'd said to her a few days before. Was it only a few days? It felt like a lifetime. She rummaged in his rucksack, looking for clothes. Her fingers curled around something small and cold, a precious stone. She examined it in her open hand. It looked like an opal. She considered asking him about it, but decided against it. She slipped it into her pocket, resolving not to tell anyone until she found out what it was.

Slowly, gently, she helped him dress, wincing every time he yelped in pain. Then she held the cup of coffee to his mouth, one hand resting on the back of his head. "Drink up. We need you standing, Nicholas."

He took a sip. "I didn't want to do what he said anymore, Elodie."

It took you a long time to realize that, she wanted to say, but there was no point. Nicholas needed all his energy to lead them to his father.

"Why did he not kill me?" he repeated. "I betrayed him. I saved you all. He punished me with the brain fury, that's supposed to kill you. But I'm alive. I can't feel him anymore. In my head. He's not screaming, he's not whispering. He's left me alone."

"You ready?" Elodie interrupted him. This wasn't a conversation she was prepared to have. She held him by the waist, and they stood together. He was so tall, and muscly – he was heavy on her, and still she supported him.

They were on the doorstep, when she stopped. There was something she needed to know. "Nicholas. On the beach, with the ravens, you told them not to harm me, and you were harmed yourself instead. Why did you stop them? You didn't need me. Not like you needed Sarah."

"I couldn't bear to see you killed."

Elodie laughed bitterly. "More deceit, Nicholas? Casting a spell on me, like you did on Sarah?" She spat out the words. All her hatred, all her anger came flooding back. The enchantment of the wounded man was broken.

"Look at me," he whispered.

She looked into his unseeing eyes. She wasn't afraid of any power he might have, of any witchcraft or magic he might use on her. She was the Brun heir, and Harry's widow, and she was angry. He couldn't deceive her.

She looked into his eyes without fear, and she saw that he had just spoken the truth.

59
Prophecies

Hidden away
In the White Tower
But he will come flying
On the wings of the raven

"Can we trust him?" Sean ran his fingers through his hair with a sigh. "Or will he lead us to our death?"

Sean, Sarah, Winter, Niall and Elodie were standing in the smoke-ravaged entrance to Midnight Hall, rucksacks piled beside them. They had left Nicholas resting on a makeshift bed in the kitchen while they readied themselves to leave.

"Well, how else will we find this gate? Only Nicholas knows where it is. You've seen the state he's in, it's not like he can attack us," said Elodie.

"Nicholas said somewhere east, and the signal we intercepted back in Louisiana, Mike and I," Niall looked away, still unable to say his friend's name without a pang of sorrow, "it came from eastern Europe, somewhere."

"There's something else," said Sarah, "something I remembered during the battle." Sarah beckoned them to follow her down the corridor and into her grandmother's study.

There was no light coming through the windows, just the black, snowy sky. The light inside the room was strangely blue, and the embers in the fireplace still glowed. Their shadows moved along the walls as they entered.

They watched as Sarah walked towards the desk and stepped behind it. She took the painting of wild horses hanging on the wall above and rested it carefully against the wall.

"I knew it," she whispered. She'd been right. The secret alcove her grandmother had shown her was there, stone shelves carved in the wall itself. And on the shelves, a thick, leather-bound volume.

"My grandmother gave me this the day before she died. She must have known what was going to happen. She forbade me from reading it until I was sure it was time. And I had forgotten all about it." She decided against telling them what had reminded her.

Sarah held the book up for everyone to see. Engraved in gold letters on the dark brown leather cover were the words *Carmina Prophetica*. "It's a book of prophecies," she explained, and opened it to where the bookmark, a red velvet ribbon, had been placed many years before.

"*A great evil will rise from the East,*" Sarah read. "*Secret people will follow the blind man.*" There was a collective intake of breath as their thoughts went to Nicholas. "*And they will lose much and suffer much, because theirs is the ruined blood of the Secret children. The soil will run red and the trees will dance as the earth opens and the shadows rise in the white tower.*"

"The white tower?" asked Sean. "Any indication of where that is?"

"Not a clue."

They stood in silence for a moment. Suddenly, after all the uncertainty and wondering and waiting, the next step in the battle was becoming clear.

"That's funny," murmured Elodie, breaking the silence.

"What?" asked Sean.

"One of the tales in the book Harry gave me. It talks about a princess in a white tower. Never mind." She gave a small shrug.

"Right. We need to get ready," said Sean authoritatively, striding out. Elodie followed him.

As she walked towards the kitchen to go check on Nicholas, the French girl silently finished her thought. *A princess prisoner in a white tower. And in the story a prince flying on the wings of a raven is the one who saves her.*

A long, cold shiver slithered down her spine.

60

One More Chance

I never thought I would
Hear your voice again

When the others left the room Sarah lingered for a few moments. She was alone, she could see that, and yet she didn't feel alone. She looked at the book in her hand, wondering if the presence she felt might be that of the person who had last held it. Morag Midnight. She shuddered at the thought. But as she walked from the room she felt a small hand entangled in her hair, and she sighed in relief. "Mairead," she whispered. "Thank you."

She ran downstairs. There was something else Sarah needed to do before they left. Alone. Just for a minute, she begged, and reluctantly Sean agreed, as long as she didn't wander out of sight. He was now standing a hundred yards from her, watching her clutch her mobile with shaking hands, her hood shielding the snow from the back of her neck.

She had to speak to them. It might be the last time. She decided to start with the conversation that was likely to be less painful. Bryony.

Three bars in the corner of the screen showed that there was a signal. She prayed that it would be strong enough. She pressed the green button.

Sarah knew that Bryony lived with her phone in her hand, and it barely rang once before Sarah heard her friend's familiar voice.

"Sarah?" Bryony sounded astounded.

"Bryony. It's me. Merry Christmas, a bit late."

"I've been trying to phone you for ages! Where are you? Still on Islay?"

"Yes."

"With Harry, or *Sean* – whatever his name is?"

"Yes."

"Are you OK?"

"For now, yes. Bryony, listen. Listen. I know you'll find this hard to believe, but you were right. It wasn't a burglar, that night in my house. I'm sorry I lied to you."

Bryony let out a deep breath. "I was right."

"Please let me finish. I'm going somewhere. I might not come back. I wanted to apologize, to tell you the truth, just in case."

Bryony sounded strangled. "Sarah! Don't do this."

"It's OK. Really, it's OK. There was always so much going on in my life, Bryony." She closed her eyes briefly. "I could never tell you. And I'm sorry about that. You need to keep safe, do you hear me? Don't go out on your own. Try and always have someone with you. And if you see something strange, be on guard."

"Sarah, you're scaring me!"

"I'm so sorry. I just want you safe. Will you do as I say?"

Bryony's voice sounded fearful. "What's going on? Are you in trouble? What is it? Have you done something wrong?"

"No, nothing like that. Bryony, you know you were my best friend."

"That I *was* your best friend?" Bryony was crying now. Sarah could hear it in her voice. She imagined her friend's face, that face she knew so well.

"I might come back." She tried to sound brighter.

But Bryony wasn't reassured. "You might. You might come back!"

There was no point in continuing the conversation. "Be safe. And please don't tell anyone about this. Promise."

"I promise, Sarah."

"Bye, Bryony."

Sarah pressed the red button as quickly as she could, cutting Bryony off before she could respond. That was hard enough. She took another deep breath, then, giving Sean a quick wave over her shoulder to reassure him that she was nearly ready, she dialled the next number. There wasn't much time.

It rang for what seemed like an eternity. Finally Sarah's heart plummeted as the answering machine kicked in. She couldn't leave a message. She tried again. It rang a few more times, and Sarah was almost ready to give up and walk back to Sean, when she heard a crackle on the line, and then a feeble, barely audible voice.

"Hello, Siobhan's phone. Juliet speaking."

Sarah felt her legs buckle from under her, and she fell to her knees on the wet sand.

"Hello? Hello?"

A sob came from Sarah's throat, and exploded in a flood of joyful tears. "Aunt Juliet! It's me! It's Sarah!"

"Sarah! Darling! I'm so glad to hear your voice. Your uncle told me you never wanted to speak to me again!"

"What? No, no! I thought you were dead."

361

"I nearly died, Sarah. It was a terrible attack. And I think they were looking for you. They mentioned your name. I had to know how you were, but Trevor wouldn't let me."

"I'm so sorry, Aunt Juliet. There's so much I'd like to tell you."

"Sarah, darling, don't. I know. I've always known that there was something strange going on in your lives. I just never wanted to believe it was as dangerous as this. Come home, my love. We'll help you, we'll keep you safe."

The offer of a home, love, security was so tempting. Sarah turned and looked towards Sean, standing waiting for her. "I can't. I need to go. I need to sort it all out, for us, and . . . for everyone. I know it's hard to believe."

A moment of silence.

"I understand," said Juliet.

"You do?"

Sarah could hear a voice in the background. Uncle Trevor.

"Bless you, my Sarah," whispered Juliet. "I need to go. I love you like a daughter, you know that, don't you?"

"I love you too, Aunt Juliet!" said Sarah, closing her eyes to a sudden gust of salty wind.

The line went dead. Aunt Juliet was gone.

Aunt Juliet was alive.

61
Love Must Be Spoken

My love for you
Is what keeps me breathing
I knew you
Before I knew you

Sean

Everybody is packing, sorting, loading the cars to head for the boats, stepping over ashes and debris. All of us are pale, frightened, determined. I watch Sarah make her calls, and then get back on her feet and slip her mobile back into her pocket. She's walking towards me, her eyes wide. Something has happened.

"Aunt Juliet survived," she whispers, smiling.

I take her hand and lead her away from the house. She looks at me for a second, in a silent question, but she follows me down the snowy slope and onto the beach, and beyond the rocks where we met Winter for the first time.

The wind cuts our faces with sheets of snow. It's so strong it hurts, and so cold that my breath is taken away. The sea and the sky are angry, and I know it's going to get much worse. But we're about to steal a moment from the world, a moment just for us.

I have to shout over the roar of the sea as I lean towards Sarah, her hair blown by the wind, enveloping me. I know we can never be together, I know that our union would betray all I believe in, all I stand for – Harry's legacy, and my duty as a Gamekeeper – but I still have to tell her. I still have to speak the only words that matter right now.

"Sarah. I love you."

The wind and the sea are so loud that they carry my words away. She has to stand on her toes and whisper her answer straight into my ear. Her breath is warm against my face, her hair caresses my cheek as she replies.

"I love you, too."